From West Yorkshire to East Berlin

Eilsa Mellor

28. 11. 23

From West Yorkshire to East Berlin

Ailsa Mellor

Matador
Unit E2 Airfield Business Park,
Harrison Road, Market Harborough,
Leicestershire. LE16 7UL
Tel: 0116 2792299
Email: books@troubador.co.uk
Web: www.troubador.co.uk/matador
Twitter: @matadorbooks

ISBN 978 1805141 532

British Library Cataloguing in Publication Data.
A catalogue record for this book is available from the British Library.

Printed and bound in the UK by TJ Books Limited, Padstow, Cornwall
Typeset in 11pt Minion Pro by Troubador Publishing Ltd, Leicester, UK

Matador is an imprint of Troubador Publishing Ltd

"Truth be veiled, but still it burneth."
— Percy Bysshe Shelley

PART 1

Jack 1

The apples fell against the window with a vehement thud before their bruised round forms bounced onto the pavement and rolled haphazardly down the road. Moments later, a door was flung open, revealing a red-cheeked woman dramatically brushing flour from her apron.

'Rascals, the lot of you!' the woman shouted as she glanced from side to side. 'If you ever throw them apples at my 'ouse again, I swear I will run after you and cut each and every one of your grubby little fingers off – and them thumbs won't be spared either!'

The woman, known as Mrs Garth, was the village butcher's wife. She was stout in stature with a ruddy face, and her hair was always covered with a scarf. The youngsters called her "Shrew" because of her long, pointed nose, which looked incongruous against the rest of her features. 'You won't 'ave fingers to throw them apples, let alone eat them, if I catch you at my door again.' Mrs Garth walked out into the middle of the street and stood, hands on hips, while she looked around. 'Mark me words. You'll regret ever coming down 'ere,' she said, before going back inside and slamming the door behind her.

At the far end of the street, where the path met the boundary to the village green, four boys were hiding in the hedgerow.

'Shrew was really angry today. D'you hear the way she was shouting? Could hear it all the way down here,' remarked the eldest boy, Tim, who was eating the apple he had been carrying.

The other boys nodded, including Jack, who was ten and already the tallest in the group. 'At least we didn't get caught. Or we'd be fingerless and thumbless,' he said, wiggling his hands.

Jack wasn't like the other boys in the village. He spent most of his free time at his father's barbershop. Otherwise, he loved to draw – the changing shape of a tree as winter morphed into spring or a posy of flowers his mother had just arranged. That's not to say Jack didn't enjoy the high jinks of knock down ginger or racing carts, but days like these were few and far between.

The boys laughed, pleased with their afternoon's game. 'Let's have some more fun,' said Abe, who had a deep scar that ran across his left cheek. 'We could wake up grumpy Frank with the apples left over. These should do the trick,' he said, pointing to a worn brown sack next to him.

'Or we could just play with our carts. Or whip and top?' Tim added, hopefully.

'I should go,' said Jack, brushing brambles from his coat. 'The shop will close soon and my father is expecting me.'

'Shame,' said Tim as he watched Jack place a cloth bag over his shoulder. 'Keep saving them apples and we'll see you tomorrow after school.'

'Maybe,' said Jack, clambering out of the hedgerow while continuing to brush away evidence of his mischief. It was already twilight, Jack's favourite time of day, and as he started to walk towards the village green, the fierce reds, bright oranges and bursts of pink lit up the October sky.

It was at his father's barbershop that Jack's love for storytelling

4

had begun. Jack visited every day after school, usually to help with keeping the place clean, swept and tidy. Other times, he helped to mix the formula that his father, Henry Jagger, was developing to create the smart hairstyle that was the fashion at the time. This he loved best of all. Jack referred to the formula as "magic potion" because this gloopy substance was responsible for keeping men's quiffs all over Halifax neatly in place. The cream was also a closely guarded secret. It could not be shared, Henry insisted, because he still had to refine the ingredients: an emulsion of water and mineral oil (and just the right amount at that) stabilised with beeswax before he introduced it commercially. The men who came through Henry Jagger's door not only knew they would get a good haircut, it was also a social place; a place to chat, to gossip and proffer advice – whether appreciated or not. And this afternoon was no different.

'Now look…' Henry whispered as Jack watched his father prepare the "magic potion" at the back of the shop. 'Most customers that come through these doors are decent folk. Some I might even call friends. But there's one or two who are special, because there's nothing they like better than the sound of their own voice. Like Mr Hainsworth over there.' Henry nodded at the young man who had just walked (limped with some degree of exaggeration is perhaps a more accurate account) into the shop. 'Hello, Dickie, good to see you again.' Henry gestured at a chair in the far corner. 'Make yourself comfortable. I won't be a moment.'

'Afternoon, gentlemen,' replied Dickie, taking off his cap and bowing theatrically in front of Henry and Jack.

Dickie Hainsworth was a decade older than Jack and for as long as Jack could remember, his father's most loyal customer loved to talk. Hainsworth also had a notable twitch that became all the more apparent when he was in the midst of sharing one of his countless tales – a generosity many tried to avoid. These tales were almost always the same: the limp he acquired after a bout of childhood polio; his adventures stationed in Casablanca during the war and his pet tortoise, Edgar, who had a penchant for liquorice. Delivered with breathless urgency, words flew from Hainsworth's tongue like sparks from a flame. Yet, despite his eccentricity, Henry and Jack were very fond of him.

'Your usual, Dickie?'

'As always, my good man, as always.' Hainsworth slid into a leather chair and nodded at Jack, who was fetching a pair of hair clippers for his father.

'How is young Jack today?'

'Good.' Jack enjoyed having Dickie's attention. It was like having an older brother.

'Well, may I ask what was on the menu?'

'Grammar in the morning, Arithmetic after lunch. Then we had nature studies.'

'Well, lad, if truth be told, and it usually always is, *my* education was done outside the classroom. Not many folks can say this but I've travelled all over North Africa, climbed the Atlas Mountains, eaten with Bedouins in the desert and haggled 'til my voice was hoarse in the souks of Marrakesh, Fez *and* Tangier. All while the war was raging around me *and* with this poor old leg of mine. Wouldn't think that possible, would you?'

Jack shook his head, wondering how Dickie could have climbed anything, let alone a mountain.

'I think Edgar could climb a thing or two if he put his mind to it. What d'you reckon?'

Jack laughed. 'I'd like to visit Casablanca one day, climb the Atlas Mountains *and* eat with Bedouins in the desert. I'm not so sure I'd want a tortoise, though.' Jack stood by Dickie's chair on the opposite side of his father, who was quietly preparing the lotion.

'Tortoises aren't for everyone. But I can see great things destined for you. Did I ever tell you the story of when I was caught in a storm on these moors here?'

Jack shook his head again.

'Terrible it was. *Terrible*. Got struck by lightning not once but three times – went through me like a sword! Now, who would think I would be here to tell the tale after being struck by lightning three times? But let me tell you, being struck by lightning was the best thing that happened to me. It's a sign of luck, you know...'

'Is that so?' Henry smiled. 'Ready for your trim, Dickie?'

'As ready as I'll ever be,' Dickie replied, winking at Jack.

Edward Oldroyd was less voluble than Dickie Hainsworth but made up for his lack of conversation in other ways, including keeping meticulous punctuality. When the clock struck five, Oldroyd appeared, exactly on the hour and not a moment before, hovering at the entrance of the barbershop with a newspaper under one arm and an umbrella tucked under the other. Despite being one of his regulars, Henry Jagger was no closer to knowing the man whose hair he had trimmed for the best part of six years, save for the fact that he always came in for his appointment every other Tuesday, was never late and always made provisions for the possibility of rain.

'Ah, Mr Oldroyd,' said Henry, greeting his last customer. 'I can always rely on you being on time. Please, over here.' Henry gestured at the chair closest to the door before placing a black gown over Oldroyd's coat. 'Isn't the weather glorious?'

'Indeed,' came Oldroyd's reply as he eased himself into his usual chair.

'Hopefully, no need of that for a while,' said Henry, gesturing at Oldroyd's umbrella.

'No,' said Oldroyd, taking the umbrella from his lap and placing it carefully on the floor.

'Good day?'

Oldroyd nodded. 'Very good. Thank you.'

Small talk may not have been Oldroyd's forte, but he did want to talk about something in particular and so, halfway through his trim, he asked suddenly, 'Did I mention that my son-in-law has opened a barbershop in Bradford?'

'Yes, I believe you did.' Henry caught Oldroyd's eye and remembered their previous conversation a fortnight ago.

'It's not always easy, though, is it, to create something that's just right? He's a perfectionist, my son-in-law, to his detriment, sadly.' Oldroyd gestured at the emulsion Henry was mixing. 'As, seemingly, you are too. You could put your heads together and come up with quite a concoction.'

'Well, I'm not so sure about that...' Henry glanced at Jack, who remained quiet.

'Nonsense.' Oldroyd waved his hand dismissively. 'You two would make quite the team.'

'Now listen,' Henry said to his son once Oldroyd had left and they were finally alone in the shop. 'What we have here is worth its weight in gold, and no one, and I mean *no one*, must ever know the ingredients. There are hundreds of Mr Oldroyds out there who want to know this and that, but we must not tell them. This is our secret and we must be patient until we are satisfied that what we have here is perfected one thousand times over.' Henry began to place items in a large oak cabinet. 'Do you understand, son? This is *our* secret. Now, please, pass me that key over there.'

'Yes, Father, I understand,' said Jack, handing his father the key. 'This is our secret.'

Life, however, had other plans. Henry Jagger's death came without warning just over a year later on a winter's afternoon in the middle of an otherwise unremarkable week. He was thirty-six years old and in his prime. A heart attack, everyone exclaimed. How could a seemingly fit young man fall victim to such a tragedy? Jack remembered how he had been promised a new coat for his birthday. Now his father wouldn't be there when he turned twelve. He wouldn't be waiting for him after school either; the two of them sweeping up the remains of the day in the shop. And he wouldn't be there to take his sons for their Sunday walk on the moors, the only time they could all be together.

The sun did not shine on that bleak January day when Eva, alongside Jack and her younger son, Harry, laid their father to rest. Menacing swathes of grey dominated the landscape as the vicar spoke of the sweetness of life, of faith and hope; soil crumbling between his fingers as it landed softly against the coffin. There were no answers, just disbelief from those whose lives Henry touched. And he had touched many lives; that much Jack could ascertain. His father's barbershop had been the beating heart of the community. It was where friendships were cemented and disagreements aired. Where now could the men of the village gather? Where now could they spend their Saturday afternoons? And where now could they find a barber as good as Henry Jagger?

Jack didn't really remember the weeks that followed, but it was as if a thick fog had engulfed his world. Nothing made sense to him. Confusion obscured his thoughts, and the speed with which his father's shop was boarded up haunted him long after the locks had been changed and the Jagger sign taken down. Yet he couldn't blame his mother for hastening things along. She was simply doing what was required. He couldn't blame his father either for leaving them without so much as a warning. As the eldest, Jack sensed an undercurrent of expectation hovering over him, like the way his mother suddenly insisted on calling him master of the house. 'You're a grown man now,' Eva would say, patting her son's shoulder. 'And your brother needs someone to look up to.' Jack didn't care about being someone his brother could look up to. He didn't care about being master of the house either. His father was gone. The barbershop was gone. Their secret – gone too.

*

'He was the salt of the earth,' said Dickie Hainsworth, who had come to pay Eva a visit some months later. 'How are you all bearing up?'

'We're getting there,' said Eva, putting her arm around Harry. 'It's been difficult, but we'll manage, won't we, boys?' Jack and Harry nodded, the two of them either side of their mother.

'Well, if you ever need anything...'

'That's very kind, Dickie, we'll bear it in mind.' Eva walked over to the kitchen table and picked up a piece of paper. 'I was wondering, did my husband ever mention a cream he was working on?'

Dickie looked thoughtful for a moment. 'Not specifically,' he said, glancing at the papers in Eva's hand. 'In as much as he didn't say anything *specifically*.'

'It's just that we have no trace of it with the shop shutting so suddenly, and I couldn't find anything when I went through Henry's belongings.'

Dickie tilted his head to one side as if trying to recollect something.

'It would be such a shame to put all his hard work to waste.'

'Well, come to think of it...'

'You remember something?'

'I'm not sure if...'

'What is it, Dickie?'

'Well, apart from your husband referring to it – the cream he used in the salon that is – as the Yorkshireman's best friend. He would say to me: *Dickie, my good man, let me put a drop of this in your hair. It's going to make the ladies swoon.*'

'Well, did it?' Eva smiled, a trace of lightness returning to her voice.

'Oh, that cream was right up there in the swooning stakes. Got me a date with Betty Bradshaw and that Gloria girl – the one whose father owned the ironmonger's on the other side of town. The last I heard, she's living the high life in London with a merchant banker husband. Gloria Barlow – that was her name. A redhead too. Quite a pretty thing from what I remember.'

'You'll find a good girl, there's plenty of time for that.'

'Oh, I don't worry about that, Mrs Jagger,' Dickie's voice began to waver as he stared at the floor, 'but I do wonder what us lads are going to do now. Your husband was a good man. A talented man.'

'I'm sure you'll find somewhere just as good…'

'I'm not so sure, Mrs Jagger. He really did have the magic touch.' Dickie glanced at Jack before turning to Harry. 'You won't remember much, if anything, about your daddy's barbershop, but it was a very special place. All of us miss it. Miss your father too – he was the best of 'em.'

'Yes,' said Eva, her eyes glistening. 'God rest his soul.'

Later that evening, Jack thought about his father, about Dickie's words and the "magic potion" that would now never come to fruition. If his mother couldn't find the formula, if it had disappeared, then where was it? Had it got lost amid the confusion and chaos before the shop was boarded up? Or did someone who knew about it steal it? But who? And how? And what on earth would they do with it? What about the possibility that his father had destroyed it just before he died? But why would he do that?, thought Jack. Unless he *knew* he was going to die. Jack lay on his bed and stared up at the ceiling. *One day, I'm going to uncover the truth,* he vowed. *One day, all of this will make sense. It has to make sense.*

*

Several weeks later, Jack and Harry were helping their mother pack the rest of their father's belongings into boxes. 'That's the thing about life,' said Eva, kneeling next to a large trunk. 'Sometimes, just when we *think* we know what's coming, a storm arrives and our best-laid plans are torn to shreds. So we have to start again, all over again. Just as we are doing now. And we should thank God that none of us know what the future holds.' Eva looked upwards; Jack and Harry following her gaze.

'Does God know what's going to happen to us?' Harry was twirling one of his father's ties.

'I think he does, son. Our destinies are mapped out for us, you see.'

'Did he know that Father was going to die?'

'Yes, I think so.' Eva put her hand on Harry's shoulder and drew him closer to her.

'Then why didn't God warn *us*?'

'Because no one, not even the hardiest of souls, should want to know their fate.'

Eva

2

The Roaring Twenties, with all their glitter and optimism, did not offer any respite. With Henry Jagger gone and Grandma Clara losing her sight, this "Golden Age" was anything but golden for the Jaggers. Grey was perhaps more apt a description, as Jack was soon to find out. Jack found out the day his teacher, Miss Simms, told the class that the tomb of Tutankhamen had just been discovered. But the thing that stuck in Jack's mind that drizzly November afternoon was not Tutankhamen; rather it was the image of his mother waiting for him outside the school gates with a strange, distracted look on her face.

'What are you doing here?' Jack asked with surprise.

'I thought I'd come and meet you.'

'But you never meet me. I always take the tram home by myself.'

'I had a meeting with Mr Duggleby, your headmaster.'

'Mr Duggleby? Why?'

'I wanted to talk to him about something.'

'Talk to Mr Duggleby?'

'Yes, and then I thought I'd wait and come home with you.'

Jack didn't want his mother to come home with him. He was still in the habit of going to his father's shop after school even though there was nothing to see now apart from the boards that had been hastily erected in front of the facade. It was as if he somehow expected his father to be waiting there for him and to tell him it had all been a bad dream. But no matter how many times Jack stared up at those boards, he knew his father was never coming back.

'I was going to wait for Tim.'

'Tim will be quite all right without you.'

'What did you talk to the headmaster about?' Jack slung his satchel over his shoulder.

'I'll tell you when we get home. How was school today?'

'Fine.' Jack glanced at his mother. 'Do you know where the Valley of the Kings is?'

'Why?'

'They've found the tomb of Tutankhamen.'

'Who has?'

'An English archeologist. I learnt about it today in class.'

'Tutankhamen's tomb.' Eva stopped and looked at her son. 'And what did he discover?'

'Jewellery, statues, a chariot. They found clothing too.'

'Well, that's a lot to fit into one tomb.'

'Miss Simms said it was a very big one.'

'It's very important to learn about the world,' said Eva, her voice suddenly adopting a matter-of-fact tone, 'but there are other important things in life too. Like responsibility to family.'

Jack nodded, half listening; wondering if there was time for a game of conkers before tea. He glanced at his mother and noticed the distracted look was still there, as if she had a thousand things on her mind. When the tram arrived, Jack stood at the front as usual while Eva found a seat nearby. Every now and again she glanced up at her son while writing a list on a crumpled piece of paper that had been stuffed into her coat pocket. The sun had set by the time they reached their stop, and when they walked past the freshly ploughed fields towards the green, it was almost dark. Henry Jagger's boarded-up barbershop could be seen in the distance. And further down, past the bakery and ironmonger's, was the confectionary shop where, on a Saturday afternoon after work, Henry would buy as a treat for his sons Black Jacks, Fruit Salads and some brightly-coloured sticky sweets that could be bought for halfpenny an ounce.

They walked through the village, Jack trailing behind his mother. They passed Grumpy Frank's and Old Shrew's houses – rows of uniform red brick that seemed to go on forever – and the scowling black cat that belonged to somebody but nobody knew who, while the trees with their bare branches looked foreboding against the skyline. When they got home, Grandma Clara was already asleep in the front room. Jack peered in through the door and caught a glimpse of his grandmother. Her head was tilted to the side with a slightly open mouth and hands clasped together as if in prayer. Jack wanted to know if she could still see things, anything – a flicker of light, the trace of a smile perhaps – or whether everything was just darkness now, but he was too afraid to ask. He quietly pulled the door towards him and then made his way upstairs. When he reached his brother's room, Harry was in his usual position: elbows on table, hunched over desk, a ruler clasped in one hand.

'Hello,' said Jack.

'Hello,' replied Harry, his back still to his brother. 'Where's Mother?'

'She came to meet me after school today.'

'Oh.' Harry turned around and frowned. 'Did you do something bad?'

'Tea is in half an hour,' said Jack, ignoring his brother's question. 'Don't forget.'

When Jack came back downstairs, Eva was sitting at the kitchen table waiting for him. 'Come here, son. Let me look at you.'

15

Jack moved closer, albeit tentatively.

'Is it me or are you growing taller every day?'

Jack shrugged and put down his satchel.

'Do you know, I have a feeling you are going to be taller than your father.'

'What did you talk to Mr Duggleby about?'

Eva rose from her chair and walked over to her son, lightly brushing his cheek with her palm. 'Well, I told him that what with your father gone, I need you to be master of this house now.'

'I thought I already was.' Jack stepped away from his mother. There was a trace of resentment in his voice, which he didn't try to hide.

'You are,' Eva paused, 'but with that comes responsibility.'

'What do you mean?' Jack began to rummage in his satchel for pencils.

'It means you need to find work.'

'Work?' Jack stopped what he was doing.

'Yes, I need you to help me.'

'But we're learning about kings. I thought maybe you could help *me*? With my homework?'

Eva sighed. 'I've just found out that the sale of the shop didn't generate enough income for us to live on. Unfortunately, we can't simply live on the proceeds.'

Jack didn't say anything. He had begun to fidget with his jacket sleeve.

'What I mean is we need more money.'

'But Father was always so busy. He turned people away. I saw them. Sometimes, the queue was so long, he'd tell them to come back tomorrow. I was there. I *saw* them.'

'Your father had debts to pay off. It was assumed he had plenty of time to repay the loan. Grandma Clara needs help too. She can't look after herself anymore.'

'What about Jo? Can she help?'

'I've had to let her go. We can't afford a daily anymore. And Grandma Clara is an extra mouth to feed.'

Jack looked at his mother and noticed how much she had aged. Her rounded cheeks, which once lent a gentleness to the contours of her face, were sunken. Those blue eyes, once vibrant and curious, were heavy from grief and overshadowed by dark circles. And her delicate hands, which her husband once claimed to be the softest in the village, were coarse from heavy chores. Living in reduced circumstances was not what Eva envisaged for herself. She had been – was still – very attractive and like Jack had artistic leanings; a combination that unwittingly drew suitors to the younger Miller daughter. Eva wasn't distracted by men like her friends were with their regular infatuations. She was interested in books and painting. Her sister Lily, who was three years older, went several steps further; making it known that it would take a remarkable man to turn *her* head.

By the time Eva was twenty, things had changed. The man in question was Henry Jagger, whose parents were friends of the family and whom Eva thought at the time seemed terribly old at twenty-five. After the initial introductions were made, she was curious to know more, which was a good sign because there was nothing Eva liked better than to have her curiosity piqued. Henry, Eva learnt, had undertaken an apprenticeship as a barber, quickly cutting his teeth in various establishments before opening his own shop at the age of twenty-three. By the time he met Eva, he had already carved out a reputation for himself as the most popular hairdresser in Hipperholme. Together, they were a bright young couple with the world at their feet, a flourishing business and a house always filled with guests. Not that there were guests to receive now. It appeared that people didn't know what to say to a young widow. Better to avoid an awkward conversation and stay away. Dickie, at least, still dropped by from time to time.

17

'It won't be forever,' Eva reassured her son. 'Once Harry is older, it will be easier. I promise.'

'But what about school?'

'You're almost fourteen, so legally you'll be allowed to leave next spring, just after your birthday.' Eva watched her son tug absently on a loose thread that was coming away from his coat. Deep down, it pained her to know that she had unsettled him. 'I can't afford to pay the school fees anymore. I'm sorry, but it's just the way it is.'

'It's not fair. Why can't Harry work too?'

'Because your brother is far too young. You're the eldest and with that comes responsibilities. But we'll make provisions for you to continue at the local church school part time.'

'Part time? What does that mean?'

'Well, that's what I spoke to Mr Duggleby about. They can make provisions for a system of part-time continuation classes for pupils like you who need to work. You will still be able to sit your School Certificate in a couple of years' time, just like your friends.'

'It's just not fair. I don't want to leave *my* school, where *my* friends are.'

'Life isn't fair, son. The sooner you realise it, the easier life will be.'

Jack looked at the floor, eyes downcast; fingers still tugging at the thread. Why did his father have to die? Why couldn't life go on as it was – afternoons in the barbershop listening to Dickie's tales, watching his father perfect their secret? Now something else was being taken away from him.

'Do you think I wished for a life like this? Without a husband, and a father for my boys? Look at your grandmother. Soon, she won't be able to recognise any of us. We've all suffered, *are* suffering, but we need to have faith there will be brighter days ahead. And there will be. I promise.' Eva moved a hand across her face, as if to brush away a tear.

'I'm sorry,' Jack said, coming closer. 'I will help you as much as I can.'

'Son, I don't expect you to understand. But I hope you can forgive me.'

Jack forgave his mother – what else could he do? – but the thought of not returning to his school was hard to reconcile. How he wished he had not been born the eldest. It pained Jack to know that his brother's destiny would be left untarnished, that Harry would sail through this fraught time unscathed. What did his brother know anyway? He barely knew their father's barbershop. He certainly didn't know about the formula. Now he would have no idea how much Jack was giving up. The only consolation, as his mother reminded him, was that he was lucky to have found a job at all.

*

Little did Jack know that his foray into the world of work would begin with Mr Garth, who was the village butcher *and* Shrew's husband. Jack certainly wasn't prepared for the feeling when he turned up on his first day in the middle of the night – it was still hours before dawn – of being the only one awake in the world.

'You're too soft, lad,' Graham Garth shouted as he watched Jack drag in slabs of meat from the delivery cart. The sky was still a dark inky blue. 'Cannot remember how many times I've told you not to carry 'em like that. There's a knack to everything, and it will make your life a lot easier if you do it my way. I've been doing it thirty year!'

'I'm trying my best, Mr Garth,' replied Jack, remembering the countless afternoons he had thrown apples at Mrs Garth's door. 'I promise to do it right next time. I won't let you down.'

'I should hope not, son. There's plenty of lads out there grateful for work like this. I don't want to have to let you go, but if you don't do it proper, like, just like I told you…'

'I'll remember next time, Mr Garth. I promise. I won't let you down.'

By sunrise, Jack was on his bicycle, cycling the five miles north to help process hops in the brewery. By the time he'd completed his second job, it was almost time for lunch. Jack looked forward to the bread, cheese and sliced apple that his mother prepared for him every day, which he savoured, especially when the sun was shining and he was able to sit outside in the meadow behind the brewery. After lunch, it was back to the village, weighing fruit and vegetables for customers at Mr Cartwright's, the greengrocer's. By the end of it all, Jack was exhausted. The days felt like months and the months felt like years. Life was monotonous, joyless and relentless. Or so it seemed to Jack as he moved seamlessly from job to job, an everyman acquiring skills that were as futile as they were essential. Once Friday evening had come around again – how he looked forward to this golden hour – weekends were spent catching up with schoolwork. Jack tried not to show resentment as he watched his friends breeze through their young lives, but the life that had been suddenly thrust upon him was hard to swallow.

How did he get through it all? Perhaps it was fear that ignited Jack's determination. Certainly, the feeling was always present. He heard it in his mother's anxious voice when she would ask someone if she could defer a payment for this or that. He could see it in the dripping tap and the draughty windows that were never mended. And he saw it in his mother's eyes when he gave her his weekly pay as she carefully counted the shillings on the table. Life was about keeping heads above water now, about survival and surviving. Accepting this was how life was. For however long.

Although it was never mentioned, Jack's endeavours did not go unnoticed. Eva expressed her gratitude in small, thoughtful ways; tokens of appreciation that she knew her son would treasure. Jack occasionally returned home to find a beautifully wrapped book waiting for him on his bedside table. Books became Jack's companions, long after his friends had abandoned him. Books allowed him to escape the tedium of his life and indulge his imagination.

They also taught Jack everything he needed to know. And what he learnt during these long dark days of butchers, brewers and greengrocers is that the only certainty in life is change.

By Design 3

'Well, son, how was it? Did the paper like your stories?' It was washday and Eva was squatting next to a large iron tub and immersing several grubby shirts in water. It was a question she was used to asking by now as she heard Jack's heavy footsteps walk through the door.

Jack didn't answer. Instead, he slumped into the nearest chair and placed his face wearily in his hands.

'What is it, son?'

'I just don't know what to do anymore.' Three years of carrying the weight of financial responsibility on his young shoulders was not over yet, but during that time he had passed the School Certificate, and because he enjoyed writing and was also rather good at it, Jack had applied for a junior reporting role at the *Halifax Courier*.

'Don't give up. Something will come of it.'

'I've tried but they don't seem to care about the weekend activities of Lightcliffe Cricket Club, and I don't just mean the usual reporting of the match and where they are in the Bradford League, but the interesting bits, the gossip. Things that readers really want to know about.'

'You just need to persist.' Eva eased herself up from the floor and peered into a pot simmering on the stove. 'The stew is ready,' she said, seasoning it with parsley. 'And it's very hot.' She handed Jack a bowl and sat down opposite him.

'What about you? Aren't you going to have any?' Jack looked at his mother's empty plate.

'I've already eaten.' Eva Jagger was not going to tell anyone, least of all her children, that she'd rather her boys had enough (for second helpings at least) while she went without. She had two growing lads and a frail mother under her roof. She preferred to keep her sacrifices to herself. 'Well, like I said, son – persistence is everything.'

'Persistence is getting me nowhere.'

'Remember, you have your exams under your belt now. You'll get a proper job soon and things will become easier. And it will be far better than you imagined.'

'You really think so?'

'Look at Dickie. For years, he drifted in and out of work, not quite sure of his direction. I've always said that everyone needs a trade. Now look at him. A businessman – his own business!'

'Strange to think of Dickie as a tailor.'

'Well, that's down to his wife's talents. She's the creative one. Dickie had the capital.'

'Capital? I didn't think Dickie had that sort of money?'

'Well, perhaps he did. Or his wife. People are dark horses when it comes to these things. But it's not our place to pry. We should only wish them well.'

'Good for him,' said Jack. 'At least one of us is making something of our lives.'

And so, after his shift at the greengrocer's, Jack continued to put on his father's old suit for luck and took the tram to Halifax; his cup of optimism no longer overflowing but still resolutely half full, hoping *this* would be the day that someone at the *Courier* would realise his abilities and offer him a job. But Jack's endeavours remained resolutely in vain and soon his reports of standing awkwardly outside the newspaper's drab building, looking up at the small rectangular windows as he waited patiently for someone to answer the bell, began to grate on him. It was becoming increasingly clear that no one was ever going to invite him upstairs, because the people inside this seemingly elusive entity were either against a deadline, out on a scoop or just not interested.

At least Eva had been right. It was only a matter of time before life changed again for the Jaggers in the shape of Albert Everson. Eva had been introduced to Albert by her cousin's husband. It was a swift courtship – Eva didn't have the time to be wooed and won over. What she needed was a man who knew how to fix a wayward floorboard, replace the tiles on the roof, mend her leaking tap and, above all, be patient with Grandma Clara and kind to her boys.

Albert had neither been married nor had children, yet he embraced his new role with a delicate balance of humour and patience. He also had a gentle manner and an easy way about him. And as much as Eva appreciated the interest he showed in Jack and Harry from the outset, Albert was careful not to diminish Henry's memory, sitting the boys down one evening shortly after he and Eva were engaged. 'Now, I know how much your father meant to you both,' he said, choosing his words carefully, 'and I will never take that away from you. But I want you to know that your wellbeing is of great importance to me, and that means you can depend on me for anything.' Albert looked at Jack and then Harry, before adding, 'Would either of you like to ask me anything?'

Harry glanced tentatively at his brother and then Albert, before saying somewhat cautiously, 'I have a question for you.'

'Yes, Harry, what would you like to ask?'

'Can we…?' Harry glanced again at Jack.

'Yes, Harry, what is it?' said Albert encouragingly.

'Can we call you Father?'

'I would like that very much.' Albert laughed and ruffled Harry's hair affectionately.

Harry jumped up and embraced Albert. He was nearly twelve but still possessed a child-like spontaneity that had long eluded other boys his own age. 'I'm really glad you are part of our family. Everything feels better already, doesn't it, Jack?'

'Yes,' said Jack, before looking awkwardly at Albert. The truth was, Jack wasn't sure what he felt, his only thought being that it had happened so quickly. One minute they were a family of four, if you included Grandma Clara, and the next Albert had moved in. They had managed well enough up until now, hadn't they? They had managed, thought Jack, because *he* had kept the roof over everyone's heads. The only consolation he felt – admittedly a large one at that – was relief that providing for the family no longer weighed on him, and that meant no more shifts at Mr Garth's. His mother seemed happy too, certainly less distracted, with an energy about her that he hadn't seen in a long time. He also noticed that she had taken to quietly singing to herself again, just as she had done when his father was alive, in that soft and melodious voice of hers. *Is this what love does?* Jack thought, as he observed Albert chatting animatedly to Harry. *Is this what love does?*

'Now off you go and finish your homework,' said Albert, shooing Harry away playfully.

'Yes, Father,' replied Harry, enjoying the sound of the word father as it rolled off his tongue. Harry ran up the stairs, into his room and, when he reached his desk, adjusted the thick-rimmed glasses that he had taken to wearing permanently to stop his squinting. Then he opened a textbook. Harry already knew he wanted to solve problems – technical problems – just like Albert, whose latest project was upgrading the lighting system at EW Worth's, a carpet manufacturer in Halifax.

Jack, on the other hand, was a month shy of turning

eighteen, and as uncertain as ever. If he wasn't going to write, then what else could he do? He liked to sketch. He liked to use his imagination. But what use was all that? He needed to make a living too, and if the paper wasn't interested in his articles, then who was going to sit up and notice his drawings of trees and flowers?

'Penny for your thoughts?' Albert looked earnestly at Jack.

'It's nothing,' said Jack with a shrug.

'You *can* talk to me, you know. I'm a great believer in a problem shared...'

Jack glanced sideways at Albert. Should he be confiding in a man he barely knew? Who wasn't his father? Would Albert even understand?

'It's all right,' Albert said, reassuringly. 'You can trust me.'

Jack reluctantly met Albert's gaze. 'It's nothing.'

'Well, if you're sure,' said Albert, rising from his seat.

Jack continued to watch Albert from the corner of his eye. He didn't care for Albert's advice, but he would have been the last to admit that he didn't want Albert to leave the room either. He wanted to be left alone *and* he wanted to be listened to. Jack looked up, his face a patchwork of irritability and vulnerability. 'Harry just seems so sure of himself and he's not even twelve.'

Albert turned around, kind eyes resting on Jack's anguished face. 'Remember, he's had it easier than you. Your experience will ultimately shape you for the better.'

Jack furrowed his brow. He was still unconvinced.

Albert smiled. 'It will come. And always when it's least expected.'

Jack wondered what his own father would have made of his son's uncertainty and whether, if Henry had been alive, he would have simply joined the family business, his future clearly mapped out. And what about the magic potion? Would the formula be commercialised by now? Would the "Yorkshireman's Best Friend" be a bestseller? It saddened Jack that he would never know the answer, and in that moment, along with hundreds of other moments, he felt his father's absence deeply.

*

Whether Jack liked it or not, Eva and Albert were married a month later, and a subtle shift altered the dynamic in the Jagger household. It took time but the resentment Jack felt towards Albert gradually dissipated. Resentment turned into acceptance, Jack appreciating the positive effect his stepfather had on everyone. It was clear Albert was good for his mother, good for Harry and, despite not wanting to admit it at first, good for him. The best thing, though, he thought, and the presence of Albert always reminded him of this, was that he never had to touch a bloody carcass again. In the absence of butchers, breweries and greengrocers, Jack spent his days honing his writing skills, always allowing himself to be swept up in the wave of his ambitions; one day fancying himself as an art critic, the next a cricket reporter. There were days that were prolific, ending, for example, with a carefully crafted feature (if Jack were to say so himself) on the fated appointment of one of the world's leading batsmen, Herbert Sutcliffe, to the Yorkshire captaincy. Other days, words eluded him, escaping his grasp as if he were digging for precious gold. Still, he was grateful. Thanks to Albert, Jack's only job now was not to give up and to keep sending articles to the paper.

And then, Albert said, they would think of Plan B.

Plan B, however, came sooner than expected.

*

'I've never seen anything like it.' Albert's excitement was palpable as he rushed through the front door.

'What is it?' Eva came to greet her husband.

27

'To think I've worked there for months now and I've only just discovered where all the marvellous ideas are generated!'

Jack looked up from the book he was reading. He could hear the animated conversation taking place in the hallway.

'What on earth are you talking about?' Eva took Albert's coat and ushered him into the kitchen, where everyone was sitting.

'Well, ideas for patterns – trees, flowers. Anything really. It's quite something.'

'What is?' Eva was becoming impatient. 'You need to stop talking in riddles, dear.'

'The design studio.' Albert waved his hand theatrically as if a revelation had been unveiled. He knew he had caught Jack's attention.

'Maybe I'll work there one day,' Harry announced. 'Do engineers work there?'

'No, it's a special room only for designers.'

'What do they do?' asked Harry, adjusting his thick-rimmed glasses.

'Well, they create the designs for the carpets, you see.'

'How many designs?' Harry asked.

'Hundreds.'

'Hundreds?' Harry repeated Albert's words.

'Yes, because carpet production where the yarn is spun starts right here in Yorkshire.'

'They don't call Yorkshire God's own country for nothing,' said Eva, smiling. 'We forget what's here on our doorstep.'

The brothers nodded, but it was Jack who felt a wave of excitement surge through his veins as he dared to imagine the possibility that this place his stepfather so colourfully described could be somewhere he might belong.

'I'd like to see these designs,' said Jack.

'And I'd like to see how the lighting works,' Harry added. 'Can you take me too?'

'Of course, son. Once I've taken your brother, I'll bring you with me next time.'

Later that week, Albert brought Jack into work and introduced him to the head designer, a Mr Bayman, telling him that his stepson, who was soon to turn eighteen, had some talent and could he possibly give the lad a job in Worth's design studio.

'What do you think makes for a good design?' Mr Bayman asked, peering over his glasses at Jack, as the three of them sat in his small windowless office.

Jack glanced at his stepfather before replying. 'Well, I think that depends on the customer.'

'Go on, lad,' said Mr Bayman.

'They tell you what they want, and then you create something around that, I suppose.' Jack glanced again at Albert, checking to see whether he had answered correctly.

'He's a bright boy – he'll learn on the job,' Albert interjected, hoping to strengthen the case for his stepson. 'And he's had a lot of experience already. We can provide references too.'

'Is that right?' said Mr Bayman, who was still looking at Jack.

'If you need anything, I can find—' Albert added.

'That won't be necessary,' interrupted Mr Bayman. 'The first rule of business – *always* keep the client happy. *Always*. No matter how demanding they are. No matter *how* ridiculous the brief.' Mr Bayman rose from his chair. 'But you appear to know that already, lad, don't you?'

Jack nodded again, his eyes darting nervously between Mr Bayman and Albert.

'I'll see to all the necessary paperwork,' Mr Bayman added, straightening his tie.

'Jack and I are very grateful for your time, aren't we?' said Albert.

'Yes, Mr Bayman. Thank you for your time,' repeated Jack, unsure what exactly had been decided, for Mr Bayman didn't appear to like giving anything away. By lunchtime, however, it was settled. Jack was to start at Worth's the first Monday of the following month.

'You've done a marvellous job, you really have,' said Eva later that evening when she and Albert were finally alone. Harry was in bed and Dickie had taken Jack out for a celebratory drink at the Dusty Miller in Brighouse. 'And I'm speaking for us all when I say how much your kindness is felt. It doesn't go unnoticed. I know how much the boys look up to you.'

'It gives me enormous pleasure to offer them a guiding hand, not having had sons or daughters of my own.'

'What would we have done without you? What *would* we do without you?'

'*That*, my dear, is something you'll never have to worry about.'

*

Jack started work at Worth's design studio in the spring of 1927, running errands for a team of six artists. He had just turned eighteen and his tall, slim frame barely filled his new wool suit, but his energy and enthusiasm made up for it. Thanks to his stepfather, a door had opened. The world of butchers, brewers and greengrocers may have been firmly behind him, but if you had asked Jack whether he still thought about his father's barbershop, the "magic potion" and everything else that happened during the cruel winter of 1920, he would probably have nodded, a trace of sadness reflected in his eyes.

'I won't let you down, Mr Bayman,' said Jack, when he was greeted by the head designer at the factory entrance on his first day of work. 'I promise.'

'Well, you'll be the first to hear about it if you do.' Mr Bayman waved Jack up the stairs. 'The trick is to make sure you don't, and then you'll be quite all right. Quite all right, I'm sure.'

Maybelle 4

THE "HALLY DANCE"

'How can you expect to meet a nice young man if you would rather sit in a corner with your crochet!' Mary Drake waved a hand dramatically in the air, her plump arm wobbling accordingly. 'If you were married, you could crochet to your heart's content, but you need to find a husband first!' Mary Drake inhaled sharply, before adding, '*And* you need to make an effort.'

Mary Drake was well known in certain circles. Although she was petite, her physique belied her forceful reputation. Even her husband, the affable, mild-mannered Andrew Drake, knew when to ignore his wife, not least to maintain a peaceful life but also because he was well acquainted with the consequences if he didn't.

'I'm perfectly happy as I am, Mother,' replied Maybelle. 'It does no one any good to fret and fuss, least of all you.' Maybelle was also diminutive in height, with eyes that appeared violet depending on the light and wavy dark hair that sat neatly at the nape of her neck. She was an only child and it seemed that the lack of sibling companionship had shaped her tendency towards solitude, which in turn brought her closer to her mother. It was a relationship that was as unique as it was overbearing, for Mary was deeply attached to her daughter.

'Well, I do, dear. But that's quite all right because we have the dance coming up and I'm sure you'll put your crochet to the side for one evening, if only for your mother's sake.'

'If it makes you happy, Mother, then I will.'

The "Hally Dance", as it was known, was an annual event hosted by the Halifax Young People's Society, and it took place on the third Saturday in April. The event was of particular importance to Mary, given the opportunity the dance provided for young ladies to be seen, admired and courted. Mary, for a few years now, had hoped for all three for her daughter, but to no avail – Maybelle didn't seem interested. Still, Mary remained positive and by the time spring reappeared and the Hally Dance was circled in everyone's calendar, she was determined *this* would be the year her daughter would be seen, admired, *and* snapped up.

*

'I have a good feeling about today,' declared Mary to her husband. 'Saturday, the fifteenth of April – it's got rather a nice ring to it, don't you think, dear?' The day of the Hally Dance had finally arrived.

'Do what, dear?' Andrew Drake bolted upright in his chair at the sound of his wife's voice.

'Oh, never you mind. Why I even bother asking your opinion about anything is beyond me.'

'Right you are, dear.' Andrew Drake closed his eyes before opening one again, just enough to see his wife hovering by the kitchen door. 'Should anyone need me, I'm just having my forty winks.'

'Forty winks. When are you *not* having forty winks? It's a good job no one *ever* needs you, least of all your family, who have learnt to manage quite well without you. As we will do this evening.' Mary stopped to study the piece of framed embroidery that was hanging on the wall, looking particularly pleased with herself as she took a few steps back to admire the lilac, narcissi and tulip detail that had taken her many hours to perfect. 'And don't wait up on our account. We'll be home late – all being well.'

The spring sun was still visible in the sky when the young people of Halifax, dressed in their finest attire, began to fill Hally Hall. Only Maybelle, who was wearing a delicate pale blue chiffon dress with puffs and ruffle sleeves, arrived with her mother, who wore a rather unflattering brown calf-length skirt with inverted front pleats.

'Go on, girl, keep moving,' said Mary, as she dramatically steered her daughter through the hall like an exhibition piece. 'We need to get past this crowd to the middle there. I'll need to see who is worthy of my daughter's time.' It was matchmaking at its least subtle and Maybelle was horrified. Once Mary had found a table – declaring it an excellent vantage point from which to watch the evening's activities unfold – she still wasn't content. 'It's terribly stuffy in here. Surely someone has the common sense to open a window and let some fresh air in! I've a good mind to complain. Now, where is that Mr Cartwright when we need him?'

'Oh, Mother, please stop. If it bothers you, I'll go over there and open a window myself.'

'Don't be ridiculous. That's hardly the place for a young lady and certainly not a daughter of mine.' Mary began to scan the room. 'Good grief! Is that the postmaster's son? What on earth is he wearing? Surely someone ought to tell him *that* went out of fashion last year! And young Betty over there! Recently engaged, pockmarks and all. Who would have thought such a plain Jane

33

would be snapped up. Well, I hope she brightens up on her wedding day. What a fright for her new husband, otherwise!'

'Oh, Mother, *please* do stop. There's nothing wrong with Betty Arnold, and I'm perfectly pleased that she is soon to be married. It's awfully mean of you to say otherwise.'

Mary, however, was not to be deterred. On she went with her tirade, becoming all the more loquacious the less she could hear herself speak. But as abruptly as the tirade had started, all of a sudden it ceased. Two familiar faces had been spotted on the other side of the room, and they were standing awkwardly as if unsure what to do with themselves, the cut of their suits overwhelming their youthful frames. It was Jack and Harry. 'Well, I never! Is that the young Jagger boys? I hardly recognise Harry with those glasses and just look at Jack! What a fine man he has grown into! What a fine young man!' Mary shot up from where she was sitting and began to gesticulate excitedly at the brothers, waving at them above the sea of heads in front of her.

Although Harry was six years younger than his brother, he was already the same height as Jack. His physique was broader too and it was often remarked upon that Harry's thick black glasses, which he had worn in some form since late childhood, framed his face handsomely. Both of them possessed light blue eyes and black hair. Jack, however, was the more distinguished-looking of the two.

'Boys, over here.' Mary waved animatedly before flashing a look at Maybelle, her eyes ablaze. 'For heaven's sake, if I've told you once, I've told you a thousand times, don't just sit there daydreaming. The Jagger boys are coming over to say hello, and Jack Jagger is a fine young man. You should do well to be polite and interested, or another lass will seize the opportunity.'

'I shall do my best,' replied Maybelle, patting down her dress.

'Get up, get up.' Mary gestured excitedly to her daughter. 'They're coming over. They'll be here any moment.'

Although Maybelle didn't realise it at the time, it was a serendipitous moment, because, despite she and Jack living in neighbouring villages their whole lives, it had taken almost a quarter of a century for their paths to finally cross. Thank goodness for Mary, Jack later mused. For it was clear that her beguiling yet taciturn daughter needed some coaxing to come out of her shell. Maybelle preferred to say little, that much Jack knew. Yet for all Maybelle's reticence, Jack sensed that Mary was happy to take over, nudging her daughter towards him with assured confidence. The kind of confidence that knew she was making a good match.

'Would you like to dance?' Jack turned to Maybelle as he offered her his hand. The room began to fill with music again and the young people of Halifax moved towards the centre of the room with their chosen partners.

Maybelle didn't reply. Instead, she glanced furtively at her mother.

'Go on.' Mary waved effusively, ushering her daughter away with an approving nod. 'You two enjoy yourselves. Harry's going to tell me all about life at university. Where are you again, dear?'

'Leeds,' came Harry's curt response.

'Well, that's a relief. More civilised than Manchester. Such an ugly, dirty city is Manchester. Leeds, at least, has its Victorian architecture to be proud about. But Manchester? I do despair…'

Jack glanced at Harry apologetically, before gently leading Maybelle towards the other dancing couples. It was twilight, Jack's favourite time of day. As the last of the sun's rays stretched across the hall, Jack looked at the woman by his side, who shyly returned his gaze as they began to move to the sound of Bing Crosby singing about love and hope in *Shadow Waltz*. And to think he hadn't even been sure whether he wanted to attend the dance. At least he had Harry to thank for changing his mind.

Twilight turned to nightfall and nightfall into the early hours of the morning. All the while, Mary was firmly – it certainly

wasn't subtle – orchestrating another meeting for her daughter.
'Now, before you leave,' Mary said firmly to Jack, 'you're to keep
Saturday free. I'm inviting you to have supper with my daughter
and husband at our home. We shall dine early because I expect
you'll want to go to the Picturedrome afterwards. I hear that *King
Kong* is all the rage now, but I'll leave that up to you youngsters
to decide. Harry, I'll expect you'll be back at Leeds. Otherwise,
you would be most welcome to join us.'

Harry feigned disappointment, his expression masking relief
at not having to accompany his brother to the Drakes' for supper.
Jack, on the other hand, wasn't sure whether to be delighted or
affronted, wondering what Maybelle thought of his seemingly
redundant role in her mother's plans. *Shouldn't I be taking the
initiative?* he thought. *Couldn't Mrs Drake leave some of the
decisions to me? Or at least make it appear she is?* Maybelle, it
seemed, was accustomed to her mother's decisiveness. Although
her intentions were unspoken, Mary was simply steering the
ship to the safety of the shore, her daughter's destiny, which had
successfully been sealed only hours earlier. The plan, it seemed,
was to cement the union between Jack and Maybelle as soon as
possible. Mary Drake was well aware that unmarried women were
a topic of much debate and conversation in the village, and she
was of the view that if her daughter were left to her own devices
– she was twenty-three after all, already in her prime *and* two
months older than Jack – there could be a reasonable chance she
would end up less Yorkshire rose and more of the wilting variety.
Mary Drake did not want anyone commiserating, congratulating
or remonstrating with Maybelle for not having secured a husband
yet, not if *she* had anything to do with it. Whenever the subject
came up, Andrew Drake, on the other hand, reminded his
daughter in the most tactful way possible (always delivered when
his wife wasn't present) to ignore her mother's silly nonsense, that
spinsterhood might actually be a good thing *and* that the path to
happiness does not necessarily equate to marriage.

'Now then, how does five-thirty on Saturday sound to you? Does it seem a reasonable amount of time to have supper and catch the evening performance at the Picturedrome?'

Jack and Maybelle nodded in assent, both privately conceding that it was best to go along with whatever plans were being made for them. It was only when Mary disappeared briefly to retrieve her gloves that Jack and Maybelle felt comfortable enough to exchange a few words.

'It's been a while since I've been to the pictures,' said Jack, smiling at Maybelle.

'Yes,' whispered Maybelle as she met Jack's gaze. 'It's been a while for me too.'

'Well, if you both decide on *King Kong*, let me know what you think,' added Harry. 'I can always watch it back in Leeds with the lads.'

Jack nodded at Harry, while Maybelle's eyes flitted between the two brothers. It was at times like these that she wished she had a sibling of her own, someone to share the weight of her mother's dominance. *A brother would have been nice*, she thought; *someone to look out for her. Or perhaps a sister; someone to confide in, someone to go to the Hally Dance with.* Maybelle's eyes settled on Jack, lowering them as soon as he caught her gaze, and the two of them smiled at each other, as if they were the only two people in the room having been let in on a wonderful secret.

*

The summer unfolded exactly as Mary Drake had hoped, and it was with immense relief and satisfaction that the following spring her daughter was finally married. The groom wore a purple tie, which complemented the delicate blush of pink English roses that decorated the church. His bride wore a gown made from silk with matching elbow gloves, and her hat, which was worn tilted on the side, was adorned with feathers, netting and brooch embellishments. Maybelle had been very precise about the style of dress she wanted to wear and selected the fabric herself, which she and her mother made together by hand, making the most of the long, light evenings. Dickie Hainsworth's wife, Celia, who at that point was heavily pregnant with their third child, had offered to help with the final touches and regretted not being able to attend the nuptials with her husband.

The wedding was small and intimate, and Jack, having quickly realised the way to his fiancée's heart was through music, privately arranged (courtesy of a colleague who was related to the vicar) a piano recital of Schubert's *Licht und Liebe* at the church service, which was held in the village at St John the Baptist, once known as the Chapel of Coleye. It was where both Jack's and Maybelle's parents had married, and Jack admired its gothic beauty, particularly the church's tall, slender, octagonal fluted columns with its moulded capitals and pointed arches. Maybelle was deeply moved by the groom's thoughtful gesture; Harry, in his role as best man, was relieved to have respite from his studies; Andrew Drake was brimming with pride as he gave his daughter away and Mary cried – no one had been sure whether she was happy or sad – while Eva and Albert marvelled at how grown up and handsome Jack looked in his morning suit.

'Now, dear,' said Mary after the church service, 'come with me.' She proceeded to lead her daughter gently by the elbow to a corner of the hall where the two of them could be out of earshot. 'I prepared your trousseau earlier in the week, which I know is of no great consequence to you but it signifies something to me.'

'Oh, Mother, there's no need to get upset again.' Maybelle reached for her mother's hand, having noticed that her eyes had started to glisten around the edges.

'Well, it's not every day that my daughter gets married, and goodness knows it took long enough. But now that you're going – gone – well, I shall miss you. Quite terribly, in fact.'

'I'm not moving to the other side of the world, Mother – we'll only be a short walk away. You know you can visit anytime. And you still have Father. We mustn't forget Father.'

Mary snorted and rolled her eyes in what appeared to be mock exasperation. 'We are here to talk about your trousseau, not your father, dear. Now, inside you'll find some useful items – household goods, linen, clothing and the like. But, and I *only* wish my mother had been as thoughtful, I've included other things that I think will serve you well in your marriage.'

Maybelle looked at her mother, her violet eyes narrowing.

'Now, don't look at me like that, child. You've still got a lot to learn, and your journey is just beginning. These things will hopefully help you along the way, including my china tea set, which I have no use for anymore. Your father and I rarely entertain now and you, well, at least it will be kept in the family.' Mary waved a hand dismissively, detracting from the little tears that were forming quietly around her eyes. Then she took a handkerchief from her dress pocket and blew her nose dramatically. 'And please don't ask me about the other items – that's all to come.' Mary smiled knowingly as she patted her daughter's arm. 'Now, go and find that husband of yours before he thinks you've changed your mind. Heaven forbid.'

'What would I do without you?' Maybelle moved towards Mary, inhaling her mother's familiar patchouli scent. 'What *will* I do without you?'

It was then that she saw him; a pink rose was still on the lapel of his jacket and in his hand was a slice of the wedding cake that his Aunt Lily had baked to commemorate their wedding. How the guests had admired Aunt Lily's cream-coloured icing, which had been painstakingly piped in elaborate detail. But, oh, her husband! *Her* husband! Now, of course, she was Mrs Jack Jagger. Maybelle repeated the words as she gazed at the man she had just married. *So this is what it feels like,* she thought as she slowly walked towards Jack, who, as if sensing her presence, suddenly turned towards her and smiled.

*

The newlyweds honeymooned on the North Yorkshire coast. But it was the weeks and months that followed, the slow discovery of one another and the sense that anything was possible, that Jack and Maybelle remembered the most. Because that's what it felt like to them; the rest of their lives a blank canvas as hopes, dreams and plans began to dot the landscape of their lives like a wide, open vista. As for Jack, he regarded these benign interwar years as being among his happiest. He was finally building a life. He was married. He and Maybelle were living in their first home – a modest Victorian terrace in Brighouse. He was design assistant at EW Worth's; his natural, creative flair having finally been given a platform as colleagues began to sit up and notice this softly-spoken young man. Maybelle, meanwhile, took to the role of homemaker with ease and couldn't wait to fill the house with children. And Mary still visited every Sunday afternoon, not least to drink from her old china teacups.

5

'I can tell something's troubling you, dear.' Maybelle was watching her husband bounce their son on his knee. Hanson was nearly eighteen months old and, to the amusement of his parents, currently had a thing for his father's ties, pulling them this way and that like reins on a horse.

'Well, I suppose I've been giving the promotion some thought,' said Jack. 'I do not for one moment doubt what a terrific opportunity it will be and quite frankly it's what I've been working towards these past few years. But must it mean leaving this all behind?' Jack waved an arm around the room as if to emphasis the perceived loss they all would surely feel. He had lived his whole life within the boundaries of this wild and rugged county. God's *own* country. He knew the moors; he knew the villages dotted around them and he knew the countless mills that underpinned thousands of livelihoods. It was the only world Jack had known for a quarter of a century and now they were moving to the Midlands, he felt a heaviness in his heart.

'Yes, if that is where your career is taking you,' replied Maybelle. 'And really, if you want to work in textile design,

41

then quite frankly, there is no other place to be.' Hanson began to wriggle about, prompting Maybelle to take her son from her husband's arms and place him in her own. 'Lest we forget that Kidderminster is *the* carpet centre of the world. And you are going to be a *carpet* designer.' Maybelle had lived in the same Yorkshire village her whole life too, but she was feeling more sanguine about a potential move than Jack. 'Besides, we can always come back for visits. It's not as if we are moving to the moon.'

'You're right.' Jack reached for his wife's hand. 'Of course you are right.'

But not everyone thought it was a wise move, namely Mary, who insisted that her daughter and son-in-law think again about the inevitable upheaval. 'It's hardly the right thing for a baby to be carted off like that,' she said upon hearing the news. 'I can't bear the thought of my grandson being unsettled by it all. I mean, is the Midlands really the right place for him to grow up?'

'But he's not even two,' replied Maybelle incredulously. 'At his age, he's hardly going to know the difference whether he's moving to the Midlands or Timbuktu. Really, Mother.'

'But *I'll* know the difference. *I'll* know that he – *you* – won't be living here anymore, barely a stone's throw from my home. With *whom* do you expect me to spend my Sunday afternoons now? With *whom* do you expect me to enjoy a cup of tea and a slice of cake at the end of a trying week?'

'With Father?' Maybelle's voice had become softer, hoping to acquiesce her mother's sudden outburst. She glanced at her husband, who remained silent.

'Don't be so ridiculous,' retorted Mary. 'Your father hasn't drunk tea for over twenty years!'

In these moments, Jack knew not to interfere in the delicate dance that was his wife and mother-in-law's relationship. Unlike his own mother, whom Jack saw intermittently, Mary still treated her only daughter like a child, ignoring the woman in front of her, the woman she had become.

'Mother, this is a wonderful opportunity for Jack. It would be foolish to pass it by.'

'Well, I don't know many daughters who can happily abandon their family like this, but you've always been different.' Mary paused before continuing, her eyes narrowing as she looked at Maybelle and then Jack. 'Then again, it's your life, so by all means go. Leave Yorkshire. Go to the Midlands. I'm sure we'll manage quite all right without you. In fact, I'm *certain* of it.'

'We shall miss you, Mother, despite what you might think. And I hope you and Father will come to visit once we are settled. Hanson will be wanting to see his granny and grandpa before too long, I'm sure.'

Mary ignored her daughter's attempts at appeasement and turned towards Jack.

'What has your mother to say about all of this?'

'Well...' Jack knew he needed to tread carefully. 'She's sad to see me go, of course – any mother understandably would be – but at the same time she's happy to see her son progress in the world.'

'And Harry? Is Harry happy for you to leave *too*?' Mary's tone was sarcastic.

'Yes, I'm sure he's pleased for me,' said Jack, glancing at Maybelle.

'Harry recently graduated with first class-honours, Mother. We have a civil engineer in the family now, and the clever boy has already secured a job in Lancashire of all places. Isn't that right, Jack?'

Jack nodded. 'Yes. Fleeing the nest for Oldham.'

Mary waved a hand in the air and turned her cheek. Her distress was visible but she tried not to show it. Maybelle looked at her husband, who nodded discreetly in return. She knew what her husband was trying to convey and that was to leave Mary to it. In time – in her own time – she would surely accept the news.

It was settled. The carpet capital of the world was to become

Jack and Maybelle's new home. But as soon as this new chapter began, the darkness and uncertainty of war shrouded the country again. It couldn't have come at a more inconvenient time, Jack remembered thinking. He and Maybelle had taken Hanson on his first holiday to Aberdovey on the Welsh coast and it was exactly as they hoped. Waves lapped against the shoreline while stretches of golden sand, which felt like velvet beneath their feet, provided hours of entertainment for a rambunctious three-year-old. With the help of his father, Hanson proudly built his first sandcastle among the dunes, adorned with flags, seashells and a fancy moat, while his mother indulged her son with Aberdovey's finest homemade ice cream. No one tried to dwell too much on what was already happening in Europe. In fact, most thought that it would be over by now, but the impending threat of invasion was never far away, and Jack, along with countless others, decided to assist with the war effort and volunteer his skills.

When they returned home, Jack's pocket-sized military training pamphlet from the War Office was already waiting for him – the only indication as to what might be in store. If there ever was a time when he would use his artistic skills for the good of the country, this was it. *The British Army School of Camouflage.* Maybelle read the words on the front of the pamphlet before flicking through the flimsy pages. 'It all sounds very intriguing. My word, it says here that your role will involve *working in total secrecy and in increasingly sophisticated and strategic ways.* Whatever do you think that means? What do you think they will make you do?'

'I daresay I'll know more soon,' said Jack, quickly reading the small print at the back of the pamphlet. 'But I expect we'll need to find lots of creative ways to deceive and distract the Germans.'

'Can I come with you, Daddy?' Hanson asked, sitting on the edge of his parents' bed later that evening, as he watched his father gather clothes into a neat pile while Maybelle folded shirts next to him.

'Daddy won't be able to take you with him.' Maybelle reached over and stroked her son's cheek. 'He's going to be very busy and he's going to be very brave. But we'll have plenty of fun while he's away.'

'But I want to go with Daddy.' Hanson began to swing his legs back and forth.

'Daddy will tell you all about his adventures when he's back,' said Jack. 'Hopefully soon.'

'When?' Hanson looked at his father and pulled a sad face.

'I'm not sure, son. As long as it takes to make sure the bad man doesn't come here.'

'Bad man?'

'Yes,' said Jack, sitting down next to his son and patting the space between them. Hanson moved closer. 'That means I have to paint things, in all sorts of ways and in all sorts of colours, so that the bad man won't be able to find his way here.'

'What things?' Hanson began to tug at his father's tie, stretching it towards him.

'Aeroplanes mostly,' said Jack, drawing Hanson onto his knee. 'I'll have to use my imagination, just like when we play our games in the garden. I'll need tricks up my sleeve too. I suspect it will be a bit like magic really.'

'Magic?' Hanson clapped his hands together and made a *whoosh* sound.

'That's right, magic,' said Jack, ruffling his son's hair. 'I shall make things disappear.'

'And then...?'

'And then...' replied Jack, watching Hanson roll onto his back, his chubby legs suspended in the air. 'And then the bad man will go away.'

Later, when Jack and Maybelle were alone, save for the hum of the wireless playing quietly in the background, Jack rose from his chair and walked over to his wife. Maybelle glanced up from her embroidery, a delicate pink peony half completed in her lap. 'Working as a camouflage officer is no guarantee of a safe passage through the war,' he said, resting a hand on his wife's shoulder as he stood behind her. 'Even so, I still consider myself to be in a fortunate position.'

Maybelle looked up at her husband and nodded, waiting for him to continue.

'Come to think of it,' he added, 'imagination and inventiveness are the only real requirements. Not a bad place to find oneself in when there are millions fighting on the front line.'

Maybelle reached for her husband's hand and gave it a gentle squeeze. 'You are still brave. Very brave. And Hanson and I are so very proud of you.'

Jack gazed down at his wife and smiled. Somewhere on the south coast was going to be his home, whether for a week, a month, or years. He didn't have an answer. No one did.

He only hoped he would make it back home.

Art, but not as we know it   6

ENGLISH SOUTH COAST

'You got family back home?' The question was as unexpected as it was sudden, punctuating the silence that pervaded the room. Jack and his colleague, Officer James Hepburn, had been assigned to camouflage an aircraft together. Both were immersed in the task: one working on the nose, the other the tail.

'A wife and young son – well, a toddler really. He's almost four.' Jack looked up from his work, brushing away small flecks of paint which were sprayed across his face and overalls. 'We've just moved to the Midlands.' Jack took a step back to examine his work. 'He would be fascinated with all the planes here. Mind you, he'd have a field day with the paint too.'

The two men laughed; a brief respite from their rigorous routine.

'Yourself?' Jack asked. 'Where is home for you?'

'Not far away, even though it feels it here. My ma is still alive – Kent girl through and through. That's where we still live – the two of us. She always said if you can't look a man in the eye when you shake his hand, then you're still a boy. She's proper into manners is my ma. Couldn't tell you nothing about my dad, though – never knew him. Impossible to miss someone you don't know. Miss my sister, though. Died when I was six. Tuberculosis. She was only ten.'

'I'm sorry to hear that. I lost someone too – my father – as a lad. What was her name? Your sister?'

'Libby. Short for Olivia. But Ma and me always called her Libby.'

'It makes us more resilient, you know, losing someone like that.'

Officer Hepburn nodded, before returning to his task. His strong, muscular arms moved methodically as he employed vigorous earthy-coloured brushstrokes onto the body of the plane. After a few moments, he looked up at Jack and added, with a hint of self-deprecation, 'Someone must've found out art was the only thing I was good for. I'll do anything to keep them monsters out. I'll camouflage the whole country if that's what it takes.'

'Did you volunteer too?' Jack asked.

Hepburn wiped his hands on his overalls, before placing his brush on a nearby table. 'What was I supposed to do? Sit back and let my country down?'

Jack followed his colleague's movements, and it suddenly struck him just how young he was.

'I want to be part of this, be part of history. Help whichever way I can, you know?'

'Well, you'll certainly be putting those artistic skills to good use in sophisticated *and* strategic ways!' Jack emphasised the words sophisticated and strategic and the two of them laughed as the afternoon light infiltrated the corner of the room; shafts of yellow stretching across the floor like stalks while the half-painted aeroplane glistened in shades of green and brown.

Everything had happened so quickly. One minute Jack was in Aberdovey, enjoying the sea and fresh air with his family; the next he had been catapulted to the Sussex coast along with countless designers, artists and other civilians. It was as if he had found himself in a new reality, a reality which hadn't quite sunk in. Now, in the midst of it all, when he had finally come up for air, it dawned on him. They were really at war. It was the uncertainty that affected Jack the most. Uncertainty as to when this chapter would end; uncertainty as to how many lives would be sacrificed and uncertainty as to when he would next see his family. He worried for Maybelle. They had barely been in their new home a year. How was she feeling about all of this? He hadn't asked her. He simply took it for granted that she would manage until he returned, but even that assumption didn't hold any guarantees.

Days turned into weeks, weeks into months; autumn into winter and winter into spring. In May 1940, the Germans began their assault on Belgium. The Netherlands and France prepared to fall, and everyone, including Jack, assumed the whole thing would be over in a few days.

'Can you believe they employed a zoologist to be deputy head of the unit here?' said Jack to Maybelle during one of the rare occasions a telephone was available. 'Apparently, the man is an expert in the animal kingdom, but whether he knows anything about disruptive patterns is anyone's guess.'

'Is that so?' Maybelle was happy to hear her husband in good spirits. 'I imagine it takes all sorts. As long as he knows what he's doing, that's the main thing.'

'How's our boy?' Jack was keen to change the subject.

'Your son appears to have developed a taste for trifle of all things.'

'Well, I can think of worse things than trifle,' said Jack, laughing.

'It's all Aunt Lily's fault. You know how terrific she is with her puddings. I made a trifle from one of her special recipes and Hanson enjoyed it so much, he insisted not only on second but third helpings and has been hankering after it ever since! My bread and butter pudding offers no consolation – it simply has to be trifle!'

Jack felt soothed as he listened to his wife speak of domestic trivialities and home.

'I have to watch him, mind you,' added Maybelle. 'I may ask Mr Phillips to raise the garden gate a notch as I'm frightened the boy will clamber over it one of these days. He's such a lively little thing!'

'Yes, might be a good idea,' said Jack with some reluctance. The thought of his wife having to rely on another man to help her around the home was not something he wanted to dwell on. It was moments like these when Jack felt helpless, as if his role as man of the house had been suspended until further notice. It also made him uneasy, and this sense of unease spilled over into his brief visits back to his family, where bursts of domestic bliss did not always flow quite as he would have liked.

'I fear you're spoiling the lad while I'm away,' lamented Jack during his latest visit. 'Our son seems to have become accustomed to drinking only cream. I wonder, since when has milk not being good enough? I saw him pulling a face this morning because there wasn't any cream left in the bottle. He's five years old, for heaven's sake! It's not as if milk is in abundance either. Perhaps it might do our son good if you explain what rationing is all about.'

'And it might do *you* good to remember that he's our son, who, if you cared to realise, is missing the presence of his father,' Maybelle retorted. 'I save up my coupons like everyone else, so why shouldn't I be able to indulge him every now and then? If I choose to give Hanson the cream from the milk while I drink the rest, then surely that's my prerogative?' In the seven years they had been married, Maybelle had rarely, if ever, spoken out of turn. Yet on matters of her son, she knew her mind. 'It doesn't do him any harm, and if I can't provide some comfort to our boy in these dark times, then for goodness' sake, when can I?'

Jack looked incredulously at his wife. Here was the woman who had barely been able to meet his gaze when they had first met, so shy was she upon their acquaintance. And now she was speaking with conviction about how she intended to raise their son – how *she* was raising their son while her husband was at war. And by all accounts, she wasn't waiting for approval from anyone. 'Very well,' said Jack, softening. 'I daresay it will make his bones stronger.'

'I daresay it will,' replied Maybelle, brushing down her apron as she reached for crockery from the kitchen dresser. 'Now, I'm sure you won't have been served roast pork in a while. Hanson and I have been eating Woolton pie until it's been coming out of our ears, haven't we, darling?' Maybelle glanced at her son, who had just wandered into the kitchen. He was waving a wooden toy soldier around and making whirring sounds, as if to imitate a plane. 'Why don't you tell Daddy how you've been helping me to plant all those carrots, cauliflower and parsnips in the garden?'

'Is that right?' Jack reached over and took Hanson's hand, scooping him onto his knee. 'I'm very pleased to hear that.'

'Why don't you tell him about Potato Pete and Doctor Carrot from your comic strip?'

Hanson tried to wriggle free, not used to having his father around, all the while looking curiously at this half-stranger. 'Have you made bad man go away yet?'

Jack looked into his son's bright eyes, whose attention returned to the toy soldier he was clutching.

'Not yet, he's a very bad man, you see, and it's taking a long time.'

'How long?' Hanson wiggled the toy soldier in the air as he spoke.

Jack glanced at Maybelle, who quickly interjected. 'Hanson, darling, why not tell Daddy about all those coupons we saved up to have pork for supper? There were so many. Do you remember, we counted them together?'

'No,' said Hanson flatly, his eye resolutely on the soldier, which he was now waving erratically.

'Yes, you do, darling. We laid them all out on the table together at the start of the week.'

'How long…?' Hanson repeated, ignoring his mother while wiggling the soldier in front of Jack's eyes. 'How long 'til bad man goes away?'

'I don't know,' replied Jack, releasing Hanson gently from his arms, sad that he couldn't provide more certainty. 'But all those brave soldiers are doing their very best to make him go away.'

'Bad man, go away! Bad man, go away!' Hanson began to jump up and down, the soldier still in his hand.

'That's a handsome soldier you have there,' said Jack, hoping to distract his son from any more thoughts of war. 'I haven't seen it before. Is it new?'

Hanson ran towards the kitchen door, before glancing back at his parents, first at Maybelle, then Jack. 'Was Mr Phillips. Now it's mine.' Jack thought he detected an air of malice in his son's voice.

Maybelle glanced at her husband. It was as if a dark cloud had suddenly obscured part of his face. She knew Hanson's words would have hurt him. 'The pork is ready but the potatoes just need a few minutes longer,' she said brightly.

'Roast pork. Now I'm the one being spoiled!' There was a forced joviality in Jack's voice as he rose from his chair. 'And pudding! I'll need to be dragged back to the coast at this rate.'

'Well, if it's quite all right with you, I like to spoil my husband every now and again.'

'It's quite all right with me,' said Jack, walking towards his wife and placing an arm protectively around her. He knew it was futile to be angry with Maybelle. There was nothing he could do about Mr Phillips, or the toy soldier, or the feeling that his son viewed him as merely someone who came to visit from time to time. This was what war was about: fragments of normality and familiarity jostling for space in a strange and uncertain world. A world that was ever-changing.

A world that could change in the blink of an eye.

7

When Jack returned to the south coast, life remained strange and uncertain but with an undercurrent of urgency. The advice now, within the unit, among colleagues, was that the enemy advance had accelerated and an expected attack was imminent. There was no room for complacency. They were operating under a ticking time bomb – at least that's how it felt – and it was imperative to prepare for the worst while terror persisted in the menacing skies above.

'Now listen, lads…' Officer Phillips, stout in stature with a jolly face, positioned himself at the top of the low-lit room and looked out at the crowd of men in front of him. 'In light of recent developments, it is now a matter of priority that we protect all of our airfields. The Germans are edging closer to our shores, threatening us with their aggression. And we need to be, as always, one step ahead of the game. And we *will* be, no doubt whatsoever, because we will *not* be beaten.'

Jubilant roars emanated around the room and men clapped excitedly, as if a great victory had already been won. Officer Phillips took this opportunity to drink from a glass of water that had been placed on a table nearby.

In the far corner stood Jack, who was leaning casually against a wall, clasping a pencil in one hand and in the other a small notepad. Every so often, he glanced up from his notepad before recording his observations, which were beginning to take shape in the form of caricatures and sketches of his fellow colleagues. Harry has no idea, he thought, an image of his brother suddenly coming to mind. No idea what is actually *going* on. Not that it was his fault, with his poor eyesight. But *was* it right that he was cocooned away in his own little world, unaware of the effort, the relentless, ongoing effort? It was as if history was repeating itself, Harry impervious to the sacrifices being made around him.

'So, lads, what's next? Well, first things first, let me congratulate you on the terrific job you are all doing, and I want to thank each and every one of you for your hard work.'

Some of the officers started clapping again, before Phillips motioned with his hands to stop.

'Secondly, we need to find new ways to keep those Jerries well and truly off the scent.'

The excitable crowd roared their approval, throwing caps in the air while Officer Phillips paused until the noise had once again dissipated. 'That means protecting our airfields as a matter of priority. We'll be using camouflage to create a rural-type landscape and simulating woodland, hedges and the like. And that's not all, because as you all know, visual deception is just as important as concealment. So, lads, how are we going to do that?'

Officer Phillips paused again, this time to retrieve a handkerchief from his top pocket to mop his glistening brow, which had started to form beads of sweat. 'Well, boys, what we're going to do is build thousands of pillboxes all over the country, which will allow our troops inside to fire at the enemy. And then we're going to let nature take its course, while these pillboxes, some small, some large, blend into their environment. They might look like unloved, derelict cottages from above, but these will be armed structures. And mark my words, if any invading troops come too close, they'll do so at their peril.'

As if on cue, another wave of fists thumped the air.

'But we won't just be employing our efforts in the countryside. Our camouflage tactics will take on an urban form too, as we prepare to build pillboxes in streets and squares across our cities. Lads, mark my words, *no* stone will be left unturned.'

Officer Phillips gestured with his hands for quiet to resume. 'We will need your expertise to do this, and in the coming days and weeks many of you will be deployed across this great land of ours to help carry out these plans. The rest of you will remain here to continue the valuable work you are doing to transform our military equipment. Thank you for your time, lads. If you have any questions, please come and speak to me or my colleagues here.'

While the crowd began to disperse, Jack remained in the room and waited. He reached inside his pocket for his pipe, before deciding that some fresh air and a brisk walk around the grounds would do him good. The sky was threatening rain, with large black clouds beginning to accumulate, and as Jack began to walk towards a row of maple trees at the back of the building, he quickened his pace. Blackbirds could be heard chirping in the branches nearby, and Jack found it strange to think that somewhere else anti-aircraft guns were conducting their own melodic cacophony, with shells whistling high in the sky like fireworks, winking brightly before extinguishing themselves.

'Funny old business, this war game,' came a voice not far behind Jack.

'What's that?' said Jack, turning around to see a man who was also smoking a pipe.

'This war business, it's a funny old game to find ourselves in.'

'It is indeed,' said Jack, looking at the man more closely. The officer was about the same age with round silver glasses, high cheekbones and a long, angular face. But it was his eyes that Jack found the most curious. They seemed ablaze with indignation and fury.

'Those Jerries think they are going to win, but they have no idea what they are up against. They may have taken Paris but they'll never take London – or any of our cities for that matter.'

'Yes, I suspect you're right.' Jack spoke with an air of detachment. 'I think we'll certainly outwit them with our pillboxes in any case.'

'Outwit them? Of course we'll outwit them. Those Jerries haven't a clue what we're capable of, because this great land of ours is *not* for the taking. Not now, not ever! Let's hope every one of them is shot down, until not *one* Jerry is left standing.'

The officer was shouting now with a vehement incoherence and Jack, shocked by his sudden vitriol, instinctively moved a few steps back to distance himself. 'It's the work of the Nazis,' said Jack, once the man had stopped shouting. 'This terrible business is the work of the Nazis. I have no doubt most Germans are as fed up and terrified as we are. They want what we want; sons, husbands, fathers returned safely to mothers, wives and children. And for peace to resume. By the grace of God, let's hope peace *will* resume soon. It's war that's evil, not men. No one wants to be in this mess.'

It had started to rain, gentle drops that seemed to arrive at just the right time. Jack put his pipe in his pocket, the lingering smell of tobacco mingling with the damp air. Before he turned around, making his way back towards the main building where only moments ago words of defiance had been spoken and the bellies of men fired up, Jack caught a glimpse of the officer's silhouette from the corner of his eye. But Jack wasn't feeling defiant and his belly wasn't filled with fire. It was filled with something else, something unrecognisable. All he knew was that he had to get away.

'They'll never beat us, you know,' the officer shouted to Jack from a distance. 'Never…'

Years later, when his son married a German girl, Jack remembered the officer with the round spectacles. Despite working at the same unit for nearly four years, they remained strangers united by a common goal. But the officer's words never left Jack's mind. And he wondered what the officer would think of his daughter-in-law, whose own father had fought in the Great War; a terrified seventeen-year-old boy trying to be brave for the sake of his mother as she bid him goodbye and watched him walk towards the unknown; praying for his safe return. The officer would probably have called Jack a traitor.

*

Jack and Maybelle were thirty-six years old when the war finally came to an end. They still had their whole lives ahead of them, and even though the war had cut short their plans for a larger family, they were content. Initially, Maybelle expressed some sadness that Hanson would grow up an only child, like herself. She also wondered whether being an only child would affect him adversely, make him different somehow. But Jack had reassured her, pointing out their son's quiet confidence and popularity. And so, thoughts of a larger family – the sister or brother for Hanson – soon dissipated. Hanson was enough. Hanson will always be enough, they conceded. They were a perfect family of three.

Other things took time. Jack remembered how the adjustment was strange at first, of no longer working under constant threat. Slowly, the images that had been a part of him for so long – the aeroplanes, the uniforms, the various quotidian noises that usually signalled imminent danger – faded to the corner of his mind. Still, Jack had much to be grateful for. So many men had lost their lives or were left horrifically injured. *He* had been spared. *He* had survived this atrocity. His only complaint was sleep that was fitful and filled with nightmarish scenes of aeroplanes in flames and burnt corpses lying one on top of the other. These bloodied landscapes always woke Jack with a start. And then the relief, the sheer relief once he realised where he was; that it had all been a dream, while a wave of gratitude swept over him. He was safe. His family were safe. They still had the gift of life.

Maybelle had her own adjustments to make, namely reacquainting herself – she had become very used to her own company – with her long-absent husband. Music (and Hanson of course) was her solace, listening for what seemed like hours to Bach and Beethoven on the gramophone when her son had gone to bed. It was ironic really, she remembered thinking at the time, to find so much comfort in these German composers whose country was now the enemy: abhorred and untrustworthy. Still, she was glad to have her husband back when so many wives had been robbed of theirs. They would be a proper family again, but, as Aunt Lily liked to remind her: remember to do something that makes *you* happy, something that is yours and yours alone. At first, Maybelle wasn't entirely sure what Aunt Lily had meant by her words. She *was* happy. She had her husband and Hanson. What else was there? As long as they were happy, *she* was happy. Besides, she had a house to run.

And then, during those long wartime evenings when she was alone with her German composers, Maybelle took up dressmaking again, something she had begun in earnest before she was married. The modest box room on the top floor just below the attic was named the "Designers' Den" because it was where Maybelle kept all of her colourful sketches and various fabrics. It was always dappled with light on a bright day and in the corner was a Singer sewing machine, a gift from Jack for her twenty-fifth birthday. It was Maybelle's space. It was where she came to think, to sew buttons back onto shirts and to darn her husband's socks. And there were plenty of those to keep her busy. It was now also a place to create beautiful dresses.

*

'Just look at the light outside.' Jack was pointing at the view in the garden one evening. 'The way the mauves and apricots blend together into the most glorious sunset. You know, I've been thinking about Venice again. I did promise that once we were married we would visit those pretty canals and fine palazzos together. But what with the war and everything…'

Maybelle laughed. Her expression had a faraway look. 'Oh, Jack, I can just see you…' her thoughts drifting towards a palette of watery pastels '…see you searching for the perfect spot to watch the sun sink into the Veneto…'

'We deserve it. *You* deserve it. I rarely tell you how much I appreciate what you do.'

Maybelle smiled shyly and it reminded Jack of when they had first met.

'It's true. *You* have kept this family going these past few years without complaint. I often think how much Hanson is growing into a fine boy and that is all down to you.'

'It's my job…'

'Yes, but you did it – *do* it – with such grace and love.'

'I do it because…' Maybelle paused. 'I do it because you and Hanson are everything to me.'

Jack reached over to touch his wife's hand. 'One day, we *will* go to Venice. That I promise you.'

It was a brave new world, and despite the horrors of the past five years, there was still hope. Hope to dream about the future. Hope to dare make plans again; however tentative, however far-fetched they may have seemed in the moment. It was 1946. Jack's idealism was as strong as ever. Yes, there were dreams of Venice, of faraway places; places which only months ago would have been inconceivable to think about, to dream about. Jack was ambitious and determined and proud. Ambitious not to squander the opportunity to do something with his life.

Determined to experience every drop of what the world offered. And proud of what he had created: a family. A family whom he could be fiercely proud of. A family he was determined to defend to the end. Because wasn't that what life was all about? Creating a family? A family to be proud of ? A legacy of sorts?

PART 2

Hanson

8

'The art teacher mentioned Dad in class today. It was embarrassing.' Hanson threw his satchel on the floor in the hallway, which landed with a thud.

'Darling, I've told you countless times to be careful with that satchel. Next time, it might catch an ornament.' Maybelle was peeling potatoes in the kitchen but she came out to greet her son, who had returned home from school. 'Now, tell me, what did he say that was so offensive?'

'It wasn't offensive, just that Mr Sykes mentioned him.' Hanson followed his mother into the kitchen. 'I just didn't like him talking about Dad.'

'Well, if you don't tell me what he said, I won't be able to sympathise.' Maybelle placed two slices of bread on a plate and gave it to her son.

Hanson slumped sullenly into a chair. 'It's about his commission, you know, the painting he's been asked to do.' Hanson reached for the butter dish and slid it towards him.

'Is that so extraordinary? I think it's rather nice that your father was asked to paint a watercolour for the school.'

'That's not what I'm concerned about.' Hanson scooped two large slabs of butter from the dish and smeared it roughly onto his bread. 'It's the magic I'm worried about.'

'Oh, darling.' Maybelle turned around and laughed. Two peeled potatoes were in her hands, their yellow skin a fluorescent hue. 'If that's what you're so worried about, I can ask your father not to perform any of his tricks when he gives the talk at the end of term.' Maybelle glanced at the butter, which now had a considerable dent in it. She had asked Hanson countless times to use the butter sparingly, told him they only had so many coupons to last them, that his father would be angry if the butter was gone before they would be allowed to buy another one, but it didn't seem to make any difference. Hanson always forgot. Either that or he was careless. The solution, Maybelle decided, was quite simple. *She* would go without.

'Have you had enough to eat, darling?' Maybelle looked at her son's empty plate before placing the potatoes to one side.

Hanson didn't reply. He picked up a newspaper instead, briefly flicked through its pages and then left the room.

Hanson was fourteen years old and very much his mother's boy. Maybelle doted on him and he in turn aired his grievances to her, many of which were directed at his father. The latest, it transpired, was his father's burgeoning interest in magic and accepting an invitation to give a talk to Hanson's art class on his paintings and the special rug he had designed to commemorate the Festival of Britain. Still, it was the magic Hanson appeared to be most concerned with. *Why can't he be normal like other fathers?* he thought. *Who decides to suddenly become a magician? Carrying apples and extra shillings with him just in case.* And a magician called Jelisto – *Jelisto* – at that? Hanson went upstairs to his room and opened the window. The air was stuffy, redolent of a late spring afternoon, and the sun sprinkled little shafts of yellow light into the room. He closed the curtains and lay on his bed. Only six more weeks to go until the end of term, he thought, as he watched the movements of a bee which had found its way inside. That meant a whole eight weeks to play cricket and see his friends. Hanson was almost fifteen and if he were granted one birthday wish, it would be to escape far away from home – from school – and for no one to be able to find him again. Leave without a trace, without any warning. Yes, that's what Hanson would wish for.

He opened one eye and glanced over at his desk. On the table, hand carved by his father for Hanson's tenth birthday, lay his homework for the weekend: geometry, geography and preparation for an English test. Dull, tiresome, homework. Irrelevant, useless homework; all of which would be forgotten by the time he left school. *Of what importance will learning about the semi-arid land of Australia really have on my future*, he thought, *or the work of Coleridge for that matter?* Hanson turned over onto his side, pulled the eiderdown over him and sighed.

On the other side of town, another bee had found its way into a room, disturbing a talk that Jack was giving to a group of textile students whose focus had been temporarily diverted. The students watched as the bee flew haphazardly around, bumping repeatedly against the glass windowpane, never quite making its escape.

'It seems a friend has come to join us,' said Jack as he tried to move the bee away with his hand. 'It's not going to sting if you all keep perfectly still. Remember, he's more frightened than all of you put together.' Jack walked to the other side of the design studio and opened the door. Moments later, the bee followed Jack's path and found a new way out. 'Clearly, our friend didn't want to leave the same way he came in,' he said, laughing. The group, which had now re-formed a circle around him, relaxed again. 'Now, where was I? Ah yes, Worcester Bridge. It's ironic that we often don't notice the things where we live. How many of you notice things around you, I mean really notice, when you go about your day?'

The students shook their heads, waiting for Jack to continue.

'We take for granted all those landmarks that strangers, hundreds if not thousands of miles away, come to see, photograph and write home about. Unfortunately, Worcester Bridge cannot be classed among the world's seven wonders, for it is purely functional, and any aesthetic beauty comes a poor second.'

Jack glanced at the students as they recorded his words in their notebooks, and he made a point of speaking more slowly.

'But should it disappear overnight, it would certainly be missed, if only for the fact that you'd drive straight down Bridge Street and into the river.'

The students laughed.

'But would anyone remember exactly what it looked like? Would any of you?'

The students shook their heads again.

'Chances are, people wouldn't. Most people might use Worcester Bridge twice a day and never actually really notice it. You may be asking what all this has got to do with design. Well, quite a lot, in fact, because it's all about perspective.' Jack walked to his desk and picked up a piece of carpet. 'What's the first thing you think of when you look at this?'

A young man with jet-black hair raised his hand.

'Yes,' said Jack, 'go on…'

'The pattern?' said the boy with the jet-black hair.

'That's right,' said Jack. 'And what else?'

'Colour?'

'Precisely… colour *and* pattern – two of the most important ingredients in carpet design.'

The students scribbled down Jack's words, glancing up only when he stopped speaking.

'But as well as perspective, carpets and painting have another feature in common. They must have eye appeal. *And* they must be emotional. I mentioned that I'm currently painting a picture of Worcester Bridge. I don't expect this to be an easy feat, because it's basically a boring old structure. Its span is nearly flat and it's not rounded like some smaller bridges. That's why no one pays much attention to it. So the problem is how to make the subject matter interesting.'

A student raised his hand. 'Why not choose to paint another bridge instead?'

Jack smiled. 'Good question. Perhaps I like the challenge. Now, the obvious answer is to include in the background what features of the skyline I can muster up – Worcester Cathedral and St Andrew's spire. But if you put those two in a painting, they fight for eye attention and you don't notice the bridge. And there we have the perspective thing again.'

Days like these were few and far between, but Jack always enjoyed engaging with the students who visited the factory and studio. It was a relatively new thing – the collaboration with the local art college and the apprenticeship programme. Some of his colleagues had dissuaded him, pointing out that they had enough work on their plates, but Jack had insisted, reiterating the importance of providing these opportunities. What had Albert told him? *You're a designer now, but don't forget the next generation of talent coming through.* It would have been easy to turn a blind eye, to keep climbing the ladder without looking back. *People are afraid. They don't want what they've worked hard for to be taken away.* These words were a sage reminder of his own struggle. To remember that his own path had been far from smooth. In fact, were it not for Albert, he would not be here at all.

It was strange to think that he had known Albert longer than his father, and he sometimes felt guilty that, as if by loving Albert, he was somehow betraying Henry. Whether his mother felt the same way was doubtful. He didn't think so. She seemed very happy. Harry, understandably so, regarded Albert as the only father he had ever known. It was true; Albert had been a blessing to them all. He'd grown up with two remarkable men. Two remarkable fathers. How many people could say that?

'Our son seems to be worried about these magic tricks of yours,' said Maybelle, greeting her husband at the door as she took his briefcase. 'Any chance you could have a word with him about it?'

'Why on earth would he be worried? He hasn't complained before.' Jack laughed dismissively as he took off his jacket and draped it over a chair.

'More to do with school. He's worried about that talk you're going to give at the end of term. He said he doesn't like the idea of you performing magic tricks in front of his classmates.'

'The lad has nothing to worry about. I'd rather he concentrate on his end-of-year exams. He really needs to pull his socks up if he's going to have any chance of passing anything.'

'Well, he hasn't come out of his room all afternoon,' said Maybelle, wandering back into the kitchen. 'Don't be too hard on him. He's trying his best.'

Jack waved a hand impatiently and disappeared into the living room with a newspaper.

'How were the students?' Maybelle had returned with a tray and a pot of tea.

'Well, they didn't say much, but they were very diligent in their note-taking so I assume they were paying attention.' Jack laughed. 'I'd like to be able to offer more, though. It's so competitive these days.'

'You're doing so much for the students already. Don't forget your son in all of this.'

'What do you mean by that?'

'Well, I suspect he might be feeling somewhat neglected.' Maybelle's voice had lost its softness as she carefully poured tea into her husband's cup.

'Neglected? How the devil can the lad feel neglected? He has everything he needs – and wants.'

'Well, I daresay it wouldn't go amiss if you asked him how he's getting on from time to time.'

'Whatever next,' said Jack, shaking his head in exasperation. He unfolded the newspaper and watched his wife, who chose to avoid an argument at all costs, walk out of the room.

The strange thing was, it had all *started* with Hanson. That's why, thought Jack, it was all the more peculiar that his son should suddenly take umbrage at what was little more than harmless entertainment. Jack had joined The Magic Circle shortly after the war ended when a colleague told him one day that his uncanny ability to make things vanish was a talent that shouldn't be ignored. So Jack decided to make enquiries and see where this uncanny ability might lead. *The basic discipline of magic is sleight of hand, and making an object vanish is the archetypal magic trick*, said the man at the other end of the phone when Jack rang about becoming a member. *Once you learn sleight of hand, there are countless things you can do.* The man was right because Jack soon realised that there were many things he could do with a shilling, and people – children – were beginning to sit up and notice. Beginning with Hanson's eleventh birthday, to everyone's delight, Jack performed an amateur set of party tricks for his son and friends. And so, when the children asked, *Where is the apple? How did you make it disappear?*, Jack was spurred on. It was only a matter of time before Jack's birthday party tricks evolved into dinner party tricks, and Jelisto soon became a household name. *Now, where's the harm in that?* Jack thought, as he remembered the trick with the spotted handkerchief and cane.

Jack wondered how his fourteen-year-old son had become so irascible. He had been such a curious, lively child. Now it seemed that Hanson needed to be pushed with everything. Privilege *and* advantage. The boy had both in abundance – everything he could want and need: a good education, a stable environment, a loving family – so what was the issue here? Was it because his mother doted too much on him? Jack did worry about that. Was it because he was an only child? He recalled colleagues at work who had the same family dynamic, but from what he could glean, those children seemed to be perfectly well-adjusted. Jack would have sacrificed his right arm to have been offered the opportunities his son had been given. Yet it appeared the more he did for Hanson, the more sullen and difficult he became.

As well as being irascible, Hanson was also increasingly secretive; locking drawers and hiding things from his parents, so it was not a surprise that the bedroom door was closed when Jack decided to go upstairs to see what his son was doing. Unlike his wife, Jack knew that quiet didn't always mean diligence. Hanson was hardly studious. He loathed having to learn and so, if all was quiet upstairs, it usually meant that Hanson (more often than not) was trying to outwit his parents. Jack stood outside his son's bedroom and knocked – gently to begin with and then louder. It was better to give him the benefit of the doubt, if only for his mother's sake, he thought. As far as Maybelle was concerned, Hanson could do no wrong. Jack was certainly more objective. Yet the one thing they did agree on was their son's secretiveness. He'll grow out of it, and you weren't much different, said Mary, when Maybelle mentioned it in passing to her mother. But when Maybelle relayed her mother's words to her husband, both she and Jack agreed that this was different. There was something about their son that wasn't apparent in other children of his age.

Jack knocked on Hanson's door and waited for a response. 'Son? Can I come in?' He waited for a reply before opening the door but Hanson wasn't in his room. Jack glanced around and shook his head. School books and notepads were placed neatly one on top of the other as if they hadn't been touched, and the bed linen was dishevelled. But it was the window, moving gently in the breeze, which caught Jack's attention. He walked over to it and leaning over the sill, he spotted his son casually throwing a cricket ball against the garden wall. 'What are you doing down there? Shouldn't you be studying?' Jack shouted.

'Hello, Dad,' said Hanson cheerily as he looked up at his father. 'Thought I'd get some practice in.'

'Haven't you got homework to do? Mum said you have to prepare for geometry and English.'

'Yes.' Hanson swung his bat to the side. 'But I've finished it already.'

'Is that right? Well, if that's the case, I shall test you on what you've learnt already.'

'How about a game first?' Hanson's response was brazen but he did not receive an answer because Jack had gone already, closing the window firmly behind him.

On his way to the garden, Jack picked up one of his drawing pencils before finding Hanson – the sun highlighting the deep auburn tones in his hair – sitting cross-legged on the grass and eating a pear that had fallen from a nearby tree.

'I've not paid for you to go to a good school, only for you to fritter the opportunity away,' said Jack, walking towards his son. 'You've only got two years left. You need to make them count, lad.'

Hanson looked up at his father and decided that this was not the moment to make a quip.

'Now, your mother tells me you have homework to do this weekend, but you tell me that you've already finished it. Well, what's it to be?'

'I was going to finish it tomorrow,' said Hanson, frowning. 'Not that any of it really matters.'

'What's that?'

'What I mean is, I can't see how geometry is going to really help much in those hotels.'

'Hotels?' Jack loosened his tie as he spoke. 'What have hotels got to do with any of this?'

Hanson uncrossed his legs, the pear still in his hand. 'I've decided I want to work in hotels. Big hotels, with lots of interesting guests from all over the world.'

'Well, that's a first,' said Jack, smoothing his tie. 'Let's see where we are in a year's time and if you still feel the same, we can start thinking about it – seriously.'

'Do I still have to do my homework?'

'Well, you won't be working anywhere – let alone a hotel – if you don't do your homework and pass your exams. It's as simple as that, son. You have to, *need to*, put in the effort now.'

Hanson leant back on his elbows and sighed, squinting at his father through one eye as the sun caught the side of his face.

'Very well,' said Jack, taking the pencil out of his pocket. 'I shall expect to see everything finished by Sunday evening. And this here...' he said, wiggling the pencil '...is what I shall be using to check that everything is in order. In the meantime, it can disappear back into its box.' Jack whisked his hand behind his back, the pencil clasped between his fingers. When he brought his hand back to his side, the pencil was gone. Jack chuckled, a glint returning to his eyes.

Hanson rolled his eyes as he bit sharply into his pear. 'Maybe you could work some of your magic spells with my homework too?'

Jack picked up Hanson's cricket ball and smoothed it between his fingers. 'Remember, son, happy people rarely sit around. They are always working towards something.'

*

Six weeks later, Jack stood before an art class of fifteen-year-old boys, and spoke about his special commemorative rug and why, more than ever, design was integral to everyone's lives. Hanson sat at the back of the class, listening to his father with a mixture of admiration and incredulity; two conflicting emotions bubbling for prominence. *How odd*, he thought, *that my classmates actually seem interested, are actually listening to what my father has to say. And if Clive Dunwell, the best batsman in the school by far, wants to know where Dad gets his inspiration from then surely he can't be that bad after all.*

'Yes, lad?' said Jack, nodding at the student who had raised his hand to ask a question. Hanson turned to his left to see which of his classmates it was.

'What advice would you give to a new designer?' The pupil in question was the popular Freddie Coleridge, who was as renowned for his sketches of cars as he was for his occasional pranks.

Jack placed his sheets of drawings on the desk next to him. 'That depends on what kind of designer they hope to become, but ultimately the principle is the same. Firstly, you need eye appeal and secondly, a sense of perspective. Cultivate eye appeal *and* a sense of perspective. Everything flows from that.'

In that moment, Jack caught his son's eye at the back of the room. 'Now, I don't want to keep you lads from your class any longer, so if you have any more questions, fire away.'

The class remained silent and, as if on cue, Mr Sykes, the head of art, stood up and began to clap. The pupils followed suit and amid the steady ripple of applause, Mr Sykes said something about talent and determination and for everyone to cultivate their own inner designer. Hanson wasn't quite sure what his teacher meant by the last part, but he was sure to ask his father later. It was the first time in a long time, certainly as far as he could remember, that he was pleased to ask him something, something that even Clive Dunwell would surely want to know the answer to.

Hanson watched his father gather his belongings and wondered whether it would have been so embarrassing after all if he had finished the talk with one of his magic tricks. Perhaps the one with the handkerchief and the ball, which Hanson always liked. Now that his father was apparently the most interesting person in the room too, if Clive and Freddie were anything to go by, Hanson also thought about the idea he'd recently discussed with his friend Eddie. Running away without taking their exams didn't seem so appealing now after all. Where would they run away to? It wasn't as if they had a real plan. Or anywhere to go.

Besides, he would surely miss his mother's trifles, especially the one from Aunt Lily's special recipe book.

That was surely worth sticking around for.

Clara ⟨9⟩

THE DARKNESS AND THE LIGHT

'It's flowers I miss most,' said Clara, while Eva placed a blanket over her mother's legs, 'especially the lilac bush. Is it still flowering, dear?' Now that summer had arrived and the days were warmer, they had taken to sitting out in the garden, making the most of the late-afternoon light.

"No, Mother, it stopped flowering at the end of May. We have roses now – lovely pale pink ones. Can you smell them? They seem to be especially fragrant this year, don't you think?'

'Roses?' Clara echoed her daughter's words, as if surprised. 'Is it that time of year already?'

'Yes, I've always thought June to be the loveliest month.'

'You know, your dear father, may he rest in peace, planted a rose bush for our first wedding anniversary. It was the most beautiful sight. A sea of cream-coloured roses climbing up the house. And so fragrant...'

'Can I get you anything, Mother? Some tea, or a glass of lemonade perhaps?'

'I'm perfectly happy just sitting here listening to the birds. Thank you, dear.'

Clara Miller was ninety-two and where once she stood tall and strong, she was now frail and stooped like a wilting sunflower. She had also been blind for over thirty years. She hadn't seen a sunrise, sunset or indeed a rose come into bloom for so long; the abyss of blackness was now the only colour she could see and it was her constant companion. If you asked Clara if she could pinpoint when her eyesight began to fail her, she wouldn't be able to tell you. It was so gradual, so surreptitious, as if someone were tip-toeing behind her and slowly stealing the light from her eyes. What Clara did recall was the moment she could no longer differentiate between her daughters. Lily, the eldest, was taller and fairer; Eva shorter and darker. Now they were reduced to two blurry silhouettes, their features and form no longer recognisable to the woman who had raised them. Only their voices remained distinct: Eva's soft and melodic; Lily's commanding.

The doctor hadn't expected Clara to live a long life – but here she was still living it, and she was grateful every day for her daughter's dedication, for the light she brought to her life. Clara was also grateful for her eldest girl, Lily, willowy Lily as she was known by her family, who, at the age of sixteen, had been almost as tall as her father. Of course, Lily was no longer a girl. But she was still being called names by village nosy parkers who had nothing better to do than engage in tittle-tattle. She had heard the rumours. If they only knew her story, she thought; these cruel and ignorant people who decided that because she still lived in the family home, having being born there, grown up there and never moved out, she must be some kind of witch. But of course she knew the real reason behind these names. Unlike her sister, Lily never married, and for most of the villagers, she was something of an enigma, not least because she appeared to relish her independence. And because Lily didn't rise to the occasion and give them what they wanted – a husband by her side, children in her arms – they believed there was something wrong with her, that she was in some way flawed. The closer Lily kept her cards to her chest, the more village tongues wagged. *What do these folk know of the world anyway?* she thought. They certainly didn't know about David, the dashing, grey-eyed soldier she had met by chance the summer she was about to turn thirty. David, who was about to go to war and promised to marry her the following spring. David, who wrote her letter after letter until one day her replies were met with silence.

Those folk didn't deserve to know about David but Lily knew – the insufferable longing, the waiting, the empty abyss of hopelessness was something she never wanted to experience again. And so she overcame her grief by baking: cakes, flans, pastries, trifles and soufflés. She baked every day, sometimes several times a day; she baked for family and friends and sometimes she baked for herself. It was a ritual as much as it was comforting. It was also her saving grace.

'How's your sister, dear?' Clara turned her head as she spoke again, not realising that her daughter had disappeared into the kitchen to wash her hands.

'What's that, Mother?' Eva could hear Clara's words drifting towards her from the open window.

'I said have you seen your sister lately?'

'Not lately, no,' said Eva, walking back into the garden with a tray. 'She's gone to London.'

'Gone to London? Whatever for?'

'To visit Hanson.' Eva sat down again, shielding her eyes from the sun. 'Perhaps Lily has gone to show him how to make a proper soufflé.'

'But I thought the boy was in Cyprus?'

'He was, but he's completed his National Service now. Do you remember we told you at Christmas that Jack secured Hanson the trainee position in London? It's one of the most prestigious hotel training schools in the country.'

'What the devil is he doing there?'

'Well, he's starting out in the kitchens and he'll work his way around, I suppose.'

'And is your sister staying there with him?'

'Yes.' Eva poured water into a glass and placed it in her mother's hand.

'All by herself?'

'All by herself.'

Clara leant forward and carefully began to take small sips from the tumbler, which Eva held against her mother's mouth.

'Lily's been given a room overlooking the Thames, you know. She takes a walk along the Strand every morning at nine and again at four in the afternoon. And she's already been to the theatre, The Ambassadors, I think she said, to see that play everyone is raving about.'

'Well,' said Clara, once she had finished drinking, 'our girl certainly gets out and about. And why not? If I couldn't do it, then she certainly can! Just like our Jack. Now, what about that other boy of ours?'

'Harry? He's quite well, Mother. Albert is helping him with the wiring, remember? Helping them settle in. I still wonder after all these years where our boy inherited that mind of his – certainly not this side of the family, nor his father's. If anything, Harry takes after his stepfather. Isn't it funny how he is so like dear Albert...'

Clara reached for her glass, her hand moving erratically in the air.

'Here, Mother.' Eva placed the glass firmly in her mother's hand. 'I'll go and refill the jug.'

'That's no bad thing,' said Clara, closing her eyes. 'But his wife, I worry about that wife of his.'

'There's nothing wrong with Molly. She's just sad sometimes.'

'Sadness doesn't do anyone any good. That girl needs to take a leaf out of Lily's book.'

Lily   # 10

Lily ordered a strong black coffee and a Cinzano with tonic
water. It had just turned seven and Hanson was due to meet his
great-aunt for an early supper an hour ago. She didn't mind the
waiting so much, it was the enquiring glances she received; the
nuisance of having to explain herself every time, followed by a
niggling doubt that perhaps she had made a mistake and was in
the wrong place. Lily glanced around the wood-panelled dining
room. It's true that her memory occasionally failed her, but she
was sure that Sampsons had been suggested by Hanson for its
roast meat; its proximity to the Savigny and for its chess. It was
a wonderful suggestion really, thought Lily, because she loved
roast meat and she loved playing chess.

'Good evening Ma'am? Is everything to your satisfaction?'

'Yes, thank you, quite all right.'

'And your guest? Are they to arrive soon? Or will you be
dining alone this evening?'

'I already explained to your colleague over there,' said Lily,
gesturing impatiently at a waiter who was hovering nearby, 'that
my nephew – great-nephew in fact – will be joining me very soon.'

'Very good, Ma'am,' the waiter replied, bowing in an exaggerated manner.

'My great-nephew is, in fact, undertaking his hotel training at the Savigny. Five years it takes, apparently.'

'Very good, Ma'am. I'm sure he'll be very happy with his training at the Savigny.' The waiter bowed again and walked away briskly, a half-smile lingering on his face.

Lily sat back in her chair and took a sip of her Cinzano. The room, which was thick with smoke, pleased her. It was the kind of establishment that would make her sister shudder – too stuffy, too noisy, Eva would surely complain – and it was true, it was both these things, but it was also teeming with life, the kind Eva would never know about, even though she at one point fancied a life like this: literary, worldly, cosmopolitan. On the adjacent table two men were playing chess, postures hunched and brows furrowed, as they attempted to gauge their opponents' next move. Lily loved chess. She had taught herself many years ago, mainly as a distraction from David, but also after reading Stefan Zweig's *A Chess Story* and being fascinated by the protagonist.

Thanks to Lily, Jack also loved chess. Hanson, however, wasn't the slightest bit interested. He wasn't the slightest bit interested in cooking either, especially the bouillabaisse sauce that he was required to perfect before he graduated to condiments. There were so many condiments to learn – at least that's what another trainee, a Frenchman, had forewarned him – a lengthy list from various countries, regions and cultures. How on earth was he to remember them all? Still, he conceded, spending time in the kitchen was par for the course, and soon he would be learning the ropes in front of house, a far more civilised part of the hotel as far as he was concerned. Hanson removed his double-breasted jacket and *toque blanche* and made his way to the staff quarters. He shared a small bathroom with eight other trainees, but he didn't mind. In fact, Hanson rather enjoyed the camaraderie of it all. He was twenty years old and finally life was just beginning.

Oh, how he had waited all those years to leave school and put those dreaded exams behind him. And now, here he was, having promised himself, and Aunt Lily, that he was going to enjoy every minute. Hanson put on a pair of grey trousers and a blue shirt then stood in front of his meagre collection of ties, pondering which colour he should wear. He settled on dark blue and, before he closed the door behind him, reached for a jacket that was draped across the chair and swung it casually over his arm. By the time he arrived at Sampsons, an hour and a half later than agreed, Aunt Lily was not amused. Still, she excused his tardiness immediately, conceding that bouillabaisse could be tricky at the best of times and because she had such a soft spot for her great-nephew.

'Aunt Lily, I am so sorry—'

'And so you should be,' Lily interrupted, undercurrents of teasing in her tone. 'I've had quite a time of it here with the waiters buzzing around me like bees, unsure, no doubt, as to what to do with this old girl. Now, I did warn you about the bouillabaisse. Remember *bouille* means to boil hard and *baisse* means slow and easy. Did you remember that earlier?'

'Yes, I did, but I just don't think I'm a natural in the kitchen. Not like you with your trifles!'

They both laughed as Hanson bent over to give his great-aunt a kiss on the cheek.

'Now tell me all about your day. I want to know every single detail.'

Hanson settled into a chair opposite Lily and proceeded to tell her about the straw-haired sous-chef, who was a Catholic from Liverpool and insisted that everyone recite the Hail Mary before the morning shift. And how he, Hanson, had objected because he was an atheist and didn't believe in Hail Marys, least of all God. 'This Hail Mary business is to set us up on the right footing, apparently, or that's how the Liverpudlian justified it. More like turning us into left footers. I don't think I've stepped into a church since the day I was christened – and I have no intention to either for that matter.'

'Good grief! How did the sous-chef react to your objection?'

'Well, he was rather taken aback,' said Hanson, smirking, 'but I explained to him, in the nicest possible way, of course, that I wasn't brought up in the Catholic faith.'

'As if you didn't have enough on your plate, what with your condiments and sauces.' Lily threw her head back and finished the remains of her apéritif. 'Now, what will it be? Gin and tonic? I'll keep you company with another one of these.' Aunt Lily waved her tumbler in the air, the remaining ice cubes clinking and crackling.

Hanson loosened his tie. 'A gin and tonic is precisely what I need, thank you Aunt Lily.'

Lily spent five days in London, four of which were spent dining at Sampsons (where to the horror of her fellow diners, she tried her first cigar) and the other at Patisserie Valerie in Soho after reading about its delicious cakes and pastries in a magazine. Hanson was able to ask for half a day off, which was made full use of when Lily decided to take him shopping after complaining that he only had one suit to his name. *You can't have only one suit to your name and live in London,* she'd said. And that was that. Aunt Lily, seventy-two years old and as sprightly as ever, was going to take her great-nephew shopping in Regent Street.

'Mum would never do this, you know,' said Hanson as he tried on a marl grey jacket.

'Do what, dear?'

'Come to London like you have, all by herself. I don't think she's been anywhere without Dad. He travels the world while she's stuck at home. It doesn't seem fair, does it?'

'Well, that's because she's married. That's what married women do. Your mother is not unusual. I, my dear, am the anomaly.'

Hanson glanced at his aunt in the mirror. 'Do you ever wonder what it might have been like, you know, if you had married?'

Lily paused as she watched her nephew take off the grey jacket and try on a navy linen one, its elegant shape accentuating his broad stature. 'I'm not sure about this one,' said Hanson. 'What do you think?'

Lily ignored her nephew's first question. 'I agree. Linen doesn't travel well. Now, what about the single-breasted jacket in black? You can't go wrong with that.'

'The trousers are too long, but otherwise it fits perfectly.'

'Shame your mother isn't closer. She's wonderful at adjusting clothes, whereas I'm terrible.'

'I could always go a tailor...'

'Haven't the Hainsworths opened a shop in London? Dickie, your father's old friend, is married to a tailor. Why don't we ask at the hotel this evening? I can pop into the shop tomorrow before I leave and let them know you need a pair of trousers altered. I'm sure they won't mind at all. In fact, I'm sure the Hainsworths will be delighted.'

'If you wouldn't mind, Aunt Lily.'

'I won't mind a jot. There's nothing worse than an ill-fitting suit. Even worse than your bouillabaisse sauce.'

Lily bought Hanson two jackets that afternoon: a black one and a blue wool mix before popping into Fricks on the way back to the Strand because she wanted to see, and show her nephew, the new replica marshmallow sofa that everyone was talking about. 'What a disappointment,' she declared, as she and Hanson stood in the large, airy store, gazing at the sofa in question. 'And to think I've been led to believe, by some magazine or other, that this is the best thing to come out of the fifties, when the reality is that it's rather, well, a huge blow to one's expectations.'

Hanson took a step back and inspected the insipid-looking sofa. 'suppose that's the thing with expectation. Better not to have too much of it, or so I've been told, as it usually disappoints.'

'Quite right,' said Lily, linking arms with her nephew. 'I imagine had I been married, I most certainly would be disappointed. And I certainly wouldn't be gallivanting across London with you.'

'Ha,' said Hanson, laughing. 'I never thought of it like that, but I suppose you're right.'

'Well, isn't it human nature to believe that happiness is to be found in someone else's garden? But I learnt long ago that's nonsense. Now, promise me you'll always be happy with your choices.'

Hanson glanced sideways at his aunt, and smiled. 'But what if I change my mind?'

'You are perfectly entitled to change your mind. I just want you to be happy.'

Hanson didn't reply. And as they walked into the fading Piccadilly light, he wondered what his aunt had meant, if she had meant anything at all.

A week later, Lily paid her mother and sister a visit. It had been raining heavily for a day and a half – a relentless downpour that didn't show any sign of subsiding – and Clara and Eva had retreated indoors until the weather improved. Lily gave Eva a speciality tea and her mother a jar of strawberry champagne preserve, both of which she had bought in Fortnum & Mason. After she described all the delicacies that could be found in the store and relayed details of the Hainsworths' shop near Fenchurch Street, Lily proceeded to tell them about Hanson. Clara laughed when her daughter told them the story of the straw-haired sous-chef, Hanson's pickle with the bouillabaisse and how he had refused to speak to the guest who complained about the temperature of his soup, which Hanson had been assigned to keep an eye on.

Eva shook her head, a hint of disapproval etched across her

forehead. 'I wonder where he gets his irreverence from. His father isn't like that at all, nor his mother for that matter.'

'Oh, he's just a lad,' said Lily, waving a hand in the air. 'He'll soon grow out of it.'

'Well, I like to hear what my great-grandson is getting up to down there,' added Clara. 'It gives me something to think about and, quite frankly, it's good for my mind to be lit up every now and again. He's a Jagger after all, and Jagger boys *always* leave their mark on the world.'

Harry

11

By his own admission, Harry conceded there were good days and there were bad. Only lately, there seemed to be more of the bad days than the good. It was strange, but no matter how many times he witnessed his wife's descent into despair, Harry never felt prepared for the relentless blackness that seemed to engulf her, disable her, render her incapable of clambering out of the well of hopelessness. *In sickness and in health, for better, for worse.* As if Harry needed reminding of the vows he made before God, but he did, sometimes berating himself for feeling that the worse part would never get better.

It was the uncertainty he found the hardest. *When will it end? What can I do? How can I help?* He asked himself the same questions every time, until the cycle repeated itself like an all too familiar pattern – hope and despair, hope and despair – insidiously embedding itself into the heart of his marriage.

Molly had been just shy of her twenty-eighth birthday and three years older than Harry when they met. It didn't take long for Harry to realise that the woman he hoped to marry was a far cry from the girls he had known while a student at university.

She was – he remembered describing to his mother and Albert, a conversation that remained as clear as the day he had uttered it twenty-two years previously – like a delicate flower who needed more sun and water than the other blooms around her. In fact, if Molly didn't receive the exact amount of water or sunlight, Harry explained, then her world would be plunged into darkness.

'Like Grandma Clara's?' Eva had looked puzzled as she listened to her son describe the woman he was clearly in love with. 'Is the girl going blind?'

'No,' said Harry. 'It's not like that at all. She's like a flower. Like one of those delicate orchids.'

'Harry, dear, just get on with *what* you are trying to say.' Eva glanced across at Albert, who responded by placing his finger to his lips, as if to dull his wife's impatience.

Harry fidgeted nervously with his glasses, pushing them up the ridge of his nose, only to readjust them again. 'I'm not sure what I'm trying to say. I suppose sometimes it seems like she's stuck in a dark cloud, a thick, heavy, dark cloud, which comes out of nowhere and she can't get out of. And being stuck under this cloud makes her *really* unhappy for days, sometimes longer.'

'About what? What exactly is she unhappy about?' Eva's expression remained puzzled.

'I don't know. It could be anything really. The weather… something she hears, reads…'

'The weather? Are you sure about this girl?'

'Of course I'm sure. She's lovely in all the ways that matter.'

Eva looked at her husband. 'What do *you* think about all of this?'

'Well,' said Albert, shifting in his chair. 'Firstly, I think it's wonderful Harry has met someone he likes. Love, as we know, is a precious and rare thing. Secondly – and I speak for both myself and your mother when I say this – I am proud that you are not discouraged by Molly's affliction.'

'Affliction?' Eva glanced from Albert to Harry.

'Yes,' replied Albert. 'It's clear to me, as I'm sure it's becoming clear to Harry, that Molly suffers from bouts of melancholia. It's a medical condition. Not much talked about, but a condition all the same.'

'Melancholia…' Eva looked at her son apprehensively. 'Did you know about this?'

'I knew something wasn't right…' Harry began fidgeting with his glasses again. 'I just didn't know what exactly.'

'Melancholia,' said Eva, as if weighing up the concept. 'What a strange thing.'

'Strange, because *we* don't know anything about it,' said Albert pragmatically. 'Unfortunately, it's not just the likes of Molly who suffer. Spouses, sons, daughters, siblings – they all suffer too. But it's by no means a life sentence. She may get better in time. In fact, I think she *will* get better in time.'

Eva moved towards her son and cupped his face between her hands, like she did when he was a child. 'Well, as long as you know what you are doing, that's all that matters.'

It was a conversation Harry recalled often, remembering his stepfather's empathy and his mother's confusion. Still, they had *supported* his choice, *cemented* his decision, *accepted* Molly.

Alice, who was born a year after Harry and Molly were married, was not only a happy surprise, she was the antithesis to her mother: light, easy and uncomplicated. Alice was the summer to Molly's winter, while Harry existed between the two extremes. From an early age, Alice had been very good at intuiting her mother's moods, quickly understanding the ways of this temperamental, delicate lady (as she once heard her mother described). Alice preferred to describe her mother as special and whom she knew not to disturb at all costs. Even if Alice wanted to show her mother something, tell her about school, curl up beside her and make the sadness go away, she knew when to make herself inconspicuous. It didn't matter when the girls in her class asked in a slightly mocking way why

Mrs Jagger never met her at the school gates, Alice's loyalty for her mother never wavered.

Her father, meanwhile, was used to the parallels within which his life existed.

A world split into two: one half underpinned by order and the other half chaos.

Bridges and tunnels: these were Harry's specialisms; a pragmatist who thrived on precision and logic, mathematical formulae, technical specifications and the concepts of physics. He was an engineer who understood the complexity of how things were made. He just didn't understand the mechanisms of his wife's mind, her intricately complicated inner world that could change direction without warning. Still, it was a life he had chosen and he was content. Harry didn't want his brother's life. Jack always seemed to be striving towards an ideal: the ideal career, the ideal family. So many expectations stacked one on top of the other. From a practical point of view, something was bound to collapse – eventually. Not that Harry would wish that on Jack. He wouldn't wish that on anybody. But wasn't that what always happened?

Jack   **12**

'It was about so big,' said Jack, relaying to his wife the length
of the python that had slithered in front of him at the Queensland
hotel he had stayed at some three months previously. 'The strange
thing was, he appeared just as my client and I were taking afternoon
tea. We weren't sure whether it was the cucumber sandwiches he
was after or the scones.' Jack reclined in his chair and laughed, his
eyes twinkling with mischief. He enjoyed the role of raconteur, not
least because these tales were always delivered with a sprinkling of
exaggeration. 'Needless to say, our visitor didn't hang about once
the hotel manager caught wind of it.'

'I daresay it didn't,' replied Maybelle imperviously. She
was accustomed to her husband's tales by now and this latest
one, which she had already heard twice, was evidently one of
his favourites. 'When do you fly to Canada? I can't remember
whether you said next week or the following.'

'The twenty-sixth – that's if we get all the samples ready on
time. That Boycott lad, our new artist, is still finding his feet and
unfortunately we're behind schedule because of it.'

'Well, Hanson promised to visit and I think it coincides with your trip. I could always ask him to—'

'Not to worry,' Jack interrupted. 'Besides, it will be company for you.'

'I know, but it's such a rarity to have us all together now, what with Hanson in London and you travelling so much.' Maybelle was used to Jack's frequent trips abroad and despite Mary telling her daughter that she must feel very lonely with her husband *always* overseas, Maybelle looked forward to the time alone. In fact, she needed it. What Maybelle wasn't used to – it had been seven years since Hanson left home – was no longer having her son around.

'The twenty-sixth it is then,' said Maybelle, rising from her chair. 'At least there's time to prepare. You'll certainly need your wool coat if it's as cold as it is here.'

*

Two weeks later, Jack arrived in Newfoundland amid ten inches of snowfall, glad of his wool coat and his wife's prudent advice. The jagged edges of the rugged Eastern Seaboard, now a nebulous haze of white, had slowly morphed into something softer. Jack remembered the strange, eerie silence while he sat in the passenger seat of the company car that came to collect him from the airport and drive him to St. John's. By the time he reached his hotel – a cosy establishment at the foot of Signal Hill with its pretty walking trails and Cabot Tower at the top overlooking the city and ocean – the snow had turned the city into a ghost town. Telephone pylons, which loomed like menacing figures against the foreboding skyline, now rendered Jack isolated from the world, with neither his company nor wife able to contact him by phone.

'I'm afraid, Mr Jagger, it will be impossible to drive anywhere in these conditions,' said the hotel manager, who was paying each of his guests a courtesy visit to their rooms. 'You see that snow out there? Well, it's just going to keep falling, and it won't be stopping anytime soon.'

Jack looked out at the vast expanse of white. 'I don't suppose with the roads closed and public transportation down, my colleagues will be able to drive to the hotel either?'

'In this weather? Nothing to do except surrender to the elements. Now, if there is anything I can do in the meantime to make your visit as comfortable as possible, please, do come and find me.'

'Thank you,' said Jack, 'I'm sure I'll be very comfortable.'

The quiet – save for the occasional bark of the hotel's resident huskies – was a welcome respite from Jack's long journey, the traces of which he was feeling now. It was strange, he thought, that in his foggy jet lag, he should remember the meditation techniques he had learnt a year earlier in Calcutta. As snowflakes swirled and twirled around him, his mind began to wander back to the place he first learnt to be still. It was amid a riot of colour, heat, chaos and beauty: India 1960.

Following a week of business in Bombay and New Delhi, Jack had flown to Calcutta on the invitation of his clients, having expressed an interest in intricate Indian carvings. Jack, by this point, was beginning to discover the philosophies of the East, Buddhism in particular, and was devouring every book he could find on the subject. His host, the affable Mr Anand Mukherjee practised meditation himself and invited his colleague to visit the antique markets in the Bengal capital and meet a revered *yogi*. 'You have come to the right place, Mr Jagger,' he said, waving a finger. 'One can't move for the *ashrams* in this city, but the trick is to find one that is authentic. It's all about removing the wheat from the chaff!' Mr Mukherjee's warm brown eyes widened like a child's and Jack had liked him immediately, not only because his English was impeccable but also because of his unaffected charm.

'You have someone in mind?' asked Jack, intrigued.

'Oh, yes, yes indeed, and I think you will be very happy. He is the most revered, the most benevolent, the most experienced, the most successful *and* the most spiritual of all *yogis*.'

That is a lot of adjectives, Jack thought, before asking, 'Have you visited him yourself?'

'Oh no, no, no, no, no!' Mr Mukherjee shook his head. 'That is not possible. I have my own *yogi* in Delhi. It is greatly frowned upon to change *yogis*. I have chosen mine already. You are now choosing yours.'

'I see,' said Jack, trying not to sound dubious. 'Well, I shall look forward to meeting my *yogi*, highly recommended by you, of course.'

Later that day, Jack was collected from his hotel and driven some ten miles to the west of the city. He had visited India several times already, but the assault on the senses never failed to surprise him. As the car navigated potholes and holy cows, Jack marvelled at the images around him: women gliding past, a kaleidoscope of colour in their silk saris; lively street hawkers selling *chai*, the distinct aroma of ginger, cardamom and cloves wafting through the air; and monkeys jumping playfully in between all the activity. When he finally arrived at the *ashram*, Jack was met by Mr Mukherjee, who welcomed him with a smudge of incense. 'To cleanse you before entering,' he said, before looking down at Jack's shoes. 'Those need to come off.' Jack carefully removed his brogues and stood in front of the threshold, which was little more than a flimsy beaded screen. 'It's all right, you go in.' Mr Mukherjee ushered Jack inside as he stepped away from the entrance. 'I'll be waiting for you here.'

Jack moved the colourful beads to one side and found himself in what appeared to resemble an Aladdin's Cave, with the most exquisite furnishings scattered around the small, dark room. Persian carpets adorned the walls and from the ceilings hung ornately carved lanterns in a myriad of colours, which flickered in the dim afternoon light. The room was cool and smelled of burning incense, a welcome relief from the heat and dust outside. In the middle of it all was the *yogi*, who was sitting cross-legged with his arms placed loosely on his lap and gesturing for his visitor to sit down.

'Welcome, please, welcome...' said the *yogi* softly. Jack eased himself gently onto the floor, mirroring the *yogi's* posture. 'Relax... take your time. Be comfortable. There is no rush here.'

The *yogi* tapped his gong, which was placed neatly between his legs. 'Let us start. Are you comfortable?'

'Yes, thank you,' said Jack, awkwardly crossing his legs.

'Then let us begin with some gentle breathing.'

And so began a rhythmic pattern of inhalation and exhalation, controlled by the sound of the gong, which was as gentle and languorous as it was urgent and loud. Jack closed his eyes and followed suit.

'Breathe. Focus on your breath. Breathe in and out. In and out.'

Jack tried to concentrate on the *yogi's* voice, but the nagging ache that he felt in his legs had begun to distract him.

'Focus. Breathe in... and out.'

When was the last time I crossed my legs like this? Jack wondered...

'Breathe in... and out.'

I'm not sure I can hold this position for much longer.

'In. Out.'

If I just shift this way, that might help. Jack moved his right leg slightly and straightened his back.

'In. Out.'

Ah, that's better, thought Jack as he inhaled sharply. *That feels much better.*

'Please, now, open your eyes,' the *yogi* instructed, gently tapping the gong. His hands were clasped together and he was smiling at Jack. 'How do you feel? Are you relaxed?'

'Yes, I feel very relaxed,' said Jack, nodding effusively.

'Very good,' replied the *yogi*. 'Now, please, watch me.' The *yogi* closed his eyes again and placed his hands in his lap, taking deep, slow breaths. 'Please. Empty thoughts. Think of nothing.'

Jack closed his eyes again, trying not to think of Mr Mukherjee waiting outside.

'We call it *dhyana*. Hindi word for meditation. Please, now open.'

Jack opened his eyes. 'When *this* becomes quiet,' said the *yogi*, tapping his forehead, 'when *this* has no more thoughts... no noise... peace... nothing. Just still. *This* is *dhyana*.'

Jack nodded, unsure as to whether he should speak.

'Everyone thinks this is easy, very easy. But no, no, no! It's very, very hard. Very hard thing to do.'

Jack nodded again. 'I think so too.'

'Many years for me. Many years of practice. One life of practice. You want to try?'

'I would like to,' said Jack. 'It would be a privilege if you could teach me how.'

Jack spent three consecutive afternoons at the *ashram*, by the end of which he had learnt the basic techniques of deep breathing and mindfulness. George Harrison and the Beatles were yet to bring the concept of meditation and yoga to the West, but Jack was already ahead of the game, excited to be discovering the connection between wellbeing and creativity and share what he had learnt with his wife. Maybelle, it seemed, was content simply listening to her husband's adventures rather than experiencing them for herself. Certainly, the Bengali *ilish* Jack had eaten the evening before and the *panta bhaat* he ate for breakfast, which he learnt from his Indian colleagues kept the body cool during the hot summer months, were not something Maybelle cared to try for herself. He knew his wife, and although she was open-minded to a degree, she often regarded things that were foreign with suspicion. In this respect, they were very different. Jack regarded travel as the great educator; Maybelle less so.

'So, how was it?' asked Mr Mukherjee, as he drove Jack back to the hotel.

'It's a wonderful thing, meditation, as you very well know, Mr Mukherjee. If more people knew about it in England, I'm sure it could calm a thousand minds and cure a thousand ills.'

'Oh yes, I think so too. My people have been practising meditation for over two and a half thousand years. It is an art *and* a science. But now you must remember to keep up the breathing back home. You think you can do this?'

'I will try,' said Jack, smiling. 'My wife will certainly make sure of it.'

Mr Mukherjee grinned and pointed at the cows who were wandering aimlessly along the road, oblivious to his bright red Ambassador and the hooting car horns around them. 'In England, the cows are not sacred, but I think they are not selfish either.' Mr Mukherjee was waving impatiently. '*Jao jao*' he shouted as he leant out of his car window. '*Jao jao!* They should know I have a very important client with me.' Mr Mukherjee emphasised the word "very" as he glanced at Jack, and the two men laughed.

'In England, we would call this a traffic jam,' said Jack. 'Being stuck on a motorway is no fun either. This here, though, is far more colourful and entertaining.'

'Yes! A wonderful, sacred cow traffic jam.'

*

And so it was in the midst of a Canadian snowstorm that Jack recalled what he had learnt under the heat of an Indian sun. He closed the heavy plaid curtains and lay down on the bed, letting his arms fall loosely to the side as he tried to remember what the *yogi* had taught him: *Start by focusing on your breath... breathing in and out, in and out.*

Wait a minute, Jack thought. *Wasn't he supposed to remind his wife to take the car to the garage today? What time was it in England? Were they five hours ahead or six?* Jack inhaled sharply as he willed the thoughts racing through his head to disappear; persistent, banal thoughts that swirled around his mind like the snowflakes outside. It took years of practice for Jack to master the art of being present. But he never forgot the *yogi's* words, the calmness he exuded and the wisdom he shared with him that afternoon.

In between these quiet bursts, Jack read, sketched or worked on a brief. He also became acquainted with the guests around him; usually over coffee and eggs at breakfast. They were an eclectic mix, Jack thought, and he began to recognise the familial chatter emanating around the dining room, which he quickly learnt to discern. Some of these included the Broussards, a gregarious couple from Louisiana. The Broussards' eldest daughter, Katherine, was studying medicine at Yale, and the couple were taking an extended vacation across the East Coast after visiting their daughter in college. Jeff Broussard had himself enjoyed a successful career as an anaesthetist before taking early retirement to spend his days on the golf course. Jeff's ebullient wife, Carolyn, told Jack that she had sacrificed her own medical training to bring up four daughters, having married and become pregnant with her first child as soon as she graduated. Jack wondered whether Carolyn Broussard ever asked herself what it was all for. Yet from their conversations he sensed a dogged determination to ensure her own girls would be different. It was an interesting decade to be a woman, Jack thought. The sixties represented choice and freedom with its miniskirts and the pill, yet despite them achieving great things, as far as Jack was concerned, a woman's place was in the home.

'How is your eldest enjoying college?' Jack and Jeff were sitting alone by the fireside in the hotel lounge.

'Oh, very much, she's a wonderful kid,' said Jeff, beaming with pride. 'Two more years to go. It's a lot of work. My word, we both remember how much, but she's a bright spark, she'll get through it. What about you? You said you have a son?'

'Yes, he's a couple of years older than Katherine. Hanson was never one for studying, or school for that matter, but he seems to have found his place. He finished his training at hotel school last year.'

'Ah, a hotelier! Where did he train?'

'The Savigny. In London.'

'Well, if I'm ever in town, I shall remember young Hanson at the Savigny.'

They both laughed. Yet, for all Jack's pride, he was well aware that Hanson had not attended the Savigny on his own merit. Yet, what of Jeff Broussard's four girls? They were bright. They were ambitious, but how would they fare in the world? Jack wondered how he would feel if he had a daughter.

'It's an interesting time to be a woman *and* a man,' Jeff said, gazing into the flickering flames. 'I mean, women are achieving remarkable things, but some of the things you hear. My niece, Simone, just graduated...'

'That's wonderful,' said Jack. 'Congratulations!'

'Loyola Law School. West Coast. The kid is real sharp.'

'A lawyer in the family is always useful.'

'*If* she ever practises. Those firms she's applying for are more interested in how many kids she's planning, less so on why she wants to do criminal law. Call me controversial. And *please* don't repeat this to my wife...' Jeff looked around the room and suddenly lowered his voice '...but sometimes I look at my eldest and wonder if all her hard work will be worth it. I don't want her to sacrifice four years of medical school when at the end of it she might just end up, well, you know, *not* practising medicine.'

It never occurred to Jack that Maybelle might like to work. 'I imagine it must be a difficult dilemma to be in,' he said. 'Yet

I somewhat find myself struggling with the notion that women can become doctors or bankers, albeit it's a wonderful thing if they do, but how is this compatible with their domestic responsibilities?' As soon as he'd spoken them, Jack was immediately conscious of his words.

'Surely you'd want the same opportunities for your daughter as you would your son?' Broussard swirled the liqueur in his glass, the amber liquid lending an effervescent glow in the evening light.

'Perhaps because I don't have a daughter, it's not something I've given much consideration to. But I should. Jeff, this has been a conversation that has shed light on my antiquated opinions. Thank you for helping me to sweep them aside.'

The two of them leant forward and clinked glasses.

'To women,' said Jeff, effusively.

'To women,' replied Jack, smiling.

'Your granddaughter will thank you for it one day,' said Jeff with a wink. 'I'll bet my bottom dollar on that.'

*

The snow was already beginning to subside by the time the week came to a close, and like colourful migrating birds flocking to warmer climes, Jeff and Carolyn Broussard prepared to return to the Deep South. 'We keep promising our daughters a trip to London,' said Jeff. 'Every year, I keep saying *next* year, but you know, maybe we'll take that trip and stay in the Savigny!' Even though he had barely known them a week, Jack immediately missed the ease and charm of the Broussards' company. That first evening, after their departure, he felt their absence and decided to work downstairs rather than go straight to his room. He didn't want to be alone.

Jack hadn't been seated long before he heard a voice – a familiar accent – behind him.

'May I join you?' A man, roughly about Jack's age, was pointing at the sofa opposite him. 'It looks so cosy here by the fire, and I must confess I'm intrigued by what you are drawing.'

'Yes, of course, do please take a seat,' replied Jack, moving his sketchpad to the side.

'Edmund Peats.' The man extended his hand.

'Jack Jagger,' said Jack, extending his own.

Edmund Peats was a chess collector from London who had just completed a successful sales trip to Quebec and Montreal and had flown east to research the potential market in Newfoundland.

'Have you just arrived?' Jack asked his new companion.

'Oh no, I was here before the snow,' said Peats, settling into a chair opposite Jack. 'I had a terrible cold, thought I'd never be rid of it, and I've been hiding away in my room. Took all my meals upstairs, nightcaps too. Isn't the maple syrup wonderful? The staff made a spectacular concoction with whisky to ease my symptoms. Never tasted anything better.'

'Sounds like it did the trick,' replied Jack. 'I'm tempted to try it myself.'

'Well, I highly recommend it,' said Peats, who had begun to shift about. There were clearly more cushions than he was used to. 'What a carry-on with the snow! Have you been keeping busy?'

Jack placed his sketches to one side. 'Yes, but I've rather enjoyed this quiet time.'

'Are you an artist?'

'A designer. Carpets. But I paint in my spare time.'

'How interesting! May I ask where you work?'

'Kidderminster. It's where most of the carpet factories are. All seventeen of them!'

'And you're here on business?'

'Yes, we export all over the world. A chap in Canada always asks me why I keep returning to his country, and I told him it's to keep our friendship in repair so that they keep buying our carpets.' Jack smiled. 'That's what I'm doing here, keeping those friendships ticking over.'

The two men laughed, a familiarity unfolding between them.

'Tell me, do you make particular designs for specific markets?' Edmund Peats was now settled comfortably, having decided to place the cushions on the floor beside him. 'If you had a design for Australia, for instance, would you have sent the same one to Scandinavia?'

'Well, designs are partly conditioned by climatic elements. Because the sun is quite bright in Australia, the colour we send there has to be heightened and sharpened.' Jack lit his pipe and small circles of smoke swirled around him. 'They also like coloured designs with flowers, whereas New Zealanders prefer plain ones. But in Denmark, or any of the Nordic countries in fact, the light is muted, so the patterns that we send there are restrained.'

'I had no idea it was so specific.'

'Yes, but there's also been a tremendous change in taste towards elegance and simplicity.' Jack picked up his catalogue and began turning the pages. 'There's been a change in colour too, which is actually more important, I think, than design.'

'What are folks asking for these days then?'

'Interestingly, colours have become clearer, more pastel, like in this picture, as opposed to the muddy, dirty colours that were popular before the war.' Jack pointed to a design in the catalogue.

'Fascinating,' said Peats, taking his spectacles out of his jacket pocket and arranging them carefully at the end of his nose. 'And how do you go about actually setting up a pattern then?'

'Well, first of all, the artist, and we have around twenty, starts by formulating an idea. Once they have an idea, which can come from something as simple as the bark of a tree or the scales of a fish, they then draw it out in charcoal. Here, let me show you.'

Jack picked up a folder next to him and began to sift through various pieces of paper. 'We use charcoal because it can be easily altered. Once the artist is satisfied and the size of scale is about right, they then transfer the pattern onto what we call square papers, which look like this.'

Peats peered at various pieces of paper scattered on the table next to him.

'You see here, each square becomes one cut in the carpet,' Jack traced the drawing with a finger, 'and we have enough yarn to go ten times around the world if it were all joined together!'

'Ten times! Good grief. How many designs do you have under production at the moment?'

'Close to a hundred, but in the range as a whole, we have around one thousand designs.'

'One thousand designs! That must keep you busy.'

Jack laughed, and the two of them were quiet for a moment.

'How did you get into it? Carpet design, I mean?'

'My stepfather. If it wasn't for him, I think I would still be throwing stones at the window of the local rag, hoping to God someone heard me. I wanted to be a writer initially, you see. Strange how all the dots connect one by one until we are presented with the sum of our life and it all begins to make sense. Of course, at the time, nothing does. These choices, these doors closing and opening, closing and opening, they all add up in the end, I think.'

'Oh, I agree. Nothing ever makes sense at the time. And you've stuck with it? Carpet design?'

'Oh yes... apart from when I left school and worked at the butcher's... but that's another story...'

'A fascinating one, I'm sure.' Edmund Peats lowered his voice, as if he were waiting to be let in on a secret. 'Do you know, I've always wanted to know the difference between a Wilton and an Axminster.'

Jack laughed. 'You've certainly come to the right place.

Might it be easier if I drew you a diagram?'

'Oh no, please don't trouble yourself.'

'It's no trouble at all.' Jack picked up his catalogue and began to flick through it again before placing it carefully on the table in front of them. 'This here is an Axminster. You won't be able to tell the difference just from this image, but each individual tuft is put separately into the back of the carpet by grippers. And with a Wilton...' Jack turned the pages until he found a carpet in glorious shades of green and pink. 'With a Wilton, here, as you can see, the pile yarn is led in from the back of the carpet and lifted from the pile. I hope that clears up matters.' Jack laughed as he sat back.

'Well, I never,' exclaimed Edmund Peats. 'You learn something new every day. Thank you.'

'Enough about carpets. What about you?'

'I'm a chess collector. Dabble in antiques too. Haven't always, mind you. Used to work in the City but quickly realised that I wasn't quite suited to the life of an actuary.'

'What a coincidence. I collect chess sets and antiques too.'

'Then you must make it part of your itinerary to visit the Farmers' Market before you leave. It is a wonderful, wonderful place to find all sorts of treasures.'

'It's already on my list,' said Jack, feeling pleased that he had met someone with whom he had so much in common. 'Let's just hope it doesn't snow again.'

'Ah, and before I forget, another item for your list is the Portobello Road market. It's an antique lover's paradise. If you ever come to London, I would be very happy to show you.'

'I should like that very much.' Jack gathered his sketches together and placed them back in his folder. 'And should you ever need advice on carpets...'

'Oh yes, I'll know exactly where to come.' Edmund Peats slapped his knee, as if he had just made an exciting discovery.

It's true. They all add up in the end, thought Jack, as he lay in bed that night. Dots connecting one by one to make a life, a story. And yet, how strange that they don't ever reveal their true significance at the time.

13

It must be bad news, thought Jack the following afternoon. He had received a message from his wife, the first time they had spoken in a week, asking him to call her back urgently. He had never gone three days without speaking to Maybelle when he was overseas. And now, as his finger turned the numbers on the telephone dial one by one, a feeling of dread began to build within him.

'Jack?' Maybelle's voice was strained.

'Hello, Belle, everything all right? Hanson all right?' There was comfort in hearing his wife's voice.

'We're both fine. How are things out there? Back to normal?'

'Yes, the telephone lines are back up again, and my meetings back on. I was going to call you this evening but you've—'

'Beaten you to it. Yes, I know. I'm afraid I have some bad news,' Maybelle said quickly.

Jack inhaled sharply as the phone's intermittent crackling threatened the renewed lines of communication between them.

'It's about Aunt Lily – and Grandma Clara.'

'What's happened?' Jack lowered his voice, even though he was the only person in the room.

'It was the snow. We've had so much of it. It arrived on Tuesday but it quickly turned to ice.'

'What happened?' The same question had reduced Jack's voice to a whisper.

'Aunt Lily insisted on visiting, despite your mother telling her to stay home. She'd made a fruitcake, you see. Well, you know how she is, and insisted on walking in the melting snow to the house.'

The telephone continued to crackle and Jack pressed the receiver against his other ear.

'She had the fruitcake wrapped up in a tin and as she walked up the garden path, she slipped and fell against the doorstep. Your mother rushed out and Grandma Clara followed her to see what all the commotion was.'

Jack was grateful that his despair – visible on his now drained face – was shielded from his wife.

'Of course, your grandmother couldn't see the ice in front of her as she stepped out of the front door. She fell, thankfully on her side, but both Aunt Lily and Clara are in hospital.'

'When? When did all this happen?'

'Yesterday – it's when all the snow turned to ice.'

'I can't believe it.' Jack looked absently around his room, as if searching for something. 'And to think I've been completely absorbed in my own world hundreds of miles away.'

'There was no way of reaching you...'

'I know, but it's just... what does the doctor say? Will they be all right?'

'He can't be sure. They are stable but not out of danger. They may need operations, which of course has its own complications, especially at the age they are. Your mother is in an understandable state of shock.'

'Have you spoken to her?'

'Yes, although it's unlikely I'll be able to travel up to Yorkshire at all in this weather. It will have to wait. Perhaps I should call Harry. He'll be coming to see your mother in any case.'

'No,' said Jack resolutely. 'I've only got two more days in Canada. I'll be there soon.'

'They'll fly by,' said Maybelle, trying to sound upbeat. 'But I need you home now. We all do.'

*

It was the last day of February and wintry blizzards had given way to brilliant sunshine. It seeped in through the large, colourful mosaic windows in the church where the vicar was giving the sermon, and it lightened the heaviness that emanated from the eighteenth-century walls with its promise of spring.

'For those of you who know,' said the vicar, as he looked out at the sea of faces in front of him, 'the two women whose lives we are praying for today are remarkable in their own ways. Clara has not once let her disability define her, despite losing her sight years ago. Instead, she chose to face her predicament with grace. She is a much-loved member of this congregation, although sadly no longer able to attend church. And I cannot remember a day when she didn't light up the room with her smile.'

Maybelle, sitting between her husband and mother-in-law, placed a hand in each of theirs. Jack squeezed her hand.

'Her daughter, Lily, is known as much for her zest for life as she is for her cakes. We here at Saint Mary's are thankful for the countless occasions that Lily has helped us raise money for various charities and especially the children's Sunday school. Thanks to her wonderful baking, we were able to take our younger members to visit Westminster Abbey last year, which was much appreciated by all.' The vicar paused, looking into the congregation. 'And so it is now that we pray as one for Clara's and Lily's speedy recovery. And I know that your thoughts and good wishes will help them, give them the strength they need.'

It was strange, Jack thought after the service, that he had never viewed his aunt or grandmother through the lens that the vicar had just used to describe them. He'd only known his grandmother as helpless and vulnerable, someone who required constant care and attention, and, as a child, he had often been too frightened to look at her, to ask her how she was feeling; *what* she was feeling. As for Aunt Lily, she had a razor-sharp wit and she was renowned for her trifles – but what of her charitable work? Jack had no idea of the fundraising she did for the church, and it made him ashamed that he knew so little of her, his mother's sister.

'Aunt Lily really is a trailblazer,' said Hanson, as five Jaggers stood outside the church. 'Ahead of her time. Does her own thing and couldn't care less what people think about her. *And* selfless too.'

'There's a lot we don't know about Aunt Lily,' said Jack, adjusting the buttons on his coat. 'I certainly had no idea she did so much work in the community. Did you?' Jack's words were directed at his wife, whose arms were linked with Hanson's; the two of them huddled together against the cold.

'I knew about the cakes she sold to raise funds for the Sunday school here,' said Maybelle, gesturing at her mother-in-law. 'Your mother told me. Keeps me updated about these things.'

Eva nodded. 'It's true. She always does so much. Never one to sit still. If anyone is going to raise money for the community, it's Lily. Of course, others do too – only the difference is, Lily never shouts about it.'

'Well, I suppose all we can do now is wait,' said Harry, who had driven up from Lancashire alone. 'Glad we've been able to see Aunt Lily and Grandma Clara at least.'

'There's no need to wait around any longer. You've all got lives to be getting on with,' said Eva, smiling at her younger son. 'I expect you'll need to get back to Molly. Is she…?'

'Not having one of her best weeks,' Harry replied. 'But there you are.'

'I'm sorry to hear that,' said Eva, touching her son's arm. 'Please give her my love, *our* love.'

'Yes,' said Maybelle, echoing her mother-in-law's sentiments. 'I hope Molly feels better soon.'

'She'll appreciate that,' replied Harry, adjusting his glasses before fiddling awkwardly with his coat buttons. Jack was never quite sure what to say when it came to his sister-in-law. It had taken eighteen years for Molly to be diagnosed with depression. And to this day, Jack still didn't understand what it all meant. He had tried to understand, tried to imagine what it must be like to be completely overwhelmed with hopelessness and despair, and he felt genuine sympathy for her. It's just that he didn't believe there was actually anything wrong. What did Molly have to be depressed about anyway? She had a nice house, a kind husband, a loving daughter. What was the root of it all? What had triggered it? What suffering had she actually endured in her life that rendered her unable to get up in the mornings for weeks on end? Jack reasoned that Grandma Clara and Aunt Lily might feel more than a little sorry for themselves, one of whom had been blind for most of her life while the other's fiancé was killed in the war. But Molly? As far as he was concerned, what the woman needed was a change of mindset.

'Will you be all right getting back, dear?' Maybelle turned to Hanson. 'You could always come down with us and take the train to London from there.'

'Thanks, Mum, but I'll be fine.' Hanson patted his mother's hand as he gently unlinked his arm with hers. 'It's a good run down to London on the train.'

Some days later, when Jack was driving back to Kidderminster with Maybelle, he thought about his conversation with Jeff Broussard. And it occurred to Jack again how little he knew. It was true what Hanson had said. Aunt Lily *was* a trailblazer because she had defied expectations and was living an independent life. Jack glanced across at his wife. Her hands were resting neatly on her lap and she was gazing out of the window, watching the ever-changing landscape like a film in forward motion.

'Penny for your thoughts?' said Jack.

Maybelle continued looking out of the window. 'I was just wondering whether I should defrost the casserole.'

'Might be sensible. The butcher's will be closed in any case.'

'The daffodils will be coming out soon...' said Maybelle, her voice becoming fainter as if retreating deeper into thought. 'I hope that our young shrubs have survived this frost.'

'They're made of strong stuff. They can survive almost anything. Just like Aunt Lily and Clara.'

Jack glanced again at his wife, whose face was still obscured from him. 'Let's hope so,' she said, finally turning towards her husband, 'because it's been a very unforgiving winter.'

Tilly 14

The two young women gazed out at the majesty of the Bavarian Alps. Even though it was well into spring, there were still patches of snow on the peaks, which glistened like diamonds in the afternoon sun.

'The sun *always* shines in Paris,' said Lotte in a faraway voice. 'And England, well, you know it never stops raining there! They like to drink warm beer too. *Wie schrecklich!*'

'Lottchen, you are not helping one bit! I need more convincing than that!' said Tilly, laughing. She bit into her *brezel* and flecks of rock salt fell onto her dress like snowflakes.

Tilly Stein was the third of four daughters born into a German family, who regarded themselves as Bavarian first, German second. She had short dark hair, a waspish waist and had taken to regularly smoking cigarettes, hoping to emulate her favourite actresses. She was close to her father, less so her mother; and her sisters were a source of amusement and aggravation in equal measure. Tilly had never lived anywhere other than the village of Weildorf, which was nestled at the foot of the Bavarian Alps. She was also more familiar with Salzburg than Munich, regularly crossing the border with her family; the former being less than ten kilometres away and, of course, boasting the best *buchteln* for miles.

Lotte and Tilly met at hotel school when they were both seventeen. The school, which was located in the spa town of Bad Reichenhall had a vast terrace where the girls almost always ate their lunch, unless it was raining. It looked out at the jagged horizon, which adopted a different mood depending on the weather. Today, the mountains appeared restless as if waiting for a storm to appear. 'Race you to the bottom?' Lotte shot up suddenly and tugged playfully at her friend's dress.

'Not if you want me to beat you,' replied Tilly, following her friend. The two of them ran down the path, their colourful *dirndls* expanding like tulips. When the girls reached the foothills, giddy and laughing, they stood for a moment catching their breath, waiting in line for the cable car to take them back to the top.

It hadn't taken long for Lotte to decide she was going to live in Paris, not least because her French was better than her English. Tilly, on the other hand, was still undecided; yet, unlike Lotte, her English was far better than her French. Now with their third year of training almost over, the summer stretched before them with promise of picnics, mountain hikes and wild swimming, but the question of where they would spend their year abroad still loomed large.

'So, what do you think?' Lotte asked, once they were inside the cable car. 'And before you say anything, you should know that I'll be very sad if you don't come to Paris with me.'

'Then I'm afraid you will be very sad. I think I want to go to England,' said Tilly, trying to sound decisive.

'But... why? Why *England*?' Lotte's voice had taken on an exaggerated tone.

'Why?' Tilly clearly enjoyed the suspense she was creating.

'*Why?* Why, the Beatles, of course!' The truth was, Tilly wasn't sure why, her reference points being as cliched as they were outdated, but with her childhood behind her, she couldn't wait to begin an adventure as far away as possible. Britain, a long, narrow island floating in the middle of a cold sea, seemed exotic and remote. Surely, along with the Beatles, that was as good a reason as any.

*

'Now don't forget to eat *and* to write.' Tilly's father, Friedrich, shot an affectionate glance at his daughter, who he was driving to Salzburg, from where Tilly was to take a train onwards to France. 'And remember to try the pork's blood – black pudding, I think it's called. Apparently, they eat it for breakfast over there.'

Tilly laughed and kissed her father on the cheek, the Bavarian countryside hurtling past them. 'Oh, Papa, I'm going to miss you! I'm going to miss you all!' But Friedrich Stein was used to these words by now. His two eldest girls had already left home. Tilly, however, was good with languages and so had dared to spread her wings further.

Having her daughters leave home one by one had become a rite of passage for Katarina Stein too, as she dabbed their foreheads with the holy water that was kept in a font by the front door. 'May God bless you and keep you safe,' she said, '*wherever* you are.' Katarina Stein knew she had done her duty. She had brought up four girls who were ready for the world, and the world was ready for them. They had to find their own way now, and she hoped she had instilled in them all the valuable lessons she had learnt from her own mother. And so, when Tilly embarked on the ship that was to take her to Dover, she looked at the rough, inky sea below, remembering her mother and the holy water and the other rituals and traditions that had been part of her for so long. Then she thought about Lotte in France

115

and herself in England and wondered how different life was going to be.

It was, in fact, going to be very different. Tilly had been posted to the Charing Hotel, a large establishment in the centre of London opposite landmarks that she had read about in books and magazines, now all on her doorstep. Mods, Mary Quant miniskirts, marmalade, bright red double-decker buses, the Beatles and the BBC – Tilly embraced it all.

Until The Cows Come Home 15

'Never guessed you were German, well, apart from your accent, that is.' Edith Smith was one of the Charing Hotel's cooks and was as renowned for her fry-ups as she was for her relentless questioning. 'How long you say you've been here?'

'Just under six months,' replied Tilly. 'It feels like much longer, though.'

'Is that a good thing or a bad thing?' Edith placed two slices of toast on Tilly's tray.

Tilly laughed. 'I'm not sure. But there are so many things I love here, like British television. We don't have programmes like that in Germany.' Tilly peered at a dish in front of her. 'Or *that*.'

'That's bread and butter pudding. There's a few sorts who like to eat something sweet in the morning.'

'Is it sweet?' Tilly pointed at the dish. 'I thought you said it was bread?'

'It's made from bread. The raisins and nutmeg make it sweet. Like I said, it's a pudding.'

'Bread and butter with raisins. For pudding?'

'That's right, love. Bread and butter pudding.'

'All right, I'll try it,' said Tilly, finally. As she moved her tray along the assortment of steaming plates and dishes, she laughed to herself. *Bread and butter pudding, just wait till I tell Papa about that.*

Edith – or Edie as she liked to be known – was one of the first people Tilly met in London, and she had taken a liking to her immediately. There was something about Edith's demeanour that was protective of the trainees that came through the hotel's door. It usually had to do with the inevitable homesickness that surfaced after several weeks of being in a foreign country and far away from family and loved ones. Not that Tilly was homesick. Or minded being in a foreign country. She loved London and was taking every opportunity to practise her English. She did this through her weekly letters to Lotte (who admitted that Paris was not as wonderful as she'd hoped) and with numerous colleagues at the Charing Hotel, including a young man called Hanson Jagger.

Tilly had noticed him immediately. He was tall, broad-shouldered, and his hair, she decided, was not quite red, not quite brown, something in between. There was something else about him too that was different. It came to her one evening during the interval of a play a group of them had gone to see, which had been organised by the hotel's social committee. It was the softness of Hanson's voice that had caught her attention, which struggled to be heard above the din around him. And this reserve had been all the more apparent as the two of them sat only a few seats away from each other during the performance. In fact, were it not for the colleague sitting between them, Tilly wondered how much longer it would have taken for Hanson Jagger to introduce himself.

'Tilly, my dear, have you met our rising star yet?' Tilly felt a hand lightly touch her knee and she turned towards her colleague, whom she knew to be Mr Carruthers, the hotel's head of personnel.

'No, not properly,' said Tilly, smiling politely.

'Well, it's high time the two of you were properly introduced… Tilly Stein, Hanson Jagger. Tilly is one of our new trainees. From Germany… it is Germany, not Austria, isn't it, Tilly?'

'That's right,' came Tilly's response.

'Do please call me Donald, dear,' said Mr Carruthers. 'Now, Hanson, Tilly is with us for a year before she returns to Germany to finish hotel school. So, if I were you, I would make the most of her while she's with us. A year flies by, you know.'

'I think that can be arranged.' Hanson's voice was barely audible as he leant across his colleague to shake Tilly's hand, his eyes momentarily resting on hers.

'Wonderful,' said Mr Carruthers, rising from his seat. 'In that case, I shall leave you youngsters to it. I'm off to find some ice cream.'

'A teetotaler.' Hanson smirked as he nodded in Mr Carruthers' direction. 'I don't know about you but I'd prefer something stronger. I'm afraid it's only wine or gin and tonic here. No beer, I'm afraid.'

'You think I only drink beer because I'm German?'

'Of course not,' Hanson said with a snigger as he gently guided Tilly out of the auditorium. 'Would you like to join me in a gin and tonic? It's one of our great British inventions, you know.'

Tilly nodded, and as Hanson walked towards the bar, she stepped aside and retrieved a Benson & Hedges from its packet, which she had taken to smoking now that she was living in England. And while she slowly inhaled her cigarette, enjoying the sensation as the smoke swirled around her, she took in this so-called rising star: the charm, the reserve, the quiet confidence.

The two of them were discreet at first, choosing not to make their union obvious, but as large as the hotel was, it was also a family affair and impossible to keep anything secret for long. 'Aha! I knew it was only a matter of time,' said Mr Carruthers to the couple some months later, proclaiming to anyone who cared to listen that the pairing had all been down to him.

'We will be forever grateful for your superb matchmaking skills, Donald. You have quite a talent for it.' Hanson winked at his colleague. 'By all accounts, I think Arnold at the front desk could do with some help too.'

Edith was also pleased. 'Now your English will be even better,' she exclaimed to Tilly once the stream of gossip had reached the staff kitchen. 'He's a right proper gentleman is Mr Jagger. You'll go back home speaking the Queen's English even better than Her Majesty.' And with that, Edith laughed, throwing her head back in delight at the thought of a German girl returning home an English lady.

Tilly, however, had no intention of returning home an English lady. In fact, just six months after arriving in London, she was preparing to move to Scotland; Hanson's posting having come to an end at the Charing Hotel. Yet for all the excitement of a fresh start, Hanson's mind was fraught with whether Tilly would be joining him. 'I won't be able to do anything about the rain up there, but if you come to Glasgow with me, I *will* promise to love you until the cows come home.'

Tilly wasn't sure what Hanson had meant by loving her until the cows came home. Should she first check and ask her English teacher what this peculiar phrase meant before giving an answer? The no-nonsense Mrs Forster, with her selection of colourful scarves, never minced her words. Then again, Tilly's next evening class wasn't until Tuesday – five days away. Or should she just take a leap of faith right here, right now, and trust that this man standing before her and gazing hopefully into her eyes was absolutely *sure* the cows would never ever come home?

'What are you thinking about?' Hanson was hoping the question would belie the anxiety he was feeling inside.

Tilly's eyes remained steadfastly on Hanson. 'I think you know the answer to that already.'

16

'I should like the sleeves long and the hem to reach just about here.' Tilly bent forward slightly, showing the tailor the precise measurements of her dress.

'And what about the neckline, dear?'

'Oh!' Tilly thought for a moment, as if she hadn't given it any consideration.

'May I suggest a boat neck? It's a very fashionable look at the moment.' The tailor took a step back and looked at Tilly before adding, 'And it would complement your figure.'

'No, I think I'd prefer the dress to have a high neck. It will look better with the shorter length, I think. Especially as we're going to be married in Rome. Well, in the Basilica di San Silvestro, to be exact.'

'Rome…' the tailor repeated. 'Sounds like a fairytale.'

'My fiancé arranged it. We are very lucky really.'

'Well, I've never been to Rome, but my daughter-in-law has visited several times. She's from a Catholic family – staunch ones at that. Are both you and your fiancé Catholic?'

'No, just myself…' Tilly paused, before adding, 'but my

fiancé very much believes in God,' which Tilly knew sounded much better than the truth.

'Well, I'm sure that doesn't matter,' said the tailor, measuring the hemline of Tilly's dress. 'Even if he were a Catholic, that doesn't necessarily mean anything these days, does it?'

The tailor was Celia Hainsworth, wife of Dickie, and she – the Hainsworths – had just opened a shop in Edinburgh, the latest city from which they were expanding their business. The job – the alteration of the wedding gown that Tilly had chosen in Munich earlier that month with her mother – was a favour too; Celia having been given the task of "taking up" and "taking in" at shorter notice than usual.

'Are you sure she won't mind?' Tilly had asked Jack, who, having heard that Tilly was fretting about the wedding dress being ready in time, arranged for his soon-to-be daughter-in-law to visit the Hainsworths' new shop.

'Mind?' Jack sounded surprised. 'I know Celia. And I know Dickie. They consider it a privilege to be involved in the preparations for the wedding.'

'I mean with it being such short notice? With Celia having to travel all the way from Bradford?'

'Consider it a favour. I've known Dickie since I was a lad, and he looked out for us, my mother especially, when my father passed away.'

'What a thoughtful couple,' said Tilly, relieved that her dress would be ready on time.

'Rest assured they are happy to help in any way they can.'

'Well, if you're sure, Dad,' said Tilly, playing with the cord on the telephone. 'I'm sure Celia will do a wonderful job. It's just such a shame that you won't be able to come to Rome.'

'I know, but Mum is loath to leave her mother. The doctor has finally sent for tests at the hospital and she wants to be here when Mary receives the results. Aunt Lily insists on baking you a wedding cake, though. Fruitcake, no doubt – or some kind of trifle concoction for Hanson,' Jack said with a laugh. 'Clearly, she's had a second wind since her accident. Who knows where she gets her energy.'

'And Clara? How is she?'

'Fragile – not much of a life anymore, I'm afraid. She's inching towards hundred – not a bad innings – but it can't be much fun being confined to a wheelchair all day.'

'But to reach a hundred.'

'If I live that long,' said Jack, 'I hope I'll still be painting.'

On the whole, Tilly considered herself lucky. What was the saying about in-laws? She'd heard the countless jokes on British television, even among her British friends: the tyrannical mother-in-law, the hen-pecked father-in-law. You either love them or loathe them. You either strike lucky or don't. If you loathe them, then you can look forward to years of being in the company of people you don't like. If you love them, then you have struck gold. Tilly had the impression that not many friends in her adopted land considered themselves having struck gold. Their in-laws were people to be tolerated, making small talk through gritted teeth, all the while waiting for it – another visit – to be over. But was it really that bad? All she knew was that she had taken an immediate liking to Maybelle and Jack. Her homeliness and his warmth had put Tilly immediately at ease, and any thoughts of being an outsider, *not* being English, *being* German, struggling with pronouncing certain words like "breath" and "oxygen" didn't seem to matter. They accepted their soon-to-be daughter-in-law for who she was and, ultimately, for making their son happy.

And if Tilly ceased making Hanson happy, what then?, she thought.

What then? She was in love. She was getting married. She was doing all the things expected of her. It's what her parents did. It's what her two eldest sisters had done. She was treading a familiar path, towards a happily ever after. One where Hanson would love her until the cows came home. Even if that meant turning a blind eye to her fiancé's occasional roving eye.

Tilly visited Celia five times in her shop just off Princes Street. She was present throughout all of Tilly's fittings, bar the fourth occasion when she was required to remain in Bradford on business. She worked diligently, demonstrated meticulous attention to detail and was attentive to Tilly's requests, almost to the point of being obsequious.

'Mr Jagger's a nice man,' Celia said, during Tilly's final fitting. 'You're in safe hands there.'

'Hanson?'

'No, his father. He's what they call a gentleman. Fathers-in-law don't come better than that.'

'Yes, I agree. He's been so kind to me,' before quickly adding, 'and Mrs Jagger.'

Celia motioned with her hands as she gestured for Tilly to move slightly to the left. 'Keep still if you can, love,' she said, removing a needle from her mouth. 'I just need to adjust the material.'

Tilly straightened her back and stood as still as she could while Celia worked quietly by her feet. 'There…' she said, getting up before taking a step back, 'I think it's coming along nicely.'

'I really appreciate this. You've been so kind to me, you *and* your husband.'

'It's the least I can do,' Celia said, looking the bride-to-be directly in the eye. 'We owe *you* so much too.'

Tilly wondered what Celia had meant by her words *we owe you so much too*, but she didn't dwell on it for long. Thoughts quickly returned to her dress, to Rome, to the wedding and to her soon-to-be husband.

*

The young couple were married in Rome at the end of August. It rained torrentially for three days and according to the priest who carried out the service, the unfortunate weather was, in fact, a very fortuitous sign. 'Is a-very good for man and woman,' he told them. 'Is a-very good for married life,' as if he were a fortune teller, mapping out their destinies. But the setting – the cool marble interior of the *basilica* with its intricate, highly detailed mosaics, which at first glance looked like paintings – made up for the absence of family and friends as the couple stood in front of the altar and privately exchanged vows and rings, leaving the church as man and wife. It had been a last-minute decision, given that Maybelle refused to leave her mother's side, was incapable of leaving her mother's side, having finally cajoled her to visit the doctor. If Maybelle and Jack couldn't be there, Tilly thought, then it didn't seem fair to invite her parents and sisters either. Yet none of it mattered. There was something beautifully intimate about sharing their day in the most heavenly of places, just the two of them.

When the newlyweds left the city for their honeymoon, travelling down to the Bay of Naples and on to Capri, it suddenly occurred to Tilly just how ironic the whole thing had been. Ironic because her new husband – a non-believer, a self-proclaimed atheist – had arranged with what seemed like relative ease to marry his Catholic fiancée in Rome, the home of the Catholic Church. It was, if one thought about it, quite frankly nothing short of a miracle.

Tilly had not even been married a week but she had already learnt two new things about her husband. The first was that he must *really* love her to have made this wonderful miracle happen. The second was that he must be very good at getting what he wanted.

The ties that bind us 17

'Rhododendrons are not my favourite,' Mary reminded her daughter as she pointed at the window. 'Don't you remember how I detested them when we had the garden that looked over the railway tracks? They look frightful when they wither. And you know I'm not fond of purple at the best of times.' Even in her fragility, Mary remained as opinionated as ever. Nothing was good enough: her tea in the morning was either too hot or too cold, she preferred to take lunch at noon and not a moment before, and she wasn't particularly taken with the view from her bedroom window.

'Really, Mother,' Maybelle responded softly, 'I can't do much about the view, less so the rhododendrons, and if it bothers you so, I can always close the curtains.'

Mary never sought to relinquish the ties she had carefully bound around her daughter, especially now that she was a widow. It didn't matter that Maybelle was herself a wife and mother; Mary continued to subtly exert her dominance. Jack was well acquainted with these subtleties, quietly respecting a bond that was as unique as it was complex; a bond that was layered with friction and fondness; a bond that was fragile yet enduring. Maybelle understood them too and realised, more than she cared to admit, that she needed her mother. It was her mother whom she had turned to for guidance when she met Jack, and it was her mother who had helped her to raise Hanson while Jack was away during the war. They *both* needed each other.

Now Mary had been diagnosed with cancer, Maybelle felt an emptiness rising within like a ball of tightly bound wool slowly unravelling with each day that passed. It was inconceivable to see her mother ill and yet here she was, thought Maybelle, becoming weaker before her eyes. She always imagined Mary to be invincible, with years of life still in her; someone who would always be there. Why did she imagine her mother to be somehow immortal, someone who could outwit death? Maybelle didn't have an answer. She only knew what she would miss. Before long, the doctor caring for Mary regretted that he could do no more for his patient. She could come home and be surrounded by her family, he said. Maybelle vowed, indeed, made it her responsibility to ensure her mother was made as comfortable as possible. This was no mean feat – Mary was critical to the end. But it was with patience and empathy that Maybelle chose to behave, all the while brushing aside something that had started to grow within her too. It was as if the ties that bound mother and daughter were reasserting themselves one last time.

The dull ache did not concern Maybelle at first. She simply put it down to the stress of her mother's demise. But then the ache in her armpit persisted, accompanied by an intense lethargy, and domestic chores she had enjoyed in the past soon overwhelmed her. Jack noticed the change in his wife and encouraged her to visit their doctor. Yet the more he persisted, the more Maybelle insisted she was fine. Besides, she exclaimed, it was her mother who was ill, not she. So she threw whatever energy reserves she had left to looking after Mary, all the while ignoring her body's own silent struggle.

Then, in the grip of winter, weeks after Mary succumbed to the cancer, Maybelle was diagnosed with the same illness. She was fifty-nine years old, still young enough to enjoy life and harbour hope for what lay ahead – grandchildren perhaps and more travel – yet old enough to have wisdom and maturity behind her. It was the irony that stung Jack the most; months of his wife sacrificing her own needs and putting life on hold, only for it to now hang from a thread. Jack vividly recalled the grey of the consultant's office where he sat with Maybelle that cool spring morning. It had barely been a matter of minutes since the doctor had left the room to fetch his wife's results, but it seemed to stretch to hours. It was a typical hospital office, and save for the harsh light squeezing its way through the slats of the dusty window blinds, the rest of the room's details were unremarkable. Still, Jack never forgot the earnestness with which the consultant addressed Maybelle, nor the kindness in his eyes as he calmly and carefully outlined her prognosis while she sat with hands folded in lap, graciously accepting her fate.

Later that evening, Jack called Hanson as soon as Maybelle had gone to bed. 'Your mother has breast cancer.' His voice wavered while he placed the telephone receiver on his lap. 'The biopsy came back today and it appears to have already spread to her lymph nodes. The consultant told us they will do all they can but we need to prepare for the worst.'

'How is she feeling?' Hanson could feel pricks of tears gather in the corners of his eyes.

'She's resting now but she's still in shock, especially with Grandma Mary passing away only a few months ago.'

'If there's anything I can do… to help…' Despite his offer of help, Hanson felt helpless.

'There's nothing you can do at the moment. Perhaps Mum will give you a call in the morning.'

When the call came the following evening, Hanson listened in disbelief. It was as if his mother had resigned herself to her illness, without resistance, without questioning the unfairness of it all. Why is this happening to me?, he wanted her to ask. Why not someone else? Why now? Instead, he was met with a quiet pragmatism; a pragmatism that unnerved Hanson with its sense of acceptance. 'I'm sure they'll do their best,' was all Maybelle could say to her son.

'Dad said the consultant is one of the best in Worcestershire. Doctors can do terrific things these days. You're in good hands now, Mum.'

'How are you both doing up there? Are you still enjoying Scotland?'

'We're both well, Mum...' Hanson hesitated, before continuing, 'It's you I'm worried about.'

'I don't want you to worry. *Please* promise me you won't worry.'

'I promise,' said Hanson, wiping away his tears.

With each day that passed, Maybelle retreated further into herself. Jack hoped his wife would share some of her anxieties, but she seemed to prefer her own company more than ever. 'I'm fine,' she replied whenever Jack asked her how she was feeling. 'I just want to rest my eyes for a while.' These stolen moments were like meditation to Maybelle, transporting her to a place of calm as she turned on the record player and let the music of Beethoven and Bach surround her, engulf her, seep into her veins. Soon, it became a daily ritual, this need to be alone, this need to close the door on the world, process her thoughts and find some kind of respite, if only fleetingly. Jack tried to understand his wife's need for solitude, despite the urge to share as much time with her as possible. But the more insidious his wife's illness became, the more Jack found himself alone with his thoughts. She had been a good wife – *was* a good wife – but she was also a complex character, as reserved as she was stubborn. Even though Jack had long accepted their disparate personalities, it still pained him to witness the very reservedness that was intrinsic to his wife's character push him away, because he knew that the luxury of time, of *being* together, was not in their favour. But what right did he – the person who *wasn't* sick – have to complain? He felt he had no other choice than to watch her slip further and further into herself.

Maybelle   18

A trip was planned in late summer to the Scottish Highlands, just before Maybelle was due to have a second operation. Hanson had been appointed to manage The Kyle, a hotel with a white facade and pretty gardens that reached to the edge of the sea, and all agreed, including her consultant, that the visit would provide a respite from the rounds of hospital appointments and treatments.

'It's a shame we haven't spent more time exploring this part of the world,' said Jack, as he joined his wife by the large bay window to look at the view from their room. 'The scenery really is breathtaking.'

'Well, we didn't have an excuse before. If it wasn't for Hanson's posting here, we would probably have returned to the Gower Peninsula.' Jack followed his wife's gaze towards the horizon: to the seagulls, to the ferry coming in to harbour and to the lapping waves that were rolling gently back and forth. He moved closer and draped an arm over her. Maybelle took her husband's hand and held it loosely. 'Did you know that Skye is derived from the Norse words "ski", meaning cloud, and "ey", meaning island?'

'Where did you read that...?' Jack asked.

'I didn't. I overheard one of the guests mention it yesterday.'

'Well, it's certainly living up to its reputation today,' said Jack. 'It looks like rain.'

A child was playing with a bright orange kite in the garden below and the two of them turned their attention to watch the boy, who had reddish hair, struggle to get it to climb.

'Reminds me of Hanson at that age,' said Maybelle, smiling.

'He seems a determined little thing. Hopefully, this wind will do the trick.'

Suddenly the boy began to cry and a middle-aged woman rushed towards him. Jack and Maybelle watched as the woman gently showed the boy how to release the kite so it could climb. When it finally took off, the boy clapped and shrieked, clutching the woman's hand as they ran after it; a vivid orange spot flying higher and higher towards an insipid, featureless sky.

'Sweet child,' said Maybelle, as she moved away from the window. 'They are always so sweet at that age.'

The following day, Jack, Maybelle and Tilly boarded the ferry at Kyle to spend the afternoon in Skye. Although Maybelle became easily tired, she insisted they continue with the planned itinerary. They explored the walled garden at Dunvegan Castle, had lunch at a pub in Portree and admired the mysterious and ancient silhouette of the Old Man of Storr. It helped that the weather was good too. Weeks of persistent rain had given way to brilliant sunshine; Tilly exclaiming how fortunate they were to have such benign weather given the unpredictability of Highland summers. But it was the quiet calm of Plockton, save for the sound of the seagulls in the skies above, that deeply resonated with Jack. He drove to the picturesque village every morning, just as the sun was rising, to capture the morning light with his camera. He was moved by its beauty – the pastel-coloured houses and sheltered bay – and by its peacefulness;

painting, weeks later, the solitary wooden fisherman's boat by the shore as it waited to sail.

Although it was already September, the light lingered long enough for walks along the Lochalsh Peninsula in the evenings. 'We have some news we'd like to share,' said Hanson, as the four of them strolled leisurely along the seafront after supper. Hanson glanced at Tilly. 'Would you like to tell them?' Jack and Maybelle suspected what was to come; words they had been longing to hear. It was what they had hoped. They were going to be grandparents. Yet the poignancy of the moment couldn't have been more stark: the excitement of welcoming new life in the spring was in sharp contrast to the life that was being taken away. Everyone knew that while Maybelle's condition was stable, it could deteriorate at any time. All they could do was hope. Hope for more time. Hope for a miracle. It was a bittersweet moment but if the poignancy was felt by Maybelle, she didn't choose to reveal it. Still, Hanson knew. He knew his mother and how she would be desperately trying to conceal her feelings so as not to overshadow the joyous news. And it overwhelmed him to think she might not be around to share their happiness. Jack knew too and in that moment he prayed for God to answer his prayers; that his darling wife, who didn't deserve this cruel, unforgiving illness, would live long enough to meet her first grandchild.

'It's terrific news,' said Maybelle, linking arms with Tilly when they were alone. 'I'm looking forward to all the hats and booties I'm going to knit for the baby. Do you think white would be best? I'm not sure about yellow.'

'I'm sure it will look lovely in either yellow or white, Mum,' said Tilly, holding on to her mother-in-law's arm. 'And how lucky it will be to have a grandma like you.' Tilly's heart ached in that moment; ached for the gentle, stoic woman beside her who chose to bear her sorrow in silence, as if it was hers to bear alone.

'White it is,' said Maybelle, patting Tilly's arm reassuringly as they walked toward their husbands; the sun fading further into the horizon, bursts of pink and mauve against the grey of the sea.

The fisherman's boat
Scottish Highlands

19

Jack didn't remember much about the period that followed, too painful was it to recall. Only some things remained in his memory, like the way he would place his wife's small, delicate hands in his while he told her about his day or how he would peel an orange or slice an apple for her whenever Maybelle had the strength to sit up in bed and eat something. The colourful fruits and bright flowers that friends and colleagues sent Maybelle cheered up the bland grey of the hospital room and the bleakness of the November skyline outside. The sun never shone once. Or maybe it did; Jack had simply forgotten.

Whether Maybelle realised she wouldn't return home, Jack wasn't sure. The consultant had said it was for the best she didn't know, that one day she would simply lose consciousness and fall asleep, never to awake again. Jack wanted to tell her that she had been the most precious wife a man could hope for, that he would give anything to have her well again. But he didn't. He couldn't. It was too final. Instead, they spoke about Christmas and whether the holly berries would soon ripen on the tree; if they could expect another "Big Freeze" and whether Tilly, who was suffering from pregnancy-induced sciatica, might prefer the guest bed with the firmer mattress when she and Hanson came to stay. Jack remembered how Maybelle's eyes lit up knowing she would see her son and daughter-in-law soon and how much comfort their presence would give her. And it broke his heart.

When Maybelle took a turn for the worse, the consultant told Jack to prepare for the inevitable and to contact Hanson and Tilly. They arrived just in time, keeping a vigil by her bedside for three days before Maybelle spoke her last words; softly whispering her son's name as she slowly slipped into unconsciousness, the morphine having quietly contained the pain that ravaged her body. In those final moments, Jack gazed at the face of the woman he had loved for thirty-seven years; the woman who had captured his heart at the Hally Dance. In that first flush of love, who stops to imagine the inevitable suffering that comes to everyone in the end? It seems that no matter how prepared one is, Jack thought, and he was, death always arrives unannounced.

Not only did death arrive unannounced, Jack wasn't prepared for the hours, days and weeks that followed. First came the suffocating silence. Longing to hear the familiar sounds of his wife nearby: the clanging of pots and pans in the kitchen, the rousing tones of Bach drifting through the house and the whirring of her sewing machine. Anything to suffocate the silence. Anything to smell the sweet aroma of his wife's fruit-filled pies wafting from the oven or the delicate fragrance of pale pink roses she expertly grew in the garden, which were so elegantly displayed in vases around the house. Jack wanted to hear. He wanted to smell. But he couldn't bear to look around. He especially couldn't bring himself to go into the Designers' Den, which had always been Maybelle's room. He knew he would find all the unfinished blankets and booties his wife had been in the process of knitting for the grandchild she would now never meet. What would he do with them now? What *should* he do with them? Throw them away? Keep them? Maybelle was *everywhere* and she was nowhere.

Neighbours and colleagues, some of whom could barely be called acquaintances, dropped by to visit. This seemingly endless stream of guests – usually widows and spinsters – would arrive unannounced with a hot dish in hand. Jack was not ready to be enticed with well-meaning casseroles and pies. Instead, all he could do was draw comparisons with his own late wife's cooking and misread the good intentions as meddling. But he continued to bear his grief stoically, at least outwardly, relieved to close the door at the end of the day and be alone again with his thoughts.

Let all moments arise and dissipate, like clouds in the sky. This too shall pass.

Lately, Jack had begun to remind himself of what the *yogi* had taught him in Calcutta. But when he recalled the *yogi*'s words, instead of feeling calm, he felt angry.

Let all moments arise and dissipate, like clouds in the sky. This too shall pass.

Jack took a deep breath. Then he closed his eyes.

This too shall pass.

It was strange when he thought about it now, but Jack had been so sure of the ease with which he would be able to apply the *yogi*'s words to his own life, despite the *yogi*'s sage warning: mindfulness is *the* most difficult skill a human being can master. How could words that hold such simplicity be so difficult to master? Was it because he was faced with his own shadow for the first time and it made him feel uncomfortable? For so long, Jack's sense of identity had been intertwined with Maybelle's, and without her he felt lost, forced to face a future that he wasn't ready to rewrite. Who would he share his designs with now? How would he spend his weekends? Retirement? The thought of retirement filled Jack with dread. What he would do to have Maybelle by his side once more, his wife who had never been demanding, who had sacrificed so much of herself so that her husband could flourish. Because she had sacrificed herself, hadn't she? He could see it clearly now, but why not then? Jeff Broussard was right: women bent towards their husbands like flowers – nurturing them, always the caregiver – but did that make them happy? Jack wondered about that a lot. And he wondered about Maybelle. Had his wife been happy?

It had never once occurred to him to ask her that question.

Jack   20

It was at the insistence of Hanson and Tilly that Jack spent his
weekends with them. Jack readily accepted. And so, every Friday
evening, he packed a small suitcase, got in his purple hatchback
and drove all the way to Perth, where his son and daughter-in-
law were now living. By the end of the winter, Jack had made the
350-mile trip to Scotland eleven times. But it was his very last
visit at the end of February – weeks before his first grandchild
was born – that Jack never forgot.

He was always tired after his long drive north but this
morning particularly so. Still, Jack was relieved. Relieved not to
be alone. Relieved to have distractions and plans. Relieved to be
with his family. Relieved to be *anywhere* but home. The routine
was always the same: after breakfast, the three of them braved
the whistling wind as they walked along the South Inch. After
lunch, Hanson returned to work, providing Jack and Tilly the
opportunity to spend some time alone together (on this occasion
buying the pram that Jack and Maybelle had promised them),
while the evenings were spent playing rummy. In between,
Jack quietly admired Perth's elegance, especially the handsome

sandstone buildings that straddled either side of the verdant banks of the mighty River Tay. And slowly, a watercolour began to take shape in his mind.

'I'd like to do a painting of the hotel,' Jack announced the following evening, as the three of them sat around the dining table. 'It has a very unusual style, with its fusion of Flemish and Gothic.'

'You're in good company,' said Hanson. 'Queen Victoria declared it her favourite hotel in Scotland.'

'She stayed here?' Jack asked.

'Yes, before travelling on to Balmoral, in the glory days of train travel.'

'I never knew that.' Jack's eyes moved to the view outside the window. 'I wonder if the Queen also spotted the bellcast eaves that I noticed earlier. There's so much detail going on up there, with the octagonal corner towers, and those charming crow-stepped gables and turrets.' The hotel's architectural details were not lost on Jack, and for that, Hanson and Tilly were grateful. That he had spent part of Saturday morning looking up at the building from several vantage points and soaking up every angle surely meant that Jack was returning to the things that brought him joy as he absorbed himself in the possibility of a painting: a gothic Victorian pile that was "home" for his son and daughter-in-law. It was true that Jack was starting to feel better, more himself. He'd certainly felt lighter these last two days, especially when he thought of the baby and the arrival of spring.

By the end of the weekend, however, everything had changed. It had also started to snow.

'Are you sure you don't want to call your colleagues and stay here a while longer?' said Hanson, as the three of them looked out of the window. 'You'd be safer staying put.'

'I'll be all right,' replied Jack. 'I've seen much worse.'

'Are you sure?' said Tilly. 'It really would be no bother, Dad.'

'Very sure.' Jack patted Tilly's arm. 'Please don't worry.'

The truth was that as much as Jack thought he needed company, he also realised he needed to be alone. Grief, he was learning, was as intermittent as it was unpredictable. Intermittent because it came in waves, rolling towards him without warning; heavy and all-consuming. Unpredictable because just when he was starting to feel better, and he *was*, there it was again: the aching and the emptiness, turning what he thought he wanted – the company of his family and *not to* be alone – back onto its head. Then there was the baby to think about, *his* grandchild. The last thing Jack wanted was for everyone's joy to be diminished by his grief. It confused him, because even though he knew he had so much to look forward to – of course he was thrilled he was going to become a grandfather – all Jack could think about was what had been taken away.

Even those bellcast eaves and crow-stepped gables couldn't lift his spirits for long.

It was early evening when Jack reached the Pennines, a place he had walked many times with his father and Harry, and the usual glorious view of the sunset as it hit the curved tips of the familiar peaks was now obscured by a frenzied blizzard. Why hadn't he listened to Hanson? What was there to come back to anyway other than a home that he couldn't bear to be in? *My wife is gone, gone from me forever. They have just sent a man up to the moon but they couldn't cure her, couldn't save her.* Why couldn't they save her? Why didn't *he* save her? Encourage her to visit the doctor earlier? Insist? *Persist*? *He* had let it come to this. It was *his* fault. *His* fault. *His* fault. *He* had let his wife down. And now there was no going back. It was hopeless. No matter how many times he turned things round in his head, remembering this conversation or that, Maybelle wasn't coming back.

Maybelle was never coming back.

Jack began to panic. He had started to lose control of the steering wheel as it veered this way and that.

Was this it? Was he going to die here? In a snowstorm?

Pay attention to your thoughts. Remember what the *yogi* had told him. *Gratitude. Practise gratitude every day.*

Grief had obscured everything. It visits when it wants. It is a servant to no one. *I'm here, you deal with me now*, it demands.

Yes, grief had obscured everything. It was too late to start again.

Was it too late to start again?

He didn't want to die.

Jack began to swerve uncontrollably. Then came the piercing screech. It punctured the freezing air as the car reached an abrupt halt, quickly overturned and slowly rolled towards a nearby ditch.

21

Jack was alive, that much he knew. He was also covered in scrapes and bruises, having managed to crawl out of his car and tear his clothes in the process. He wasn't sure if he had broken any bones. He was too weak to move. The car lay next to him, as if bearing the weight of his accident; his trusty purple hatchback now itself dented and disfigured. I'll freeze to death if I don't get home soon, he thought, as he tried to move his body. But the pain was too much to bear, and wrestling with these thoughts, he hoped that someone would miraculously find him as he began to murmur the words of Othello to help him stay awake:

From year to year - the battles, sieges, fortunes, that I have passed...

Jack tried to remember what followed but to no avail. As he lay stiff and helpless, the cold and pain taking over his body, snowflakes circled around him, softly, softly...

And the soliloquy was abandoned.

22

'Are you all right, Mister?' A young man peered into Jack's face, looking for signs of life. He checked Jack's pulse and felt his brow. Then he took off his jacket and placed it carefully over the stranger. 'Everything is going to be all right, Mister. An ambulance is on its way. I'm going to wait here with you. Everything is going to be all right.'

Snow had been replaced by brilliant sunshine, which was streaming through two large Victorian windows. The patient, who had been admitted to a hospital near Penrith the night before, was being informed by the nurse looking after him that he'd had a very lucky escape. 'Someone must be looking out for you up there, Mr Jagger,' the nurse said, nodding upwards. 'The young lad who came with you in the ambulance told me that the roads were completely quiet around the Pennine Way and he was lucky to have spotted you. Don't suppose you remember him, but he waited a while before he had to leave. Wanted to see you were all right.'

'Bless him,' said Jack, nodding at the nurse. 'I'm very, very thankful.'

'We'd like to keep you under observation for a couple more days. It will have been a shock to the system, what with the hyperthermia too.'

'Thank you.' Jack wondered who this young man was that had saved his life.

'It's life-changing, you know, what you've just been through. We see it in so many patients, but all these emotions you're feeling are natural, if not a little overwhelming at first.'

'Yes, life-changing,' repeated Jack, echoing the nurse's words as she helped him into an upright position. Jack wasn't religious, but he had decided whoever had given him a second chance "up there" – he wasn't going to let them down.

Anna 23

Hill Country, Ceylon

Grief hadn't left completely. Sometimes it returned for a few hours, sometimes a few days; always unannounced. When grief tried to have the upper hand and outstay its welcome, Jack remembered the stranger who had saved him and he thought of all the goodness in his life, namely the arrival of Craig, his first grandchild. And then one day, as if out of nowhere and without any warning, grief packed up its bags and never returned. Of course, it wasn't as abrupt as that, but something had shifted. Instead of feeling *hopeless,* Jack began to feel *hopeful.* There was new life; a reason to celebrate. And as difficult as it was to think of Maybelle gone forever, Jack knew that the only way to move forward was to focus on the things he still had: his family, a career he loved and his painting. Still, there was one crucial element that was missing: marriage.

Jack *liked* being married. He certainly didn't like being alone; a widower, companionless. What he wanted more than anything was to share his life with somebody again. But what could he do about it? The answer was simple: find a new wife.

And that's exactly what he did. Less than eighteen months after Maybelle died.

Not everyone shared Jack's happiness – namely Hanson. That his father could replace his mother so easily – or so it appeared – was incomprehensible. It didn't matter that his father had known Anna over many years. It didn't matter that his mother had known Anna too – that felt even more strange. What mattered was the adjusting; the new dynamic thrust upon them, a past haphazardly brushed aside to swiftly make way for the new. More to the point, Hanson thought, it was not only new, it was different. Two opposing forces that had won his father's heart.

The root of Anna's grief had begun five thousand miles away in Ceylon where she lived with her husband, Christopher, and their young daughter. Christopher came along just shy of Anna's thirtieth birthday while he was on leave from his post working for the British Government overseas. He was staying with his aunt and uncle in Stourport-on-Severn and spending all of his free time at Malvern Tennis Club, where Anna was also a member. There was no doubt the two people who were practising their serve on that bright Saturday morning liked tennis; so engrossed were they in trying to perfect their form that they barely acknowledged the other's presence. Until, that is, a stray ball brought them together.

'So sorry!' Anna shouted from the other side of the court, where Christopher had gone to fetch her ball. 'I hope I haven't disturbed your practice!'

'Not at all,' replied Christopher, who was smiling broadly. 'In fact, I'm rather pleased to have been disturbed.'

Christopher walked towards Anna and she was struck by how dashing he looked in his tennis whites, with his tall, athletic frame and tanned limbs. 'Christopher,' he announced confidently, offering Anna his hand. 'And you are…?'

'Anna,' came the girlish reply. 'Pleased to meet you too.'

It transpired that Christopher had turned thirty the previous year and had lived in Ceylon all his life, having been born in Kandy to a father who was a general and had overseen the building of the country's railway system. But Christopher, Anna learnt, didn't care much for trains. His passion was tea and he told Anna how he had worked his way up the ranks to tea plantation supervisor at the Gold Leaf plantation in one of the hill stations. It was clear Christopher took delight in describing the vast estate he managed and lived in, which, he was keen to add, overlooked a garden of billowing bamboo, whistling pines and a lawn edged by overflowing borders of hibiscus, hydrangeas and lilies. 'I think you would approve.' Christopher's eyes twinkled as he mimicked the movement of a tennis swerve. 'I even have my own tennis court, but it can be lonely without someone to practise with.'

Anna returned Christopher's light-heartedness with her own kittenish behaviour, for she had learnt enough from her friend Deborah about men. 'Is that so?' she replied coyly.

'So much so that I've decided it's high time I had a young lady by my side.' Christopher placed his racket on the court beside his feet. 'Goodness knows how many times well-meaning friends have tried to pair me off, but this matchmaking business is… well… life as a bachelor, it's not always easy. What do you think? Would you care to solve my dilemma, Anna?'

Christopher's charm worked splendidly on Anna. From the moment they met, they flirted with each other like the game they were trying to perfect, batting compliments back and forth until they realised that their destiny was sealed. After three months of courting, Anna was to join Christopher as soon as possible in Ceylon.

The Gold Leaf plantation, which Anna gladly left the Midlands for, was one of hundreds dotted around the lush, fertile landscape, cloaking the region known as Hill Country in a thick carpet of emerald. It was a vast estate, far larger than Anna imagined, and she was immediately smitten with the views, with its delicate morning mists and spectacular orange sunsets. Away from the chaos of Colombo, Hill Country meandered along to its own rhythm and, much to Anna's delight, for she was careful to avoid the sun, it was infinitely cooler and quieter; a sanctuary from the dust and heat below. When she first arrived, Anna recalled how she could make out patterns in the slopes from the thousands of planted tea crops when the sun was at its brightest. Further still, scattered haphazardly across the hills, were the cheerfully painted houses: mint green, earthy pinks and primrose yellows. But it was the silvery thick-trunked eucalyptus trees that Anna loved most of all. It was there, under their shade on the verandah, that she drank her morning tea thousands of miles from England. Everyone thought that Anna would be homesick, but she exclaimed – insisted – that she never felt more alive than in Ceylon. The life she had chosen suited her. She loved the expat parties, rounds of gossip and leisurely afternoon teas, where scones with clotted cream and strawberry preserve sat happily alongside *masala chai, roti* and *parippu*. She loved the way everything just seemed so much more colourful, brighter. In fact, she loved everything about her world; until, that is, her young, fit husband collapsed playing tennis one morning before work, changing everything. Anna suddenly found herself a widow in her prime, having to uproot from a life she had built on the other side of the world, only to reluctantly return to her parents and the home of her childhood; the drizzly Midlands she never imagined she would live in again. She would return with a daughter but without a husband, and grief would accompany her across the world and stay until there were no more tears left to cry.

'It's so grey here,' declared Anna's daughter, Elizabeth, who was born in Ceylon and now found herself in less temperate climes.

'The sun shines in England too, sweetheart. Not often, but when it does, it's worth the wait.'

'What about breakfast? Can I still have kedgeree and mango?'

'Well, there aren't any mango trees here, but you'll love porridge just as well.'

'What about my friends?'

'You'll make new friends in no time.' Anna ruffled her daughter's wild hair, which was curly and red. 'It'll be better once we've settled in. I promise, Lizzie.'

Elizabeth was seven years old, yet she already knew where her heart belonged. And it certainly didn't belong to a grey Midlands town in the middle of a British winter. She was a child of the Indian Ocean, with its white sand and brilliant turquoise sea. So Anna did what she thought was best and enrolled her daughter in a boarding school some thirty miles away, where new friends could hopefully provide consolation for the inclement weather and some distraction from what she had left behind.

With Elizabeth settled in her new school, Anna returned to work. She remembered thinking at the time how easy it had been to slip back into her former role in the design team. There were new things to learn – things had changed so much – but she enjoyed being back among all the familiar faces, including Jack, the one she had looked forward to seeing most. Both privately conceded that it felt as if time hadn't changed anything at all, except now something was subtly shifting between them. It helped that Anna had an easy way about her, some might go as far as to say flirtatious – and Jack, like others, had been drawn to her effortless charm. It was only now as a widower that Jack saw Anna in a completely different light. And as he caught sight of her in the studio one morning sketching a design, it suddenly occurred to him that she would, in fact, make rather a lovely wife.

24

'I have some news,' said Jack, over the phone to his son one evening. 'You remember Anna, don't you?'

'Your colleague? The lady you've been spending time with recently? Yes, why?' Hanson felt uneasy, because although he had asked a question, he already knew the answer.

'Well, we've decided to get married.'

'Married?' It was a few moments before Hanson responded.

'That's right, we're getting married.'

'But you barely know her,' Hanson snorted. 'Are you sure you're not rushing into things?'

'Rushing into things? We are not exactly in the first flush of youth. We certainly don't have the luxury of time either.'

'Age isn't an excuse to rush into things.' Hanson's reply was curt.

'We are not rushing into things,' said Jack, disappointed at his son's evident disapproval. 'I have known Anna a long time. She's wonderful. You'll see for yourself when you meet her.' Yet, despite his disappointment, Jack also understood. He had expressed the same concern when his mother married Albert. He had also wanted his mother to claim it inconceivable that anyone could ever take her husband's place. He had also wanted things to stay the same, even though by very virtue of the fact that his father had died, things would never be the same again. What Jack had feared the most was change: someone new replacing and diminishing his father's memory. It was wrong. It was disloyal. It was not the way things were supposed to turn out. When Albert died, Eva told her sons that God had blessed her with two wonderful husbands and she had loved them both differently. Henry had been her first love but it was with Albert she had built a life. It was Albert she grew old with. It was Albert who had saved her. Maybelle was Jack's first love. But now it was Anna he hoped to grow old with. It was Anna who had saved him.

'It just seems so sudden,' said Hanson to Tilly, once he got off the phone to his father. 'He didn't even mention Mum. It's as if he's erased her from his memory to make way for Anna and his new life.'

'If Anna makes him happy, then who are we to interfere? Isn't that the main thing?'

'I know, it's just...'

'Remember what your father was like a year ago. Like a fish out of water. I think meeting Anna is the best thing that could have happened to him.'

'You think so?'

'Without a doubt. You want your father to be happy again, don't you?'

'Of course. I was just thinking of Mum...'

'*That* will never stop. But we both know Dad could never be happy without someone to love.'

*

Jack and Anna were married in the spring. Jack wore a single white freesia pinned to the lapel of his cream jacket, and Anna, who was wearing cream too, carried a bouquet of sweet peas and irises. Jack gained a stepdaughter, Elizabeth a stepfather; Anna a stepson, and Hanson, whether he liked it or not, gained a stepmother.

Someone had told Jack before the wedding – a thrice-married Australian client from Cairns – that the merging of a new life together in middle age was not something to take lightly. It was difficult, his colleague had said, presumably speaking from experience. Neither party wants to give up their independence. Neither wants to bend to the other's rhythm and routine. Inevitably, something has to give. Jack wondered whether his colleague was simply trying to forewarn him that his mid-life union was doomed. Should he be worried? Hardly, but it did get him thinking about the idea of compatibility. *If my first wife listened to Bach and Beethoven*, he pondered, *while my second wife enjoys watching daytime soap operas, what does that actually mean? Moreover, what does that actually say about me?* Jack never did find the answer. Perhaps he had simply made an unconscious decision to be with someone who didn't remind him of what he had lost. But as far as those close to the couple could ascertain, the union between Jack and Anna worked. In fact, they seemed to bring out the best in each other. Jack's introspective tendencies were a foil to Anna's frivolous nature. Anna, who was ebullient and outgoing. Anna, who loved fashion, tennis and catching up with friends at the Women's Institute. Anna, who read *Vogue* and was a popular member of her local swimming club. Anna, who made friends easily – always adding to her expanding list. Anna, who was the antithesis of Maybelle.

Elizabeth, who had recently finished university and was about to relocate to Singapore to work in a school, told Jack shortly after the wedding that she was glad he and her mother had found each other. He told his twenty-two-year-old stepdaughter, just like Albert had told him, that she could always count on his support. Neither Jack nor Anna realised that Elizabeth (neither did she at that point) would never return to England again to live. It was as if she had waited to give them her blessing before she returned to her roots; a child of the Indian Ocean.

*

The following autumn, Isla was born, and Jack became a grandfather again, delighted to have a girl in the family.

'It's a pretty name,' he remarked. 'I like it.'

'We've also taken to calling her Bobby – thanks to Craig,' said Hanson, laughing. 'He wanted to meet his "Bobby sister" straight away, and when he first said hello to Isla at the hospital, he said, rather sweetly, "Hello, little Bobby sister," instead of baby sister. The name stuck. Suits her too.'

Jack smiled and closed his eyes. He was imagining his granddaughter; what she might look like, whom she might take after. 'Our family is growing,' he said after a few moments. It was what he had always wanted: a family to be proud of, a legacy to leave behind. *This* was what life was all about.

Hanson sensed the joy in his father's heart and he realised that for all the pain of losing his mother, a pain that was still raw, his father deserved to be happy. 'We can't wait for you both to meet her.'

Isla's christening took place on a crisp, bright morning the Sunday before Christmas at St Mary Magdalene's Church in Perth. It had snowed heavily the evening before and Tilly worried that the guests would not arrive on time. Lotte and her Welsh husband, Tim – whom she met in Cologne but was now living in Surrey with – had taken the train all the way from Lewes. Lotte's French was still better than her English and at the age of twenty-nine, she still wore her blonde hair in two plaits on her head, ignoring Tilly's jibes that all she needed to complete the look was a mountain goat by her side. Jack had driven up to Scotland with Anna the previous day, collecting his mother, Aunt Lily and Grandma Clara on the way. Aunt Lily, who was now Great-great-aunt Lily, had, of course, insisted on baking a fruitcake to mark the occasion. She had also insisted on being part of the celebrations, having missed Craig's christening three years previously. Eva was thrilled that she had a great-granddaughter, and Clara, having recently turned a hundred and one, announced that she wanted to be in the presence of her whole family for the last time before it was too late.

The christening was memorable for several reasons, but two stood out in particular. It was the first family gathering Anna had been invited to and she was now officially part of the Jagger clan. The second was the moment Clara held Isla. 'This is your great-great granddaughter,' Hanson said, as he gently placed his seven-week-old daughter in her great-great-grandmother's arms. For a moment, Clara was incredibly still, imagining Isla in her christening dress as she felt the silk, lace and ruffle detail against her skin. Her eyes, what colour were Isla's eyes?, she wondered. Blue like Eva, Jack and Hanson? Green? Or brown like her husband's had been? She touched Isla's face, gently caressing the soft, downy hair and the contours of her smooth, warm cheeks.

'What colour are her eyes?' Clara asked suddenly, looking straight ahead.

'Well, they're still a bluish grey. But that will change in a few months, just like Craig's. He has brown eyes now,' Hanson said, crouching next to Clara.

'Yes, of course, how I forget these things.' Clara's head moved in the direction of Hanson's voice.

'Here, feel how tiny her hands are.' Hanson guided his great-grandmother's hand and placed it gently around Isla's tightly furled fist.

Oh, my darling girl, Clara thought, tracing the outline of a finger. *You are just at the beginning, the very beginning. And I am so very, very glad to have met you.*

Eleven weeks after Isla was baptised – she was now Isla Isabella Lily Jagger – Clara died peacefully in her sleep. Lily moved in with her sister and continued to bake cakes until her death three years later. Eva passed away not long afterwards, just before her birthday. Mother and daughter were buried together at the Anglican church just outside Hipperholme. Ten miles away lay Eva, alongside her beloved Henry and Albert.

PART 3

Giles

25

THE ARMCHAIR AND THE ELECTRIC CHAIR

'A phoenix from the ashes? Well, not quite, but certainly a change from humble origins and lack of formal education to being elected a Fellow of the Royal Society of Arts, champion of the Textile Institute and Fellow of the Royal Society of Artists and Designers.' The speaker gestured to Jack, who was sitting next to him. 'And lest we forget. He is also a college governor and an exhibitor of watercolour paintings at various societies. Without further ado, may I introduce you to Mr Jack Jagger.'

Jack rose from the table, acutely aware of the expectant faces looking at him. 'Thank you, Charles.' Jack cleared his throat and glanced around the room. 'And thank you all for coming today...

'...I left school when I was fourteen. And the only subject in which I showed any real merit was drawing...'

Jack paused, recollecting the short speech he had rehearsed so many times in his head, and glanced again at the audience, in search of a familiar face.

'...And so it was on the strength of this that my stepfather on his own initiative went to EW Worth's carpet manufacturers and asked to see the head designer, a Mr Bayman. He told him that his stepson had some talent and could he give the lad a job in Worth's design studio...

'...It was settled and the rest is history. But I have not invited you here today to talk about my youth. It's the other side of the coin I want to talk to you about that we all arrive at eventually. Retirement...

'...I believe once we reach a certain age, there are two chairs that kill: the armchair and the electric chair. Especially when we no longer have a job to fill our days. Only the luxury of time stretched out in front of us...

'...But for too many folk, and I see it every day, life seems to stop once they don't have a job to occupy them. They simply give up, no longer interested in engaging with the world, forgetting all the joys to be had. And that's a terrible shame. Because life can take on new meaning once we are no longer defined by our work.'

Jack took a sip of water, glancing again around the room. Most were from the Probus Club, but there were others whose retirement was imminent – teachers, nurses, council staff – whom Jack hoped to inspire to join the Arts Society. Alongside these were his fellow members, who had recently elected him as their president to mark the society's fortieth anniversary.

'...If I could encourage more people to pursue their passion, hobby, whatever you want to call it, I am certain it would cure many of today's common ailments. To have a reason to get up in the morning is not to be taken lightly. It's *the* best form of medicine we can give ourselves.'

There were several nods and exchanged glances.

'...In fact, we don't need to settle for either the armchair *or* the electric chair.'

Some people laughed; a few looked puzzled.

'...I'm sure you've probably all gathered by now that *my* passion is painting, and I'm hoping after today yours will be too.

Now, does anyone here have any questions?'

'I have a question.' A woman in a blue coat held up her hand. 'How long has the club being going?'

'Well, I've lived here since nineteen thirty-eight, the same year we established the Arts Society – so exactly forty years.'

'How many paintings do you complete, say, in a year?' Another woman – one of the nurses from the local hospital who had introduced herself to Jack when she arrived – took a small notepad out of her handbag.

'That all depends. I can paint anything from twelve to twenty-five in a year – sometimes more.'

'And what gave you the idea to create something like this?' Another hand shot up and Jack's eyes moved to the far corner where a young man – boy – was hovering in the doorway, as if he wasn't quite sure whether to stay or to leave.

'Well…' said Jack, keeping his eyes on the boy, 'a group of us thought we'd like to start something for like-minded folk, people with an interest in art and painting, and develop a kind of community from that. I had just moved here and I suppose it was a good way to meet people, to feel part of something.'

The boy nodded, and Jack noticed his eyes darting around. 'And the paintings – what do you paint?'

'Well, there is absolutely no expectation – you just come along with your easel and paint whatever you like. In fact, we had one chap, our previous president actually, who painted portraits of the Queen Mother. Very good they were too.'

'But what do *you* paint?'

'What do I paint? Local scenes mainly but other places too that capture my interest.'

'And your medium? Which medium do you paint in?'

'Almost entirely in watercolour – although occasionally in oils. Pastel summer gardens; muted autumn scenes; watery, dark seascapes. Things like that.' Jack wondered why the lad was so interested.

The boy nodded again, seemingly satisfied with Jack's answer.

'If anyone else has any questions, please do come and find me. In the meantime, help yourself to tea and coffee over in the far corner.'

'Just one more question,' the boy said, raising his hand tentatively.

'Yes, please,' Jack said.

'Are the rest of your family artistic?'

'My family?' Jack repeated the boy's words. 'Well, my wife has considerable talent – as has my stepdaughter. My son, on the other hand, hasn't, and it remains to be seen whether my grandchildren will develop any artistic leanings in the future. They are still young but we'll see.'

The boy nodded and buried his hands in his jacket pockets.

'I hear you've submitted some paintings to Hillmans for consideration – local ones, I suppose?'

'Yes, indeed,' said Jack, relieved to hear a familiar voice as he turned to greet a fellow Probus member. 'Mind you, that was some time ago now. I have a feeling they may have settled on someone else. I wonder, how many people do you think will consider joining up today?'

'It's difficult to say – there's certainly an assortment of faces here, which is quite refreshing. You need to get the youngsters in to balance things out, though.'

'Yes, that lad over there...' Jack motioned discreetly at the boy with all the questions and was startled to see him staring back at them. The boy nodded and, to Jack's surprise, began to walk towards them.

'Hello,' said the boy when he came over. He still had his hands in his trouser pockets.

'Hello,' said Jack, extending his hand. 'Jack Jagger, and this is a colleague of mine, Clive Arnolds, from another club that I belong to. The Probus Club.'

'Hello,' came the reply. 'I'm Giles,' taking his hands out of his pockets to shake Jack's hand.

'And what brings you here today, Giles? Do you paint?'

'Not really. Well, yes, sometimes. I studied it at school, art, but I work in retail now.'

There was something about the lad, thought Jack, which reminded him of his own youth. His demeanour had the air of someone who was still looking for his place in the world. 'Where do you work now?' Jack asked. Meanwhile, Clive Arnolds, not wanting to interrupt the conversation, discreetly motioned a goodbye before walking away.

'I work at Hillmans. My uncle recently found me a job there. It's a trainee position, a role he said was best not to pass by. They only take on a few people every year.' Giles looked uneasy, his eyes darting between Jack and the floor. 'Though, recently, I've been given more responsibility, sourcing artwork for the store, which I'm looking forward to, I suppose.'

Hillmans was Worcester's largest store. Jack knew it well. It was where he had recently submitted several of his paintings for consideration, which, if he was successful, were to be displayed across various departments.

'Your accent...' Jack said. 'Salt of the earth, if I'm correct?'

'Are you from Yorkshire too?' Giles smiled for what seemed like the first time.

'Yes, I spent almost the first thirty years of my life there.'

'That's funny, I'm from Elland. My Great-grandpa Edward still lives in the same town I grew up in.'

'Well, strike a light. I was born in Hipperholme and I can't say I've met many here from the same area!'

Although there was nothing unusual about this coincidence, it still struck a chord with Jack.

'I'm thinking of joining this place,' said Giles, looking around. 'If that's okay? It's not too far from Worcester, and I can come down on the train once a month.'

'Of course. Having you join us would quite frankly bring a breath of fresh air to the group. I always say that young people add a new dynamic and energy.'

'Thanks,' said Giles, the bashfulness returning again.

'Now, my wife and I are planning a trip to Worcester soon, and we usually have a browse around Hillmans after a spot of lunch. Which department did you say you worked in?'

'Haberdashery. It's on the ground floor. Near the escalators.'

'Right, yes. Well, I hope we will be able to see you in Worcester soon.'

They shook hands, man and boy, Jack reiterating how pleased he was to have met Giles.

By the time he arrived home, however, Jack was feeling very out of sorts and he couldn't shake off his growing sense of unease. He was sure Giles' face was familiar, yet uncertain as to where he knew him. 'It's odd,' he said to Anna when he told her about Giles, 'but I just can't put my finger on it. He was perfectly pleasant, and there was even something endearing about the lad.'

'Maybe you are just reading into things, although I do wonder why he came all the way to Kidderminster to hear you talk. Surely there are similar societies in Worcester?'

'It didn't even occur to me, but yes, you're right. Why did he come all that way?' Jack reached for his pipe in the pocket of his jacket. 'And did I mention that he's from Yorkshire? – a stone's throw from Hipperholme. Elland of all places!'

'It's a small world,' said Anna, who had gone back into the kitchen.

Jack decided to call his old friend Dickie Hainsworth. It was a while since they had last spoken and Jack felt compelled to tell him about Giles. Dickie was now in his eighties and recently retired, having finally transferred control of the management of his tailoring business – eleven express tailor shops – to his three children. He was also as voluble as ever.

'Hello, Dickie, it's Jack. How are you?' Jack waited to hear the familiar sound of his friend's voice, a voice that immediately reconnected him to his past, which few people could.

'Young man, hello!' replied Dickie cheerfully. 'I can't complain and all the better for hearing from you. Celia and I have just returned from the Caribbean.'

'The Caribbean? Lucky you!'

'Oh, it's a dream, that place. Sailed around for the best part of a month. Absolute paradise—'

'And why not,' said Jack, interrupting Dickie's enthusiastic flow of words.

'Well, we're still fit enough – just. Not difficult when you have eight grandchildren, but there'll come a time. How is Anna? And the grandchildren?'

'Everyone is doing well. It must feel good to finally be able to hand over the keys to your clan and take a back seat?'

'Oh, it's terrific, but I still need to keep an eye on them,' said Dickie, laughing. 'Make sure they're not up to mischief. Now, my good man, how is life treating you?'

The two hadn't spoken in months, but as Jack proceeded to tell Dickie about the encounter with Giles at the Kidderminster Arts Society, he felt grateful not only to have a confidant but also a link to his past. 'There's just something about the boy. It's as if he's held up a mirror to my youth and reminded me of things I'd long forgotten. Do you remember meeting an Edward at my father's salon? It's the lad's great-grandfather apparently. He's from Elland. He didn't give me a surname.'

Whether Dickie recalled an Edward was not immediately apparent. He was quiet for a moment, as if deliberating on advice he might proffer. 'Well...' he said eventually '...there's nothing wrong with that, but I think you might be reading into it. Giles is just a lad you happened to meet – nothing remarkable there. Well, apart from you both being from God's own country. And that can't be a bad thing, eh?' It was clear Dickie was keen to steer the conversation towards lighter matters: the forecast, the impending cricket season and the probability of Yorkshire winning the trophy.

'Perhaps,' said Jack ruefully. 'Perhaps the lad reminds me a little too much of myself when I was a boy.'

'I think that's it, son.' Dickie started to laugh. 'You've just met someone who's reminded you of your younger self. Now, if anyone remembers young Jack, it's me. Quite the dreamer you were too.'

'I still am, I'm afraid,' said Jack, laughing.

'You know, perhaps Harry might remember a thing or two. Jog your memory a bit...'

'Harry? He doesn't remember anything really. He was five when Father passed away.'

'Yes, of course he was. How is your brother?'

'Oh, it's not easy, what with Molly and the depression. I'm not sure how things are at the moment. We don't speak very often, but I imagine it's the same. It's always the same with Molly.'

'Do you ever call him?'

Jack was surprised by the question. 'Well, yes, not every week but now and again, yes.'

The truth was that Jack couldn't remember the last time he had spoken to Harry. It's not that there was anything specific that had brought them to that point. He just didn't feel the need to share the minutiae of his life the way other siblings did, and Jack assumed his brother felt the same way. They never marked each other's birthdays, neither did they visit each other at Christmas, and Jack couldn't remember the last time he actually picked up the phone simply for a chat with his brother. *What would we talk about anyway?* Jack thought, *I mean, really talk about?* They were just so different.

'It's a two-way thing – relationships, friendships. We need to keep them ticking over. Now, my friend, I won't keep you any longer. Give my best to that lovely wife of yours and we'll speak soon.'

'Goodbye, Dickie. Please give my love to Celia and thank you – for listening.'

'Always a pleasure, you know you can always count on me to lend you an ear.'

After speaking to Dickie, Jack did feel better, but he still couldn't get Giles out of his mind. Meeting him had brought back uncomfortable memories; memories of his father, the barbershop and the stolen formula. But what now?, he wondered. He couldn't talk to Anna about it. What would he say? His father's barbershop felt like a world away, and memories of it seemed childlike and irrelevant. With Anna, Jack wanted to look forward, not back. No, he decided, when he found Anna in the kitchen absorbed in the details of a recipe, he wouldn't mention anything about what Giles had ignited in him. It was only a feeling after all.

'Everything all right?' Anna looked up at her husband, her spectacles perched on the bridge of her nose.

'Yes, yes, fine. Is there anything I can do to help?'

'The plates and cups. Could you bring those through, please?'

Every day at exactly the same time – eleven in the morning and four in the afternoon – Jack and Anna enjoyed a pot of tea and a slice of cake. This simple tradition was the bedrock of their marriage. It was the bedrock of their social circle too (something he would never have done with Maybelle) as friends and acquaintances took turns to provide cake, conversation and company on a rotating basis. On this warm September afternoon, things were no different. Jack and Anna gazed out into their garden, admiring the kaleidoscope of colour before them.

'The garden looks so vibrant,' said Jack. 'It would be a shame not to capture it in full bloom. Perhaps a painting of the camellias with the pear tree in the background. What do you think?'

'Wonderful,' said Anna, herself a keen painter. Even if she

didn't think it a good idea, Anna rarely disagreed with anything or anyone, always maintaining a measured balance of charm and deference. They had been married for nine years and it was Anna's malleability that ensured the happy equilibrium between the couple remained intact.

'What with the weather being so fine, how about a trip to Hillmans on Friday? The lad I mentioned earlier works in the haberdashery department. I promised we would drop in to say hello.'

'What was his name again?' Anna was carefully dividing her slice of cake into small pieces.

'Giles – not sure about the surname. He didn't give me one.'

'I've always liked that name.' Anna placed her teacup on the table beside her. 'I once knew a Giles at the tennis club and he always seemed such a good sport. So polite and friendly.'

'Well, that's settled then,' Jack said, reaching for his crossword. 'Friday it is.'

As fate would have it   26

The late-afternoon light sprinkled the medieval and Tudor buildings on the Cornmarket and Friar Street with a deep golden hue, while the River Severn, which weaved its way snake-like through the centre, glistened in the autumn sunshine. Just off Deansway stood Hillmans, Worcester's oldest department store, where Jack and Anna found themselves one quiet Friday afternoon as they made their way to the haberdashery section. Jack recognised Giles immediately. His awkward silhouette was hunched over a catalogue, while a middle-aged couple stood behind the counter, considering the swabs of colour and material in front of them.

'I'm not so sure about the paisley,' Jack overheard the man say as he and Anna came closer.

'Well, how about the plain velvet in turquoise if you don't like the pink?' said the woman.

'I'm not sure.' The man looked flustered. 'If I'm honest, these are all just a bit too colourful for me.'

'Slate grey?' Giles held up a plain swatch. 'It's a very popular choice and it complements most decor.'

'We'll think about it,' said the woman, glancing at her husband. 'We don't want to rush an important decision like this, do we, John?' Jack watched the couple gather their things and wondered how something as inconsequential as curtains – he was certainly guilty of it – was given so much consideration. He looked at Anna and they both smiled, remembering the countless times they had deliberated on colour and pattern.

'Hello again,' said Jack, as he walked toward Giles. 'This is my wife, Anna. Anna, this is the young man who came along to the Arts Society on Wednesday. He's interested in becoming a member.'

Giles blushed as Anna reached out to shake his hand and while the two exchanged pleasantries, Jack noted the surname on Giles' badge. 'Illingworth…' Jack said. 'Strong Yorkshire name you've got there.' Giles smiled awkwardly, his eyes characteristically darting back and forth before resting momentarily on Anna's ring. The lad is clearly out of his depth, thought Jack. He may be working at Hillmans by virtue of his uncle's position, but it was very apparent he was ill-suited to the role.

'My wife and I have just been for a walk along the river. Do you know Worcester well?'

'No,' replied Giles evasively. 'I don't really know anyone down here.'

'That's a shame.' Jack watched Giles fidget with a measuring tape. 'How's work?'

'Maybe it's the good weather, but I've only had a few customers so far this morning.'

'Don't you find the day drags if it's quiet?'

Giles pointed at the rows of fabric in front of him. 'It's all the dilly-dallying that annoys me. Who cares about curtains? The sooner I can start doing more of the arty stuff, the better.'

'Oh,' said Jack, taken aback by Giles' sudden bluntness, before turning to Anna, who was murmuring something about denier.

'It was lovely to meet you,' she said, addressing Giles. 'We hope you join the Arts Society.'

'Thank you,' said Giles, giving a little wave before Anna made her way towards the escalators.

'That eggshell blue linen over there has caught my eye.' Jack hoped that with Anna gone, Giles might feel more at ease. 'The colour is really striking.'

'Yes, some of the stuff here is nice,' said Giles, picking up a piece of fabric. 'My uncle says I need to spend at least six months in every department, but I'm not interested in retail. And I'm definitely not interested in curtains.'

Jack laughed. 'I gathered that. Do your family live nearby?'

'No, they're all in Yorkshire. Different parts of Halifax. I live with my uncle down here now.'

'Oh, I see. You must miss them, having them all the way up there.'

'Not really. Dad is always working and Mum helps out when she can, which is basically all the time.' Giles was still fidgeting with the measuring tape and Jack wondered what could absorb so much of his parents' time.

'It sounds like they are very busy.'

'Well, he's a barber. I suppose it's to be expected.'

'A barber,' Jack repeated, as if he had misheard. 'A barber...?'

'Yes,' said Giles, placing the measuring tape to one side.

'And your father – has he been in the business long?'

'As long as I can remember. Grandad, Dad and Mum – they all work there. That's all they *ever* do.'

'Have they always lived in Yorkshire?'

'Yes – pretty much.'

'I see.' Jack averted his gaze, for he was conscious of staring at Giles. 'So this business has been in your family for a while?'

'Yes, for as long as I can remember. It never interested me what they did but I know their barbershop is very popular. So I suppose they must be doing something right.'

171

'Well, if the customers keep returning, that's always a good sign.'

'I think so. It must be their trade secret.'

'Trade secret?'

'Yes, you know, the thing that makes them special.' Giles glanced around to see if there were any customers nearby. He also wondered whether his manager, whom he could see observing them, minded that the man he was deep in conversation with didn't appear in the least bit interested in buying curtains.

'I don't suppose you know what makes your father's barbershop popular, do you?'

Giles placed the measuring tape back in its drawer and picked up a piece of fabric, undecided whether to fiddle with it. 'I'm not sure. Grandad and Dad don't talk about it much. They've always been secretive about stuff.'

Jack nodded, gesturing for Giles to continue. One by one, he was putting the pieces of a puzzle together.

'Mum used to say she thought Dad and Grandad were up to no good. They were always so guarded about the cream. Grandad didn't seem to have many friends either. He said family was everything to him and that he didn't need anyone else, well, apart from his customers, of course.'

Jack nodded again, careful not to betray any emotion.

'I suppose that's why Mum didn't question things as business seemed to be going well. I guess that's all that mattered.'

Four specific words played on Jack's mind: *family, guarded, business, secret*. They swirled around his head as he desperately tried to recall his father and the barbershop, the regular customers, the familiar faces; so many of them coming through that handsome black door and Jack in the middle of it all, a young boy.

Now he knew why Giles had unnerved him so much during that first encounter.

The downward glance. The eyes darting back and forth.

'And your great-grandfather, the one you mentioned the other day? Edward?'

'Yes, Pa Oldroyd. He's the one who lives in Elland. He started things really. I mean, with helping my grandad become successful. That's what my parents always said: *We have Pa Oldroyd to thank for everything.* He's getting on a bit now – ninety-four – but he still likes to know what's going on with the business.'

Edward Oldroyd, who always had a newspaper and umbrella tucked underneath his arm when he came in for his trim. Edward Oldroyd, whose penetrating gaze had followed Jack and his father with a sinister strangeness. Edward Oldroyd, whose son-in-law was a barber and who suggested – no, had constantly persisted – that his son-in-law work with Henry Jagger.

Oldroyd, who always asked questions but gave nothing away.

The downward glance. The eyes darting back and forth.

How strange to have life come full circle like this, Jack thought. Now, sixty years on, here was Edward Oldroyd's great-grandson standing before him, oblivious to the storm he had created. Jack stood very still as he processed Giles' words. He didn't need anything else. The truth he had been searching for all this time had been unlocked in the haberdashery section of Hillmans; unravelling before his eyes like the fabrics on the counter.

'Your grandfather is right, family *is* everything. It is to me too, as it was to my father.' Jack's words were cold, deliberate and ambiguous, lacking their earlier warmth.

Giles nodded politely. 'Well, I best be getting back to work too. My manager—'

'Of course,' said Jack, interrupting Giles. 'Well, good luck here. I hope it all works out.' Jack spoke with a trace of finality, and as he turned away and walked towards the escalators – was hosiery on the ground floor or first? – he knew he needed to get as far away from the haberdashery department as possible.

Four paintings 27

The incident at Hillmans faded into insignificance. Once he had mulled over his conversation with Giles, Jack knew it would be futile to pursue what was ultimately a hunch, albeit a very strong one. A hunch, which if stripped down to its bare bones, was accusing Edward Oldroyd of stealing his father's invention. He knew he had to let it go. What use would it be to seek justice in something that belonged to the past; all those lives he would turn upside down without any concrete evidence. Who would he accuse anyway? It wasn't Giles' fault and Edward Oldroyd was now frail and old. On top of that, he couldn't talk to Harry about it; there was no point, he wouldn't remember; and Anna, well, he didn't want to drag her into it either. Hanson? No, his son would think him rash. Tilly would only worry, and if he mentioned it to Dickie, he would just tell him that he was reading into things.

October arrived, bringing with it a crispness to the air and an unexpected letter. When Jack opened the envelope, it wasn't so much the elegant handwriting beneath Hillmans' familiar gold logo that struck Jack; rather, it was the sheer timing of it all. Why now? he thought, reading the letter carefully, as if searching for a vital clue. Why now?

Hillmans has been at the heart of Worcester's community for 150 years, welcoming customers from near and far to enjoy its traditional surroundings and experience its impeccable service.

Jack went to fetch his diary from the study. When exactly had he submitted his paintings? He knew it had been several months ago, and he assumed the store had simply declined his proposal. Jack picked up the letter again and reread the last two paragraphs.

Further to your submission, I am delighted to confirm our decision to appoint you as Hillmans' chosen local artist. We therefore invite you to select four paintings of the city of Worcester, which will be exhibited throughout our store.

In the first instance, we kindly ask that you contact the number below to make an appointment at your earliest convenience.

Jack reread the whole letter several times before putting it back in its envelope. He then put the kettle on and decided to give Hillmans a call later that afternoon. In the meantime, there was the crossword to finish and a walk to clear his head. Then he would have lunch. Anna was still out when Jack returned from his walk, and he remembered, it being a Thursday, that she had her weekly hairdresser's appointment, or weekly gossip hour as she liked to called it. Jack couldn't imagine what his wife and her stylist had to talk about. But he suspected it had something to do with the Australian soaps they both had a penchant for.

After lunch, Jack called the number on the letter. A curt-sounding voice came on the line. 'Good afternoon, Hillmans.'

'Good afternoon,' said Jack. 'I'd like to speak to Mr Watson, please.'

'Speaking. How may I help?'

'Mr Watson, my name is Mr Jagger. I'm calling about the letter I received this morning. It's about the paintings you'd like to purchase for Hillmans, the ones of Worcester.'

'Ah yes, Mr Jagger, very good to hear from you. In fact, I was only just talking about you the other day with Giles.'

'Giles?' Jack replied, taken aback. 'Giles Illingworth?'

'Yes, Giles Illingworth. He works with us here at Hillmans. Do you know him?'

'Yes, yes, I do, although I wasn't aware he discussed my paintings with you.'

'Well, I'm very glad he did, because he has done nothing but sing your praises. Not that we needed persuading.'

'That's very kind of you,' said Jack, moving the telephone to his other ear. *Why on earth was Giles discussing my paintings with Mr Watson?* he wondered.

'The competition was stiff. It always is, but your paintings of Worcester Cathedral and the cricket ground are precisely what we're looking for. You know, it was something Giles said that really brought it home; something about customers appreciating tradition...'

Jack listened to the voice at the other end of the line. He'd hoped to move on from the Giles incident.

'At your convenience, of course, I think the next steps would be to arrange a time for you to come in and meet the team. How does the first Tuesday in November sound?'

Jack reached across for his diary and quickly flicked through the pages until he reached the entry for November. 'Tuesday the first. Yes, that's perfect. I shall look forward to it.'

Watson cleared his throat before continuing. 'My secretary will be in touch with all the details.'

Jack placed the telephone back on its receiver and took a deep breath. He wanted to collect his thoughts before Anna returned home. He was veering between feeling part incredulous and part delighted, and he needed to decide which mood to greet his wife with. He went into the kitchen and cut a slice of apple tart, which Anna had taken out of the cupboard earlier. Surely, Watson had made a mistake about Giles. The lad was a trainee, after all, who was currently being shown the ropes in the haberdashery department. Would he really have a say in deciding which local artist Hillmans was going to appoint? It seemed the more Jack tried to forget about him, the more Giles seemed to remind him of his presence.

*

The first Tuesday in November arrived; the air thick with autumn. Jack drove to Worcester in the early afternoon with four paintings in the back of his hatchback, the sun already low on the horizon. He had already planned to pop into the art shop on his way home and perhaps see whether he might pick up a couple of early Christmas presents for Craig and Isla. Watson and the personnel team were based on the top floor, and Jack estimated that he would be in and out of the meeting within the hour. He had also made a point of avoiding the haberdashery department on his way in, deliberately using the store's front entrance rather than the more convenient side, which made it all the more surprising to see Giles sitting expectantly at the opposite side of Watson, the latter of whom greeted him jovially when Jack arrived in the boardroom.

'Mr Jagger, how very good of you to come. Let me take your coat and these,' he said, pointing to Jack's paintings before gesturing to Giles. 'I'm sure no introductions are needed here.' As if on cue, Giles stood up and extended his hand towards Jack. Was it his imagination or did Giles seem happy to see him?

'Before we begin,' said Watson, 'may I just reiterate how pleased we are, and I speak on behalf of everyone in this room, that you will be working with us. Of course, Giles was an integral part of that process, weren't you, Giles?'

'Yes,' came the reply. Jack noticed that Giles was fidgeting with a napkin, which he was methodically folding and unfolding. Jack nodded politely at Giles and was relieved when a sharp knock on the boardroom door interrupted their small talk.

'Ah, the tea and biscuits have arrived.' Watson clapped his hands enthusiastically. 'Yes, come in, do come in.' A young woman entered the room pushing a silver trolley, which had on it two large silver teapots and two plates of assorted biscuits. Everyone remained silent, waiting patiently as the woman arranged teapots and plates on the long glass table and then proceeded to carefully pour tea into four teacups. As soon as she left, the conversation resumed, milk was poured, biscuits were passed around and two more colleagues came in to offer their congratulations and to welcome Jack on board. There was talk of the possibility of Jack creating more artwork for the store, perhaps twenty pieces in total, including the four he had brought with him. Everyone was pleased with Jack's initial selection, which he was informed would be hung on each floor at the beginning of the new year. Jack was delighted, but at the same time, he had been acutely aware of Giles' presence. He was sure – he had been careful to avoid eye contact – that the lad had been staring at him the whole time.

When the meeting finished, Jack made his way down to the ground floor. Had Giles really played a part in his paintings being chosen? he wondered. And if it wasn't for the lad, would he even be here? The city's lights were already on when Jack stepped onto the street, which emanated a soft golden glow. Jack walked briskly now that he was relieved of his paintings, occasionally glancing into shop windows as he made his way towards the art shop. Whatever it was: a business deal, a lucrative hobby or sheer luck, four paintings had been agreed and sixteen were in the pipeline. And, despite the feeling of unease rising within him, he was still rather pleased with himself.

It was only when Jack was driving home that it occurred to him: would it be possible to avoid Giles now? Did he even have a choice? He wasn't so sure anymore, because he began to sense that something greater was at play.

Zauberhaft   28

The reds and russets of autumn faded into the coolness of winter. It was a week before Christmas and Jack and Anna were on their way to London. Hanson had been appointed to manage the same hotel where he and Tilly first met as trainees fifteen years earlier. The move from Devon was supposed to signify an exciting new chapter; to lessen the wrench of leaving friends, school and Fluffy, their stray tabby, behind. That's not how Isla described it as she walked towards the entrance of what was to be their new home for the next five years. Isla stared at the foreboding grey building in front of her and looked forlornly at her mother.

'Mummy, what have we done wrong? Why are we going to live in a prison?' Tilly would forever remember the words that her daughter impressed upon her that hazy November day. Isla didn't remember Perth – she was a baby when she moved to England – but she did remember Devon, and her world up until now had been the pretty stone cottage that was surrounded by fig trees and strawberry fields. Everyone knew each other in the village and everything was always just a short walk away. Isla had been a shy child – was still a shy child – and she struggled with starting school, which made it all the more difficult when she had to say goodbye to her best friend, Rebecca, wondering whether she would ever make a new best friend somewhere else. Tilly offered words of comfort, hoping that her daughter would adjust to her new life, but it took time, because so many things in this sprawling, noisy city alarmed Isla, and she wondered how her world could have changed so drastically.

The Tube was the first thing; the way the carriages rattled as they hurtled furiously through the tunnel and screeched to an impatient halt at every station. Then there were the endless crowds of people on Saturday afternoon as Isla and Tilly walked down the Strand, past the Civil Service Store with its bright blue clock towards Covent Garden; waves of humanity swarming past them: mods, punks, theatregoers, tourists, beggars. Everyone always seemed to be in a hurry and Isla noticed how her mother had also quickened her pace since she arrived in London, as if she too was adjusting to the city. But it was the people sleeping on the street whom Isla's gaze would be drawn to, and when she momentarily caught their eye, these people with their blankets and belongings around them, she wondered how they had found themselves, like her, so far away from home.

Jack and Anna arrived the day before Christmas Eve. The hotel was already closed and the usual bustle of guests had been replaced with an eerie silence. It was felt in the long, dark corridors – the hotel's creaking arteries Jack called them – with their endless narrow passages, and on the winding mahogany staircase, which looked like a solitary serpent dangling from the ceiling. Even the hotel's roof terrace – out of bounds, a forbidden place – had nooks and crannies from which to play hide and seek. In fact, the whole place felt like a big adventure playground to Craig and Isla; every corner waiting to be explored, preferably on roller skates, preferably with their grandpa in tow and preferably without their father knowing. Hanson did not like the idea of his children running around the hotel, no doubt causing havoc, without his knowledge. He was strict, certainly more impatient than his own father had been with him, and less tolerant than Tilly. It was no wonder Craig and Isla admitted they felt relieved when Dad wasn't around.

On Christmas Eve, Tilly filled the apartment (located on the hotel's fourth floor) with her traditional festive German biscuits. 'I'm going to teach you how to bake *Weihnachtskekse* one of these days,' she told her daughter, who had wandered into the kitchen. 'Your *Oma* taught us four girls and I want you to learn too.'

Isla peered into a biscuit tin, wondering which *Kekse* to try first. She pointed at a golden-coloured biscuit, which was lightly dusted in icing sugar and shaped into a crescent half-moon. 'What are these called again?'

'*Vanillekipferl*. It means vanilla crescents in English. Do you like them the best?'

'No, the chocolate ones, but I want to try these.'

'Please use a plate, *Schatz*; otherwise, you'll get crumbs everywhere.' Tilly watched in exasperation as Isla began to lick the icing sugar with her fingers. 'And please take a napkin too. Otherwise, everything will be sticky.'

'Mummy, what does *Zauberhaft* mean?' Isla was watching her mother stir something on the stove, its sweet scent filling the kitchen. 'I heard you say the word to Aunty Ulrike yesterday.'

'*Zauberhaft?*' Tilly added orange peel and a cinnamon stick to the pan. 'It means magical.'

'What was magical?'

'The Christmases we had.' Tilly dipped her finger in the pan and glanced over her shoulder at Isla, who had scrambled on top of one of the work counters; legs dangling down the side, plate in hand and biting into her crescent half-moon. 'Would you like to hear a story?'

Isla nodded her head enthusiastically.

'I remember one *Heiligabend*. It was really cold outside but the kitchen was warm and cosy, and I remember how the scent of freshly baked cookies filled the air. Just like the ones you are eating now. Everything was quiet. *Opa* had just brought the tree inside, a beautiful fir, and he carried it all the way upstairs without us seeing it, this huge tree for *Oma* to dress in secret.'

'Why was it a secret?'

'Because that was tradition in Germany, for children to first see the tree all lit up on Christmas Eve.'

'Why isn't it like that here?'

'Because it's different here. Now, imagine us four girls all eagerly awaiting the sound of *Oma's* bell. That was always the sign that she had lit the candles and we could enter our parents' room to catch a first glimpse of the tree. And when we saw it, shimmering in candlelight, *that* was magical.'

'Tell me about *Krampus*.' This half-goat, half-demon folklore figure fascinated Isla, and no matter how many times she had already heard the story, she still wanted to be transported from the grey London drizzle to snow-filled Bavaria.

Tilly laughed, stirring the simmering pot. 'Well, we always knew that *Krampus* was coming by the sound of his footsteps on the snow. We would sit by the kitchen fire in winter to keep warm, and every year, just before *Nikolaustag*, *Krampus* would trudge in through the door unannounced, giving us four girls always such a shock. Of course, we always screamed and ran towards *Opa*, who in turn slid under the table with fright, which made us even more terrified.'

'And what did *Krampus* say?'

'*Krampus* always asked *Opa* if we'd been good that year. If we hadn't, then he said he would take us away in the large cloth sack that was slung over his shoulder. *Opa*, by the way, was still hiding under the kitchen table.'

'And what did *Opa* say?'

'At first, he didn't say much – just hummed and hawed while

his four terrified daughters begged and promised never to be naughty again. Of course, our promises never did last long – a day at the most. And we never did ask Papa where Mama was when *Krampus* came to visit.'

'*Krampus* sounds scary,' said Isla, hopping down from the kitchen counter.

'Yes, but you see, *Krampus* would always visit just before *Nikolaustag*, and if children had been good, and in the end poor *Opa* always said we were, then *Sankt Nikolaus* would give us presents. So, I suppose we had two Christmases in a way.'

'Would you put me in *Krampus*' sack if he ever came here?'

'Only if you hadn't eaten your vegetables.' Before Isla could respond, Tilly quickly turned around and scooped up her daughter, shrieks and laughter filling the kitchen while the pot simmered away quietly on the stove.

Later that evening, Tilly went to Midnight Mass at the small Catholic church near Covent Garden, and the following day, Christmas Day, Jack and Anna took the children to an Anglican service on Piccadilly. On Boxing Day, a family tradition began when Hanson took Craig and Jack to watch Arsenal at Highbury. Anna, meanwhile, embraced her own tradition – a trip to the sales. Isla had asked to come along if only to see what all the fuss was about. She also wanted the opportunity to ride on a big red double-decker bus, in this case the number fifteen, and look at London from what felt to her like the top of the world.

Isla marvelled at the festive lights, already sparkling in the late-afternoon light as crowds of people weaved in and out of the shops. The bus drove past Hamleys and Isla jumped up when she saw the huge Santa Claus in the window, remembering the first time she had been taken there by her mother. The children's book department was situated on the top floor and Isla had spent at least an hour choosing from the hundreds of books scattered between two interconnecting rooms, eventually settling on Frances Hodgson Burnett's *The Secret Garden* as her stocking filler. That was Isla's favourite part of the store. Her second favourite was the doll section. Isla had asked Father Christmas for a Sindy House, replete with garden and a garage. She had never seen so many dolls in her life: Barbies (and Kens!), Sindy Dolls, Tiny Tears and Strawberry Shortcakes. You won't find these dolls in Devon, Tilly had craftily told her daughter, taking the opportunity to find something positive about London. It was no coincidence that her very first visit to Hamleys was also the moment Isla started to like her new home. Adapting to life in the city, at least for Isla, had taken time. It helped that there were matinees at the theatre, parks and museums to explore and with it being Christmas, trips to department stores with sparkling displays and toys that were on every child's wish list. Luckily for the Jagger children, it was all on their doorstep.

Anna's favourite shop was located midway down Regent Street. She took her step-granddaughter's hand and led her into the store; its bright lights both dazzling and obtrusive. Isla watched as Anna sifted through rails of sales clothes, highlighting to Isla the quality of a dress or the cut of a wool blazer. Anna bought two silk blouses in pastel shades, a cream jumper and a checked skirt. As a surprise treat for her husband, she also picked out a light pink tie. 'I think Grandpa will like this, don't you?'

Isla nodded. She knew her grandpa's favourite colours were pink and purple.

'Now, how about you, sweetie? Shall we find somewhere to have a hot chocolate before we return home?'

'Yes!' Isla squeezed Anna's hand. 'I know the best place.'

When they had found a café and settled in a booth by the window, Anna turned to Isla, a look of concern on her face. 'Is everything all right, dear? You seem a little quiet all of a sudden.'

'Aunty Anna, can I ask you a question?'

'Of course you can, dear. What is it?'

'What were your parents like?'

'They were very nice. I only wish I'd had a brother or sister to keep me company.'

'Were your mummy and daddy ever angry with each other?'

'Not that I remember, but I don't think so. Why do you ask?'

'It's just that Mummy and Daddy never argue, and my best friend at school, *and* another friend, tell me that their parents fight all the time. They said their parents told them it was normal.'

'Well, maybe it's because Mummy and Daddy have nothing to argue about. That's possible too.'

'But sometimes Mummy and Daddy don't even talk. There's a big silence between them that goes on forever.'

'Well, that's what grown-ups do sometimes when they have nothing to say to each other. They keep quiet.'

'But is it *normal*?' Isla stressed the word normal as she carefully began scooping the cream from her mug. 'You and Grandpa aren't like that. You always talk.'

Anna laughed. 'We do, but it doesn't mean that silence between two people is wrong. In fact, silence can be a sign of two people being very comfortable with each other.'

Isla took a sip of hot chocolate, which left traces of cream around the corners of her mouth. 'Maybe,' she said, contorting her face in a way that revealed she was not wholly convinced with the answer she had been given.

The Jaggers spent the rest of Christmas playing board games, wearing silly hats, watching films and enjoying each other's company, knowing it would be a while until they would be together again. Isla and Craig played with their new toys, and Tilly caught a glimpse of her father-in-law – the paterfamilias smiling contentedly at three generations around him – knowing how much this gathering meant to him. For an outsider looking in, they seemed like the perfect family.

When Jack drove home with Anna later that week, he began to reflect on the past decade. Was it controversial, he wondered, to conclude that these last ten years had been his happiest? He had remarried, his two grandchildren had come into the world, he was painting prolifically and he had settled into the rhythm of retirement. He was also in robust health. Perhaps more importantly, for fear of becoming consumed by the past, he was determined to forget about the business with Edward Oldroyd and that Giles lad once and for all. *Even* if they managed to infiltrate his thoughts now and again.

It didn't matter. He had everything he wanted.

The only way to keep looking, Jack decided, was forward.

Pippin

29

'Strike a light, the piece of metal can actually talk!' exclaimed Jack to his friend Geoffrey Tanner, as the two of them read the computer magazine Tanner had brought with him while they waited for their assigned slot at the bowls club.

'Remarkable *and* all the rage now,' said Tanner, as he showed Jack images of computers. 'My grandson wants one of these for his birthday. It can do all sorts apparently.'

Jack peered closely at the image – an IBM PC. 'How safe is it really for a small box to hold so much information, though? Call me old-fashioned, but I'm rather dubious about all these modern fads.'

'It's the eighties,' said Tanner with a shrug, 'and these boxes, whether we like it or not, are here to stay.'

The world was moving so fast, thought Jack, and his grandchildren were introducing him to things that were inconceivable only twenty years ago: calculator watches, video games that could be played on the television and portable cassette players with headphones from which to listen to music anywhere. And now computers! As long as he had his books and his paintings, his chessboards and his Leica camera, Jack was happy. Still, for someone who embraced the future with the fervour that he did, Jack was unusually behind the times. That's not to say that he didn't enjoy learning from his grandchildren – he did very much – but he also liked to think they could learn from him, valuable lessons that no amount of technology could make up for. These lessons always took place during Craig and Isla's summer visits to Kidderminster, lessons they never forgot.

Away from home, they enjoyed the freedom their visit provided: no strict rules and stiff formalities of hotel life. It was the antidote to everything Craig and Isla knew, and they relished the novelty, especially the freedom of being able to play with neighbouring children, running in and out of each other's homes without having to get past the peering eyes of porters and receptionists first. For the majority of children, this was normal. To Craig and Isla, it was new, along with helping to water the flowers in their grandparents' garden and going to the supermarket to choose ice cream. Craig and Isla hardly ever went to a supermarket with their parents because Tilly – one of the perks of being a hotelier's wife – ordered her weekly groceries through the hotel kitchen. Yet Jack couldn't help but wonder whether his grandchildren were in some way disadvantaged by their unconventional upbringing. He knew they craved to be like everyone else, to be like their friends and live in a house or flat that stood in unity with countless others. He remembered his own childhood: the village games with the other lads, the freedom to explore uninhibited. "Pippin" was a place where Craig and Isla could be like other children, if only for a week in the summer.

Pippin was also a bungalow and Jack and Anna had recently moved there during a heatwave – the summer of 1983 – because, at seventy-four, Jack thought it a sensible move. Their previous home, "Apple Green", so-called because its slate roof perfectly embodied the colour of an apple, had two flights of stairs and a large garden. It had been a difficult decision for the both of them but it was beginning to prove too much, and what had once brought hours of pleasure was now deemed overwhelming. Yet the large, rambling garden, with its pear and plum trees and pink roses that trailed delicately up the house, still retained its beauty until the end.

Craig and Isla remembered the summer of 1983 not only for the heatwave but also for the lions in the safari park, the huge slide at Stourport, climbing Peckett Rock at Habberley Valley, picnics by the Severn and the visit to Mr Richmond at Kidderminster Hospital – especially the visit to Mr Richmond. Jack wanted the week to be enjoyable, but he also hoped to give his grandchildren something to think about; something they would one day understand. He knew how challenging life could be and he wanted them to be able to deal with things better than he once had. And he knew exactly how to go about it.

'Is this where people come to die?' Isla was clutching her Rubik's Cube as she walked towards the grey concrete building with her grandpa and brother. They were about to visit Mr Richmond, whom Jack knew from his bowls club and who was now convalescing in hospital.

'No, darling, it's where people come to get better,' replied Jack, whose hospital visits to friends were alarmingly – to his dismay – happening all the more frequently.

Isla glanced nervously at Craig, who was bouncing a football up and down.

'Now listen,' said Jack, his tone firm, which Isla and Craig took to mean that their grandpa was about to say something serious. 'Mr Richmond has suffered two strokes this last year, and the second one was quite bad. He's out of danger but he'll be in hospital for quite a while, and having visitors cheers him up.'

Isla put her Rubik's Cube in her pocket and Craig tucked his ball under an arm and followed their grandfather through the hospital glass doors. They walked past the reception area and down a long white corridor where on the far left was Mr Richmond's ward, which had three other people in it, all lying in bed, all of them sleeping, bar Mr Richmond, who was wide awake.

'Hello, Colin, how are you?' said Jack cheerfully. 'These are my grandchildren, who are staying with me at the moment. We thought we'd pay you a visit.'

Isla was immediately struck by the insipid pallor on Mr Richmond's face. *So this is what ill people look like*, she thought, observing the slowness of Mr Richmond's movements as he cautiously raised himself up on the bed and extended his hand to each of his visitors. It disconcerted Isla that Mr Richmond didn't seem at all happy to see them.

'I've been better. My arm still aches and I feel stiff in my right leg. I expect I'll soon feel terrible all over.'

'Remember what the consultant said. These things take time, and just think how much progress you've made.'

Mr Richmond mumbled something about how his hand had begun to bother him, resisting Jack's upbeat mood.

'It's all about the power of the mind. If you believe you will never get better, then you won't. But if we focus on positive thoughts, then that strengthens our resolve and determination.' Jack took three books out of his bag and placed them one of top of the other on the table beside Mr Richmond's bed. 'I've brought some books for you, Colin – an anthology of Keats' poems and this one here is Trollope. *Barchester Towers*. I enjoyed it very much.'

There was definitely something birdlike about Mr Richmond, thought Isla, as he lowered his head and peered through his glasses, first at the books and then at Jack. 'It's all very well, but I've nothing to be positive about. Joan died two years ago and the children never visit. They don't even call. No one cares, not really. I could die tomorrow and no one would notice.'

'Nonsense. I care for a start, as do Craig and Isla, who have come especially to visit you today.'

'Yes, I see that.' Mr Richmond smiled weakly at Craig before turning to Isla.

'Now look,' said Jack, 'I don't think it does anyone any good to sit here and talk about one's life in this way. There are people who care about you. You just don't want to see it. If you continue like this, you'll be on this ward for weeks, and nobody wants that, least of all me. I want to see you back at the club playing bowls with the rest of us.'

Isla detected a flicker of recognition in Mr Richmond's eyes. She knew he had understood what was being said. He just needed time to assimilate it, away from the intense gaze of his three visitors.

'Well,' came the sheepish reply, 'shall I be expecting you at the same time next week?'

'You most certainly will,' said Jack. 'Enjoy the books in the meantime.'

'Thank you,' said Mr Richmond, raising a hand limply in the air, his dark eyes darting between Jack, Craig and Isla. 'Thank you all for coming to see me.'

'That's quite all right,' said Jack, placing his hands on Isla's shoulders. 'I shall send your regards to everyone at the club, and we are all looking forward to your return.'

As soon as they left the ward, Jack turned to his grandchildren. 'I'm very proud of you both for behaving so well. I'm sure Mr Richmond enjoyed meeting you.'

'But he didn't say anything to us,' said Craig, resuming the bouncing of his ball.

'Not in here,' said Jack. 'Wait until we get outside.'

'He just looked sad the whole time,' said Isla, taking her grandpa's hand.

'That's right,' replied Jack, 'but that's not to say that he didn't enjoy meeting you both. He just forgets how to be positive sometimes. He just needs reminding. Unfortunately, Mr Richmond needs reminding a lot. But positive thinking is like medicine. It can cure anything!'

'What if people forget to remind him? What happens then?' Isla looked concerned. 'Will he die?'

'No, he won't die. But it will take him much longer to get better. Positive thinking is just like medicine, you see. It can cure *anything*.'

'Can it cure Grandma's sneezing?' Isla looked up at her grandpa. 'She's always sneezing.'

'No, darling,' said Jack, laughing. 'Your grandma has hay fever. That's different.'

Jack was pleased that his grandchildren had recently begun to address Anna as Grandma. It was, Jack remembered thinking at the time, something that happened seamlessly. One minute Anna was Aunty and the next she was Grandma. Jack knew how much it meant to his wife to hear Craig and Isla call her that, even though he suspected Hanson didn't approve.

'What about Uncle Harry's wife? Mum says she's always sad,' said Craig. 'Why not tell her to just think positively?'

'Because that's different,' said Jack, rummaging in his pocket for his keys. 'Aunty Molly has depression, which means that thinking positive thoughts doesn't always work.'

'But you said that positive thoughts can cure anything.'

'That's true and I believe that for most things. But depression is a complex thing.' Jack hadn't expected Craig to ask about Molly. Jack wasn't sure how to even answer his grandson's question, because his sister-in-law still remained a mystery to him.

Back in the car, Isla thought about Mr Richmond and her grandpa's words. Mr Richmond's sadness had made her uneasy. She wondered how he felt, day after day, lying alone in that ward with his aches and pains. Would he ever get better? Did he even want to get better? Was it true when he said that no one really cared? It was only later – when she was much older – that Isla understood what her grandpa had tried to instil in them during their visit to Mr Richmond (who, everyone was happy to hear, went on to make a full recovery): that the power of the mind is extraordinary. She also knew that life wasn't as simple as that. The "be positive" mantra might have worked for Grandpa, but it didn't work for her. Besides, life could throw unexpected curveballs, as she was to find out.

PART 4

Tilly # 30

Jack didn't want to believe it at first. It was as if an ideal had been dismantled, an ideal he assumed would last. Tilly told him over the phone one evening, while Jack listened at the other end of the line, baffled as to how this seemingly perfect family could break into two halves. Admittedly, he had seen it coming. The laughter and familiarity the last time they were all together had been replaced by awkwardness and silence; everyone tiptoeing around each other as if navigating imaginary jagged edges. It was like Hanson had erected an invisible barrier in preparation for what was to come. By removing himself emotionally from those around him, including Anna and Jack, he could retreat into his own private world. In fact, it was becoming increasingly clear that Hanson longed to be anywhere other than with his own flesh and blood. Now, Jack knew why. After Tilly explained that Hanson had moved out to live in the hotel he bought six months earlier, Jack had heard the worst. 'Is there anything we can do?' he asked Tilly, trying to imagine what she must be going through. 'Anna and I will do whatever we can to support you.'

It was a conversation Tilly had dreaded, not least because it was made all the more difficult over the phone. Hanson had left her to pick up the pieces, and part of Tilly's "to-do" list included not only finding a new place to live but also informing her father-in-law that his son had left the family to begin a new life elsewhere. Of course, the writing had been on the wall. Her husband always had a roving eye. She just never expected him to be unfaithful. 'That's very kind of you, Dad. I really appreciate your support.' Tilly's voice wavered, grateful she still had Jack and Anna, given her own parents had already passed away. 'If you could spend a few days with Isla during the holidays, it will give me a chance to finalise things here.'

'Of course – and Tilly…'

'Yes…?'

'I want you to know that no matter what's happened, you will always be part of this family and you will always be a daughter to me.'

There are moments and conversations that remain with us long after they have taken place. For Tilly, this was one of them. She would forever remember these words, spoken to her from the heart of her estranged husband's father. Once she had disentangled them and sought to understand their true meaning, it was then she realised. Jack had decided whom his loyalties would lie with. Despite Hanson being his flesh and blood, Jack had chosen to side with her.

*

'You do know you don't have to do this alone,' said Lotte, who had come up from Sussex to help Tilly pack the rest of Hanson's belongings. Lotte was going through her own separation from Tim but had already found herself a new boyfriend, an Irishman called Seamus. 'You know, once you're settled, found a routine, you can look for a man.'

Tilly stopped what she was doing and looked at her friend, trying to hide her incredulity. 'Lotte, I do not need a man. I have my children and they will always be my priority.'

'Yes, but wouldn't it be nice? You could do things together like go to the theatre or for a meal.' Lotte waved a Wisden cricket almanack in her hand. 'Are these going too?'

Tilly nodded. 'Yes, those boxes over there are for Hanson's books.'

'Well, it's true. You don't want to be single. Who wants to be single?'

'But I'm not even divorced! Lotte, please, I'm quite happy with my own company. And anyway, I'll be far too exhausted with work to even think about going out in my spare time.'

'But that's my point! If you had a new man, you wouldn't need to work. I mean, why wouldn't you want to continue the lifestyle you've been accustomed to? Why go it alone?'

'Perhaps because I can't think of anything worse than bringing a stranger into my home, the *home* I will be sharing with my children, who, by the way, need stability right now, not more change and upheaval. Is that so odd?'

'No, of course not,' replied Lotte sheepishly. 'It was only a suggestion.'

Lotte was a strange concoction. She claimed to be independent, reminding all and sundry that it was indeed *she* who left her husband. There was talk of travel, lots of it, once the children were older, of course, but all Lotte had done was trade in her husband for a newer model, and as far as Tilly could ascertain, Seamus Brennan was certainly not an upgrade.

'Lotte, I really appreciate how much you've supported me throughout all of this, I really do, but I think you need to think long and hard about your own life too.'

'I'm working on it,' said Lotte, averting her eyes. 'And Seamus is too. It's just that he doesn't seem to have much money, not even for all that travelling I'm itching to do, unless I end up paying for him, which is probably what he's secretly hoping for. Why can't I just meet someone normal?'

Tilly laughed. 'Sounds a bit like Tim, remember. Just be careful. I don't think you're jumping from the frying pan into the fire, at least Seamus can hold down a job, but it wouldn't hurt to think about your next steps. Remember, your children need stability too, a proper home. Think how this is affecting them.'

Lotte was playing with her hair, which now hung in a long plait down her back. 'Yes, I know. I know all that. And they're fine. Matthew and Sophie are fine. They like Seamus.'

'If you want my advice, I think Seamus is probably just trying it on. But if you put your foot down, trust me, I'm sure he'll start putting his hands in his pockets.'

'I don't know – maybe he's just mean. I've only just forgiven him for ignoring my birthday.'

'Oh, Lottchen, you know there is an alternative to all of this. Being *alone. Not* settling.'

'It's all very well you saying this, Tilly, but you're still attractive.' Lotte twisted her plait up above her head like she did when she was a girl. 'I just feel that he's my last, well, my *only* chance now. Someone like me should grab her happiness when she can. *Even* if that happiness comes in the shape of Seamus Brennan.'

'Lotte Bennett.' Tilly waved a hand in the air. 'And you call yourself a free spirit!'

'Braun, I'm back to Lotte Braun again. I never liked my married name anyway.'

Eight months after Hanson had gone to live in Norfolk, Jack and Anna drove to London to spend Christmas with Tilly and the children. They now lived on the periphery of the city, a far cry from the luxury of hotel life. It was certainly less salubrious than Jack was prepared for; more urban and gritty; its landscape blighted with boarded-up businesses and shops. Still, it was where Tilly had decided to settle – as if she had thrown a dart at London and wherever it fell their future lay – if only until Isla finished school. There had been no plan. She had simply asked one of the hotel staff whom she was on friendly terms with if she could recommend an area that was affordable with good transport links. Looking back, it was ridiculous really that she couldn't even ask her own friends for advice because they were all the wives of hotel managers, and their world was Tilly's world. Until now.

After weeks of trudging around properties, which were always located at the end of one line or other, Tilly found something suitable. It was within the price range she could afford, it wasn't too far from Isla's school and it was within reasonable walking distance of the Tube. Tilly was determined to buy a place that she and her children could finally call home, and using money an unmarried aunt had left Tilly and her sisters when she died, she put down a small deposit. Tilly had liked the bright, airy flat immediately. It was a far cry from what she was leaving behind, but she didn't care. She was going to make this work.

'We got a little lost once we were off the North Circular, but you certainly can't miss this place. It's a handsome building, with its red brick and ornate roof detail.'

'Hello, you two.' Tilly laughed as she embraced Anna and Jack. 'Trust you to find the beauty in the detail, Dad. I'm very glad you made it. We've been really looking forward to seeing you.'

Jack placed an arm over his daughter-in-law's shoulder. 'Now, my girl. You've done a marvellous job painting all these rooms, but tell me, how on earth did you manage to scrape all that wallpaper off?'

'Oh, it was terrible,' said Tilly, hanging up Jack's and Anna's coats. 'But we got there in the end.'

'Well, I admire you,' said Anna, 'for being independent. Jack's eye consultant, Doctor Mason, well, I heard through Jenny at the WI that his daughter remarried in no time. I can't imagine where she had the time to find him with four young children.'

Tilly nodded, careful not to say too much. 'What do you think of the colour in here? I wasn't sure about the yellow to begin with,' she said, changing the subject, 'but it's growing on me. Dad, what do you think?'

'I had no idea you were such a dab hand with the paintbrush! I think you've done a terrific job, my girl.'

The five of them squeezed around Tilly's table in her new kitchen, festive aromas filling the air as everyone listened to Jack's fantastical stories. It was as if nothing had changed. Yet underneath the cosiness and cheer, he knew scars were forming. Tilly, for one, appeared to be always smoking, a constant puff of grey trailing behind her, while Isla, whose body was morphing out of her delicate frame into something fuller, was quiet and withdrawn. Meanwhile, Craig, on the precipice of manhood, was no longer the boy Jack remembered. *Is this what Hanson has done to them?* he wondered. *Is this what my son has done?*

'How are things?' Jack watched Tilly uncork a bottle of wine, before pouring it into two glasses. Everyone else had gone to bed and Tilly suggested having a nightcap.

'To your good health.' Tilly raised her glass to her father-in-law, skirting his question. 'It's so lovely to have you both here. It means everything to me and the children to spend Christmas together like this.'

'We're family,' Jack replied, 'and families need to stick together. Now tell me, *how* are you?'

Tilly looked at Jack, unsure whether to tell the truth to the man sitting in front of her. *Blood is thicker than water*, she reminded herself. *Remember, this man is not your father. You shouldn't burden him with your troubles. And you most certainly shouldn't expect his loyalty.* 'It's been a lot of work, redecorating the whole place and sorting everything out,' she said eventually, in between sips of wine.

'That's not what I meant. I want to know how *you* are coping, how *you* are feeling.' Jack moved closer and pressed Tilly's hand reassuringly as if to say to her, *you can trust me, you can talk to me.*

'Well, it's been tough – for all of us.' Tilly stopped herself from saying more. She didn't want to tell Jack how difficult she found juggling night school and a job with looking after the children. She didn't want to tell him she worried about rising interest rates and paying the monthly mortgage on her modest salary. The irony of it, she remembered thinking at the time, was that her separation should coincide with one of the most punishing economic recessions since the war. She certainly didn't want to tell her father-in-law that she wished she had left her marriage sooner.

'You're a strong woman, Tilly. You should be proud of the way you've dealt with everything. Just please don't think you have to do this alone. You have us.' But Jack also stopped himself from going further. He didn't want to tell Tilly how intimidated he felt when he had gone to buy a newspaper and had spotted a couple of youths dealing drugs around the corner. He chose not to reveal his concern for Isla walking home from school after dusk, past the junkies and the rowdy drunks loitering by the Tube. He didn't ask if any of them managed to sleep with the relentless sirens that whizzed past on the busy main road all night. And neither mentioned Hanson and his new life in Norfolk. It was like an unspoken agreement, but whatever Jack and Tilly chose to keep from each other that Christmas, the ties that bound them to each other were as strong as ever.

*

Several months later, Jack was sorting through some old photographs when he came across a black and white image taken in Volendam, a small town northeast of Amsterdam.

He was immediately struck by the photo. Gathered around a mantelpiece, dressed in traditional Dutch costume, were Jack, Maybelle, Hanson and a family friend, each holding a specific object: Jack an accordion, Maybelle a book, Hanson a pipe and the friend a hat. Only the friend beamed incongruously at the camera, while the rest of the group had thrown themselves into their momentary roles, gazing seriously at the photographer. Jack looked at Maybelle, a young wife and mother still in her prime, her fate already awaiting her; then at Hanson, perhaps no older than ten, adored by his mother and now estranged from his father. Then there was Hanson's friend, the young blonde boy who sat in front of him beaming at the camera. Jack studied the boy – the curve of his cheekbones, the deep-set eyes and the thick, wavy yellow hair – and tried to recall his name. But the only thing he remembered was how happy Hanson had been to have him, this nameless lad, join them on that holiday. It was so many years ago now, but the sentiment of the photograph, the four of them sharing a moment of spontaneity, made Jack sad. Perhaps because there was still so much life ahead, so much hope; their world not yet a dark place. Jack gathered the photographs together and when he put them away he decided he would write Hanson a letter.

The following morning, after three attempts at trying to articulate his thoughts into words, Jack was satisfied. He carefully folded the letter in half, sealed the envelope and put it on the table in the hallway ready to post that afternoon. Then it occurred to him: what would Hanson make of it? And how would he respond, if indeed there was going to be a response at all?

Of course, Jack knew the answer. Despite Hanson being his son, there were no guarantees.

Hanson

31

NORFOLK

It didn't take long for Hanson to decide he wasn't going to reply. He had reread the letter several times, revisiting it afresh as if expecting a different outcome, but there was nothing new to discover. The words remained the same. Of course, he had half expected to hear from his father. In fact, he was surprised it had taken this long. Yet the more Hanson thought about it, the more agitated he became. It didn't help that he initially read the letter in a rush. It was on the morning of an important staff meeting, one where he had to decide which employees he was going to keep on and whom he would have to let go. Confrontation was not Hanson's forte. He would much rather delegate difficult conversations and have everything smoothed over nicely on his behalf. 'People can be so dramatic sometimes,' he said, adjusting his tie in the bathroom mirror while Maggie, his girlfriend, stood next to him applying lipstick, a bright red. 'But it has to be done. I suppose I am the boss,' as if it had only just occurred to him.

'You *are* the boss, sweetheart,' said Maggie, 'and a very handsome one at that.'

'Fingers crossed then.' Hanson planted a kiss on Maggie's cheek, leaving his girlfriend in the bathroom to apply her make-up and quietly closing the apartment door behind him. As he descended the spiral staircase to the ground-floor boardroom where his colleagues were waiting, he pressed the letter further into his suit jacket and with it, all thoughts of his father.

It was a typical seaside hotel, painted in traditional maritime blue and white, with a grand front facing directly onto the sea. Despite its faded glory, the Connaught still attracted holidaymakers, many of who were American and in search of a quintessential British experience; replete with fish and chips, rain, fairground piers and traditional tea rooms. Then there were the regulars, whom Hanson liked best of all: the diehards who returned year after year irrespective of what the weather had in store for them; to eat in the same restaurants, lie on the same beach, browse in the same shops and drink in the same establishments, with now the added charm of Hanson's easy hospitality. When Hanson raised a glass to his guests, bringing to them from the cellar his best wine, they saw someone who was attentive, discreet, easy-going. Someone who seemingly struck the perfect balance by asking all the right questions but managing never to give anything away. Certainly not what he was really feeling inside. Then again, no one asked. Hanson had that way about him, garnering a degree of respect that others sensed; a knowing not to overstep the mark. Still, he conceded, it made sense to keep people at arm's length now. Too many questions demanded too many answers.

That is, with the exception of Marty. Marty was the Connaught's popular resident pianist who had been tinkling the ivories – Sinatra songs mainly – on his beloved Steinway for the best part of fifty years. Their camaraderie was immediate, a connection that surpassed any differences. Hanson saw in Marty a kindred spirit, someone he could trust, someone he might let his guard down with. He also liked Marty's no-nonsense approach and eccentric old-school ways; the flamboyant ties and shirts and the different hats he wore while entertaining guests. Marty was a seaside entertainer, someone so far removed from his former life that there would be no chance of the two worlds ever colliding. And that's how Hanson kept it: everything compartmentalised and in its place. No one was privy to the inner turmoil that raged in Hanson's mind as he floated about his establishment greeting employees and guests with his signature calm reserve. Not even the morning he had read his father's letter. *Especially* the morning he had read his father's letter. Of course, Hanson had known he wouldn't get away with his actions lightly. There were going to be repercussions. It just hadn't occurred to him that his own father would take the side of his estranged wife.

Besides, blood is thicker than water. Shouldn't that count for something?

'It's a good job you like Ol' Blue Eyes too, because I'm afraid that's all I know.' Marty was going through his repertoire with Hanson. They were alone in the hotel lounge – most of the guests were spending the evening at the pier, having committed to watching a mediocre comedian entertain them for two hours with his bawdy sketches – and were making the most of the quiet.

'Sinatra's been a favourite of mine too for as long as I can remember,' said Hanson.

'*Don't Make a Beggar of Me, Misty, Autumn Leaves.* You can't beat him. He was a musical god.'

Hanson smiled.

'Do you ever miss London?' Marty's question came as a surprise.

'Occasionally, but that's not to say we can't ever visit. I've come to realise that I've never been one for the city.'

'What about your children? Do they still live there?'

'They do, yes, but with their mother, so I don't see them very often.'

'My daughter's all the way in New Zealand,' said Marty, taking a sip of his gin and tonic. 'Married a fella from Auckland. Haven't seen her in four years, or my grandson. If you were to ask me what Alfie's like, I wouldn't have a clue where to start because I haven't met the nipper. He'll be three in August. And it breaks my heart every day not to be able to give him a cuddle.'

'I'm sorry to hear that. It must be difficult for you to be so far away.'

'What about you? Do you miss yours?'

Hanson had started to fiddle with a stray thread that had come undone on the upholstery. No one had dared ask him this before, not even Maggie, who at the age of twenty-nine was still digesting the aftermath of her own marriage and knew enough not to ask her new boyfriend whether he missed elements of his former life. By all accounts, she certainly wasn't missing hers.

'More to the point, Marty, I'm not sure they miss me.' Hanson rose from his chair, bringing two empty glasses with him, and walked towards the bar.

'You won't know until you ask them.'

Hanson turned around and smiled, appreciating Marty's objectivity. Jovial, good-natured, down-to-earth Marty was the foil to Hanson's snobbery and sneering. It was the unlikeliest of friendships but somehow it worked.

'You're right, Marty.' Hanson placed two gin and tonics on the table. 'I won't know until I ask.'

Maggie   32

Jack didn't have anything against Maggie. He simply had a perfectly nice daughter-in-law already and didn't feel the need to change anything. And therein lay the problem. Hanson hoped that Maggie would become part of the family, acknowledged by his father and stepmother at the very least. Yet the more time went on, the less likely it looked. It was clear that the odds were stacked against her; minds had been made up before she even had a chance to prove herself. So where did that leave them?

An outsider was what Maggie told her friends when describing her role within the Jagger family. 'In fact, there's absolutely no place for me at the table,' she said emphatically.

'Well, you can hardly blame them, can you?' retorted her best friend, Shona, a fellow Glaswegian, who was visiting for a long weekend. 'You only went and stole their husband and father. I would be the same.'

'It's not fair. I didn't do anything wrong. It was *his* free will. *His* choice to leave them. He asked me to join him here. I didn't pressurise him. Just as he didn't pressurise me to leave my husband.'

Maggie leant back in her chair and lit another cigarette. They were in the Marina, the main restaurant at the Connaught, which she referred to jokingly as her new kitchen diner.

'Ah yes, the ex,' said Shona drily. 'How long were you married? One? Two years?'

'Two – and that was long enough, believe me.' Maggie let out a little laugh before shifting awkwardly in her chair. 'It was a mistake. We both knew that. It didn't take Hanson to break us up. He was the catalyst.'

'But you still had an affair behind Adam's back. Imagine what the poor bloke must have thought, you trading him in for a man twenty-five years older. Ouch!'

'Are you enjoying making me squirm here?'

'Yes.' Shona reached out to touch her friend's arm. 'No, of course not. Just trying to offer you a different perspective, how the other half might be viewing things, you know?'

'Look, I know it doesn't look great and of course I think about what's happened. But there's no use crying over spilt milk, is there? The future is what I'm interested in. Which reminds me, I've been thinking about what to do for my thirtieth. What do you think? A wee party in here?' Maggie waved her hand around. 'It would be so much fun and Hanson wouldn't mind.'

'I'm sure he wouldn't.' Shona sniggered. There was an undercurrent of sarcasm in her voice. 'With us youngsters running around enjoying the jelly and ice cream, it will be good practice for him with all those bairns you're going to have.'

'Not if I have anything to do with it. Seriously, Shona, you say some outrageous things sometimes.' Maggie leant back in her chair and swept her thick raven hair away from her face. She had been living in Norfolk with Hanson for six months now, her former life a distant memory, so easy had it been for her to walk away and start again. Her husband had graciously accepted his wife's decision, calmly stepping aside for his university sweetheart to leave their marriage, a marriage that had barely made it to three years. There had been objections, of course, from Maggie's family, notably her mother. She'll come round, Maggie reassured Hanson when she told him her mother had threatened to stop speaking to her if she continued with a married man. 'Once they meet you, they won't be able to resist your charms. Then they'll realise what all this was for.' That was almost a year ago and Maggie still hadn't heard from her. Her father, with whom she was considerably closer, had been less judgemental, perhaps realising the futility of punishing his daughter and risking losing her. *They*, at least, were on speaking terms.

'Someone needs to get back to work.' Maggie tilted her head as she finished the remains of her wine and pushed her untouched crème brûlée towards her friend. 'But you relax and enjoy the rest of this for me. I'm afraid I can't just swan around enjoying long boozy lunches with my friends. Otherwise, Hanson will replace me with a younger model. Not as competent as me, mind you.' Maggie laughed before reaching over to give Shona a kiss on the cheek, a woman she had known her whole life. It had been their plan to leave Glasgow and the dreigh weather to study in London. Only Shona reneged at the last minute, deciding she was not quite ready to leave the familiarity of home for a new adventure elsewhere. 'So pleased you are staying for a few days,' Maggie said, touching Shona's arm. 'Don't forget we are having drinks on the pavilion at seven. It's for those new clients I told you about, so wear something pretty.' Maggie winked at Shona before giving her a hug and then she left the table.

By late afternoon, the hotel's grand pavilion was being transformed. Waiters busied themselves with various last-minute details: tables dressed with starched linen tablecloths, bar stools placed strategically around them, while glasses of various sizes were carefully perched one on top of the other atop a makeshift bar, everyone keeping their fingers crossed that it wouldn't rain. Meanwhile, Maggie and Hanson were getting ready to receive their guests.

'That Gill fellow is the epitome of new money,' said Hanson, standing in front of Maggie while she knotted his tie. 'And what really grates on me is that the man has no idea about business. Or how to run a hotel for that matter.'

'Does it really matter, sweetheart?'

'Well, yes, because if he invests in this, he'll want to have a say in how things are done around here.'

'Not if I have anything to do with it. Leave it with me. He'll know what's what once I've had a word with him.'

Hanson laughed, for he knew how persuasive his girlfriend could be. As tough as her negotiation skills were in business, she could also be tough with him. A woman occasionally rendering him speechless with her brusqueness was certainly not something he'd experienced before, but he didn't mind. He knew how much he loved Maggie; how much he had given up to be with her. 'What would I do without you?' he murmured, gazing at the woman in front of him as if noticing Maggie for the first time: the roundness of her shoulders, those bright eyes and the way her hair fell softly in waves.

'There…' said Maggie, as she took a step back to observe Hanson. 'I think we are ready to face the world.'

It was early spring and there was an unexpected warmth to the air when Maggie and Hanson stepped onto the pavilion just before seven. Given it was Maggie who insisted the drinks event take place outside rather than in the more formal banqueting room, she was not only relieved it wasn't raining but that the rough sea breeze, always present, had decided to take the day off too.

'See, I told you,' Maggie said, nudging Hanson's elbow.

'Told me what?' Hanson said with a smirk, not ready to concede his girlfriend had proven him wrong again.

'Told you that we should have the drinks out here. Much better for doing business, sweetheart, you'll see.'

'Oh dear,' said Hanson under his breath, the intimate exchange between them cut short. Maggie followed his eyes and gasped at the sight of Shona waving at them animatedly; one hand in the air, the other clutching a bottle of wine.

Maggie exchanged looks with Hanson and began walking tentatively towards her friend. By the time she reached Shona, it was clear she was already tipsy. 'You weren't supposed to start without us,' Maggie said, glancing at the half-empty bottle. 'This is supposed to be business, not a spin the bottle party.'

'Since when have you been holier-than-thou, Miss Forest? You don't fool me. We go back too far for that.'

'Come on – this is not the time to let the side down. Hanson won't be amused.'

'Well, it's too late for scolding.'

'What do you mean?'

'See that man over there? With the striped shirt?'

Maggie looked to where Shona was pointing and saw a man staring back at them with a trace of amusement in his eyes. His whole demeanour reminded Maggie of a walrus: his dark, receding hair was slicked back sparsely and the contours of his face were heavy and flabby. 'Shona McConney, what have you done?'

'Just a wee bit of sounding out,' she said mischievously. 'Oh, come on, you know as well as I do these people here need loosening up. Didn't we always say the best way to get what we want is to employ the Shona and Maggie trick?'

Maggie shook her head incredulously.

'Don't look at me like that. Thanks to me, I think he's about to part with some serious money.'

Maggie took Shona by the elbow, her steel-blue eyes narrowing. 'What did you say to him?' Shona tried to shake herself from Maggie's grip but her friend held on to her firmly. 'Shona McConney, tell me right now what you said to him.'

'Well, I… it's just that I…' Shona tried to detangle herself from Maggie but her friend remained steadfast. 'I just thought I would give you a helping hand. You know what these middle-aged hounds are like – anything for a bit of attention from the likes of us. I'm just playing the game we've always played. Thought I'd hurry your deal along, you know...'

'And...?' Maggie glared at Shona.

'And nothing. Just a wee bit of flirting – from both sides,' Shona added quickly. 'Nothing that you and I haven't seen before. It really was all very innocent.'

Maggie released her grip. 'You know these things are important to Hanson. We're supposed to be here to support him, not to create havoc. What if he doesn't trust me with this again? It will be your fault.'

'I was trying to do you a favour,' replied Shona, reaching for her glass of wine. 'What happened to your sense of fun? We've given every man we've ever met a run for his money. What's different now?'

'The difference is *this* is business.'

'Business, pleasure, it's all the same to me.'

'I think you've had enough, don't you,' said Maggie, grabbing the bottle from the table.

'If everyone is as uptight as you down here, ach, I'd rather be back home,' retorted Shona.

Maggie looked hard at her friend – for a fleeting moment, they were like teenagers again – and then she turned away. She was disappointed, angry even. Most of all, she was embarrassed. It wasn't meant to turn out like this. She was meant to show Hanson that she was capable, responsible, was his equal in business. Thanks to Shona, she was none of these things right now. She could see Hanson in the distance, engrossed in conversation with two women; his grey suit a silhouette against the white of the terrace. Maggie glanced again at the two women. They were attractive, older, and from what Maggie could see, emanated an elegance and confidence that surpassed the luminosity of youth. She felt a slight pang in her stomach as she suddenly wondered if she was enough for Hanson, or whether he would eventually tire of her too, just like he had tired of his wife.

Maggie glanced behind her and was relieved to see that Shona had already left and was making her way towards the seafront. Still, she felt unsettled. She didn't like the thought of Hanson having a good time – he was definitely having a good time from what she could see – in the company of two attractive women. She slowly made her way towards the group, her heart beating a little too fast, and when she was close enough, she caught Hanson's eye. There was a look of annoyance in his demeanour, a look she knew so well but one that had never been directed at her, until now.

'I hope I'm not disturbing you.' Maggie glanced at the women, who were now in her mind the enemy.

'Not at all. It's fine.' Hanson's smile was cordial; aloof. Maggie knew that things were far from fine. In fact, she was sure she was being punished because of Shona's behaviour.

'What were you all talking about?' Maggie immediately regretted her words.

The two women glanced at Hanson, and Maggie felt a wave of insecurity surge through her. *What's going on here?* she asked herself. She was the one with youth on her side, for heaven's sake, reminding herself that Hanson would never be interested in an older woman. So why was *she* feeling threatened?

'Well, Tara here…' Hanson gestured at the willowy woman to his left. 'Tara here was just telling me about the vineyard she helps to run in the South of France. It's been in the family for years, hasn't it, Tara?'

'That's correct.' Tara's crisp Home Counties accent irritated Maggie. 'I was just saying to Mr Jagger that he ought to come visit us one spring and sample our wonderful selection of wines. We have so many to choose from.'

'An invitation difficult to resist,' replied Hanson, his eyes still on Tara while Maggie and the other woman, whose name Maggie still didn't know, stood there awkwardly in silence.

Maggie didn't want the group to see the pricks of tears that were threatening to well up around her eyes, or the indignity of being ignored, and so she quickly made her excuses and left. She felt like an admonished child. Had she just seen Hanson's true colours? Was this what he was really like? Had she made a mistake coming here to start a life with him? Worse still, would he do to her what he had done to Tilly? Tilly, the mother of his children, whom he had been with for more than twenty years.

She had barely been with Hanson for one year. And already she felt like she was hanging on by a thread.

Maggie was still outside on the terrace when Hanson returned to the apartment later that evening. She hadn't seen Shona since their earlier confrontation and assumed that her friend had gone to bed already. As for Hanson, it was a strange feeling to have this atmosphere between them. They never argued, rarely disagreed about anything. Still, she could shout could Maggie Forest, could always win an argument. Fight her case, stomp her feet, throw plates if necessary. She had been good at that. Hanson must bring out the best in her, she thought, because all she wanted to do was love him. She gazed out towards the sea and lit another cigarette. The distant sound of waves could be heard lapping against the shoreline, while muted fragments of conversation could be heard in the next room. She looked at the freshly lit cigarette before quickly stubbing it out. She didn't want to smoke. What she wanted was to be the first to apologise. And so she smoothed down her hair, opened the patio door and stepped inside.

'Much obliged – I'll let her know.' Hanson was hurriedly scribbling down a number on the back of a newspaper. 'Yes, goodnight, and thank you very much again.'

'Who was that?' Maggie asked while tentatively hovering by the doorway.

'The manager of the Great Eastern.' Maggie was relieved to hear that Hanson's tone was conciliatory. 'Shona checked in there earlier this evening. By all accounts, your friend could barely stand up when she arrived.'

'Oh, sweetheart, I'm so sorry. It's all my fault for inviting her. I forget how inappropriate she can be.'

'It's not your fault. But I think we need to watch Shona with the wine from now on. I have a feeling she could even drink me under the table.'

Maggie laughed. 'What about Mr Allen? Shona told me she spoke to him.'

'Mr Allen? He's very well. In fact, I had a conversation with him while you were talking to that Tanner fellow and he wants to invest in us. He's to confirm in the next couple of days, but I have a feeling that it's going to be a rather large yes. Must have been something in the water.'

'Really?' Maggie looked up at Hanson as he drew her towards him. She decided not to mention how Shona had flirted with him on the pavilion. 'And Mr Gill? What about him?'

'Well, funnily enough, he's had a change of heart. He's now set his sights on casinos; big, brash casinos; and quite honestly, I think he'll do very well out of it. It's the perfect match.'

Maggie looked up at her boyfriend before burying her head in his chest. 'I thought for a second you might run off with Tara to that vineyard of hers.'

'And leave you here? Not a chance! You're my right-hand woman and always will be.'

'I thought...'

'It was just business.'

'But you—'

Hanson didn't let Maggie finish. Instead, he brushed her hair to the side and kissed her tenderly on the forehead. To anyone who didn't know the couple, it had all the markings of a father consoling a child.

Craig   # 33

THE END OF THE LINE

It wasn't so much *that* he left; it was the *way* he left. Isla hadn't understood her brother's words when he first said them. Now that they were being repeated during a conversation with their grandpa, she knew exactly what Craig meant. Her brother was right. His belief – or disbelief – in the way their father had gone about things, leaving the family without so much as a goodbye, let alone an explanation, meant Craig refused to visit Hanson if Maggie was going to be there too.

'People separate every day,' Craig said matter-of-factly, as he, Isla and their grandpa sat around their grandparents' dining table. '*That*'s not the problem. The problem is, Dad left without telling us where he was going, let us *believe* he might return, left Mum in the hotel to sort everything out by *herself*. That's the problem I have with the situation.'

Jack smoothed down his napkin, unsure as to how much he should get involved. He was stuck in the middle, wedged between two generations: his seventeen-year-old grandson, who was in the right, and his fifty-one year-old son, who was in the

219

wrong. And it pained him to see his family fractured like this, two sides refusing to meet in the middle.

'I understand how you feel,' Jack said diplomatically. 'And I'm sure your father will too. It's not as if you have refused to see him at all. That's a different matter entirely.'

'Exactly.' Craig shook his head in exasperation. 'I even suggested meeting him halfway, somewhere between London and Norfolk. But he wanted Maggie there too. I said I'm not going to come unless it's just the two of us.'

'She's not that bad,' said Isla. 'Seems to make Dad happy anyway.'

'Look, if things had been different – let's say she didn't have the affair with Dad and they'd met further down the line, then of course we might have had some sort of relationship with her.'

'You mean like a stepmother?' said Isla, trying to imagine Maggie as someone maternal.

'Something like that. It can work, that kind of thing.'

'I had a stepfather,' said Jack. 'Albert was a great support to my mother and me and your Uncle Harry. He changed our lives in so many ways.'

'What did he do?' Isla asked.

'Well, he was pivotal in helping me find my first proper job, and Harry, well, Albert inspired and encouraged him to become an engineer. He nurtured us.'

'Good man,' said Craig, 'but I'm still not going to meet Dad with Maggie – halfway or not.'

'How's the studying going?' Jack hoped to steer the conversation away from Maggie and Hanson even though Tilly was still in the kitchen with Anna. 'Do you have any ideas what you might like to do when your exams are finished?'

'Well, I know that I don't want to work in hotels. Dad is so set on me following his choices.'

'I think your father just wants the best for you, but ultimately you need to find your own path.'

Craig was adamant that his path was to finish his education as soon as possible. Free from the constraints of his father, Craig planned to put a lid on the shackles of learning as he called it and leave school as soon as his exams were over. Of course, Tilly was disappointed. Desperate even. She had pleaded for her son to stay on; pleas that continued for days and weeks, from morning till evening, hoping he would eventually see sense. Craig had been resolute, however, and deep down Tilly knew her efforts were futile. What could she do apart from force him? Craig had made up his mind and there was no turning back.

'Actually, Grandpa, I've decided that once my exams are over, I'm going to work in a bank.'

'A bank?' Jack repeated while he inwardly processed his grandson's news.

Craig half expected his grandpa to side with his mother, to make him see sense, to drum into him the importance of continued learning and then onwards towards the ultimate holy grail that she thought was university.

'Well, my boy, if that's what you want to do, I mean *really* want to do, then you are doing the right thing by following your heart. You can never go wrong with following your heart.'

'Really? You mean it?' Craig was astonished that someone could actually be on his side.

'This needs to be your decision. Your mother can only guide you.'

'I know I'm making the right choice. All I want to do is get out into the world and start work.'

Jack remembered the time Hanson had told him he wanted to work in hotels. How old had he been? Fourteen? Fifteen? Hanson had been resolute too, never one for studying; a plan already in place. Looking back to his own youth, Jack had been desperate to stay on at school, had begged his mother to let him stay. But why? Because it was being taken away from him? Because of the friends he was leaving behind? Because he knew that his brother, Harry, wouldn't have to go through the same thing? Jack wasn't sure. He only knew that he never had the privilege of deciding his future. It had been decided for him and, granted, thanks to Albert, things had turned out well in the end. And even though the circumstances were completely different, Jack knew it wasn't his place to pressurise Craig into doing something that would ultimately make him unhappy. He was well aware of friends and acquaintances whose offspring had been pushed towards a career in medicine or the law and it didn't always end well. He didn't want that for his grandson. Least of all a grandson who needed all the encouragement he could get right now.

'I can train on the job too, you know,' added Craig, hoping to build a strong enough case for himself.

'Now listen, my boy. I left school at fourteen but that didn't stop me getting where I wanted to be. You can achieve anything you want if you put your mind to it! University isn't always the answer.'

'If you wouldn't mind telling Mum that,' said Craig, lowering his voice, a faint smile forming on his face.

Jack's words came at a time when Craig needed to hear them the most. He was almost eighteen and the thought of sitting in a classroom for two more years learning things he knew he would have no need for in the real world made Craig all the more determined to do things his way. What he needed was to earn money and be independent, for freedom was now within his grasp. His father couldn't tell him what to do anymore, which was ironic really given his father had detested studying too.

Spring edged into summer and Craig sat his final exams in the middle of an oppressive June heatwave and left school at last; sad to leave his friends behind but certainly not his teachers. Especially not the headmaster, with his liberal use of the cane. In August, Craig started work in a bank in West London. He still had to wear a suit, which reminded him of his school uniform, but he loved the camaraderie, team spirit and the Friday night drinks. He especially enjoyed the thrill that came with receiving his first pay packet, and he relished the fact that he needn't pick up a book again if he didn't want to. A month into the job and Craig had a new circle of friends, most of whom were his age and, like him, lived for the weekend.

He was not yet an adult but for the first time in his life, Craig could taste what it was to be one.

*

'Where on earth have you been?' Tilly was sitting in the kitchen eating breakfast, having decided to get up early to make a start on the Christmas shopping. It was one of those clear December mornings: the sky a brilliant blue without a cloud in sight.

'I walked home.' Craig slumped into a chair and began to loosen his tie.

'From West London?'

'From the ends of the earth more like. At least that's what it felt like.'

'*Meine Güte*! What on earth happened?' Tilly looked at her son, a flash of concern etched across her face. 'And why is your shirt all smudged as if you've climbed down a chimney?'

'I was on the last train home and missed my stop. I woke up in the middle of nowhere. Stranded.'

'Stranded? Where?' The sound of the toaster pinged as two slices of toast jumped up, announcing their arrival.

'At the end of the Bakerloo Line.'

'Harrow and Wealdstone?'

'Yep.'

Tilly put her hand to her mouth. '*Meine Güte!*' she exclaimed again, as if once wasn't enough.

'You don't know the half of it,' said Craig.

It probably was a good job that Tilly didn't know the half of it because only hours earlier Craig was weighing up his options, having lowered himself carefully onto the Tube tracks and peering with some trepidation at the mouth of a pitch-black tunnel; dust and uncertainty awaiting him. He had caught the last Tube from Oxford Circus and fallen asleep shortly after it pulled out of Paddington. The carriage, from what he could remember, was teeming with revellers, and a faint, unpleasant stench gave a heaviness to the air. It also felt like a thousand conversations were going on around him, each vying to be heard above the others. Craig had managed to find a seat, weaving his way along the narrow aisle; past dozing City boys, their heads nodding along to the rhythm of the train, while young women shivered in flimsy outfits, wishing they'd brought a coat with them after all.

The next thing Craig knew was that he had woken up in an empty carriage in a deserted station at the end of the Tube line. He was completely alone, save for a group of pigeons who were hovering on the platform edge. He had no idea how long the train had been stationary and no idea why no one had bothered to wake him up. Craig rose from his seat, his hangover making its presence known as he walked out into the freezing air. There was something eerie about the station, Craig thought, as he looked around in the suspended half-light. In the station's abandoned state, the milky fog that hovered above him like a thin, translucent veil made everything look sinister. Craig glanced at his watch. It was nearly two-thirty and that meant the Tube wouldn't be running for several hours yet. *Surely I'll freeze if I wait around. Freeze to death and I haven't had a chance to ask Carrie Bradley, the new girl in the bank, out on a date yet.*

Craig eased himself onto the platform edge, his legs dangling over the side, and wondered how long it would take to walk the six stops home. Two hours? Three? He had no idea. Still, it had been worth it, smiling at the unexpected way the night had turned out. They had all ended up somewhere on the fringes of Soho; three floors of house music booming while a mass of humanity thronged on the dance floor. Craig shivered, realising it was too cold to sit. He needed to stand up, keep moving. Better not to take a risk with that thing, he thought, looking at the tunnel again. If I'm to have any chance with Carrie at the office party next week, I need to make sure a train doesn't get me first.

And so, burying his hands in his pockets, Craig made his way up the stairs and then took a left turn out of the station. He was going to follow the tunnel path, which had its own precarious network of brambles and branches to contend with. Anyone looking at him from a distance, with shoulders hunched and head lowered, might assume he had the weight of the world thrust upon him. They couldn't have been further from the truth. It was freezing, yes. There was a long way to walk still, but it didn't matter. He would live, he was living, and the weekend had only just begun.

'Promise me you'll get a cab next time,' said Tilly, the sound of coffee percolating in the background. 'I don't want you risking your life like that ever again.'

'I will,' replied Craig, unbuttoning his shirt. 'God, it's good to be back.'

'You must be starving. Shall I make you something?'

'Thanks, Mum – I'm ravenous.'

Tilly finished her toast then walked over to the fridge to find some eggs.

'What about Isla? Is she up yet?'

'At seven in the morning?' said Tilly from behind the fridge door. 'What do you think?'

Isla 34

THAT'S THE WAY LOVE IS

Unlike some of her friends, Isla was not a daddy's girl. Perhaps she was her grandpa's girl. At least his life was one she hoped to emulate; a blueprint of what she wanted her world to be filled with one day: art, books, travel and everything else that was important to him. And Isla needed this perspective more than ever. She had just turned sixteen and already knew that life could deal unfair cards. Was it fate or the result of wrong choices? she asked herself. Whatever it was, she only had to look at her mother's life to realise it had taken on a sharper reality, underpinned by precarious financial instability and the aftertaste of an acrimonious separation. Isla didn't mind her new life. She was glad she didn't to have to walk through the hotel foyer anymore, past the prying eyes of receptionists and porters on her way to school. She was glad she didn't have to listen to the shrill sound of the hotel fire alarm either, which always seemed to go off while she was trying to have a lie-in, or worse, in the middle of the night. Most of all, she was glad that her parents were no longer together.

Even though her parents never argued – not once had she heard a heated exchange – it was the stubborn silences she couldn't bear. Still, aside from the threat of fluctuating interest rates and adjusting to life in a different part of the city, Isla knew that her mother had gained much more than she had lost. She had her independence, she had her children; she still had Grandma and Grandpa and she had her friends. More importantly, and this Isla was most grateful for, her mother didn't seem the slightest bit interested in looking for a new husband like some of the mums she heard about at school. In fact, Eileen O'Reilly's mum had not only brought a new man into her home, but his three sons too. Everyone knew about it, because Eileen wasn't at all pleased, complaining about the new "domestic situation" to the whole class one day before register. *Thank God*, Isla thought, *thank God my mum would never do something like that.* But *if* she did, Isla already knew that she would never forgive her.

'Don't be foolish like I was,' Tilly began to tell her daughter. 'Promise me you will be wise. Be independent. *Live* your life.'

'Of course, Mum,' Isla's reply was always the same.

Tilly repeated these words often, as if to bury her hopes deep within her daughter's psyche, lest Isla ever forget. *Don't be foolish like I was. Promise me you will be wise.* And in turn, Isla began to repeat Tilly's words back to herself, wearing her mother's wisdom around her neck like a warning. As far as Isla's teenage self was concerned, she would never be foolish like her mother had been. Love doesn't last anyway, she decided, and certainly not a lifetime, especially if you're young. Her mother was proof of that. And her parents were proof that twenty years of marriage was more than enough. Yes, people should not expect forever, and if they do and it doesn't work out, then more fool them.

*

'Crazy,' Isla exclaimed. 'Cuckoo and crazy.' She and her best friend, Anita, were sitting cross-legged on her bedroom floor. They were poring over magazines while Radio One's Top 40 played in the background.

'What is?' Anita's fingers were idly tracing the outline of a woman in a wedding dress, its tiered layers of silk and satin giving the appearance of an extravagant cake.

'I don't understand why women think their wedding is supposed to be the best day of their lives.'

'I don't know,' replied Anita. 'Isn't it?'

'God – please don't tell me you believe it too. *Anita!*'

'Well, the thought of meeting my Prince Charming and being married sounds really nice. I hope it happens to me. One day anyway.'

'Prince Charming? Next thing you'll want is to get married in a castle, moat and all! If you're going to get married, then at least be original about it.' Isla laughed and threw a cushion at her friend.

Anita chewed the side of her mouth, which Isla referred to as Anita's "thinking" face. 'Look at Princess Diana. She met her Prince Charming and is living happily ever after with their two little boys.'

'I reckon they are not as happy as they would like us to believe. I'll bet they'll get divorced.'

'Isla, you are *so* cynical.'

'Nope, just realistic. And if you believe in happy ever after, then you're an idiot.'

Isla took hold of the magazine and suddenly thrust a picture of the beaming bride in full view of them both. 'See this? She's definitely a bridezilla, all dressed up like a meringue. She's got that scary "nothing's going to get in the way of my special day" look. She's probably been obsessing over the colour of her bridesmaids' dresses and flowers since the day she was born.'

'Probably *before* she was born!' Anita laughed, joining in with Isla's jibes.

'Don't you think it's just so yucky? So, so…'

'Predictable?'

'Yep, I will *never* be like that.'

'I know what you mean.' Anita pulled her hair into a ponytail. 'My cousin got married last year, the one I told you about, and she behaved exactly like that. Was kind of desperate to be married by twenty-seven. It was like a massive goal for her.'

'Yeah – and what for? Fast forward fifteen years and she'll be divorced and on to the next.'

Isla burst into another fit of giggles and rolled onto her back, tears streaming down her face as she marvelled at the maturity of her insight and wisdom. She suddenly reached for Anita's arm and brought her friend down with her, and as the two rocked back and forth in childlike mirth, Anita said, 'I never thought of it like that.'

'What? Divorce?'

'Yeah.' Anita paused for a second before continuing. 'Mum says it's much better to get married later.'

'Mine too. If you think about it, *your* parents are divorced and mine soon will be. *You'll* get married, *You'll* have children. *You'll* get divorced. *Your* children will get married, *they'll* have children, *they'll* get divorced. Do you really want that life?'

'Oh my God, Isla, it's scary when you put it like that.'

'Someone has to say it.' Isla was still lying on her back, her hands resting behind her head. 'So many weddings are like something out of a Disney fairytale. They think nothing will go wrong, that their marriage will last forever.'

'Yeah, I see what you mean.'

'And the idea of being the centre of attention like that makes me want to puke.'

'*Especially* if they're in a big pouffy dress,' said Anita, joining her friend on the floor, their shoulders touching. 'My mum didn't wear a big pouffy dress, though, and *she* still got divorced.'

Donna Summer came on the radio and the girls stared up at the ceiling, lost in their own private worlds.

'Wait, wait,' said Isla, suddenly bolting upright. Bruno Brookes' show was a regular fixture in her and Craig's weekend, and they both routinely recorded their favourite songs, which they had now perfected to a tee. 'Listen, he's just announced that Ten City is about to come on. I want to tape it.' Isla's hand was flapping around excitedly.

'Which song?'

'*That's the Way Love Is.*'

Anita scrunched her nose. 'I like '*Looking for Linda.*' Who sings that?'

'Hue and Cry.'

Anita placed her hands behind her head. 'I like the song. It sounds nice.'

'Well, they're in the top ten, so we're bound to hear them too.' Isla peered into the machine to check she had enough space on her cassette before she pressed the radio's record button. 'I hate it when I miss the start of a song. Even worse when the tape cuts out. It's so annoying.' Isla placed a finger in front of her lips. 'Shh, here we go...'

She turned up the volume and began singing along to the lyrics, bobbing her head back and forth.

When the song ended, Isla flung herself onto the floor again, the lyrics still floating around in her mind. What was it her grandpa said about love? Something about love overcoming anything, everything. If love is so powerful, she thought, then why is there so much suffering in the world? Why is love so closely associated with hate? Why do the heroines in the Hardy and Brontë novels always end up tragically? And if love conquers all, then why were her *and* Anita's mother failed by it?

'I wonder if my cousin will ever get divorced...' said Anita.

'Probably,' Isla said with a chuckle, kicking her legs in the air.

'God, imagine if my cousin found out we were trying to predict her future.'

'Well, she shouldn't have been so predictable in the first place then.' Isla laughed as she hoisted herself up from the floor. 'I'm hungry, let's go and find something to eat.'

*

Two years can make all the difference. Inevitably, a gap begins to close and the childish opinions once harboured slowly begin to fade. This was certainly the case for Isla. The fateful novels of Brontë and Hardy were soon replaced by the charm, wit and irony of Austen; impressing her with stories of mischievous matchmakers and chivalrous, misunderstood men. Isla had blossomed. Or at least it could be said her edges had softened, her opinions broadened, and her heart, while not yet open, was curious. And, much to Tilly's delight, her daughter's hair appeared to be going through its own renaissance, with its new-found mass of waves and curls.

'Where on earth has *this* appeared from?' Tilly said, running her fingers through her daughter's chestnut mane. 'Everyone keeps saying how lovely it looks. I hope you realise that hair like yours can't be bought in a bottle, *Schatz*.'

'*Everything* can be bought in a bottle now, Mum,' retorted Isla. 'It's 1990.'

Giles 35

Giles swivelled in his chair while he absently flicked through the pages of a magazine. His uncle was never on time; always running to this meeting or that, a look of perpetual agitation etched across his face as if constantly racing against something. He closed his eyes. The recorded voice of the store tannoy system announcing that Hillmans would be closing shortly drifted over him. Giles liked to think that someone who brought such good news could surely do no wrong. How he looked forward to hearing that kind, benevolent voice at five on the dot knowing that the end of the working day was imminent. It had been another tiring afternoon answering customer enquiries and carefully logging in requests. When would it ever end, Giles wondered, this daily drudgery? He had completed his time in electronics, which wasn't so bad; menswear had been pleasant enough too, but now he was working in kitchenware, a department that was, in his opinion, far worse than haberdashery. At least in haberdashery, Giles thought, he had all those different designs to distract himself with. Still, he was learning the ropes to management. And once he had that under his belt, he would take his experience elsewhere. Somewhere far more interesting.

Giles opened one eye. A butterfly was hovering outside the window and he turned his attention to it, noticing the dark flecks on its delicate white wings. The butterfly reminded him of long, lazy summers spent with his family in Provence. The walled garden of their renovated stone farmhouse, a vibrant medley of lilac, lavender and salvias, was a magnet for wildlife, and even as a young boy he had loved how peaceful it was to be among all that nature. How many years had it been since they were all there as a family? Ten, twelve? All his parents ever seemed to do now was work.

'Ah, you're here,' said Giles' uncle, his head peering around the door. 'I wasn't sure you would be waiting.'

'I had no other choice. You told me it was important.'

'It is indeed. These end-of-year reports always take up so much of my time, as you know.' Peter Illingworth placed a stack of papers on his desk. 'Now, I want to talk to you about something.'

Giles shifted in his seat, waiting for his uncle to continue.

'I realise it isn't an ideal situation for you, and I know you didn't want to go into the family business. However, most people would bite their hand off for the opportunity you've been given here.'

'I'm not sure I understand what you mean.'

'It's just that we've had a number of complaints – about you. Customers who've not been entirely happy with the service you've given them. Apparently you've been suggesting they shop elsewhere.'

'It happened once. Okay, twice, but that's because they couldn't make up their minds!'

'That is *not* how we do business here.' Peter Illingworth's voice was firm, with an authority usually reserved for colleagues. 'At Hillmans, we move mountains to make our customers happy.'

'Yes, I know all that.'

'Then why are you doing the contrary? We don't shoo our customers away to a competitor. We offer to *find* alternatives for them, make them think that they've wanted the alternative all along.'

Giles looked down at his hands, trying to avoid his uncle's gaze.

'Now, another thing…'

Giles continued to stare at the floor.

'You're a fine young man and there are plenty of girls out there who I'm sure would be delighted to be on your arm. Just not the granddaughter of a very important client.'

Giles looked up and ruffled his hair.

'Either way, it can't continue.'

'Why? What have I done wrong?'

'Business is business. It's not appropriate behaviour given Hillmans' relationship with Mr Jagger. *Our* relationship with Mr Jagger.'

'What do you mean? *Our* relationship with Mr Jagger.'

'Exactly what I've said. It's about business ethics. You enter into a contract. You don't expect it to be violated.'

'But what has Isla got to do with Mr Jagger's contract?'

'It's just not appropriate to enter into a relationship with a client's granddaughter, and if you want to keep your traineeship here, keep climbing the ropes towards management, have a good reference…'

'This is ridiculous.'

'It's the way the world works, I'm afraid. And if you see any kind of future for yourself…'

'I'm not giving her up.' Giles looked his uncle squarely in the face.

'You barely know her.'

'I've known her almost four months. Long enough to know that I want to be with her.'

'She's eighteen years old, for heaven's sake. And you're twenty-six. Do you not think there will be others? For the both of you? Love, whether we like it or not, eventually runs out of steam.'

It had been a bright midweek afternoon when he first spotted her, having noticed her on one of his lunch breaks. Now that the weather was getting warmer, Giles had taken to spending his free time outside walking through the sun-dappled cobbled streets. He wasn't sure whether it was the way her hair fell in waves like a Pre-Raphaelite painting or the way she held on to Mr Jagger's arm as they stood with their backs to him outside the small independent gallery. Either way, Giles knew that Isla was the most interesting thing that had captured his attention in a while. Isla, of course, recalled a different version of events. 'You just looked well, so...awkward, the way you smiled when I turned around. It's funny but I just *knew* you had been staring at us all that time,' she said, half earnest, half teasing. What they both agreed on was the way they felt about each other. Giles was smitten, Isla intrigued. And so their story began. Isla had taken Giles by surprise, of course, not least because Mr Jagger had never mentioned a granddaughter. The ease with which Giles was able to find Isla again was also surprising, having somehow managed to persuade a hapless colleague from personnel to give him access to Hillmans' files.

'I'm only doing what I've been told,' Giles had told the man from personnel.

'Can I ask why, Sir?' the man had asked, trying to assert some semblance of authority.

'The artist, Mr Jagger, we need to contact him urgently about one of his paintings.' It had been that simple; the violation of privacy that was so carefully guarded in a grey metal filing cabinet. No one thought to question the nephew of a Hillmans director. Then again, no one knew how determined he had been either to see the girl with the Pre-Raphaelite hair, the girl he was certain he was in love with already. Yes, Giles had to find her again and *this* was the only way.

*

'Did you know it was me? I mean, did you remember me from the gallery that day?' Giles was lying on the grass next to Isla, one hand plucking a dandelion, the other draped loosely over her waist.

'Of course,' she smirked, remembering the letter Giles had written asking her if she'd like to meet him in Worcester for a drink. 'It was so sweet, especially where you'd signed off *Giles – the one who smiled at you outside La Peinture in Worcester*. It's a good job my grandparents didn't see it. There would have been so many questions.'

'Just for the record, I've never done that before, written a letter like that to a girl.'

'Really? I thought that was how you asked out all your dates.'

'Very funny. Seriously, though, there was no other way to contact you. I couldn't exactly have called you at your grandparents' house.'

'Suppose not,' replied Isla, plucking a daisy and twirling it between her fingers. 'But I don't agree with what you said about not doing this for anyone else. Of course you would.'

'Why do you say that? You know you are special to me.'

'Am I?' Isla had a hint of provocation in her eyes. 'The problem with you, Giles, is that you are far too sentimental.'

'I'd like to think that fate brought us together that afternoon.'

'By stalking me?' Isla laughed, tossing her hair to the side. 'Now don't go all funny on me. You know I'm teasing.'

'You know what *is* fate, though?' Giles propped himself onto an elbow and gazed down at Isla, who had positioned her face towards the sun; eyes closed.

'Hmm?' Isla brushed a fly away from her cheek.

'The fact that I met your grandpa years ago at an event. At a local art thing.'

'Really? Why haven't you mentioned it before?'

'Because I'd kind of forgotten about it. And then, after he came to visit me at Hillmans with his wife, your grandma, I had the sense that he was upset with me about something.'

'Upset with you? Why would my grandpa be upset with *you?*'

'I don't know. He only visited me once and then when he found out I was on the Hillmans arts committee, it kind of made matters worse. He couldn't even bring himself to talk to me.'

'My grandpa? That's nuts. Are you sure you're not imagining it?'

'Maybe. I don't know. Look, forget I ever said it. It's not important…'

'Well, you've kind of said it now. But anyway, you obviously misread him. Grandpa isn't like that.'

And so Giles decided not to tell Isla about the awkward conversation he had with his uncle, a conversation which still unnerved him. The two of them had been inseparable up until then: Isla somehow managing to steal a couple of hours with Giles each day without arousing the suspicion of her grandparents; offering to run errands for them or announcing that she was going into town or on long walks by herself. Instead, she had taken the train to Worcester, timing it to coincide with Giles' lunch hour, which he always took as late as possible. That's when his uncle had seen them and asked who the girl with the chestnut-coloured hair was. The rest of the time, Isla spent wandering around the shops until Giles finished work; the two of them walking reluctantly to Shrub Hill so that Isla could catch the 5.30 back to Kidderminster. Sometimes, Giles came with her on the train – it was the only reasonable way they could extend their time together – both of them wishing the journey would never end.

This set-up continued until Isla had to return home to prepare for her first term at university. Giles insisted they keep their union a secret, saying it was for the best, not least to avoid upsetting her grandpa any further, and Isla, not thinking anything of it, agreed. Unsure whether she and Giles would last the summer, she didn't see the point in telling her grandparents anyway, or her mother. Giles was right; why complicate things? Their paths were diverging and there was no telling whether they would survive the distance. Three years was a very long time, she thought, between Durham and Worcester.

For Giles, their secret represented something greater. His uncle's threat loomed like a foreboding shadow, one that had the potential to throw his future into jeopardy. He had been at Hillmans for almost eight years now. It wasn't perfect, but it was something. He was on the arts committee and he was a trainee manager with good prospects. And if his uncle was more concerned with *upholding business ethics*, whatever that meant, at the expense of his nephew then what did family actually stand for? What did *his* family actually stand for? Giles didn't know. He only knew that they mustn't find out about Isla.

Jack

36

Jack stood by the window, staring at two birds perched on a branch, and wondered how on earth it had come to this. After several years of silence, Hanson had finally written to his father, having typed his thoughts on the Connaught's letter-headed paper. It was cool, detached and lacking the conciliatory tone he had hoped for. His family, the one he was so proud of, was now shattered into fragments, and he had no idea which pieces to save and which ones to let go of. It was the tone Hanson adopted that disappointed Jack the most, along with the ultimatum he had been given: either give Tilly up or his son.

'I'm trying to understand,' Jack told his old friend Edmund Peats over the phone one evening, 'but I'm still not sure what I've done to provoke such a reaction. I've accepted Maggie. I accepted Hanson's decision, despite my having to find out through Tilly. Yet why is he so adamant that she should not be part of the family still? Without her, when would I see my grandchildren?'

Edmund Peats was one of Jack's closest confidants and despite having only seen each other twice since first meeting in

Newfoundland – Peats had taken Jack to Bermondsey Market in 1982 and a year later invited him and Anna to dinner at the London home he shared with his wife – they remained in regular contact by letter (which Jack always looked forward to and found great comfort in reading) and telephone. Peats, unbeknown to Jack, was also going through his own family upheaval.

'You've done nothing wrong. Unfortunately, I have the opposite dilemma with Gail...'

'I thought you got on well with your daughter-in-law.'

'I did, until she and Leo separated. He hasn't seen his daughters, and neither have we, for over a month. She won't even talk to Leslie and me anymore or acknowledge our existence as grandparents. Yet she prides herself on being a good mother.'

'Oh, Edmund, I had no idea they had separated. I am so sorry.'

'It's still very new. I had harboured hopes they would get back together.'

'It's a terrible situation to be in. I'm so sorry.'

'It happens.' Edmund shrugged. 'What do you think you'll do about Hanson?'

'I'm not sure.' Jack stared into his teacup. 'The thing is, I just don't know how I'm meant to reply to something like that. To think I gave that lad everything.'

*

Two more years went by. The distance between father and son was like a ship sailing further and further away from the shoreline. How could Hanson expect Jack to accept his ultimatum? Choose between the two? Couldn't he choose both? Tilly and *his* son? Or was he breaking the rules by undermining the old adage that blood is thicker than water? It might have been easier to choose, Jack thought, while sitting alone in his study one afternoon, but choosing would have gone against everything he believed in.

Instead, he busied himself with painting, setting out to complete the last of his Worcester series – a set of three pictures of the cricket ground. Craig, like his father, was an ardent cricket enthusiast; three generations of cricket enthusiasts trickling down the Jagger family. Now the natural order of things had been disturbed and they would no longer be three generations united by a love of cricket. They weren't united anymore. They were divided. Jack looked at his watch. It was almost time to pick Anna up. She was having lunch in Worcester with friends and she had taken the train in. If he left now, he could quickly pop into the art shop beforehand to buy the watercolours and the cold press paper he had run out of.

As Jack approached Worcester, one eye on the road, one eye on a vacant parking space, he noticed a young couple to his left walking along the pavement. They were casually meandering like young couples do, swaying together hand in hand as if with no destination in mind. There was also a familiarity in the way the couple walked, Jack thought, narrowing his eyes as he glanced at them again in his rear-view mirror. Was that Isla? With the Hillmans lad? But before he could look at them properly, the couple faded from sight. Jack made a swift left turn and drove down a side road so that he could get another glimpse of the couple on the main road again. Surely he must be mistaken. *It can't be them*, he thought. Isla was at university and Giles...

Sure enough – and Jack made a special point of driving slowly so as to get a closer look – it was his granddaughter with Giles. Isla's hair was styled in a ponytail – unusual for her – but he recognised the rich chestnut hue and the distinctive way she walked: lightly and quickly. Giles was less distinguishable. Certainly, the way his arm was folded protectively over his granddaughter's shoulder was not something Jack was familiar with, nor wanted to be. Jack looked again and then he recognised the hair that fell in soft waves, framing a still boyish face despite the ten years that had passed between them. He drove slowly, keeping one eye on the road and the other on the young couple.

Jack couldn't believe it. He didn't want to believe it.

Well, I'll be darned, he thought. Of all the young ladies, he had to choose her.

'You are never going to believe who I saw earlier,' Jack said, helping Anna into the car.

'Who?' Anna smoothed down her skirt before making herself comfortable in the passenger seat.

'That lad from Hillmans' haberdashery department walking hand in hand with a young lady.'

'Who?' Anna glanced up. Her forehead was knotted into a frown.

'That chap, Giles, who works at Hillmans. He was interested in joining the Arts Society but never followed it through. It was years ago now but I introduced you to him. Maybe you don't remember. Anyway, I saw him with a young lady earlier.'

'Oh! That's lovely,' said Anna.

'I found it rather odd myself.' Jack realised his words sounded ridiculous but Anna wasn't even paying attention. She was looking through her address book, searching intently for something.

'You seem distracted,' said Jack.

'I'm sorry. It's just that Deborah Hart's husband recently passed away and I want to check that I still have her address. You remember Deborah, don't you?'

'Vaguely,' replied Jack, feeling irritated. 'Can't that wait? I'd like to talk to you about something.'

Anna continued to look through her address book, unaware of her husband's distress. As for Jack, how could he ever confront Isla about Giles' unsuitability if he hadn't even confronted Giles about his family's past? Yes, it was a hunch, he thought, and he had no way of proving it, but he was certain Giles knew more than he was letting on. It was in the way he was insidiously creeping into all of their lives. And now there was no way of stopping it.

Tilly   # 37

'I've been thinking…' Jack's conversations with Tilly began the same way every week. 'I've been thinking about why there is so much discord in the world. And I've come to realise that it all boils down to religion. Muslims don't see eye to eye with Hindus; Catholics and Protestants are at odds, and I've never understood why Jews and Christians share the Hebrew bible but interpret it differently. Why can't people just find love in their hearts for their neighbour?'

Tilly rang Jack and Anna every Sunday just after five. It was a routine that had started after Hanson left, and there was some comfort to be had from speaking with her in-laws regularly. These phone calls were filled with minutiae and provided a sense of connectedness. It drew Tilly away from her own world; a world dominated by long commutes and keeping on top of the mortgage payments, and she seemed to enjoy the distraction. Jack, on the other hand, used these conversations to tackle life's big questions: does God exist? Why does religion cause so much conflict? And, if there is such a thing as reincarnation, did Tilly think it possible for our souls to reincarnate into, say, a bird or a fish?

On this particular Sunday, Jack wanted to discuss the Eucharist. 'Now, Tilly, as a Catholic, you believe that the bread and wine actually *turn* into the body and blood of Christ, yes? Whereas my church believes that it *stays* bread and wine and *only* represents Christ. Small details, but it's these small details that turn into wars. Why can't people just accept these differences?'

'I'm not sure.' Tilly lit a cigarette and inhaled sharply. 'Like you say, Dad, it shouldn't matter.'

'Yes, but it matters to the millions of Catholics and Protestants who can't stop arguing about it.'

'I know. It's terrible what goes on in the world.' Tilly was not quite sure where the conversation was leading, but she was used to her father-in-law's questions by now.

Jack had never been religious but with each year that passed, he found himself edging closer towards God. And it seemed to challenge him, this new-found faith, with all these questions looming in his mind. 'I suppose what I'm trying to say is that we understand each other, don't we, despite you being Catholic and my being from the Church of England?'

Tilly laughed. 'Of course we do, Dad.'

'It seems the Buddhists have got it right, though. I'm reading a book on the Dalai Lama. Did Anna mention they offer meditation classes at the town hall now? She's going to her first one next Monday.'

'She didn't, but how interesting.' The truth was, Tilly wasn't in the slightest bit interested in meditation. Even if she was, she thought, when would she fit in the time to be still? She always had so much to do, so much to tick off. And then there were Jack's questions waiting for her at the end of the week, as if she had all the answers.

'Now, before I forget,' said Jack, broaching a subject he had been trying to skirt since the beginning of their call, 'I spotted Isla in Worcester with a young man yesterday.'

'That's not possible, Dad. Isla's in Durham.'

'Well, I'm certain it was her.' Jack paused. 'Has she ever mentioned a special gentleman friend to you?'

Tilly laughed. 'Not that I'm aware of. Perhaps it was just a friend you saw with her. Not a *special* one.'

'No, it definitely looked like a special friend to me.'

'Well, I'm sure she would have said something if she wanted us to know.'

'I think the chap she was with was more than a friend. Quite a bit older than Isla too.'

'Oh! How much older?'

'Ten years, I think.'

'But Isla's barely twenty. She's far too young.'

'The problem is, Tilly, I don't think that's what you should be concerned about.'

'Concerned about?'

'I'm concerned about this chap's background. His *family*.'

'His *family*?'

'Yes...' Jack took a deep breath before he continued. He had only told Anna about his suspicions, and that hadn't been easy, but now that Isla was involved, Tilly had a right to know who her daughter might be seeing. 'The thing is, I have reason to believe his family – well, his great-grandfather to be exact – carried out an injustice towards my father.'

'Oh?' Tilly's Sunday calls with Jack were always interesting, but she hadn't been expecting this.

'My father was working on a hair formula, you see, before planning to release it commercially. When he died suddenly, the ingredients, everything, disappeared. When my mother went to pack up her husband's belongings and close down the shop, she couldn't find the cream anywhere.'

'And you're sure the man Isla's with, I mean, his great-grandfather, has something to do with this?'

'Unfortunately, I can't prove it but I have reason to believe it's true. I met Giles when he was a lad some years ago in

245

Kidderminster and then again at Hillmans where he works with his uncle. He told me his family are barbers, with salons across Halifax. Of course, there's nothing unusual about that, but when he told me his great-grandfather was Edward Oldroyd, that's when I began to suspect something. I remembered the name immediately. Oldroyd was a customer of my father's and a strange one at that, always asking questions. I just knew it was him. It was all very odd, looking back.'

'But can you really be *sure*, Dad? I mean, there must be hundreds of barbers in Yorkshire.'

'It's not so much the fact they are barbers, it's the fact they have a thriving business. And that, Giles said, was all down to the best-selling cream they sell. Yes, there are hundreds of barbers in Yorkshire, but it's too much of a coincidence that their cream was launched around the time my father died. They *must* have stolen my father's formula.'

'So you think they patented your father's work and sold it as their own?'

'I'm certain of it. Who else could it be? The formula was stolen before my mother could do anything with it. When she couldn't find the formula, she just assumed it was lost and didn't take it any further. But I knew then something wasn't right.'

'I can't believe it.' Tilly took a drag of her cigarette. She needed to calm her nerves.

'Tell me, Tilly, do you think I'm being rash?'

'No, no, I'm sure I would think the same. And you're right, Isla needs to know. Have you told Anna?'

'Yes, after I spotted Isla with Giles. It was never the right time before. I had resigned myself to letting it go. What could I have done anyway? But with these developments...'

'It's not going to be easy, Dad, especially as you have no conclusive evidence. Let me speak to Isla...'

'That's the problem. I have absolutely nothing to prove that any of this is true. But I really think Isla needs to know.'

Later that evening, Tilly rang her daughter. She had never spoken to Isla about relationships or boyfriends before, let alone one whose family her grandpa suspected of committing a crime. She dreaded Isla's reaction as much as she dreaded the thought of her being mixed up with someone she didn't approve of. Isla, however, listened calmly as she took in her mother's words. 'It's fine, Mum,' she said with an air of indifference, 'but what do you want me to do? I mean, it's not as if Giles had anything to do with the formula. He's a good person, and as far as I'm concerned, he's got nothing to do with any of this.'

'How long have you been with him?'

Isla hesitated for a moment. 'Two years…'

'*Two* years – and I don't know about it? *Schatz,* why didn't you want to tell me about Giles?'

'It was his choice. He didn't want *anyone to* know about us.'

'So his family don't know about you? But why? Why do you think that is?'

'I don't know…' Isla sounded doubtful, as if a seed had just been planted.

'Don't you find that strange?'

'Well, yes, and no…'

'You don't find it strange that your boyfriend of two years doesn't want anyone to know about you?'

'What I mean is he had his reasons. He didn't want to upset Grandpa for a start.'

'He didn't want to upset Grandpa? What did Giles tell you about Grandpa?'

Isla remained silent for a moment as she tried to recall the conversation she'd had with Giles in Worcester. They had been in Gheluvelt Park, and the only thing she remembered was that it had been an unusually warm September afternoon and she was wearing blue polka dot leggings with an oversized white tee-shirt. 'I don't remember exactly. It was so long ago. I didn't go into it with him. It didn't seem important at the time.'

'You weren't curious to know why Grandpa might have been upset with your boyfriend? If someone told me they needed to keep me a secret because of some upset, *I'd* want to know.'

'It wasn't like that. It sort of made sense at the time and, anyway, neither of us knew where this was going, if we would even last when I went off to Durham, so I was fine with keeping us a secret anyway.'

'*Schatz*, isn't it clear to you? Giles obviously knows about his family's past and he's ashamed.'

'That's ridiculous.'

'Look, I'm not saying he's to blame for any of this, but by keeping you apart from his family, he thinks you'll never find out about their past. Their family secret will remain... well, a secret. Can you imagine how they would feel if they knew Giles was with the granddaughter of Jack Jagger?'

'How do we know, though?' said Isla, starting to feel uncomfortable. '*How* do we know any of this is actually true? We only have Grandpa's word. Maybe Grandpa was upset with Giles about his paintings. I don't know, maybe Giles didn't like his work and said something silly to Grandpa about them. He can be a bit weird sometimes, a bit awkward with people, and blurts things out without really meaning them.'

'Just be careful, *Schatz*. I'm not telling you to stop seeing Giles, but, please, just be careful.'

*

When Tilly spoke to Jack the following Sunday, she reiterated her conversation with Isla. 'She didn't seem upset and it certainly hasn't put her off seeing him again, and she's right, none of this is his fault.'

'Did she mention introducing him to you at some point?'

Tilly laughed. 'No. Doesn't want to scare him off probably. There's time. She's still young...'

'I still find this whole thing rather odd. I mean, why Isla? Why did he choose Isla?'

'I don't think we can choose who we love, can we, Dad?'

'I'm not sure it's about love, though. It's just all too much of a coincidence.'

'What can we do apart from tell Isla to stop seeing him?'

Jack was quiet for a moment but he couldn't think of anything to say.

'How was Worcester by the way? Did you buy anything?' Tilly was keen to change the subject.

'Watercolours. I'm always out of greens and blues.'

Tilly imagined Jack's mind ticking over, if not about his granddaughter, then about something else he had been ruminating over that week. What a luxury to be able to ruminate, thought Tilly, recalling all the times her father-in-law had shared something he had been mulling over. The truth was, by the end of the week she was usually too exhausted to even think about what she should have for supper, let alone cook anything substantial. She wanted nothing more than to close the door on the world, defrost a pizza and pour herself a glass of wine. That was the extent of Tilly's life now: a relentless balance of work, keeping on top of the mortgage payments and household chores. But she didn't mind; duly accepting her lot because she knew she had been given more than her fair share of a charmed life.

How she had loved entertaining: inviting friends over for drinks then sauntering downstairs to the hotel restaurant for supper. Entertaining without having to step into the kitchen once. It had been so easy. A four-course meal for eight without having to buy the ingredients, do the cooking, or the washing-up. It was a good life, an *easy* life, and Tilly rode the wave long before the tide turned. It had been six years since Hanson left, and that day, a bright, warm April before Easter, was still clear in Tilly's mind. Now the divorce had gone through – she had matter-of-factly filed the decree absolute in a folder as if it were a bill – there was a sense of finality to things. Not that she ever expected her husband to return (despite him never making it explicit that he was leaving her either,) but when she thought about it, looked back at her forty-nine years, it was with relief, regret and sadness. Regret that she couldn't turn back the clock and have the chance to do things differently; sadness that she hadn't been able to make her marriage work and relief that she knew she could do it alone. Relief because she had not just got back on her feet, she was walking confidently towards a future that she was building all by herself.

*

Tilly bit into her pizza, and as she settled into another evening in front of the television, she rather enjoyed the ordinariness of it all. The glamour had been stripped from her life and there was washing-up to be done now – plenty of it – but it grounded her and gave her the impetus to ride a different kind of wave – one of survival. The sea had become calmer as she'd learnt over time to navigate the highs and lows of the ocean: by herself, with her children, always looking ahead, never giving up.

Anna 38

Anna sat at the dining table and wrote Deborah Hart a condolence card. She chose her words carefully, imagining the grief engulfing her friend in the wake of her husband's death. It had happened so suddenly, and just like that, Bob was no longer the energetic, jovial, easygoing chap that everyone knew: the man who could cycle for miles; the man who ran three marathons for charity; the man who had recently built a treehouse at the bottom of the garden for his grandchildren to play in. How wonderful, everyone said, admiring Bob's deft handiwork as he ceremoniously unveiled his wooden masterpiece, which was lodged between two oak trees. Instead, Bob would now be remembered for the stroke that had struck him like lightning.

A stroke was perhaps the cruellest condition of all, thought Anna. Of course, Deborah would be fine once the shock of it all was over. She had four children, whom she clung to even tighter now that their father was gone.

'I can't imagine life without them,' said Deborah Hart several months later while she and Anna sat in the Harts' garden. She was knitting a hat for her seventh grandchild and smiling contentedly. 'They are my world, really they are.'

Anna nodded, pleased that her friend seemed to be in good spirits.

'John and Clare have decided to call him Alfie. Isn't it sweet? There's something rather old-fashioned about the name. What about you, Anna, have you heard from Elizabeth recently?'

'Not since Christmas,' said Anna, annoyed that her friend always asked the same question. 'But that's not unusual for Lizzie – she's so busy with the school; and what with living so far away, she can't just hop in the car to visit.'

'Yes, I suppose Singapore is rather far away for that.'

'She's happy and that's the main thing.'

'Well,' said Deborah, picking up a half-knitted wool hat and holding it against the light, 'I expect she must be quite lonely out there.'

'Actually, Lizzie loves living in Singapore – the weather, the food, the culture. I don't think she'll ever come back.'

An air of silence descended upon the room while the two women looked at each other furtively. 'What is it?' Anna shifted uncomfortably in her chair. 'Why are you looking at me like that?'

'It's just that, well, I just feel so terrible for you. You have a daughter who lives thousands of miles away who you never see for months on end and, well, what's the point of it all?'

'What's the point of what?'

'What's the point of having children if you never see them?'

'What an absurd thing to say,' said Anna, shaking her head. 'Really, Deborah, whatever next?'

'Well, it's true. If my children flew to the other side of the world and decided to park themselves there permanently, I'm sure I would have something to say about it.' Deborah waved her arm around the garden like a helpless bird. 'Who would look after me if I became ill? Forgive me if I'm wrong, but isn't that the whole *point* of having them?'

Anna had known Deborah for most of her adult life, long before she married Jack. They had met in their late teens at Malvern Tennis Club, where they were both members; a friendship that was solidified by endless rounds of tennis practice. Yet, with each choice the other made, their worlds drifted further apart. Anna recalled what a fit young woman Deborah had been back then, but it seemed with each year that passed, Deborah had let herself go more and more. Still, Deborah didn't seem to care. She had a husband, she had four children; she had everything she wanted. And besides, she protested, staying slim was hard work. Yet for all Deborah's indifference to her physical demise, she had been canny when she was younger. She had been determined to marry young and she wanted to marry well. And, although she was attractive – Deborah had once likened herself to a ripe, shapely pear – she didn't possess the effortless beauty that Anna exuded, whose willowy frame gave an elegance to everything she wore. Bob, however, had been smitten, proposing to his "Dee" within three months, who carried her newfound status with an authority Anna found alarming. *I'm a real woman now*, Deborah exclaimed when she got married just before her twenty-second birthday.

It would take more than a decade for Deborah to congratulate Anna on reaching the same milestone. Marriage had found Anna, rather than Anna finding it. It arrived without fanfare, without expectation, and without any sense of urgency. Yet the intervening decade had not been without judgement. 'You really need to get on with it,' Deborah told Anna during a weekly swimming session. It was strange how these conversations always took place in the local pool, thought Anna, as if the water were a safety net for frank exchanges. Anna always swam in the lane next to her friend; feeling soothed by the water, wondering whether this was what it felt like to be a baby growing in its mother's womb. The truth was, Anna had not met anyone she cared to marry. Most of the men were away fighting a war, and it didn't seem likely they were coming home soon. Still, Anna's glass was always half full. She had a good job in the design studio at the carpet factory in Kidderminster, and her parents didn't seem to mind their daughter living at home with not a marriage offer in sight. Besides, she wanted to travel and had quietly resolved that once the war was over, she would take off and see the world with whoever cared to join her.

There are plenty of Deborahs in the world, thought Anna, as she sat opposite her friend. She could see it in Deborah's own daughters, who themselves had married young and now, at middle age, full of restlessness and resentment for dreams that were no longer theirs, wondered if there had been more to life after all.

Anna looked at Deborah, whose expression had taken on a puzzled hue. 'As long as Lizzie is happy, I'm happy. She is doing wonderful things. The art department has really taken off. She has plans to start a painting club, and she even has her own exhibition space at one of the galleries there. What have your daughters achieved? Aside from having children?' Anna had never spoken so boldly before and she would never speak with such conviction again. But in that moment she knew she had to say something. Deborah Hart had lived her whole life by the book. She had been born less than twenty miles from where she settled to raise her own family, and she knew she would never leave. For where would Deborah Hart go? The extent of her world was so limited, and she patronised anyone who didn't fit the mould she had created for herself. As far as Anna was concerned, Deborah Hart was living but she wasn't really *living* life.

'I'm very confused...' Deborah Hart spluttered. The large piece of cake that she was about to put into her mouth – she never ate with small, delicate mouthfuls – had fallen back onto her lap, crumbs darting everywhere. She dabbed the corners of her lips with a napkin and then picked up her knitting needles, before putting them down again. 'I expected more sympathy from you today, quite frankly, what with Bob and everything. You've made me quite upset. In fact, I think you should leave.'

'I'm terribly sorry for your loss, Deborah, I really am.' Anna rose from her chair. 'Bob was a good man and we shall all miss him terribly. But there's many ways to live a life,' she said, before quietly closing the door behind her.

Hanson   39

It was Maggie who suggested extending the olive branch, but she did it selflessly, knowing that Hanson's family would never know the months of persuasion it had taken to shift her boyfriend's stubbornness towards conciliation.

'Your father won't be around forever,' she said one evening. 'Imagine how you would feel if anything should happen to him, all because you were trying to make a point.'

Hanson knew if anyone could persuade him to do something, it was Maggie. 'All right,' he conceded. 'It won't do any harm if we invite them to stay. We can put them in one of the suites and then they can please themselves.'

'I don't think you'll regret it, sweetheart. Things will be back on track in no time.'

'We'll see. He needs to accept our invitation first of all.'

'He's your father. Of course he will.'

'That doesn't count for much, not if Tilly has anything to do with it.' Hanson's bitterness, this feeling of misplaced loyalty, came in waves. If his mother were alive, he thought, she would never have betrayed him like this. She would never have betrayed her own flesh and blood. She would have stuck by him; supported him no matter what. Even now, after all these years, the ink long dry on the divorce papers, Hanson was astounded to learn that his father was closer to his ex-wife than ever.

It didn't make sense at all.

*

The painting, which had been carefully placed on the dining table, was looking less likely (the more time went on) to provide the much-needed ice breaker between the four people who were peering down at it. Jack and Anna were in Hanson and Maggie's apartment, having arrived earlier that afternoon, and everyone was running out of small talk.

'I think it's a keeper,' said Maggie, attempting to lighten the heaviness in the room. 'What do you think, sweetheart?' Maggie looked at her boyfriend, trying to gauge his mood.

Hanson offered a weak smile. It was clear he was not ready to extend the olive branch yet.

'Do you think you might like to hang it somewhere in the hotel?' Anna glanced nervously at her stepson. Like Maggie, she was searching for a spark.

'Quite possibly,' came Hanson's cool reply. Anna and Jack exchanged glances, quietly acknowledging that the task of rebuilding a relationship was not going to take place over a painting of Holkham Bay.

Jack and Anna had been given a small suite at the opposite end of the hotel and were told by Hanson to come and go as they pleased, which meant taking breakfast, lunch and dinner in the Marina, along with the other guests. On the first two mornings, they took brisk walks along the seafront. Afternoons were spent browsing in antique shops in nearby villages or driving through country lanes; the landscape shifting into new shapes and colours the further they explored. And when the sun began to fade, reds and yellows disappearing into the grey sea, they drove back to the hotel for dinner. To anyone at the Connaught, Jack and Anna were just another couple enjoying a weekend break by the sea. Still, Jack was glad for the anonymity and felt some comfort from the low din of individual stories emanating from the tables in the restaurant around them: families, friends, colleagues, strangers – celebrating, reminiscing, consoling, repairing. Jack wondered how many people were here to repair a relationship. By the sound of things, he didn't think very many.

This routine continued on the third day, by which time Jack and Anna still hadn't seen Hanson or Maggie. What should they expect? Jack reasoned to himself. It's a bank holiday. The hotel is full. Everyone knows that hoteliers work around the clock. Running a business is a full-time job. His son was in charge. As long as they saw them at *some* point. There had been sightings at least; Anna catching a glimpse of her stepson disappear into what looked like a boardroom, while Jack had seen Maggie laughing with the girls at reception on his way to fetch something from the car. He had planned to say hello to her when he returned, but she was already gone. Had she seen him? Did she deliberately leave before he had a chance to talk to her? The whole set-up was starting to feel rather odd – as if Hanson and Maggie were avoiding them. By the evening, however, in between their main course and pudding, Jack and Anna were interrupted by someone who did appear keen to meet them.

'Good evening, Mr and Mrs Jagger.'

Jack turned around, surprised by the appearance of the stout, round man who was grinning broadly at them. 'I'm Marty,' said the pianist effusively, offering his hand to Anna. 'Welcome to the Connaught. My office is just around the corner there,' he said, pointing in the direction of the Players' Lounge.

'Thank you,' said Jack. 'Pleasure to meet you.'

'How are you enjoying your stay so far?' Before Jack could

reply, Marty interjected. 'Expect you'll have had some catching-up to do, the four of you, eh?'

'Yes,' replied Jack. 'The restaurant is certainly popular.' He didn't know what else to say.

'Ah yes, must be the chef's fish and chips. I'm sure Mr Jagger told you about the hiccups at the beginning, though.'

'The hiccups? No. Anything to be concerned about?'

'Concerned?' Marty laughed heartily. 'Oh no, thankfully, it's all water under the bridge now.'

Jack nodded at Marty, saddened by the realisation that there was so much of his son's life he was no longer privy to. He was proud of him, proud of what he had achieved, *was* achieving, and he wanted to tell him that. But how could he when they had barely exchanged more than a few pleasantries? They were strangers now, he thought. Perhaps that's all he should expect.

'I wonder what that was about?' said Jack when Marty had left. 'The hiccups, I mean.'

'Well, I can't expect it's easy to run a place like this.'

'I suppose you're right.' Jack looked around the restaurant as waiters darted about frenetically, balancing silverware on their arms like precious jewels. There was so much he didn't know about his son's life now. But how on earth could they sort things out if they never saw each other? Three days and they still hadn't spoken to Hanson and Maggie.

Why had they been invited? Why were they *even* here?

On the fourth day, Jack and Anna drove to Happisburgh as planned. They lingered in picturesque villages dotted with thatched cottages and ancient churches, and they explored the rolling chalklands and watery patchwork of the Norfolk Broads, Jack every so often stopping the car to take a photograph. Anna dozed lightly, her face turned towards the sun, and Jack recalled the coolness with which Hanson had spoken to her when they first arrived. The nonchalance was palpable. Anna was simply trying to make things better in the gentle, easygoing manner that was characteristic of her, only for her actions to be thwarted. Had it really come to this because his son wanted a different life? Because deep down Hanson knew his father didn't approve? Because he had ignored his son's ultimatum? But what if Jack changed his mindset? What if *he* accepted Hanson's behaviour rather than Hanson change his? More to the point, what if he accepted Maggie as his new daughter-in-law? Things certainly might be easier.

The more Jack thought about it, the more he wondered whether *he* was the problem and not his son.

'Do you think it's me?' Jack turned to Anna, before motioning at a nearby bench. 'Do you think if I was less focused on Tilly, more focused on Maggie, things would be different between Hanson and I?'

'Only you can know that,' said Anna, the sound of seagulls squawking around them. The beach and Happisburgh Lighthouse glistened in the sun, while children's laughter could be heard in the distance, and Anna wondered what kind of child Hanson had been; something she always found difficult to imagine. 'At least Maggie is making an effort. I'm sure she'd have preferred for us to stay with them in the apartment rather than squirrel us away at the other end of the hotel.'

'I agree,' said Jack, taking Anna's hand. 'At least that's something.'

They sat in silence. Two boats were bobbing on the horizon and coming closer to shore. Anna closed her eyes and shielded her face from the sun while Jack continued to gaze out to sea. 'I don't think, though...' said Jack after a while, 'I mean, as pleasant as Maggie is, and she does seem to make Hanson happy, I don't think I could ever really consider her a part of this family.' What Jack really wanted to say was that Maggie wasn't Tilly. She would *never* be Tilly. Maggie was who she was, his son's new partner – perhaps wife one day – and Jack was prepared to accept her for just that.

'I overheard a guest say that Norfolk has been inaccurately described as flat.' Jack was watching Hanson prepare four drinks in the small kitchenette. 'Yet there doesn't seem to be anything that rises above a few hundred feet. If you think of all the hills in Scotland, the landscape couldn't be more different.'

It was Jack and Anna's final evening at the Connaught, and they had been unexpectedly invited for dinner in Hanson and Maggie's apartment, after finding a note under their suite door instructing them to keep Monday evening free and to arrive no later than seven. Maggie was cooking supper, which, according to Hanson, was a rare occurrence.

'Precisely,' said Hanson, pouring gin into three tumblers before preparing a ginger beer for Anna. 'The landscape is certainly what makes Norfolk unique. In fact, I read somewhere that it's exactly these big skies, windswept vistas and boats drifting across a shoreline that drew the likes of Turner and Constable here.'

Hanson nodded towards the window and the group gazed out towards the horizon. It was a simple observation, but Jack knew his son had tried to find common ground with which to take the first real step toward conciliation. Jack felt relief sweep over him. 'Ah yes, the eponymous *Great Yarmouth Harbour*. If anyone can capture the colours of the sunset and sea, it's Turner.'

'What does it look like?' Maggie asked Jack.

'It's all about the sunset. But what makes it special is Turner's use of colour and composition, the way he's created an ethereal quality to the sky against the darkness of the lighthouse. It's quite something.'

'Perhaps we could find a copy and hang it in the hotel. What do you think, sweetheart?'

'How about Dad paints one for us instead?' Hanson smiled at his father, a smile that was as sincere as it was unforeseen. 'Maybe several, depending if you'd like to paint a series of local scenes.'

'That sounds wonderful. Don't you think, Jack?' said Anna, encouraged by the sudden benevolence in her stepson.

'Might I suggest…' added Maggie, clearly pleased with the burgeoning enthusiasm in the room, 'that Jack do a painting of the Connaught? It's occurred to me that we don't have one, and every hotel needs its very own painting. What do you think, sweetheart?' Her face beamed as she looked at everyone in turn.

'I think it's a terrific idea,' said Hanson. 'As long as Dad has the time.'

'Yes, of course,' said Jack, smiling. 'I would be delighted.'

'Well, that's agreed then.' Hanson smiled again at his father. 'What time were you thinking of heading off tomorrow? You might want to take some photos here beforehand. I have a staff meeting at ten, but we could meet at nine, or a bit later…'

'Nine is a good time,' said Jack. 'We'd like to get an early start on the traffic.'

When Jack returned with Anna to their suite, he chose to only focus on the positives. That the breakthrough with his son – there was no other way of describing it – had taken place on the final evening wasn't important, nor the fact that they had barely seen Hanson and Maggie over the last four days. Jack's unanswered letter and the years of silence that ensued – also irrelevant. All that mattered was that he had achieved what he had come to Norfolk for. They were talking again.

An early-morning mist was slowly giving way to a glorious blue sky. From Jack and Anna's vantage point – the bay window in their room – the horizon looked like a brilliant canopy above the sea, while yachts bobbed between larger ships and glistened like white gold beneath the sun's rays. 'I almost wish we could stay longer,' said Jack, as he and Anna gazed out at the view.

'Well, I can't imagine either of you leaving it too long before we meet again.'

Jack smiled. 'We mustn't forget to buy some Cromer crab. I hear that Smiths by the harbour sells the best for miles.'

'Cromer crab *and* a gift for Hanson and Maggie,' said Anna. 'They've really been so kind.'

Hanson was already waiting by the Connaught's side entrance when Jack returned from loading the car. 'All set?' Hanson had a bundle of papers wedged underneath his arm.

Jack nodded as he walked towards his son.

'And the photos? Do you think they'll be good enough to use for the painting?'

'I think so.' Jack noticed that Hanson looked distracted. 'Anna is just returning the room keys. She'll be here shortly.'

'Actually, I was hoping to catch you alone.' Hanson had lowered his voice. 'There's something I wanted to talk to you about, something I've been meaning to say...'

'Oh...' Jack glanced back at the hotel and hoped that Anna was caught up in conversation, for now would not be a good time to reappear. He had been waiting for this moment for nine years. If it wasn't going to happen here, it never would.

'Maggie and I really enjoyed having you stay.' Hanson spoke carefully, enunciating each word, as if to avoid any misunderstandings. 'Hopefully, we'll be able to do this again soon and not leave it so long this time.'

I am never going to let this happen again, thought Jack. *If Hanson regrets his actions, realises the error of his ways, I'll forgive everything. We'll start anew with a clean slate.*

'However, I want you to cut ties with Tilly. Completely. It doesn't make any sense and it's not fair to Maggie.'

'But what about the children?'

'The children have nothing to do with this. They're adults now. They can visit you by themselves.'

'But they always visit together. The three of them. That's how it's always been.'

'Well, perhaps it's time for a change. I just don't think it appropriate for Tilly to be in your life any more than it is for Maggie's father to be in her former husband's. Not that he is, but it's the only analogy I can think of.'

'But Maggie doesn't have any children. There is a subtle difference here.'

Jack knew from his son's face that he would be punished for those words. Hanson glared at his father; his expression, which only moments before had been warm and amiable, was now that of a stranger again. Jack dared to say what Hanson hadn't wanted to hear, and now there would be consequences. He was most certain of that. All the good work undone; those first steps towards some kind of conciliation unravelled. They were back at the beginning.

'Ah, there you are,' said Anna, who was carrying a large book and a small wrapped package under her arm. 'Your very kind pianist has given us this beautiful book on Norfolk. He left it with the girls at the front desk. Do please give him our thanks.'

'How very kind of him,' said Hanson drily.

Anna and Jack exchanged looks, the same look they had given each other when they first arrived.

'I was just saying to Dad you'll have a nice run back on a day like this.' There were no embraces. No goodbyes. After Hanson spoke, he simply turned around and walked away; the grey of his suit becoming fainter in the soft morning light.

'Dear oh dear,' said Jack as he and Anna stood there, watching Hanson's silhouette disappear from view.

Anna opened the car door and placed the book Marty had given them on the back seat along with the thank-you gift she had bought for Hanson and Maggie, while Jack took one last look at the hotel with its faded blue and white facade.

And then he shook his head sadly.

Isla   # 40

The trip had been planned for several months. Isla had wanted
to visit Yorkshire for some time; discover the place where
generations of her family lived, and Giles decided it was time
for Isla to finally meet his parents. They had survived the
distance between Durham and Worcester and now that Isla
was (reluctantly) living back at home in London, Giles' mind
was more and more on the future; their future. So, one late
September morning, the two of them set off in his car from
London and headed north.

'You have one toe in the Big Smoke and the other in that
beloved German *kapital* of yours.' Giles glanced over at Isla in
the passenger seat as they headed towards the M1. 'You're like a
mistress. You can't live in two places at once.' Isla was offended by
Giles' flippancy because it was a complex situation; this affiliation
with Berlin and sense of disconnect with London. She mulled this
over as they drove northwards; away from the noise and pollution,
the chaos and crowds towards something calmer. He was right,
she knew that, and that's why it stung, this sense of not belonging
anywhere. She began to wonder whether it was her unusual

childhood—the hotels, the transience, the feeling of living in a "bubble" – that caused her to feel this way. Giles was proud of his Yorkshire roots, and the fervour with which he arranged their trip, painstakingly going through each detail as if afraid to make a mistake, was proof to Isla that Yorkshire provided a sense of identity or whatever it was that Giles called home.

Why shouldn't she spend time in Berlin? A university friend had recently moved there and she had loved the city ever since she first visited as a teenager. She loved how spacious it felt compared to London. She loved being able to cycle through the city with confidence – in the centre, around different neighbourhoods – and feel completely safe. She loved how Berliners had turned a derelict, unloved pile of rubble into a thing of beauty; examples of which were everywhere. Berlin wasn't home, but it had the potential to be. The rent was cheap for a start. And it offered her a lifestyle she could never afford in London. Besides, here she was at twenty-four and living at home again. She couldn't afford to rent somewhere because she was currently flitting between one admin job and another while applying for roles that required the elusive experience she didn't yet have. Giles didn't understand because he didn't have her life. He'd only ever had one job – Hillmans – which he hadn't even had to apply for, thanks to his uncle. In fact, Giles didn't have a clue. At least Grandpa had a clue, she thought, remembering the conversations he had with her about his early life. Whenever he told her stories about all the letters he had written to the local paper when he left school, letters that were never acknowledged, she always felt better. Look where her grandpa was now, she thought.

'I think you'll like the guesthouse,' said Giles, when they turned off the motorway. 'It has all that spa stuff you love.'

'Sounds great,' Isla replied, still lost in her thoughts.

'Hey, don't look so worried!'

'I'm worried because *you* look worried.'

'I'm sorry, I just want everything to go to plan. This trip means a lot to me.'

'And for me too.' Isla reached over and squeezed Giles' hand. 'I'm really looking forward to it.'

They drove on in silence; the grey of the motorway had been replaced by rolling green hills, while trees jutted out into the horizon. Isla was trying to focus on the trip but lately, Tilly's words kept infiltrating her thoughts with greater frequency, like seeds of doubt waiting to root themselves. *Schatz, isn't it clear to you? Giles knows about his family's past. That's the reason he's keeping you a secret.* So why, she thought, is my boyfriend finally prepared to reveal me to the world? It had never really concerned her before. But now that it was finally happening, she couldn't help but wonder, why *now*?

'Look, we're almost here.' Giles turned into a cobbled lane. 'Down here is the Little Yorkshire Rose Inn, our home for the night.' The car jostled from side to side and Isla admired the pretty apple trees that lined the lane on either side; their fruit jangling from branches like jewels. Giles parked the car in the courtyard in front of the guesthouse and, as if on cue, a door opened expectantly to them; the proprietor having observed the couple from the hallway window.

'Good afternoon, Mr and Mrs Illingworth, welcome to the Little Yorkshire Rose. My name is Rose Hemsworth.' The woman ushered them in and Isla noted how the freshness of the lady's cheeks, plump and ruddy, reminded her of the ripening apples they had driven past moments before. 'You're on the top floor, the best view in my opinion, and here's your key. If there's anything you'd like to know, it's in the guest book upstairs. Otherwise, breakfast is served sharply between seven and nine.'

'Thank you,' said Giles. 'We'll let you know if we need anything else.'

'Right you are then.' Mrs Hemsworth raised an eyebrow before disappearing into an adjoining room. Less than a minute later, she reappeared. 'Being the weekend, mind, breakfast will be served until nine-thirty.'

Giles waited until the door closed a second time and the two of them laughed before climbing the three flights of narrow stairs to their room.

'It's lovely,' exclaimed Isla, opening the bedroom door to reveal a spacious attic room with a view of the Dales.

'I thought you'd approve. Did you also like what Mrs Hemsworth first said when she welcomed us?'

Isla looked blankly at Giles. 'What do you mean?'

'She called us Mr and Mrs Illingworth.'

'Oh yes, so she did.' Isla began to unpack her belongings; smoothing out the creases in her two dresses, which she laid out neatly on the bed, unaware of Giles staring intently at her.

The following morning, Isla woke to Giles talking urgently on his phone. He was in the corridor outside their room and she could hear him pacing up and down as snippets of muffled conversation floated towards her. She clambered out of bed and tiptoed towards the door, edging closer until the conversation became clearer. 'I can't put it on hold...' The padding of footsteps was followed by muted words and Isla instinctively recoiled back into the room, feeling guilty at eavesdropping. She quietly crept back into bed, pulling the duvet over her. *What can't he put on hold and why is he being so secretive?* she thought.

'Ah, you're awake,' said Giles when he returned. 'I've just been talking to my parents. You were still asleep and...'

'Everything okay? I mean with us visiting them still?'

'Yes, fine,' said Giles, putting his phone to one side. It was like a big black brick, Isla thought, glancing at his Motorola. When he'd first bought it, he was the only person she knew with a mobile phone (apart from her father but that didn't count), and she would joke that it was like having a third person in the relationship; this bulky contraption that Giles brought everywhere. 'They're expecting us later and said we can stay as long as we like. But that all depends how everything goes, of course.'

'How everything goes?' Isla propped her head against a pillow. 'You make it sound as if there are conditions to be met.'

'Well, there are. Sort of.' Giles gently brushed a stray wave from Isla's forehead. 'But I don't want you to worry. Everything is going to be fine.'

The rain arrived later, covering Hipperholme in a heavy greyish hue. 'This is it,' said Giles, as he and Isla turned into a long street. 'I'm not sure of the exact number, but it would have been one of these down here.' Isla looked at the row of red-brick mid-Victorian terraces; homes that seemed to stretch as far back as they rose high.

It was not how she imagined it, and yet, it was *exactly* how she imagined it.

'What's wrong?' asked Giles, as they watched two pigeons on the roof of a nearby house. Two colourful banners advertising a day nursery were erected on either side of the building and they were flapping furiously in the wind.

'Nothing's wrong,' said Isla, burying her hands in her jean pockets. 'I'm just taking it all in.'

'They wouldn't have had those in your grandpa's day,' said Giles pointing at a skip. 'Grim-looking things, aren't they?'

Isla glanced from house to house, sparks of individuality emanating from each one, and wondered which one had belonged to her great-grandparents. 'It could be any one of these,' she said, as her eyes darted from side to side. 'I'll never forget my grandpa's stories, the ones about his childhood. He got up to all sorts of pranks, most probably in this very street.'

Giles laughed.

'Like the one with the apple.'

'The apple?'

'Yes, Grandpa and his friends would throw apples at people's doors and then run off before anyone got caught.'

'I can't imagine your grandpa doing that.'

'Me neither.' Isla smiled as she and Giles moved towards the edge of the pavement.

'Are you okay?' Giles put his arm around Isla and drew her closer to him.

'It's just, well, knowing that Grandpa lived *right* here, knowing that he didn't have it easy with his father dying so young and so suddenly; so much opportunity taken away from the whole family, well, it's really brought it home.' Isla looked at Giles, waiting for some kind of reaction. But Giles was distracted and eager to move on. He reached for Isla's hand and led her away from the street and towards a small green which could be seen in the distance. 'Come, I want to show you something,' he said. Soon, he thought, there would be no going back. In a matter of hours, in front of his family, he would wait to learn his fate. 'That over there would have been where the villagers bought their essentials. And got their hair cut at the same time!' Giles pointed to a row of shops, the nearest of which looked like a café and as they got closer, Isla began to make out the bright red lettering with its broken "C", so the storefront read: *Hipperholme Fish and hips*, the letter "C" dangling precariously in the air.

'What's this?' asked Isla.

'I know it's probably not what you imagined. But this is what it is *now*. Not what it was like *then*.'

Isla stared at the unkemptness of it all: the dirty, peeling plaster; the faded grandeur. 'What is it?'

'This...' said Giles excitedly, '...this was your great-grandfather's barbershop. Over there was the original doorway. It was twice the size – extending all the way to the back with a facade and *HW Jagger Barbers* in black and white and...' Giles was about to show Isla a separate entrance, his enthusiasm palpable, but she cut him short.

'How do you know... I mean, how did you know it was here?'

'I thought you'd be happy.' Giles clasped Isla's hand but she withdrew it immediately.

'Why? What do you care?' How on earth did Giles know exactly where her great-grandfather's barbershop was? she thought. Grandpa must have been right after all.

'Because I knew how much seeing all this would mean to you.'

'You know so much about my family. *How* do you know so much about my family, Giles?' Isla's tone was accusatory.

'I did my research before we arrived. I've learnt so much! Did you know that my great-grandad, Pa Oldroyd, was actually a regular customer of your great-grandfather's right here in this very spot? Can you believe it?'

'Your great-grandfather knew mine?' Isla was still hoping her grandpa had made a mistake.

'Yes, isn't it a coincidence? Just think, our families are kind of connected.'

Isla looked away. This was not what she had wanted to hear.

'Everyone knew him. Your great-grandfather had customers for miles around. *Everyone* came to get their hair cut here.'

Isla's heart was thumping. She *had* to say something. *Now* was the time to say something. And yet, she was still hoping that deep down her grandpa's suspicions were unfounded.

'I know,' she said, finally turning towards Giles. 'I *know.*'

'Know what? What do you mean?'

'Look, I know what your family did, Giles. I know why you've kept me from them all this time.'

'What my family did? What are you talking about?'

'The formula my great-grandfather was working on. The hair formula. It was stolen from this exact spot when he died.' Isla pointed at the fish and chip shop.

'Stolen from here? What are you talking about?'

'Giles, please stop pretending. There's no point lying to me anymore.' Isla folded her arms and turned to face her boyfriend.

'Your great-grandfather, Pa Oldroyd, stole the hair formula from Henry Jagger, *my* great-grandfather, and gave it to his son or whoever. Stop pretending that you don't know. My mum told me everything.'

'But Dad has his own formula. They've been selling it for years.'

'No, your family stole the formula from this place. My great-grandfather died unexpectedly and must have left it lying around before the place shut down.'

'What? This is crazy. Why haven't you said anything before?'

'Why didn't *you* say anything?'

'Because it's the first I've heard about *any* of this.'

'You're lying, Giles.'

'I'm *not* lying.'

'I don't believe you.'

'Well, you're going to have to believe me.'

The two of them looked at each other, arms folded.

'Why didn't you tell me...' said Giles. 'If you knew about it, why didn't you just tell me?'

Isla shrugged.

'How long have you known about it?'

'A while...'

'Were you ever going to tell me?'

'Yes, of course I was. It's not exactly an easy conversation to start, though.'

Giles stared at the ground, trying to take everything in.

'It didn't matter at the time,' said Isla. 'I thought to myself, it happened so long ago, it has nothing to do with you. Why should I even concern myself with something *you* didn't do?'

'And then...?'

'Then... well, then I just kept thinking what my mum told me. She told me to be careful, that it wasn't normal you were keeping me a secret from everyone.'

Giles looked up, his tone accusatory now. 'So just to be clear, what you're basically saying is that my great-grandfather was a thief? That my family's business is basically built on a lie? I'm just trying to get my head around everything here.'

'Think about it, Giles. Your family has a thriving business, barbers everywhere and a best-selling hair cream.'

'And…?'

'Well, their hair cream became a bestseller *right* after my great-grandfather died and his formula disappeared. Don't you think it's too much of a coincidence? It *has* to be them.'

'But where's the proof?'

'There is no proof. That's the thing. That's why I didn't really want to mention anything to you.'

Giles looked away. He was trying to process everything all at once.

'What I want to know is why you have kept me away from your family all this time. How long have we been together and I haven't met one single member of your family? And please don't say it's because you didn't want to upset my grandpa. Remember what you said? You told me Grandpa had been upset with you at Hillmans, something to do with his paintings?'

Giles shook his head. 'It's not what you think. There was something else I didn't tell you.'

An elderly woman appeared from the side of the building and began to sweep up around the entrance. 'Can I help you, love?' the question appearing not to be addressed to anyone in particular. The shop door had been left open and two men could be heard chatting inside, while the smell of fried fish drifted towards them.

'Excuse me, but I was just wondering, how long has this shop been here?' Isla asked the woman.

'Oh, about thirty year now.' The woman looked up briefly, peering at Isla before resuming her sweeping. 'Were an ironmonger's before that, and then it were derelict for a long time. I just work here. The family that own it live in the next town. We never see 'em. They just let us get on wi'it.'

Giles ruffled his hair nervously, willing the woman to go back inside; to leave Isla to her questions.

'I keep saying to them that own it, you should visit from time to time. It could do wi' a lick of paint. Give it some love, like.' The woman paused and wiped her brow before continuing. 'They're not like them that owned the barber's. It were his proud and joy, this place. Such a tragedy, what happened.'

Isla felt her heart beat faster. 'Do you remember them? The family... and the barbershop here?'

'Do I remember them?' The woman let out a hoarse laugh. 'I used to work for 'em! Mr Jagger were a good man, and his son were only two year younger than me. Did the same thing for them what I'm doing now. That's all I've been good for, but I've got some stories to tell.'

'We have to go,' said Giles, tugging Isla's arm. 'My parents are waiting. We don't want to be late.'

'I'm here every day. Weekdays... eight while four. You can ask for Louisa. That's my grandson George inside – he helps out every now and then. But you'll find me. Hard not to in this village.'

Pa Oldroyd

41

'Are you going to tell them?' Isla stared out of the car window while Halifax whizzed past like a film in forward motion; the handsome red-brick buildings the only remnants of its Victorian past. For most of the journey she had refused to talk to Giles, blaming him for making her leave before she had a chance to ask the old lady from the fish and chip shop any more questions. Now that they were getting closer to where his parents lived, she needed to be absolutely sure about something.

'Of course I'm going to tell them. Do you think it's been easy for me to hear this?'

'No...' Isla glanced at her boyfriend and saw the distress etched across his face.

'If my parents have lied to me all of these years, then I won't be able to forgive them.'

'And what if they are innocent? What if Grandpa is wrong? Nothing's proven after all.' Giles' words suddenly frightened Isla, as if she had only just realised the significance of what was at play.

'We'll cross that bridge when we come to it. In any case, I believe your grandpa and that's what's important right now.'

Isla glanced at Giles, thankful that he was on her side, even though she was more confused than ever. Giles could still be lying, she thought, as she watched the town morph into suburbia. But Isla didn't have time to ponder because after some minutes she could see the beginnings of a long driveway, at the end of which was a magnificent oak tree and a large house with elegant bay windows; each sill decorated with French lavender. The first thing she noticed about the Illingworths' house was the striking front door. It was a resplendent green with a mosaic motif and two pairs of black wellies placed on either side, standing to attention like soldiers. Waiting by the entrance was a tall, slender woman with a fuchsia-coloured scarf draped over her shoulders. 'Welcome – both of you. So lovely to see you. Now, you must be—'

'Isla,' Giles interjected. 'The girl I've been telling you about, Mum.'

'Pleasure to meet you, Isla,' said Faye Illingworth warmly. 'Do come in – and please, let me take your bags.'

Isla was struck by the elegantly cut figure that was Giles' mother, her bright scarf creating a dramatic visual dissonance against the backdrop of brown wood panelling behind her. Somehow, Isla had imagined her differently.

The three of them stood awkwardly in the doorway for a moment, exchanging pleasantries and details of the journey. Isla glanced into a room on her left, noticing a wall painted in a rich burgundy, which seemed in perfect contrast to the colourful tapestry on the opposite side, while a William Morris print sofa took centre stage.

'Come with me,' said Giles, taking Isla's hand. 'I have a feeling you'll like this one.'

Isla followed Giles through the narrow hallway into a large side room, and the first thing that caught her attention was the Labrador warming itself by the fire. On either side of the mantelpiece stood two huge bookcases, brimming with literary classics. Isla walked towards the one nearest the door, lightly touching their spines as her hands skimmed the row of titles, not wanting to disturb their quiet order. 'I didn't realise you had a dog.' Isla bent down to stroke the Labrador, who had sauntered towards her.

'Nor did I. My parents bought him a few months ago. But as we know, they keep secrets. He's called Mungo.'

'He's gorgeous and so is the book collection – it's really impressive. Are they big readers, your parents?'

'I don't think so. Knowing them, it's probably just for show.'

'Oh.' Isla laughed nervously.

'I mean they don't *devour* books. Not like some people.'

'Your mother seems nice, though.'

'Does she?' Giles glanced behind him. 'Between you and me, she has her moments.'

Isla could hear the strain in Giles' voice: the dismissive way he spoke about his parents, the tension that now gripped him, and she began to regret the conversation she'd had with him earlier. Perhaps she should have waited, she thought; waited before confronting him with her family's suspicions. His family seemed nice, normal, in fact. Not the kind of people who would be capable of the kind of things her grandpa suspected. But Giles' obvious discomfort only increased Isla's nervousness, and when Faye Illingworth kept referring to her as the "first lady" in a teasing manner, Isla wondered (with some relief) if the reason he didn't want to tell his parents about her was because he had never brought a girlfriend home. Even Anthony Illingworth, Giles' grandfather – a man of few words was how he had been described – had made a special visit to meet the young lady his grandson had brought home. Isla was a "first" and so by very virtue of that fact, all three of them assumed she must indeed be very special.

'We understand that your grandfather is a Yorkshireman.' David Illingworth was elaborately carving the roast lamb –

everyone quietly observing the task at hand as if an intricate ritual was being performed – but at one point he glanced amiably at Isla, his perfectly white teeth gleaming against tanned skin. It was clear that he was enjoying the attention of his family and his guest. 'Salt of the earth, us Yorkshiremen,' David Illingworth added, winking at his wife.

Isla nodded agreeably. 'He was born not far from here – Hipperholme. Do you know it?'

'We've just come from there,' interrupted Giles. 'Isla wanted to see the street where her grandpa grew up.'

'And to find his father's barbershop,' Isla added. 'Although sadly it's not what I expected.' Isla wanted to express how disappointed she was to learn that the original building where her great-grandpa's business once stood was now a dilapidated fish and chip shop, but she decided against it, steering her words towards humour instead. 'It's remarkable how Giles knows so much. Anyone would think he was a Jagger. Although there's no harm in you being an honorary Jagger,' she added, touching his arm.

'Do start, everyone,' said David Illingworth, nodding at Isla. 'I think the mint sauce is my best yet.'

'Oh, please stop boasting to the girl, David.' Faye Illingworth rolled her eyes from the other side of the table.

'It's a small world, isn't it?' Giles said all of a sudden. 'My girlfriend came here to learn more about her family and I learnt something new too – about mine.'

'Terrific!' David Illingworth picked up his napkin and dabbed it lightly against his mouth. 'Always good to learn something new. I only wish you had told us your plans earlier. Perhaps we could have helped in some way with your research, Isla.'

Giles laughed. 'Oh, come on, Dad. You know you were hoping to keep our little family secret hidden as long as possible.'

'Excuse me…' David Illingworth stared at his son.

'How dare you talk to your father like that. Apologise immediately,' said Faye Illingworth, who Isla imagined must have been very attractive when she was younger.

'I'm not going to apologise until the truth is told. Grandad, would you like to start?'

Isla glanced nervously around the room. She had never heard Giles speak like this before – his assured confidence seemed to come from nowhere – but she looked on as her awkward, unassuming boyfriend commanded the attention of everyone around the table, seemingly unperturbed as to what he was about to say.

'If no one is going to start, then I will,' said Giles boldly. 'Pa Oldroyd was a regular customer at Isla's great-grandpa's barbershop. He used to come in for a straight, slicked-back side-part. It was all the rage. He must have done a good job as he kept returning, week after week, month after month…'

'My father-in-law, your great-grandfather, Pa Oldroyd, was a customer, yes.' Anthony Illingworth spoke slowly as he looked around the room, his attention resting on each guest before settling on Giles. He was a tall, slight man, although his back was now considerably stooped, and Isla imagined him to have possessed the same characteristic lankiness as Giles in his youth. Still, she couldn't imagine someone so frail being capable of betraying anyone. 'Your great-grandfather always told me that Jagger was the best,' Illingworth continued. 'He reckoned he couldn't get a better side-part in the whole of Yorkshire.'

'He must have been quite distraught when the salon suddenly closed then. Of course, not as distraught as Isla's grandpa and the rest of the Jagger family. They were devastated.'

Isla looked incredulously at Giles, who was speaking in a tone that was entirely unfamiliar to her.

'Of course he was distraught. Everyone was. The place was popular,' replied Anthony Illingworth.

'Then why did he do it?'

'Do what?' Anthony Illingworth looked at his grandson calmly.

'For heaven's sake, that's enough,' interrupted David Illingworth from across the table. 'I don't know what's got into you but I think we've heard enough this evening. Have some manners, boy. I'm sure Isla doesn't want to spend her whole evening listening to this rubbish.'

'Oh, I'm sure she does,' said Giles, pushing his plate to the side. Mungo had sauntered into the room, oblivious to the turmoil around him. 'To think I fell for Uncle Pete's lame excuse forbidding me to see Isla because her grandpa was a client of Hillmans. Unethical was the word he used. Seems ironic now.' Giles sat back and looked at his grandfather. 'Well, Grandad…?'

Anthony Illingworth shifted in his seat. 'It was a long time ago. A long time ago. I don't remember.'

'That's okay, I'll remind you,' said Giles emphatically. 'Henry Jagger was working on a formula and the only people who knew about it were his family. I guess once he'd got to the stage he was happy with it, then the plan was that he would commercialise it. Thing is, Mr Jagger died before his invention came to market.'

Silence fell on the room. Only the sound of Mungo's heavy breathing could be heard.

'And that's where Grandad comes in. You see, Pa Oldroyd knew about Henry Jagger's formula. And he knew all the right questions to ask because his son-in-law – Grandad here – was working on a similar lotion. The Jaggers were the competition and it was Pa Oldroyd's role to glean as much information as possible, without making it too obvious, of course.'

Isla wasn't sure whether it was the fading light outside that had turned Anthony Illingworth's complexion an ashen hue or whether the colour really was draining from his face. Either way, a chord had seemingly struck.

'So when it was announced that the Jaggers' salon would

be closing,' said Giles, 'who came to sneak around the premises under the guise of a good friend visiting to say goodbye to the place…?'

Anthony sat motionless; eyes downcast, his hands flat on the table.

'Well, Grandad, is it not true? Did Pa Oldroyd visit Jagger's salon just before it shut down?'

Anthony Illingworth began to shake his head; his lips pursed into a thin, sharp line.

'Grandad seems to have lost the ability to speak, so I'll speak on his behalf. You were right, Isla. My family *did* steal something from Henry Jagger, something that he had been working on for months and years. But while your family were denied that legacy, my family clearly benefitted from it.'

'That's not true, it wasn't like that!' David Illingworth banged his fist vehemently on the table. 'Look how you've upset your grandad. Look at him!'

'Nonsense,' said Giles, gesturing around the room. 'How many homes do we have, Dad? I never know whether to include that rental property in the South of France.'

Isla's gaze remained steadfastly on Mungo, who was lying next to her. She was afraid to look up and she was afraid to speak. Moreover, she was afraid of what she had unleashed.

'Have you said your piece?' Giles' mother had remained silent up until now. 'Your grandad does not deserve to be spoken to like that – especially at his age.'

'Well, he should have thought of that before he stole Mr Jagger's formula.'

'Get out,' shouted Giles' father suddenly. 'Get out now!'

'Oh, don't worry, we will.' Giles rose from his chair and reached for Isla's hand. 'And to think I thought this – the houses, the holidays, everything – was once down to our family's work ethic.' Giles laughed scornfully. 'Let's face it, we are little more than common thieves.'

Isla's face was still lowered when she followed Giles out of the room. 'Wait here,' he said, when they reached the hallway. 'I just need to go upstairs to collect our stuff.' Isla stood nervously by the front door and waited. She could hear Giles above her; the heavy creaking of the floorboards sounded to Isla both strangely comforting yet sinister. It was a beautiful house, but she wouldn't want to be here alone, lost in the capaciousness of it all.

'It's not the evening we had planned for you both,' said Giles' mother, walking towards Isla with something in her hands. 'I don't know what's got into my son. Here, I hope you like tarte tatin. It's not homemade but it's Giles' favourite.' Faye Illingworth presented Isla with a large square box and pushed it towards her like a peace offering. It was secured by a red velvet ribbon and tied into a large bow, and Isla was struck by how beautifully wrapped it was.

'Thank you,' said Isla, 'it's very kind of you,' immediately regretting her words, because they sounded flimsy and insincere, and because she thought Giles' mother neither kind nor deserving of her gratitude.

'I just wanted to say that I'm sorry. We didn't plan for the evening to turn out like this.'

'So we should just forget about it?' Giles had reappeared on the landing. 'It's too late for regret. We can't turn back time, but we can look forward, which is what I intend to do with Isla.'

'Giles, please don't leave like this. Think about what you are saying. Stay the night as planned and we'll talk about it together. Isla – I hope you don't mind being our guest still?'

'I'm sorry, but we're leaving.' Giles quickly walked down the stairs and when he reached the hallway, he brushed past his mother in a final act of defiance before opening the front door, Isla admiring the delicate stained glass motif and the immaculate black wellies one last time. And when they drove away, Isla could see the faint outline of Faye Illingworth with the perfectly wrapped box and its beautiful red bow still in her hands.

It was not long after nine that Giles and Isla returned to the Little Yorkshire Rose Inn, which they had only checked out of that morning. Fortunately, Mrs Hemsworth still had their room available, and under Giles' instructions, a bottle of champagne and two glasses were to be sent up to them straight away. Isla had been too exhausted to talk in the car – her mind a battleground – and was relieved to find Giles equally preoccupied with his own thoughts. The last thing she expected was for them to have a celebratory drink. After all, what on earth could they want to celebrate after this?

'What's with the champagne?'

'I thought we could celebrate.'

'But why? What's there to celebrate? The evening was awful.'

'Nothing quite like meeting the parents, eh?' said Giles, as he helped Isla remove her coat.

'We don't have to drink tonight. I'm tired.'

'Just one glass?'

'Why didn't you tell me what your uncle said? It would have made sense then, this keeping me a secret.'

'I was scared. I didn't want to complicate things.'

'But look what you've done now – it's a mess. I don't know what to believe anymore.'

'At least we still have each other.' Giles patted something in his jacket pocket.

'I don't want to talk about it. I'm really tired, Giles…'

There was a knock on the door. 'Ah, the champagne!' Giles opened the door to Mrs Hemsworth, who was holding a plastic tray with a bottle of champagne and two flutes in her hands. She smiled expectantly at Giles and then at Isla and then she looked at the unpacked suitcases.

'Well, you enjoy yourselves and see you in the morning. Breakfast is—'

'Thank you again, Mrs Hemsworth,' Giles interjected. 'We really appreciate it.' He closed the door gently and turned to Isla.

'Too tired for a glass of the very best champagne this side of Hipperholme?'

'Giles, what's going on? You're behaving really strangely.'

Giles poured the champagne carefully into two glasses, before giving one to Isla. 'This is not quite how I'd planned it. But it's the next best thing given the circumstances.' Isla sat on the edge of the bed as she watched Giles retrieve a small box from his pocket. She took a sip of her champagne, watching the bubbles rise to the surface of her glass.

'Isla Jagger. Isla Isabella Lily Jagger...'

Isla looked up and met Giles' gaze, his eyes full of sincerity; her eyes narrowing suspiciously. *Oh God, please don't do this, not now*, she thought, as she glanced down at a ruby nestled between two small diamonds.

Giles' gaze was steadfast and calm.

'You know how I feel about you.'

Isla's eyes moved from Giles to the open box and then back to Giles, unsure as to where she should look. She glanced back at the box, resting her gaze on the ruby; the warm glow of a table lamp lending a crimson hue to the precious stone as it shimmered in the soft light. 'It's perfect,' she said, leaning closer. 'But I can't, Giles. I'm so sorry, but I can't.'

Giles   42

Approximately eight miles away, Faye Illingworth was rinsing dishes in the sink of her Italian grey marble kitchen. Normally, she would have put everything in the dishwasher but this evening she was glad for the excuse to wash up. Her son had arrived fifteen minutes earlier, incandescent with rage, shouting something about his family having ruined his life. Giles had left Isla in the guesthouse at her insistence, taking his belongings with him. It was, Faye Illingworth conceded, not the most successful dinner party she had ever hosted, the remnants of which still remained. It was like two dogs fighting, she remembered thinking; flesh and blood at each other's throats. With each raised voice, she had become obstreperous, slamming cupboards and clanging pots and pans, as if attempting to either drown out the noise or convey her own anger.

'My girlfriend has just told me, in so many words, that she wants nothing more to do with me.' Giles had let himself in and marched straight to the dining room to face his father and grandfather, who were eating their tarte tatin in silence.

'Oh,' said David Illingworth, dabbing his mouth with a napkin. 'I'm sorry to hear that.'

'Are you?' Giles was shouting now. 'She thinks I'm lying. That I knew about this all along.'

David Illingworth looked at his son, unsure as to whether to say something.

'You know you're going to be found out, right? Stealing the formula, the lives you've ruined.'

'Now listen here, what you are accusing us of is nothing short of tendentious nonsense.' David Illingworth waved his fork in the air like a child with a toy sword. 'If you would just take a moment to listen to the facts at hand, you might be less inclined to accuse us of iniquity.'

'You can't pretend anymore, Dad. There's no use lying to yourself, or to *anyone*, anymore.'

David Illingworth looked impatiently at his father, who returned the look with a reluctant shrug, his bony shoulders rising in an act of resignation as if he no longer cared what happened. 'All right, all right,' David said, inhaling sharply. 'I concede that we took matters into our own hands when Jagger passed away.'

'Finally!' Giles shouted, his voice emanating all the way back to the kitchen. '*Finally!*'

David glanced at his father and Anthony Illingworth nodded, as if to give his consent.

'Well, what else was there to do?' David Illingworth motioned with his hands in the air. 'If it wasn't for Dickie, it wouldn't even have crossed our minds!'

'Dickie?' It was the first Giles had heard of the name.

'Dickie Hainsworth. He was a friend of the Jaggers. He knew where the formula was. He said we would be doing Jagger a favour by safeguarding it. We didn't steal anything. We were *doing* the family a favour.'

'Except you didn't safeguard it, did you? You didn't keep it safe. You commercialised *their* formula, and then took all the credit for it. Just admit it! *Please* just admit it!' Giles banged his fist on the dining table.

David watched as his son lurched precariously before him, his expression contorted.

'Well, I… you see… the thing is…' David's voice trailed off.

Giles turned his attention from his father to his grandfather, whose eyes betrayed no trace of emotion. 'I suppose you have nothing whatsoever to say about this. Nothing whatsoever?'

'Don't…' interrupted David, 'he's too frail to get dragged into this.'

Before anyone could speak, Faye Illingworth walked into the room, a damp tea towel draped over her shoulder. At first, she just stood there, her eyes moving between three generations of men – father, son, grandson – before they finally settled on the one whose expression she felt the most sorry for. 'I am fed up to the teeth hearing the three of you at each other's throats. If you could only see yourselves.' Her voice was measured but it was also full of sadness. '*We* are meant to be *family*.'

'Isla's broken up with me,' said Giles, despair etched across his face. 'She thinks I lied about the whole thing, that I used Uncle Pete as an excuse. Now I know *his* excuse about Mr Jagger being an important client was just a cover-up, so I would keep Isla away from you all.' Giles slumped into a chair, curling into a ball like a child as he placed his head between his hands.

Faye Illingworth walked over to her son and gently placed a hand on his back. Giles flinched. 'Look at what we've done,' she said to her husband. 'He deserves to know the truth, and if you're not going to give it to him, then I will.'

'I don't think—' But before David could finish his sentence, his wife interrupted him.

'That he deserves to know? Or that we should continue to hide the truth?' Faye Illingworth sat down in the chair next to Giles and reached across the table for the nearest bottle of wine, the remains of which she carefully poured into a glass. 'I think we've already caused enough distress for one evening.'

'Well, if we're going to get things straight, then we need to start with Dickie,' said David Illingworth.

'I'd never heard of Dickie before and now he's everywhere.' Giles still had his head in his hands, addressing no one in particular.

David Illingworth nodded at his wife, who in turn took a large sip of wine, before turning to speak to her son. 'Dickie was a friend of the Jaggers and an acquaintance of your great-grandfather's. Dickie found the formula at Jagger's salon, just before it was due to be boarded up and sold on. That's as much as we knew, or at least as much as he told us.'

'I've gone through this already...' David interrupted.

Faye Illingworth shot a look at her husband. 'I haven't finished,' she said, before continuing. 'Dickie said it would be a great shame for the formula to get lost, to have all of Jagger's work undone. And because Dickie wasn't in the business, so to speak, he asked your great-grandfather, or rather your grandad, if he might find a way to commercialise it.'

'So, just to be clear,' interrupted Giles, 'this Dickie fella stole the formula from Henry Jagger's salon, without asking anyone, without permission, basically without anyone knowing, and gave it to Pa Oldroyd?'

'Well, yes,' said Faye Illingworth sheepishly.

'And Pa Oldroyd gave it to Grandad here, who basically traded the formula off as his own?'

'Well, I suppose that's what it probably amounted to.' Faye Illingworth looked at her husband.

'What I don't understand...' said Giles, moving his hands away from his head, '...is what was in it for Dickie.'

'We paid him, of course, for the formula, which at the time would have been a substantial amount. I don't suppose you remember how much exactly, do you, Anthony?'

Anthony Illingworth narrowed his eyes, his brow furrowed in concentration; trying to recollect the one thing he had been asked. A few moments passed. Everyone remained silent.

'Never mind, Dad,' said David impatiently. 'It was a long time ago.'

'But I suppose whatever *you* paid was worth all that money you went on to make,' said Giles sarcastically.

Husband and wife exchanged glances, while Anthony Illingworth continued to eat his pudding.

'So, what's next? What are you going to do about it?' Giles stood up and began pacing the room. 'It can't just end here. Surely you didn't think this would be it?'

'We hadn't thought that far ahead. It's a lot to think about in one evening.' Faye Illingworth watched her son move across her dining room.

'What I mean is how are you going to pay the Jaggers back? You *are* going to pay them back?' Giles said.

David Illingworth suddenly rose from his chair, smoothing the creases in his shirt. 'Your mother is right. We need to talk about this properly.'

Anthony Illingworth, who had remained silent up until now, coughed loudly. Everyone turned to look at him. 'You have *my* word that the Jaggers will receive every penny we have taken,' he said, pushing his plate to one side. 'On *one* condition…'

The letter   43

The fish and chip shop wasn't open when Giles arrived just after eight the following morning. He had left his parents' house before anyone could ask him where he was going, and despite the lightness in the late summer air, Giles' heart was heavy. He had lost Isla, all hope of her, and the realisation seeped through him like an unwanted poison. He had half hoped that she might have retraced her steps back to Hipperholme, to make sense of everything that had happened the evening before, to be waiting for him; to even accept his proposal. But deep down he knew he would be waiting in vain. Isla had probably gone straight to London.

Louisa didn't recognise Giles at first, only when he mentioned Isla – the girl with the wavy chestnut hair was how he described her – did her memory seem to jolt into action. She took him to the back of the shop where it was quieter, and Giles glanced around the shabby room, imagining what the place might have looked like when Henry Jagger owned the premises: slick, definitely bustling, and at its heart an ambitious barber with a thriving business and a well-wrapped secret that simmered beneath the surface. Only it wasn't well wrapped and it didn't remain secret for long.

Giles told Louisa everything: meeting Isla, his uncle's threat, about Mr Jagger and the unravelling of his parents' secret. Louisa listened without judgement, her beady eyes narrowing only once. Just as he hoped, without wavering, without hesitation, she confirmed everything. Yes, Dickie had known where the formula was kept. Yes, Dickie had taken the formula when the shop was about to be boarded up. Yes, Louisa could confirm that Dickie went on to sell the formula to Edward Oldroyd, whom, she added, she was rather scared of as a young girl. And yes, Mrs Jagger – God bless her soul – wasn't aware of anything.

'Why didn't you say anything at the time?' Giles tried to imagine Louisa in the first flush of youth.

'I don't know...' Louisa shrugged her shoulders. 'Besides, Mr Oldroyd... he had this way about him.'

'What do you mean?' Giles wondered what it was about Pa Oldroyd that had intimidated Louisa.

'I were too scared to say anything to him. Even if I wanted to, I were too scared.'

'And Dickie?'

'Dickie were not much older than me. Not much ruffled his feathers. He were always teasing and joking with everyone.'

'But why didn't you say anything at the time? Report him at least?'

'Because I didn't think he were doing anything wrong. I thought he were doing Mr Jagger a *favour*, helping to tidy up, keeping that cream from getting into the wrong hands.'

Only it did get into the wrong hands, Giles thought, *his* family's hands.

'Besides, there was the letter...' she added. The letter, which Louisa said she still had in her wooden box of "important things", was like a precious jewel that had suddenly been unearthed. 'That's what stopped me from saying anything.'

'The letter?'

'Yes, the letter. Everything you need to know is in the letter.'

Louisa met Giles the following morning, having promised to bring with her the letter that provided evidence of Dickie's wrongdoing. She had described the wooden box and its place under her bed, and the letter, which although now faded, was still legible and in its original envelope. It was as if Louisa had waited for this moment all these years, and now her time had come.

'Keep it,' she said, pressing a flimsy envelope into Giles' hand. 'I've no need for it anymore. It's yours.'

'Are you sure?' Giles looked down at the envelope, which had Louisa's full name written in faded, elaborate handwriting. 'Don't you want to keep it? I mean, just in case...'

Louisa snorted. 'I'm old. It's of no use to me now. You do something with it. Make things right again.'

Dear Louisa,

How are you? Are you and your parents keeping well? And brother Tommy?

You are probably as shocked as I am at the sudden death of our friend Mr Jagger. He was one of those people who won't be forgotten easily, and I know we will all do our best to keep his memory alive.

I know you would want the best for Mr Jagger, and that's why I don't want you to concern yourself with matters that you wouldn't understand anyway. Just please know that I am trying to help the man in his death by protecting the things that were important to him during his life. The last thing I want at this terrible time is to disturb his family with worries on top of everything else.

Well, Louisa, I know you will do right by Mr Jagger and not tell a single soul about the cream I took when you helped me clear up that afternoon. All you need to know is

that Mr Oldroyd is kindly taking care of it. And by a single
soul, I mean your good parents and brother Tommy too,
who I know is looking forward to a visit from Edgar soon.
Don't forget the liquorice!

  I know you are a good sort, and a lass who can keep
a very important secret, so my words here are just a
reminder. In fact, I think you should read this letter often
so you don't forget. Keep it safe too.

  Finally, if you are ever asked about the cream, just say
you don't know – anything. I'm a great believer in keeping
things simple. And by doing that, I promise Mr Jagger
will be looking down at you from above, pleased that you,
Louisa, can be trusted.

  Yours,
  Richard Hainsworth (Dickie)
  Lightcliffe
  (29th January 1921)

As Giles stood there in the soft September light, he felt at once
relief and revulsion, incredulity and horror. He had read the
letter in front of Louisa, and now that he was alone, he read it
again, rereading it ten, twenty times. He had the final piece of
the jigsaw in his hand; the final piece that would be the downfall
of his family. His overriding emotion was shame. Ashamed to
be an Illingworth. Ashamed to be the great-grandson of Edward
Oldroyd. Ashamed it had taken him this long to discover the
truth. Despite the shame, Giles wasn't ready to leave his parents'
house yet.

  He had one more thing to do.

  Then he would decide on his next steps.

Jack   44

The truth, in its entirety, was like an avalanche of revelations hurtling towards Jack, one on top of the other. Not only was there the Illingworths' betrayal to contend with but Dickie Hainsworth's too. At least he had been prepared for the Illingworths' wrongdoing – there was certainly relief in having decades of suspicion finally come to light – but to discover Hainsworth's shameless perfidy brought with it the strangest sensation. The fact that Dickie could have betrayed him like that left Jack feeling totally bereft and questioning his own discernment. 'I had an inkling there was something not quite right with Oldroyd. But Dickie? I thought he was a *friend*. My father's friend. My mother's friend. *My* friend. To think he had been our enemy all along and no one had any idea who the man really was. The whole thing is just utterly incomprehensible.'

'But you weren't to know,' replied Anna, trying to offer words of solace.

'What a mess,' Jack said with a sigh as he gazed into the garden; the afternoon light casting a long shadow against the trees. 'To think he offered to help my mother, take us boys under his wing when my father died. Now we know he was little more than a wolf in sheep's clothing.' Jack's eyes followed the movement of a squirrel and, for a second, he drifted momentarily into its world before his thoughts returned again to his family. His family, a fragmented family, a family that had also been betrayed.

Jack was also strangely sorry – strange, because he never expected to feel that way – that Giles had left the country and was now teaching English at a remote school in the Himalayas, as if all this were the poor lad's fault. He glanced across at the bureau with the large brown envelope on top. Inside was a handwritten note from Louisa and her letter from Dickie. A separate letter had arrived from Faye Illingworth, which, underneath meticulous handwriting, included an email address. An email address? Jack had never used an email address. If Faye Illingworth expected a reply, then she would receive a handwritten letter. Jack had read Louisa's note first, which struck him as being almost child-like. She had introduced herself as *Mr Henry Jagger's assistant, the lass from Brighouse with two brown braids.* According to her letter, Louisa Ainscough began working for Mr Jagger when she was thirteen years old, *helping to keep the place clean and proper.* At first, Louisa and her childlike words drew only confusion in Jack's mind, but then slowly an image appeared: a girl standing in his father's salon with a broom in her hand. Someone who was always present but whom nobody had taken much notice of, least of all Jack.

Now it was all coming back, like a wave gathering momentum.

'Oh, Dad, how awful,' said Tilly, during one of their Sunday phone calls.

'It's Dickie I'm hurt by the most. He was a friend, Tilly, a *friend.* A father figure in many respects. Someone I looked up to. It's remarkable really.'

'Come to think of it, Celia said something to me once when

she was working on my wedding dress. Something that sounded a bit odd at the time.'

'About the formula?'

'No, no, I can't remember exactly, something about being indebted to us. It was just a strange thing to say. It didn't really make sense but then with the wedding coming up, I didn't read into it too much. What do you think you'll do now?'

Jack's voice had a trace of resignation. 'There's not an awful lot one can do. Apart from forgive.'

'I meant in terms of the money? Do you think you'll accept it? Under the conditions they stipulated?'

'I'm really not sure...' Jack could hear Tilly drawing on her cigarette and imagined her sitting in the chair by the hallway window, looking out at the waning crescent moon.

'Isla said she received a copy of your letter from Faye Illingworth. She's still very angry with Giles. Says he mislead her. She refuses to believe his side of the story, whatever that was.'

'It's been a shock to everyone,' said Jack, sighing. 'But Louisa's letter suggests that Giles only wanted to help unravel the truth. She wrote that he visited her to find out whether she may have remembered anything when she worked for my father. When he confided to her his family's secret, it was then Louisa told him about the letter. The poor lad was devastated.'

'And from that, Dickie and the Illingworths' betrayal was able to be proven, I suppose?'

'Yes. Isla and Giles really set the wheels in motion.'

'But how did Giles know where to find her in the first place?'

'Louisa wrote in her letter that they met by chance when they visited my father's old premises.'

'And what about the terms and conditions?'

'Yes, there's the matter of that too,' said Jack, sighing. 'The Illingworths' terms and conditions.'

The next person to call on Jack's list was Harry. As far as Jack was concerned, Harry had been left relatively unscathed from the fallout of the Illingworths' betrayal. It was *Jack* who had supported his mother when their father had died. It was *Jack* who had sacrificed his education and found work. But the little voice in Jack's head started to reason with him, reminding him that it was petty to view life like this; silly, begrudging, pointless. None of this was Harry's fault, no more than Jack could have avoided his own early fate. Jack was beginning to realise that the problem with Harry was *him*.

'Hello, Harry. How are you?' Jack's tone was formal and cool, a tone that was in complete contrast to the tone he had used with Tilly. 'Are you free to chat for a few minutes?'

'Of course. Everything all right?'

Jack shifted in his chair. It was a while since they had last spoken. 'Well, yes – and no. Do you remember Dickie Hainsworth? He used to visit us when Father died. He would have been a young lad at the time.'

'No, I don't think so… no…' Harry paused. 'Why?'

'Because I have something important to tell you about Dickie and Father.'

Jack took a deep breath and proceeded to tell his brother about their father's formula; about Edward Oldroyd and Dickie's betrayal; about Giles and Isla's relationship, their revelatory evening with the Illingworths and now the letters. Harry listened attentively, only interrupting once. It was a question Jack wasn't prepared for, not least because it had taken him by surprise. 'Does Hanson know about any of this?'

'Well, I haven't told anyone apart from Anna and Tilly.'

'Don't you find it odd that you've told Tilly, but not your own son?'

'Not really. It's just the way things are.' It had been almost two years since Jack and Anna had seen Hanson. Ever since their visit to Norfolk, they had not heard from him or Maggie. It saddened Jack not to share something so significant with his son, but why would he tell Hanson about the legacy now? Hanson had made it clear there would be no going forward if things stayed the same, if Tilly was still in his life. 'Remarkable really, of all the men Isla could meet, it had to be that Illingworth lad.'

'You say that, and call me a fool for suggesting it, but perhaps there is an element of fate at play here. Put it this way, if Isla and Giles had never met, you would most likely never have got to the bottom of all this.'

'Yes, I suppose, when you put it like that...'

'Now I don't for one minute want to appear as if I am excusing their behaviour, but at least the family has said sorry and offered to pay compensation.'

'But what about the betrayal of our father? Aren't you angry?'

'Why would I be angry? It happened so long ago. We were lads. These things happen.'

Jack shook his head, glad to be at the other end of a phone line rather than face to face with his pragmatic brother. 'I wonder, do you have email by any chance?'

'Email?' Harry laughed. 'Doesn't everyone now?'

'Oh,' said Jack, somewhat taken aback.

'Everyone uses it these days to correspond and communicate.'

'Everyone apart from me, it would seem.' There was a hint of self-deprecation in Jack's voice. 'The letter, by the way, came from Faye Illingworth. As for Dickie, I don't suppose he harboured any remorse. Not that I'll ever know. He died eighteen months ago, about a year after his wife. Cancer. I even went to the funeral.'

'Shocking to think he took something like that to the grave.'

'The thing is, none of what Dickie did actually altered his behaviour towards me. He remained as affable and friendly as ever. When one thinks about it, it's quite psychopathic really.'

'Dickie made money from the formula too?'

'Yes, they built up a large network of express tailor shops all over the country, but it's managed by the children now. To think I didn't find it odd then.'

'What do you mean?'

'Well, the ease with which Dickie established the business and became successful. You need some capital for that. *Now* I know where he got it from.'

'And the Illingworths? What have you decided?' Harry's tone was perfunctory.

'I hoped to ask your opinion before I did anything.' Jack hesitated for a moment. He wanted to talk about the barbershop, the secret formula and how sad he was that the Jagger name would never receive the recognition it deserved. But he wasn't even sure Harry would understand. How could he? His brother barely knew their father and what he had worked so hard for.

'I don't see what there is to decide. If you want my opinion, go ahead and accept the conditions as they are. It's only right that the profits are returned to the family.'

'And you think not involving the law and settling it between ourselves, which is obviously their preference – the terms and conditions they stipulate – is the best way to deal with this?'

'I don't see the point of making a fuss. Just accept the terms and conditions.'

'And everything our father worked towards, his legacy... we should just let the Illingworths continue to take credit for it? Take credit for their best-selling cream?'

'It's done and dusted. Life moves on. As long as the profits are returned, it makes no odds to me who takes credit for it.'

*

Some six months later, Jack received a cheque from David Illingworth. Nothing was enclosed apart from a small Post-it attached to the inside of the envelope with the words *Kind regards, the Illingworths.* Jack held the cheque in his hand for a long time. *So this is what my father's legacy has amounted to,* he thought. *A legacy that took years to perfect is now a flimsy piece of paper to be deposited into my bank account.* He didn't feel triumphant or self-satisfied. He wasn't upset either. He simply felt at peace.

Jack already knew he wasn't going to keep the money. What would he do with it anyway? He was in his eighties and he had lived his life. He also had everything he wanted; except, that is, a relationship with his son. And all the money in the world could not bring Hanson back. What Jack wanted to do was invest the money in the future; the next generation, *his* family. How could he put the money to good use? How could he help them? He knew he didn't want his daughter-in-law to be left in the precarious position of trying to pay off the rest of her mortgage after she retired; after everything *she* had been through. He also wanted to help Isla. Young people don't have it easy, thought Jack, with getting on any kind of ladder these days. He knew Craig had dreams beyond the bank and he wanted to help his grandson realise them. He wanted to help his stepdaughter too. He was so proud of what Lizzie was achieving in Singapore, what she could *still* achieve. *This* would be his father's legacy.

When Jack told Tilly his plans, he didn't see the tears that had begun to form around her eyes. Here was her father-in-law – technically ex-father-in-law – who was prepared to make life easier, more comfortable for her. Jack didn't owe her anything, but he had shown her, not only in that moment but all along, what the notion of family truly meant to him. Tilly wiped her eyes and felt her tears; salty and sticky against her cheeks. She wasn't really sure why she was crying. She only knew that Jack's generosity had deeply moved her, that sorrow and joy were closely aligned and that they had come to her in equal measure.

Craig

45

'It's not for the faint-hearted, you know,' said Jack to his grandson, who was pouring the contents of an ice-cold can of Coke into a tall glass. 'There's long hours and staff to pay. Expertise to invest in too. Not forgetting the weekends you'll have to give up. Are you really sure about this?'

Craig had long wanted to extricate himself from the banking world. The procedures, the bureaucracy, the suits and ties. They made him feel like a caged animal. 'I've never been more sure, Grandpa. If it's my own business then I'll put absolutely everything into it. *Even* the weekends.'

'But why a pub?' Tilly was playing the role of devil's advocate in the corner of Jack and Anna's living room.

'Because I like pubs,' said Craig with a smirk. 'And I think it's something I could really make a success of.'

'Be serious,' retorted Tilly. 'Can you really imagine giving up your free time? All the things you love doing?'

'I'll employ staff once I've established the business. I know it's not going to be easy, but I'm willing to put in everything I've got. There's no way I'm going to work in the bank for the rest of my life.'

The conversation continued; Jack and Tilly teasing out every eventuality of what could go wrong until it was clear that Craig's dream had not been built upon some fantastical notion conjured up on a whim. After some minutes, Jack sat back in his chair, seemingly satisfied with his grandson's answers. 'In that case, if you are absolutely certain, then like I said, I'm going to help. I'll provide the capital, help you invest, and you can build your business from there.'

Craig stared incredulously at his grandfather before glancing at Tilly and Anna. He was waiting for laughter to ensue and to be told this had all been a silly joke. But there wasn't any laughter, and Tilly and Anna were sitting upright in their chairs, reverently marking the significance of Jack's words.

'Are you sure about this? The capital – it's a lot of money. How can I ever repay you?'

'I'm only passing on what has been returned to the family. There's no need for repayment.'

'I don't know what to say. Grandpa, this is a game changer.'

Jack smiled; the characteristic mischievous smile that he wore when all was well in his world. 'Well, my boy. Let's just say that life has come full circle.'

Isla   46

Isla had flown straight to Berlin not only to escape the aftermath of her break-up with Giles and the revelations that followed, but also because she couldn't bear to be back in London. She was staying with a friend in the north of the city whose Greek husband, Freideríkos, had recently relocated for work. Isla had initially envied the seeming simplicity of Abigail's life: the impressive home they were renting with its airy, palatial feel and the absence of worry that came with simply having nothing more to do than to follow one's husband around the world and conduct an internal debate as to whether white bath towels might be better than grey. Until, that is, Isla saw the reality of the situation. It wasn't so much what Abigail had become. It was how drastic the becoming had been: the anger and disappointment that was etched around the sharp angles of her friend's face had shocked Isla the most. That first morning, Isla had cautiously watched Abigail in the kitchen complaining about the loss of another night's sleep. 'I don't know where Angelo gets his energy from to keep me awake like that. I mean, what do other mothers do?'

As if I have all the answers, Isla thought.

'Freddie of course was out for the count. He sleeps through everything and then wonders why I'm irritable the next day.' Abigail began to chop a banana. 'I swear if he doesn't stop, I'm going to move to one of the guest rooms. Permanently.'

'Why don't you just put Angelo to bed and if he starts crying then just leave him? He'll soon tire himself out surely.'

Abigail stopped what she was doing and froze.

'I mean, I'm no expert, but I read somewhere that babies thrive on routine.'

'That's right, you are no expert,' retorted Abigail, turning round. 'You haven't the first idea what it means to have a baby, let alone look after one. I have to do what's right for Angelo, not what some dusty book tells me to do.'

'I was only trying to help.'

'Wait until *you* become a mother and see how bloody hard it is to never have a moment to yourself, to walk around with vomit on your shirt and in your hair, no matter how many times you've cleaned yourself that day. Hoping to God your baby stops crying so you can finally get a few moments' rest.'

'If it's so bad… it's just, well, it's just that you don't really seem to be enjoying it…' Isla's voice trailed nervously into what was barely a mumble. 'I mean, why did you—'

'Have a baby?' Abigail interjected.

Neither said a word, and for a moment the two women looked at each other suspiciously.

Abigail turned around. '*Nobody* told me it would be this bloody difficult.' She pointed at a piece of unfinished toast and its residual crumbs tossed from its plate onto the dining table; at the soft toys strewn around the room and at the large pile of soiled bibs that lay on the kitchen counter. 'Don't you want to have all of this one day?'

Isla pulled a face. 'I'd like to see the world. The *whole* world.'

Abigail picked up a soft toy from the floor.

'Did you know there are almost as many penguins in Patagonia as there are people?'

But Abigail wasn't paying any attention. She was standing very still with her finger pressed against her lips and she was slowly tiptoeing towards the door. '*Scheisse*. Can you hear Angelo crying again? I only put him down an hour ago. What's wrong with him? What does he want *now*?'

It had been somewhat of a revelation to see Abigail like this. Moreover, Isla felt sorry for her friend for having settled. Everyone knew that Abigail was only telling half the story, the side she wanted people to see. She had been at a crossroads and Freideríkos turned up at just the right time. Abigail insisted it was fate, of course; boasted about the trips to Paris and New York and how she and Freideríkos met in a bar in Malaysia thousands of miles away from home. Fancy that, Abigail exclaimed, trying to convince herself and others of the fortuitous serendipity at play. Yet scratch away at the surface and Abigail began to admit, reluctantly at first, that she wasn't attracted to Freideríkos; that he sometimes repulsed her. He's growing on me, she announced one day, as if Freideríkos were an experimental fungi she were trying out for size. Even when Abigail's mother had tried to reason with her that marrying a man whom she wasn't in love with might not be the best idea, her daughter refused to renege. She was going to get married and that was it. The rest can follow, she had reasoned, and besides, she no longer wanted to go back to her previous life. She had outgrown it and Freideríkos was the exit she was looking for.

'I'm going to take him out,' said Abigail, hoping the fresh November air would induce sleep in her sleepless son. 'How about you? Any plans?'

'I was going to hang out here for a bit if that's okay.'

'Lucky you,' said Abigail. 'I can't remember the last time I sat around all day doing nothing...'

When Abigail left, Isla tiptoed nervously around the house, enjoying the silence and the sensation of cool marble against her bare feet. She wandered into the living room, her eyes settling on a silver framed wedding photograph. It had been a classy affair, elegant and intimate. She remembered the sound of the jazz band and the intense aroma of cheese and smoked meats floating around them while Greek guests politely sidestepped the British; and as they toasted the couple in their huge garden with its views of Athens in the distance, Freideríkos had dramatically lifted Abigail in the air (although he had clearly struggled with the exertion – poor Freddie, thought Isla) as if she were a prized doll that he had won.

Isla was still staring at the wedding photograph when she heard the sound of her Nokia ringtone. She reached into her pocket, glad to see her mother's name on the tiny screen. '*Mein Schatz*, how are you?' said Tilly, and Isla smiled at the familiarity of her mother's voice. She placed the mobile phone against her ear while carefully replacing the frame back on the table.

'I'm fine, Mum. What about you?' Isla let her body sink to the floor and listened to Tilly relay the news about her grandpa and the money from the Illingworths.

'He knows how difficult it is for young people to get on the ladder these days, especially in London, and he, well, he knows how happy you are in Berlin. You don't have to make a decision now, but give it some thought.'

The gentle hum of the dishwasher was whirring in the background and Isla was relieved that Abigail was still out with Angelo. Her heart was racing. She hadn't expected this. She simply assumed she would do it alone. One day, maybe all her savings would amount to something. Her mother certainly had never been in a position to help her with a deposit, and her father – well, she never dared ask him for anything. She didn't want to rely on a man either. Where was the sense of accomplishment in that? Besides, weren't those men always much older or controlling? Either way, it didn't sound like a good idea. Isla placed her head in her hands and tried to steady her breathing. There had already been so much to take in – Giles' proposal, the Illingworths' lies, the hair formula – and now this. Grandpa was going to help buy her a flat? Help Craig set up a business? Help her mother? From the Illingworths' compensation? Now technically her ex-boyfriend's family. It seemed so unreal.

'*Schatz*, are you all right?'

'Yes, just taking everything in…'

'I know. It's still very fresh…'

'And this – it means I can really live here?' Isla spoke slowly, not quite believing her own words.

'Yes, if that's what you want. *Is* it want you want?'

'Yes, I think so.'

'Grandpa will help Craig with his new venture.'

'How can we ever thank him?'

'Well, you can start by calling him first thing. He'll appreciate that. When are you coming home?'

'End of next week,' said Isla, lowering her voice. 'Unless Abigail throws me out first. Things aren't great here. She's really rattled with the baby *and* her husband. Poor Freddie. And there I was thinking she was living the perfect life.'

'Like I've always said, *Schatz,* we never know what goes on behind closed doors.'

'Especially these doors,' said Isla, easing herself up from the floor. 'I'd better go, Mum. I have a feeling Abi will be home soon.'

Isla wandered into the kitchen and scribbled something on a piece of paper. Then she placed it where her friend was likely to see it – in front of a worn paperback that was propped up against a series of cookbooks on the kitchen counter; one of the many books Abigail still insisted on finding the time to read. Let's hope art doesn't imitate life, she thought, glancing at the paperback. It was Gustave Flaubert's *Madame Bovary*.

The cold northerly wind whipped Isla's face as she headed towards the station. It was a quiet neighbourhood, safe and unassuming with its neat row of shops and *gasthaus* at the end of the main road and a *biergarten* that thronged with people in the warmer months. Now the days were darker, the camaraderie took place inside, and men with ruddy cheeks and red noses drank their afternoons away while their wives indulged in *kaffee* and *kuchen* in the main café at the opposite end of the street. The air in the *U-Bahn* was warm and Isla loosened her scarf as she made her way towards the trains going into the city. She found an empty seat and rested her head against the glass pane, recalling all the times she had been here: first as a teenager, two years after the fall of the Berlin Wall, to now on the precipice of twenty-five; the city a shiny bright magnet for creatives. Isla never knew Berlin as it was: divided, intimidating, full of secrets. Only what it was morphing into: a city of possibility, a place to start over.

Outside, the late November sunshine cast a hazy film over the skyline. Oranienburgerstraße still looked the same. The imposing solemnity of its most significant landmark, the Neue Synagoge, looked incongruous next to the stream of restaurants and bars nestled on either side of the house of worship. Isla walked towards Café Orange, and felt an overwhelming sense of wellbeing. Her life had changed irrevocably in less than an hour and it would never be the same again. She found a table near the window, her favourite spot, and browsed the menu with new eyes, even though she had read it countless times before. Isla ordered a coffee and the lunch special: salmon on pumpernickel with a cup of beetroot soup.

'*Noch was?*' asked the waitress, a trace of nonchalance in her voice.

'*Nein danke. Ist schon gut.*'

As the waitress wrote down the order, Isla noticed her sinewy arms. Both were marked with tattoos, including a tiny heart motif on the side of her left wrist with the words *love rules* inked on it. Isla had always envied the lives of people living in this city, the effortless way they *lived* their lives. Life was within reach here. In London, everything seemed out of reach, unobtainable. Now, though, things would be different. She would be *living* in this city, in her *own* apartment, no longer the observer. She would live alone and please herself, find a job on a local magazine, come here for coffee as often as she liked.

And she wouldn't miss home at all.

47

'We thought you'd gone missing,' shouted Abigail from the upstairs bathroom as Isla walked through the door.

'Gone where?' Isla shouted back.

'Gone missing!' Abigail's response was more like a bellow.

Isla took off her coat and placed it on a peg by the front entrance. Freideríkos was at the kitchen table, poring over a newspaper. He was wearing a white vest, which was partly tucked into his jeans, and his forehead had lingering beads of sweat on it. 'Hello, Freddie.' Isla said cheerily as she came into the kitchen. 'How was your day?'

'Oh, you know...' he began, his English heavily accented. 'This and that. My boss is, how you say, a real pain in backside.' Freideríkos put his newspaper to one side and brushed crumbs onto a plate, which had the remnants of a half-eaten *Berliner*. 'German way is not same as Greek way.'

'How do you mean?' Isla poured herself a glass of water.

'Well, the German way is very... how you say it?' Freideríkos used a chopping motion against the table to emphasise his point. 'Strict. Very strict. It's too much strict.'

'At least they get things done,' said Abigail, who had reappeared. She was carrying Angelo in one arm and in the other a heavy wool coat. 'Here, take him for a moment, please. I need to finish getting ready.' Freideríkos extended his arms towards his son and gently eased him into his chest.

'Good afternoon?' Abigail asked as she turned to Isla, draping the coat carefully on a kitchen chair.

'Yes, I had lunch at Café Orange.' Isla glanced nervously at husband and wife, waiting for the inevitable dynamic to play out between them.

'How I wish I could have time to gallivant about.' Abigail was standing in front of a mirror carefully applying mascara; all the while keeping one eye on her husband and one eye on her son.

'Are Greek bosses better to work for?' Isla sat down opposite Freideríkos. 'Because my experience of the two English ones was pretty awful.'

'Greek boss no better,' said Freideríkos, his mouth full of the half-eaten *Berliner*.

'Freddie!' Abigail shouted from across the room. 'I can't believe you are eating a doughnut and we have a dinner reservation in an hour!'

'I was hungry.'

'And why aren't you dressed? I'm sure Isla doesn't want to see you with just your vest on and stomach hanging out.'

Freideríkos rolled his eyes and Isla could see from his expression that his wife's remarks had embarrassed him. 'I'll take him if you like,' said Isla, gesturing at the baby. 'It's okay, you get ready upstairs.'

Freideríkos shifted in his chair as he tried to manoeuvre it towards Isla, but the sudden movement woke Angelo, who immediately began to cry. 'I think he needs changing,' he said, holding the baby in the air.

'I apologise on behalf of my husband,' said Abigail, marching towards him. 'Anyone would think Freddie is the baby here,

311

with jam all over his face, sticky fingers and crumbs everywhere.'
Abigail disappeared into the nursery and Freideríkos sighed
dramatically as he rose lethargically from his chair.

'At least you won't have to cook this evening,' said Isla,
watching Freideríkos walk wearily towards the stairs. He waved
a hand in acknowledgment before disappearing from view. Poor
Freddie, he can't help the way he is, thought Isla. She could see
the resignation in his eyes; the reality of his marriage playing out
in full view of the world like an Ibsen play. Still, Isla felt more
sorry for Abigail; for all the frustrations her friend harboured
towards her life, a life she had somehow imagined otherwise.

Later that evening, Isla was sitting cross-legged in the
nursery; a pen in hand and notebook on her lap. Angelo was
asleep nearby in his cot and she was listening to the rhythmic
sounds of his breathing. He had cried at first and resisted Isla's
attempts to try and comfort him. But eventually, as she carried
his heavy body from room to room, his warm, wet cheek pressed
against hers, he acquiesced. And when she laid him down,
Angelo had clutched Isla's finger with his tiny, chubby hands as
if to bid her goodnight. She hadn't noticed his long eyelashes
before. Or the way his grey eyes sparkled when he broke into
a dimpled smile. She only knew his cries had been relentless
and Abigail's anger was like a boiling pot waiting to implode.
But tonight had been different. Isla picked up her notebook
with its half-written list of neighbourhoods – Charlottenburg,
Prenzlauer Berg, Schöneberg – she thought she might like to
live in and wondered whether she should tell Abigail how easy
it had been with the baby. That it just required a little bit of
patience, some tenderness. And then she decided against it. For
everyone's sakes.

PART 5

Maggie

48

'I was thinking of cooking the Namibian beef stew,' shouted Maggie from the upstairs bathroom. 'Do you remember we tried it last year in South Africa?' Maggie was staring at her reflection in the mirror. She was not sure whether Hanson had heard her, but as she began to pick at the silvery threads in her hair, it suddenly occurred to her that she needed to start thinking about recipes for Isla and Max's visit. Maggie's bathroom ritual took longer these days. She was forty-four years old and her thick raven hair was not what it was. Maggie had first noticed the greys a few years ago, and it was then that she began toying with the idea of dying her hair blonde. Dark just seemed so impractical now.

They had moved to the house in Old Buckenham while Hanson was in the process of selling the hotel; both agreeing it was nice to finally live somewhere that felt like a real home. Hanson had looked forward to retirement. Forty years in the industry was more than enough, he had told Maggie, and he wanted to step away before too many hotels were ruined by brash international buyers with money and no clue; a concoction that made him shudder. Now he would have time for all the things he enjoyed. The only catch was that Maggie wasn't going to be spending it with him. She had taken on a management role at another establishment, excited by a new chapter. Hanson was excited for her too. Although, and he would never admit this, he thought increasingly about the age gap between them. There was something comforting in growing old together without having to wait for Maggie to catch up. Of course, she would never catch up. She had a long way to go until she was at the point that he had already reached.

'I'm thinking of going blonde and cooking the beef stew we enjoyed so much in Africa,' Maggie announced, finding Hanson sitting in the garden with his headphones on.

'What was that?' Hanson removed an earphone from his ear.

'I can't keep up with all these greys so I've decided to go blonde. And I've decided to cook the beef dish we loved in Africa, you know, for Isla and Max's visit.'

'Not at the same time, I hope,' said Hanson, smirking.

'No, sweetheart, I think I'll tackle the beef first. Do you think you'll like me blonde?'

'Why not? I think you would even look fabulous with pink hair if you felt so inclined.'

'You know that's not what I meant.' Maggie removed a newspaper from Hanson's knee and positioned herself in its place. 'You've always said you've never been one for blondes.'

'I should hope not. Nor brunettes, redheads or raven beauties either. You're the only one that I'm interested in.' Hanson took Maggie's hand and kissed it.

Maggie laughed and wondered where her newfound insecurities stemmed from. She was still a woman in her prime yet couldn't help but feel her youth was something she had long ago wrapped away in a box. And she was worried Hanson might start seeing her that way too. 'What were you listening to?' she said, wriggling free from Hanson's strong, tanned arms.

'The Test Match.' Hanson shielded his eyes from the sun as he watched Maggie walk back towards the house.

'I wonder what your father makes of it all. No doubt he'll be watching too.'

But Hanson didn't reply. He had put his headphones back on and his eyes were already closed.

*

It was one of those evenings that could have gone rather well were it not for Maggie's nerves. 'A Namibian dish,' she repeated to herself as she paced up and down the kitchen, flapping her oven glove around as charred meat lingered in the air. 'A Namibian dish! Who on earth cooks a Namibian dish in Norfolk!' Maggie opened the fridge door and glanced at the champagne, which was intended for Isla and Max's arrival. She picked it up and held it against her face, feeling the coolness against her cheek. It wouldn't hurt to have a glass already, she thought, as she began to twist the cork upwards. The sharp tang of the crisp bubbles tasted bittersweet in her mouth and she felt immediately soothed. She knew what this weekend meant to Hanson, not least because his daughter had never introduced a boyfriend to her father and this in itself was a big deal, but also because he hadn't seen his daughter for eight years. And Maggie, if she was completely honest with herself, was slightly anxious about the whole thing.

'You made it,' said Hanson warmly, as he took Isla's and Max's bags and placed them at the foot of the stairs. 'How on earth did you get lost, though? I thought my directions were good.'

'They were,' said Max nervously, for he was well aware of the Jagger history. 'It's just, well, I've only recently passed my test. And I don't really know this part of the world.'

'Well, you are both safe and sound, that's the main thing,' said Hanson, leading them into the living room. 'Do you drink champagne, Max?' asked Hanson, turning towards him.

'No, thanks. I'd prefer a soft drink, please.'

'Ah, a teetotaller in the house,' said Maggie. 'We don't usually entertain teetotallers, do we, sweetheart?'

Max exchanged looks with Isla and, from her expression, he knew she was thinking the same: it was only three hours to midnight but it was going to be a very long evening.

'Diet Coke okay?' Maggie asked.

'Great, thanks.'

'Now, I need to warn you that supper is not exactly what I'd planned. You both eat beef, don't you?' The guests nodded politely. 'Well, this is going to be a Namibian beef stew. Just a slightly overcooked version.'

Isla found it strange that Maggie should go to all the effort of making a South African dish, when she knew Maggie didn't really enjoy cooking. Even more strange, she thought, was that her father should have chosen two very different women. In fact, the only obvious thing her mother and Maggie seemed to have in common was that they both smoked. As far as Isla was aware, her father had never smoked in his life, and as she watched him follow Maggie into the kitchen – cat wrapped in his arms, he and Maggie clearly wrapped up in each other – she wondered, *is this what people mean when they say love is blind?*

'Now, I hope you don't mind me stealing your boyfriend for a while, because I want to give him the grand tour upstairs,' said Maggie, coming back in the room. 'Your turn will come.'

'Of course not,' said Isla, shrugging nonchalantly, as she watched Max follow Maggie into the hallway.

Isla glanced around the well-curated living room. She remembered how the bookshelves and her father's books – cricket almanacs, sports biographies, first editions – were the only things he had insisted on taking with him from London. Isla picked up a silver frame on a table nearby and looked at the photograph. It was of Grandma Maybelle. She was wearing a mustard-coloured coat and holding a bunch of heather in front of a tree; red and gold leaves scattered around her. Isla wondered whether her grandma loved autumn as much as she did. It was strange, she thought, how little she knew about her.

'Is Barbra Streisand in or out?' Hanson had come back into the room, catching his daughter unawares.

'In,' said Isla, turning around.

'Good. I wasn't sure what you youngsters listened to these days. We'll keep her on then.'

'Babs can definitely stay.'

'How's the flat?' Hanson scooped up a black cat, who was lying on a chair. 'I thought the plan was to live in Berlin?'

'It was,' said Isla, not sure how much she wanted to tell her father. 'I decided it would be better to have it rented out first.' The truth was that Isla hadn't been able to find a job in Berlin. She had applied to several magazines, to no avail; all of them requiring the perfect German she couldn't deliver. And so, lost between cities, Isla returned to London, to a dull office job, to her friends and to her mother, and it was there that Max had found her.

'Max seems like a nice fellow.'

'Yes, he's nice.'

Isla was thankful to have her attention diverted to the black cat, who had jumped off her father's lap onto the floor and was now beside her feet, looking up at her.

'She likes you,' said Hanson. 'It's not often she does that. Blitz prefers to size people up first.' Blitzen continued to look at Isla, weighing up whether this might be a good place for a nap. 'Go on Blitzy, go to Bobby.' After some deliberation, Blitzen jumped up on the sofa, stretched out her velvety legs and settled down next to her new friend.

'How old is she?' said Isla.

'Getting on now. Nine this year but still loves to explore. Donner is the homebody.'

'They're both cute.'

Hanson glanced at the ceiling. 'Well, I certainly hope she's not giving him the longer tour. The poor boy won't ever want to come back. What do you think, Blitzy? Do you think Max will want to come back?'

Isla looked at the cat and wished her father would change the subject.

When Max and Maggie reappeared some minutes later, Max looked embarrassed and Maggie looked pleased. 'We're back,' she said triumphantly, 'and we had lots of fun, didn't we?' Maggie held on to Max's arm while she put her shoes back on; a pair of black high-heeled courts she had taken off before going upstairs. Max nodded vaguely and Isla imagined him silently screaming, *what madhouse have you brought me to? Please tell me we can go home now.*

'I've decided that one grand tour is enough for the evening,' said Maggie, nodding at Isla. 'Next time, though.'

'Well, how did you like the tour?' Hanson asked Max, uncorking a wine bottle. 'You need to be careful up there. Those low beams can really catch you out.'

'It was good,' said Max, exchanging awkward glances with Isla. It was clear he didn't know what else to say.

A variant of Namibian beef stew was served at some time around midnight, followed by malva pudding, another South African delicacy, which Maggie served hot with custard. No one felt like eating by that point, at least not a rich two-course meal, but they all showed appreciation to the cook, who was clearly exhausted by the ordeal. No one felt like talking either. Everyone was sleepy and subdued after too much wine and heavy food, which was a good thing, Isla thought, given she would soon be alone with Max for the first time that evening and she was dying to know every little detail of the tour Maggie had given him.

'She swore me to secrecy,' Max said in hushed tones when they were finally alone. The two of them were sprawled across the bed in their room. 'Of course I'm going to share it with you. Just not here.'

'Why would she tell *you* a secret? She barely knows you,' said Isla, looking puzzled. 'Is it to do with my dad? Oh God, it's to do with Dad, isn't it?'

Max pulled Isla towards him. 'I'm paranoid this place is bugged or something. It doesn't help that it's so old and creaky. All these Tudor beams and little nooks and hideaways are kind of freaking me out.'

'I know what you mean,' said Isla, 'but there's only three rooms up here. It's not exactly a grand tour, is it?'

'I think it was just an excuse for Maggie to get me alone.'

'So will you tell me tomorrow? After we've left?'

'Of course.' Max began to stroke Isla's hair. 'You know, meeting your dad was always going to be significant. Finally, all your little ways are beginning to make sense.'

Isla shifted uncomfortably in Max's arms. 'What do you mean?' There was a prickliness to her tone.

'Don't be like that. I meant it in a good way.'

'You're the one who started it, implying that there's something *wrong* with me.'

'There you go again, always jumping to conclusions. I just said—'

'Forget it…' said Isla, turning round to face the other way. 'I don't want to hear it.'

The following morning – well past eleven – there was still no sign of Hanson and Maggie. Isla was sure she had reminded them that they needed to leave by midday so that Max could make his evening class. At the same time she was relieved they were still asleep and goodbyes could be avoided. It was better this way, she conceded, as she and Max tiptoed out of the kitchen while Donner and Blitzen looked on as if their presence made them complicit bystanders. Isla glanced quickly at the note she had left on the hallway table, thanking her father and Maggie in large, neat handwriting for their hospitality and that she hoped to see them soon. She wondered whether they felt the same way, or whether they would pretend, like her, that everything had been perfect.

Maggie wasn't mentioned at all during the car journey home. In fact, Isla and Max barely spoke at all. It was as if a gulf had been created between them, like an insidious seed growing stronger, pushing them further apart. This continued for another day. When they finally began speaking again – it took the appointment of a new prime minister to break their silence – there was still no mention of what Maggie had said. While Isla didn't want to push the matter, apprehensive of what might be revealed, she was curious to know what her boyfriend thought of her father's one-line email response to the letter she had left on the kitchen table. Max, it appeared, didn't have an opinion either way. 'What were you expecting? It's not as if you two are close.' His nonchalant attitude surprised Isla and she wondered where it had come from, this sudden indifference.

'What's got into you? Every little thing I do seems to annoy you. I daren't breathe anymore…'

'Maybe we are just spending too much time together.'

'Is this to do with what Maggie said to you? Or my dad…?'

'No…'

'What then?'

'It's just that everything about you is, well… so complicated. Things should be easy.'

'Well, I'm sorry if I come with a little baggage.'

'That's not what I meant. You're just so defensive all the time.'

'If you want a fairytale, why don't you go and watch some Disney cartoons.'

'I don't need fairytales. I just need someone who's not always looking for a battle.'

Three days later, they broke up, Max citing the need for space as if Isla were a piece in his game of chess. They had been together a year, and while Max's decision was half expected, she was still hurt by what she perceived as his giving up on her. Isla didn't like endings, especially endings she had no control over. Apart from the small matter of collecting the few belongings she had left in his flat just off the Old Kent Road – as *soon* as possible, he had iterated – there was a finality to their connection; the sense a barrier had been erected that would be impossible to climb over, not least to retrieve the answers he seemed determined to keep to himself. Perhaps Max was simply trying to protect her from something. From what, and why, she had no clue.

Tilly   49

'Only you could drag a Christmas tree home by yourself,' laughed Isla, as she and her mother sat around the kitchen table, the last of the afternoon light filtering through the shutters.

Tilly waved her hand dismissively as if it had been easy. 'It wasn't that heavy and some kind people helped along the way. But I was glad to get home. And what a lovely surprise to find you here, waiting for me.'

Isla still thought it strange for her mother to call the cottage home, even though Tilly had moved in just less than a year ago. Perhaps because the transition had been so subtle: weekends here, birthdays there, a few holidays in between and then, after the sale of the flat had gone through, Tilly left London and moved to Devon. Many thought it inconceivable that a woman who had just turned sixty should move to a place all by herself and start again. But people didn't know their mother as well as Craig and Isla. Their mother was made of strong stuff; fiercely independent and claiming that the only company she liked was her own.

'Shame Craig won't be joining us,' said Isla, getting up to boil the kettle. 'Won't be the same without him.'

'Unfortunately, that's what happens when you have your own business. You can never switch off.'

'But he could close the pub, couldn't he?'

'And lose all that business over Christmas. It's one of his busiest times.'

'I suppose so,' said Isla. 'It's good he has Lia to help him. They make a good team.'

'Yes, they are good for each other.' Tilly's eyes narrowed, and Isla knew what was coming next. 'It's just such a shame about Max. Whatever did happen between the two of you? I had such high hopes.'

'Oh, Mum, it's not that big a deal. It just didn't work out.'

'But I liked him. He just seemed... well... like he had some oomph about him.'

'Yes, but it's not just about having oomph, is it, Mum? And remember, he broke it off with *me*. You know, I still wonder why Maggie confided in him. She didn't even know him.'

'I've no idea. Perhaps she had no one else to talk to.'

That night, while Isla lay in bed, she remembered something Max had told her; the way he alluded to the absence of upheaval in his own childhood and how that had made him feel less interesting, as if his parents were to blame for their "normality". But that was before their visit to her father, before Maggie's secret. Why did Max suddenly want to reconnect with her after two years of silence? The Facebook friend request came as much as a shock to her as did his profile picture – the insipid grin peering over black statement specs. Was it possible for someone to overhaul their image so quickly? Or had the Max she had known waited to morph into the person he was meant to become? Without her by his side? Isla turned over, soothed by the absence of noise. The relentless city sirens had been replaced by a gentle cooing, which her mother said came from the resident owl who lived in the trees at the end of the garden. Isla wasn't sure whether she had even seen an owl before, and it suddenly struck her as being rather sad; this lack of a connection with nature. Since her mother had moved to Appledean, Isla wanted to know everything: names of birds and different trees and the stars in the sky. Perhaps it was inevitable, this being tired of London. Tired of people bumping into her, all vying for precious space. And there she was in the middle of it all, floating around like a piece of driftwood.

When Isla came down for breakfast shortly after eight the following morning, Tilly was already at the kitchen table, surrounded by her endless scraps of paper and several packs of Wrigley's Extra Peppermint gum, which, to the relief of her children, had helped to replace her smoking habit. In the centre of the chaos was a cafetière and two slices of toast smeared thickly with butter and marmalade. 'So much to do still,' said her mother, waving an arm around the room.

'But it's Christmas Eve,' exclaimed Isla. 'Please don't tell me you will be spending it balancing the books.'

'*Schatz*, there is so much to do before year end. This guesthouse isn't going to run itself. I still have all the bookings to confirm. Then I need to get all the accounts ready. It's never-ending.'

'I thought this was the age to start winding down? Doing less work?'

'Me? Winding down?' Tilly gave a deep, hearty laugh. '*Schatz*, you do say some silly things.'

The magnificent spruce tree was ready to be lit when Isla walked through the village later that day, and it occurred to her what a huge leap of faith her mother had made. Tilly had started afresh in a place where she had known not a soul, and now it seemed every soul knew her, if the number of people that dropped by the cottage or said hello to her in the street was anything to go by. Strange to think that her mother was now one of these villagers and who, by her own admission, couldn't imagine living anywhere else now. It was remarkable how she had assimilated and adapted, shrugging off the cloak of her former life that hadn't always been easy, and Isla remembered wondering what it was about the cottage that resonated with her mother so much.

Now, of course, it was easy to see why. The cottage was picturesque, with a kitchen garden that wound all the way around the building. Although it had been somewhat neglected, one of the first things Tilly did when she moved in was to plant kohlrabi, strawberries, blackcurrants, cucumber and lettuce. Tilly had said that the first year's crop had brought back memories of being back in her childhood home again; wandering around the garden barefoot with her sisters, each with a bowl in their hand; the bowl never quite filling up as the girls ate their pickings absent-mindedly. The second thing she did was turn the outhouse, which was formerly used as a stable, into a small two-bedroom guesthouse. The set-up, wholly her grandpa's idea, seemed to work. Since Tilly didn't have space for an additional dining room, she brought her guests breakfast to their room – muesli, croissants, scrambled eggs, whatever they fancied – which she left outside their door with a packed lunch. The guests always dined out, usually one of Tilly's recommendations, and conveniently stayed out of her hair (Tilly's words) until it was time for bed. From early spring to mid-autumn, the two rooms were always occupied. Tilly liked *almost* everyone who came to stay, although the Americans were usually demanding – or was it obnoxious, she could never be sure – the Germans annoying and the French particular. Her Irish guests, however, were never a problem.

The village, of course, was pretty too, and as Isla walked towards the neat row of independent businesses, which formed a pleasant circle around the green, she noticed something had changed. Indeed, it was so subtle, she could easily have missed it were it not for several men queuing up outside. It was nestled between the arty café on one side, with its flat whites and artisan bread, and the florist's, La Petite Fleur, on the other. How strange her mother had never mentioned anything. Now, as Isla stood outside trying to peer in through the open door, she thought she could still smell the fresh paint on the immaculate grey facade.

'Can I help you, love?' a voice called out to Isla. The man was standing at the entrance with a shaving brush in his hand.

'Oh no, it's fine.' Isla felt embarrassed. 'I was just having a look. It's—' Before she could finish, he had cut her short.

'No worries, love,' before quickly adding, 'Merry Christmas.'

Isla glanced up at the sign, which read JCJ & Sons Barbers in large green lettering. A family business, she thought, as she headed next door to the arty café, the one which now sold Tilly's festive *Lebkuchen* and *Vanillekipferl*. She joined the queue, remembering how she had encouraged her mother to sell her Christmas biscuits to them. The café was busy, which always seemed to surprise Isla, and she smiled, as she always did, when she spotted her mother's biscuits nestled in between the *Panettone* and *Kransekake*; each bag tied with a red velvet bow.

'Hey, Isla! How's it going?' came a familiar voice from behind the counter. 'I haven't seen you in ages.'

'Hello, Carrie. Just checking up on Mum's biscuits,' she replied with a wink. 'All good…?'

'Do you know, we've sold about fifty bags already. They're proving more popular than our mince pies over there! Tell Tilly she'll need to up her game next year and double her baking efforts.'

Isla laughed. 'I'm sure she'll rise to the challenge. Do you have any more of that delicious caraway seed bread left? I bought it the last time I was here. It's delicious.'

'You're in luck. We have one loaf left.' Carrie pointed to a dresser in the corner with a selection of fresh bread on it. 'I'd grab it while you can. And don't worry – it's on us!'

'Thanks, Carrie – that's kind of you. Merry Christmas if I don't see you beforehand!'

'*Fro… hey…* Oh, I always forget the…'

'*Frohe Weihnachten!* I know, bit of a tongue twister!'

'Fro, Hey, Wine, Nakten.' Carrie laughed.

'By the way, d'you know how long the barber's has been here?'

'Two months – and already the most popular barber for miles.'

'Thanks, Carrie, see you soon.' Isla weaved through the waiting customers into the fading December light; past the barbershop with its slick facade and past the florist's with its poinsettias and pretty bunches of hypericum. And then she thought of him. She went through phases of thinking about him all the time and then not at all. And now here she was again with thoughts of Giles. But why? Because of the new barbershop? Isla wasn't sure but as she walked towards the village pond where a group of carollers were gathering around the Christmas tree, she wondered for the first time in a long time how he was. It had been seven years since she had last seen him and the only thing she knew about his life now was that he had moved abroad. It was only when she was halfway back to the cottage that she realised she had forgotten to buy a poinsettia for her mother. It was too late to go back now. She would return later. Perhaps when the melancholy that was starting to rise within her had disappeared.

'Why didn't you tell me about the barber's?' Isla glanced around the kitchen, wondering what she could eat. The Christmas tree was still propped against the wall and the scraps of paper still lying on the kitchen table. 'Mum, you home?' Isla took the bread she had bought earlier out of its brown packaging and began to cut the loaf into thick slices. Unsettled by the silence, she turned on the radio. As she stood there, a woman with long silver hair and a green leather coat walked past the kitchen window while a man trailed behind her, a mobile phone to his ear. Isla instinctively recoiled before catching another glimpse of the couple. The man had caught up with the silver-haired woman and they now stood together while he appeared to show her something. Isla was still peering through the window when Tilly suddenly walked through the door, a folder in one hand. 'Ah, *Schatz*, you're back,' she said, a burst of cold air escaping into the room. 'A couple from New Zealand, the ones out there, are looking for somewhere to stay. I told them we're closed for Christmas. They're not having much luck.'

Isla moved towards the window again. 'I thought for a moment we had weirdos trespassing around.'

Tilly laughed and lowered her voice. 'That's the thing, you just never know who is going to turn up.' She joined her daughter at the window and the man suddenly gestured upwards with his thumb. 'Well, that's good, they've obviously found something,' she said, mirroring his action. 'How was your afternoon? Did you manage to buy some bread?'

'Why didn't you tell me about the barber's?'

'What do you mean? Which barber's?'

'The one that recently opened. It used to be a newsagent's.'

'Oh that.' Tilly began to take things out of the fridge. 'I didn't think you'd be interested. We don't seem to have any cheese. Could you go back and buy some? And milk. We need milk too.'

But Isla's mind was already elsewhere. It had been transported back a hundred years to her great-grandfather's barbershop, just like the one in Appledean. She could see him at work: trimming and styling, laughing and talking; a man with plans and dreams. She could see Giles too, looking up with her excitedly at the faded facade. She knew now that Giles had brought her past to life so that he could be a part of her future. And it had taken her this long – weeks, months, years – to realise it. To realise everything he had done had been for *her*. The futility of it all, the helpless futility of where to begin.

'*Schatz*, are you all right? It looks like you've seen a ghost. *Schatz*…?'

Giles   50

'Good morning, Mr Illingworth.' The familiar chorus of
voices which greeted Giles every morning always made him
smile. Where were they all now? he wondered, staring out of the
window towards the city, which was still obscured by a damp grey
fog. He remembered his students so clearly; his diligent, patient
students who were always so eager to start their day's learning.
The classroom, the one where he had spent nearly three years of
his life, looked out onto a dusty courtyard where nothing ever
seemed to grow, so long had it been neglected. Until one day,
he decided to plant three rhododendron shrubs in the middle
of that courtyard. When spring arrived, his students marvelled
with him at those first pink blossoms – such a splendid splash of
colour amid the rubble, everyone exclaimed – proudly bursting
from the long-neglected soil.

Giles stood by the window a few moments longer before
walking towards a small kitchenette at the far end of his office. He
poured himself another coffee. It was his fourth that morning,
and he still hadn't eaten breakfast.

'Mr Illingworth?' A clipped voice floated upwards and Giles leant over the glass division to the floor below where his PA was standing with a black diary in her hands. 'I just wanted to remind you that you have your nine-thirty with Mr Jamieson. Would you like to take it down here or upstairs?'

'Up here will be fine, Lara. Thanks.'

'Oh, and Mr Illingworth?'

'Yes, Lara.'

'Your ex-wife called.'

'Oh?'

'Something urgent has come up. Says she's bringing in your daughter today after school instead of tomorrow.'

'Did she say what it was?' There was an undercurrent of annoyance in Giles' voice.

'No, she didn't mention anything as such, Mr Illingworth.'

'Fine. Thanks, Lara.'

It must have been at least two years since Giles had asked Lara to address him by his first name, but she seemed to prefer the formalities. Still, she was indispensable really, he thought, and all things considered, she had been very good to him during his divorce. And what a divorce that was. Svea, Giles' ex-wife, was Swedish, the two of them having met in Nepal at the school where they were teaching assistants. When Svea returned to university to complete her degree, Giles had followed her back to Stockholm. He wasn't able to teach and so he waited tables instead. Then, when Svea graduated – demanding everyone call her a polyglot because she had spent the last four years learning Arabic and Mandarin – they married. The wedding itself was held in Uppsala; entirely organised by Svea's mother who insisted that only gravlax and schnapps be served at the reception and that the cake should consist of two tiers, not three (too common was the reason she gave). Yet what Giles remembered most about that day, apart from the pickled herring they had eaten straight after the church ceremony – a wedding family tradition, exclaimed Svea – was the number of times Giles felt bad whenever he was asked why he hadn't invited any family or friends of his own.

'Don't worry, babe,' Svea told him when they sat down one evening to draw up the wedding list. 'My family is your family now and you'll make new friends.' Giles never told Svea the truth, because the truth was, she had never really asked about his family. Then Freja came along and that golden time for discovering each other, the secrets couples tell each other, was gone.

Giles finished his coffee and picked up one of the newspapers, which were delivered to the gallery every morning. The headlines still carried the same story that had been running for a week: *London's Day of Terror.* Whenever anything about the city came up, Giles automatically thought of Isla. He had thought about her a lot these past weeks, wondering whether she had been caught up in the bombings during her morning commute, whether she was even living in London anymore. He imagined her anxious face, frightened by what the city had become. Yet the hardest part was not knowing, because Isla had made her feelings clear. Still, how could he ever tell her that he had crawled back to his parents, accepted their offer – peace offering they called it – to help him back on his feet? After everything *he* said. It hadn't been an easy decision, but he reasoned that he couldn't be estranged from his parents forever, that Freja deserved to know her grandparents, and the money would help finance a very sticky divorce.

So here he was, a forty-one-year-old single father living in the centre of Leeds in a New-York-style warehouse with exposed brick tiles and a state-of-the-art coffee machine. Well, at least she would be pleased that I made it back to Yorkshire, Giles thought, as he made his way downstairs in preparation for Mr Jamieson. 'Lara, would you mind popping next door and picking up a bagel for me, please? The usual, if possible. I seem to have forgotten all about breakfast today.'

'Certainly, Mr Illingworth,' said Lara, quickly grabbing her handbag from the coat rack. 'I won't be long.'

Lara was longer than expected because some time had passed before Giles heard an unexpected tap on the window. When he turned around to see who it was – an elderly man with one hand cupped against the pane and the other leaning on a stick – Giles quickly glanced at his watch. It was exactly nine-thirty, but when he looked again, it wasn't Mr Jamieson who was standing outside waiting for him. It was Mr Jagger.

Jack 51

Jack knew he didn't have much time left; a handful of years if he was lucky. As long as they were good years; years he wanted to make count. He was in his nineties and although his back was beginning to stoop and the aches and pains followed him everywhere now, he could still get around. And he wanted to make one more trip before it was too late. A photography gallery had opened up in Leeds with landscapes of the Yorkshire countryside alongside numerous portraits the gallery owner had taken during his time spent living overseas. There were portraits of children playing in the street, portraits of women gathered together on cobbled steps and portraits of men high up in the mountains. But it wasn't the gallery Jack was interested in visiting; it was the man behind it. And it was time for Jack to pay him a visit.

'It's not often we see you in these parts,' said Harry, greeting Anna and Jack warmly at the door. 'Molly and I are so pleased that you've come to Lancashire, aren't we, Molly?' Harry gestured to his wife, who was sitting in the corner of the living room. Molly smiled at her guests but made no attempt to rise.

'She's feeling a bit down today. Can't seem to get her out of the armchair at all.'

'Dear oh dear,' said Jack, glancing at Anna. 'We really wouldn't have put you to all this trouble had we known that Molly wasn't feeling well.'

'Don't even think of it,' said Harry, patting his brother's back. 'It will be good for Molly to have people around.'

'Hello, Molly,' said Jack to his sister-in-law. 'No need to get up. I just want to say how nice it is to see you.'

Molly looked up and smiled again, with a trace of detachment. 'Thank you,' she said, and it occurred to Jack how very childlike Molly had become. Yet Jack had never known Molly to be anything other than childlike, even at the beginning. And now, watching her with hunched shoulders and vacant eyes, he felt a huge wave of pity for her. That Molly should have been at the mercy of her emotions for most of her life was terribly sad, and Jack thought of how things might have turned out if she didn't have depression. It had taken him long enough – by Jack's own admission, he was ashamed of the views he once held – to appreciate what it all meant. Harry had done a stellar job – was doing a stellar job – and Jack admired the fortitude and resilience his brother had shown in taking care of his wife. It couldn't have been easy, but Jack had never heard his brother complain once.

Not that Harry had ever confided in Jack about it. Was it really because they were too different? Too entrenched in their individual stories to appreciate the beauty in their opposite characters? Harry the pragmatist, who saw the world as it was, and Jack the philosopher, who imagined the world as it should be. The artist and engineer ever at odds.

'Now tell me about your plans,' said Harry, putting a plate of sandwiches on the table; his large, sturdy hands revealing a life spent making things. 'It's been years since I was back there myself. There's a Morrisons where the hall used to be and the church has been turned into one of those fancy exercise centres. Oh, it's not the same, I'm afraid. Everything changes in the end.'

'Well, we know that Father's salon is a fish and chip shop now.'

'Yes, I remember you saying. Wonder if it's any good…'

'Isla mentioned something about it looking a little unloved.'

'How's she getting on in Berlin? Any regrets about leaving that Giles fellow?'

'I'm not sure,' said Jack. 'I just don't think it's right for a young woman to be alone like that out there.'

'You don't think she felt too young?' Anna had come back into the room, having caught the tail end of the conversation.

'What do you mean?' said Jack, looking up at his wife.

'Perhaps Isla felt she was too young to get married. She was only twenty-four after all.'

'True,' said Harry, pushing his thick black glasses up the bridge of his nose. 'Youngsters like to live a bit these days before they settle down. And who can blame them?'

'Well…' Jack paused for a moment. 'There's also the small matter of the legacy. By accepting Giles' proposal, I suspect Isla thought she would be betraying her family.'

'Nonsense,' said Harry. 'It had nothing to do with the lad.'

'In fact, that's exactly why we're here,' said Jack.

'All sounds very mysterious.' Harry bit into a sandwich. 'Tell me more.'

'Well, we're going to spend a couple of days in Halifax and Hipperholme. Then we're going to make a detour to Leeds.'

'Why Leeds?' Harry looked at Jack and then at Anna. 'I know it's excellent for shopping…'

'Giles has a gallery there. Photography. He's doing very well by all accounts.'

'How do you know?' Harry asked. 'I thought you had no more contact with the Illingworths?'

'I read about him in the paper. Quite the success story too. And if the reviews are anything to go by, the lad has considerable talent. It's not been an easy decision, what with the history between us, but I feel it's the right thing to do for Isla's sake. Because if it wasn't for Father's stolen formula, things may have turned out quite differently for them.'

'But what if he's married?' said Harry. 'Or has a girlfriend?'

'Oh, I've done my research,' said Jack, his eyes twinkling. 'The article mentioned neither.'

*

Jack peered through the windowpane, his warm breath forming a ring of condensation on the glass, and waited for some kind of acknowledgment; a sign that he had been recognised. It surprised Jack how familiar Giles looked. Although he had broadened out and his face was less angular, there was still the characteristic floppiness to his hair, which had flecks of grey now. It also surprised Jack how spacious the gallery was once Giles motioned for him to come inside. The first thing to catch his eye was the neon lettering dangling above him: *Create the Space.* He really liked what Giles had done with the room.

'Mr Jagger.' Giles looked at Jack in astonishment. At least twenty years had passed since they had seen each other at Hillmans. 'What a wonderful surprise to see you. But I'm not... I mean... I wasn't expecting you.'

Jack walked slowly towards Giles. 'I've been reading about your gallery in the paper and wanted to see it for myself. You may have already gathered that Mr Jamieson won't be coming today. I hope you don't mind my being here in his place.'

'Yes, I see that.' Giles ruffled his hair. He was trying not to fidget. 'And no, of course I don't mind. May I take your coat? Would you like tea? Coffee? Lara, my PA, should be back any moment.'

'Tea would be lovely, thank you.' Jack looked around the room, his eyes flitting between images on either side of the whitewashed walls. 'You have a nice set-up here. But I didn't realise you were so interested in photography.'

'I wasn't. Well, not until I started travelling. The colours in Nepal and India are breathtaking.'

Jack gestured with his walking stick at a series of photographs displayed across the far wall. 'It's interesting then that your medium is overwhelmingly in black and white.'

Giles smiled and walked towards one of the images, tracing his finger across the contours of a woman's face. Her eyes, melancholic and soulful, were deeply etched with lines. 'You can't capture the essence of someone, their beauty, their spirit, with colour. It just doesn't work.'

'You're absolutely right. You should be proud of what you've done here. And your parents...' Jack hesitated. 'They must be proud too.'

'Well, yes, I suppose they are. They...'

Before Giles could reply, Lara came into the office, slamming the door behind her. 'Oh, hello, Mr Jamieson, Mr Illingworth.' Lara looked flustered as she placed a large paper bag on her desk. 'Would either of you gentlemen like a coffee?'

'Lara, this is Mr Jagger.' Giles gestured awkwardly at Jack, who in turn extended one hand towards Lara. 'Mr Jamieson cancelled his appointment. He won't be coming in, but Mr Jagger here is an old friend. And we have a lot of catching-up to do.'

'Very nice to meet you,' said Jack, smiling. 'No coffee for me, thank you. I'm a tea man.'

'Right you are, Mr Jagger. Will you be going upstairs, Mr Illingworth?'

'Yes. And would you mind bringing those bagels up too, please, and perhaps a couple of pastries.'

'I will indeed.' Lara watched the two men ascend the staircase, one with the help of a walking stick, the other whose gait was slightly clumsy, and wondered what on earth had brought them together.

'Charming girl,' said Jack, when he and Giles reached the long white table at the end of the room.

'She is… In fact, she's been great really, especially during my divorce. Please, take a seat.' Giles gestured to a white plastic chair. 'They are more comfortable than they look.'

'Your divorce?' Jack slowly eased himself into the chair, immediately regretting his words.

'Yes. We both taught English in Nepal and then I moved with her to Stockholm. Before I knew it, her mother had bought a hat. She's Swedish, my ex-wife. And her mother – very bossy. Takes over the whole show.'

Jack nodded, pleased that Giles had been willing to share something private. 'I understand.'

'It just didn't feel right. Even before the wedding, it just didn't feel right.'

'It seems we have been in similar situations. My late wife, Maybelle, had a very domineering mother – took over the whole show too. Had her daughter's whole courtship planned out right before my eyes. Never mind my say in the matter. It's a good job I fell in love with the girl the moment we met. And I never stopped loving her.'

'Then you are a lucky man,' said Giles. 'I think people only really find that once.'

'Twice,' replied Jack, quickly. 'Anna is my second wife.'

'Ah, Mrs Jagger, yes, I remember. How is she?'

'Very well. I believe she's in the Victoria Quarter as we speak. I hear Leeds is excellent for shopping now.'

Lara's footsteps could be heard coming up the stairs. 'Please excuse me.' Giles rose from his chair and went over to meet her.

'Will that be all, Mr Illingworth?' Lara handed Giles a large wooden tray.

'Thanks, Lara. That will be all.' Giles returned to the table and arranged the pastries and bagels on a plate. 'I hope you don't mind, but I haven't had breakfast yet. Do please help yourself. They're very tasty.'

'They look rather like doughnuts.'

'They're bagels,' Giles said with a smile, pouring Jack's tea into a mug. 'But yes, they do look like doughnuts.'

Giles and Jack sat in silence for a moment: Giles eating his bagel and Jack drinking his tea, both treading water for fear of saying the wrong thing.

'I've often thought about your family,' said Giles suddenly. 'And about what happened.'

'Giles… it's not—'

Giles interrupted. 'You see, I couldn't face what they did, so I disappeared as far away as possible.'

'I know, but you are not to blame for any of this.' Jack could see the anguish in Giles' face and reached out to touch his arm. 'It's all water under the bridge now, this thing between our families. Your parents have recompensed us. They've acknowledged their wrongdoing. We can all move forward and put the past behind us.'

Giles looked away. There were so many things he wanted to tell Mr Jagger but he didn't know how to begin.

'It's taken me many years to make peace with things that have happened in my life and to let go of the past,' said Jack. 'And I want you to do the same.'

Giles met Jack's gaze, and in that moment, they appeared to each other exactly as they had all those years ago at the Arts Society. 'Thank you,' said Giles. 'Hearing you speak these words, coming to find me. It means a lot.'

'Well, there is another reason why I'm here. I'm sure you haven't forgotten her.'

Giles' face softened but he didn't respond.

'You haven't forgotten her, have you?'

Giles put his mug down on the table. 'The thing is, Mr Jagger, I stayed away because it was the right thing to do. I stayed away because I thought *you* wanted that. I thought *you* wanted me to move on. And I did – with Svea – and now I'm...'

Jack leant forward and looked Giles in the eye. 'If you want to find her, then you have my blessing to do so. She's living in Berlin now, in a renovated apartment block that used to be a design factory, near to lots of galleries that look exactly like this one. What did she call it? Bohemian – yes, that's how she described the area to me once.' Jack reached into his jacket pocket and took out a small crumpled piece of paper. 'Isla's address – I'll leave it here with you if you ever decide you want to find her.'

Giles picked up the piece of paper and stared at it. 'Thank you, Mr Jagger. For everything. And for coming to find me.'

Jack shook his head. 'Not at all, lad. And, please, call me Jack.'

Hanson 52

It happened quickly. One minute Hanson was enjoying a gin and tonic with Maggie in the garden, laughing in the late-afternoon sunshine; the next he had keeled over; his life – indeed, their life as they knew it – over. It had been a particularly warm spring, and the pale blossoms had seeped seamlessly into the verdant hues of June along with the promise of alfresco lunches and evening apéritifs. Oh, how glorious the summer was unfolding, at least that's what Hanson and Maggie remembered, before the unexpected incident threw a fork in the road and forced them to change trajectory.

Even now, Maggie couldn't say whether she had recognised the warning signs; nothing to indicate what was to come. The only thing Hanson had mentioned with regularity was that it was turning into a stellar season for the cricket, which usually meant that Yorkshire were doing well. He was what one would call a sun worshipper, Maggie said; someone who sat outside for hours following both the County Championship on the radio and the sun as it moved around the garden. 'Well, it could very well rain next week,' he had told her, his skin already a deep golden hue. 'We can't expect this to go on forever.' Maggie hadn't forgotten those words. *We can't expect this to go on forever.* It was as if Hanson had a premonition that something terrible was going to happen; as if their contented state was finite. They had been content, hadn't they? Now Maggie wasn't sure. She had read somewhere that a broken heart can mimic a heart attack. Broken heart syndrome was the phrase used to describe it. Is this what Hanson had? A broken heart? A heart so broken it rendered him unable to look after himself anymore.

When Maggie sat on the edge of Hanson's bed in the nursing home, she desperately wanted to ask him that question. Hanson, who had been her partner for twenty-five years, the man whom she had given everything up for, and he her. Now it seemed he had given up on both of them. 'Did you hear the rain this morning?' Maggie decided to ask instead as she held Hanson's hand. 'The flowers will be happy. I'm not so sure about the cricket, though.'

Hanson smiled and Maggie wondered what he was thinking as she tightened her grasp around his fingers. It was strange; the age gap had never been an issue for her. Now she felt it acutely, two people at opposite ends of the ocean: Maggie with miles to swim before she reached the shore, Hanson already there. 'What did you have for breakfast this morning, sweetheart? Did they give you eggs again?' This was how the conversation unfolded whenever Maggie would visit. Yet the irony was not lost on her. It was true; Hanson was nearly as old as her father but now the roles were reversed. Of course, the whole thing had been inevitable. It just never occurred to her that it would come so soon, and so unexpectedly. Hanson was only in his early seventies, for heaven's sake. This wasn't the plan. This wasn't what was meant to happen. Hanson nodded; his eyes, once sparkling and bright, were now dull. And this made Maggie sad, because his eyes were one of the first things she had fallen in love with.

Maggie rose from the bed. 'Would you like me to ask if you could have plain toast instead? No butter?'

Hanson nodded again, his eyes following Maggie's movement. 'Leave it with me,' she said. 'I'll sort them out.' Before she left the room, she winked at Hanson, waving a hand behind her.

The more comfortable rooms were on the ground floor and Maggie was pleased that she had been able to secure one of the larger ones for Hanson, with a little private patio, a table and two chairs. 'It's like being home from home,' Maggie had joked when they first arrived. 'The only thing is, you'll no longer have to put up with my cooking.' Maggie had joked a lot with Hanson at the beginning and she still did. She kept other things to herself, like the first time she spotted the communal area, which, when she had heard it first, Maggie had likened to a madhouse. The image of those patients (whom Maggie surmised to be not much older than Hanson) slumped in armchairs, erratically pacing around the room or talking and laughing to themselves had left Maggie feeling horrified as she peered through the door; horrified that Hanson was now part of it all, realising there was no way back. Hanson's heart, which she had once captured, would never be mended again.

'Excuse me,' said Maggie, as a young man in a blue tunic walked towards her. 'My partner is in one of the rooms down there, and he's not a fan of eggs. Is it possible to arrange for him to have toast instead? No need for butter – dry toast will do.'

'I'll see what I can do, Madam.'

'I'm only asking for toast. A simple slice of toast.'

'That's fine but I'll need to check.' Maggie could tell from the man's demeanour that he was a stickler for the rules.

'I'm only asking for a simple slice of toast here.'

'I understand, Madam. We'll see what we can do. I'm sure it will be fine.'

'Thank you.' Maggie turned around quickly. She could feel pricks of tears threaten to unravel the cool exterior that up until now she had so excellently worn. She didn't want the man to see that they had already started to trickle down her cheeks, stubbornly leaving their trace against the sun cream she had applied only hours earlier; a faint mix of salt and verbena. *How has it come to this?* she thought, spotting an empty bench outside in the garden grounds.

The bench was next to a large willow tree whose long, stooped branches reminded Maggie of the people in the common room. How had their lives come to this? How had it come to this? Maggie turned the question around in her mind as she tasted the saltiness of the tears that flowed down her cheeks, over her mouth and down the curve of her face. Hanson had been such a fine man; tall, broad and handsome. There was something about him that had set him apart from the rest – and, crucially, set him apart from Adam. It was the way Hanson could command a room when he walked into one. It was the way he left an impression on people, whether good or bad. And it was the way he garnered respect from everyone he met despite being soft-spoken. So how dare the nurse in the blue tunic, with his rules and regulations, say that the man she loved might not be able to have toast in the morning? He obviously didn't know who Hanson was. What he had been. He only knew what Hanson had become.

Maggie sat underneath the willow tree and wept. By the time she returned to Hanson's room, he was asleep. The window had been left open and the chirruping sound of birdsong could be heard as a fresh breeze floated in. It had all the markings of late summer; warm and balmy with an undercurrent of change. Autumn was on its way and Maggie wasn't sure how on earth she was going to get through it.

The first thing she did when she got home was switch on all the lights. Not only did Maggie dislike the dark, but it was exactly the moment when the sun disappeared into the horizon and she could see the milky outline of the moon that she always found the most depressing. She was never sure whether sunset meant it was twilight or dusk, but Maggie didn't particularly like this time of day anyway, and so, as she always did at this hour, she poured herself a large glass of wine. Now that Hanson was no longer living in the house, Maggie felt lost in it. In fact, she couldn't remember a time when she felt more alone. She had been in relationships all of her adult life. Relationships had come to her easily, effortlessly; never the pursuer, always the pursued. She had moved from each one seamlessly; never looking back, always forward, because the future was the only thing she was interested in. It all began with young Tommy, whose heart she had broken when they were fifteen. His father had been offered a job somewhere in Ayrshire – Dullsville, Maggie had called it – so she broke up with him. Then there was Cameron, with whom she smoked whole packets of Embassy Gold after school. Cameron wasn't particularly good-looking but he was clever, and that's how Maggie remembered him: clever Cameron who was good at French. He was also a fool because for two years he had let her copy his homework and now she was off to London to study modern languages. He assumed they would continue seeing each other; she was hoping never to see him again. Now Maggie suspected she had broken Hanson's heart too. Perhaps he missed his children and father more than he cared to admit. Perhaps she hadn't done enough to prevent him slipping from his past. Perhaps – and this was the worst one to reconcile – she should have insisted he attend his annual check-ups, not take no for an answer, especially after the flutters, which came and went without warning. It feels like a butterfly is trapped in my chest, was how Hanson had described it. Hanson's fragile, delicate butterfly. To think how much destruction it had caused.

Maggie was still standing by the kitchen window, the moon now visible in the sky, when she realised her glass was empty. That's what happens when you have no one to talk to, she thought, as she absently poured herself another. She reached for her mobile phone and began to scroll through her address book. She had never been particularly good at keeping up with her friendships, apart from Shona, but even that was tenuous now. She hadn't heard from Shona since her marriage to a man from Belfast. Hanson hadn't been invited to the wedding and so Maggie didn't attend either. Still, she wondered about Shona now and about everyone else; all these pieces of her jigsaw. There were Hanson's jigsaw pieces too whose names she had taken from his phone – Jack, Anna, Craig, Isla – and saved them in her own in case she would ever need them. Marty was the only person to have visited Hanson since the move to the home, and she knew how happy Hanson had been to see his friend, sitting on the edge of his bed talking about Sinatra and the seaside. Good old Marty, she thought, faithful to the end. Still, it was strange to think that Hanson was the closest person to her in the world and yet she hardly knew the people who were his flesh and blood. And the thought of reaching out to them, one by one, especially Craig, who had resolutely kept his distance – it had made her heart race.

It was also a conversation Maggie had been dreading, not least because she had no idea how Craig would react to her, what he would be thinking. 'He's comfortable, that's the important thing,' Maggie had said with reassurance as she tried to imagine Craig at the other end of the line. 'And he has a lovely room – south facing – so the sun shines throughout the day.'

'That's good,' said Craig, matter-of-factly. And Maggie realised then that the gulf between them would never be closed. 'Did the doctor say what caused it?'

'Not specifically, which I know isn't very helpful. It's just, well, your father seemed on such good form – enjoying the sunshine and the cricket. He kept saying what a good year it was for the cricket.'

'Yes, it's been a great year for Yorkshire. Not so great for Worcestershire. But it's been enjoyable all the same.'

'I know your father would very much like to see you both. Obviously, the circumstances aren't ideal, but I know how happy it would make him, and I don't know how long he—'

Craig interjected. 'I'd like that. We'd like that. I'll speak to Isla and we'll arrange something soon.'

Two weeks later, Craig and Isla were in their father's kitchen with Maggie. Donner walked with a limp now and this had caught their attention, which, thought Maggie, provided enough decent material for small talk. 'It's her own fault,' she said, scooping up Donner. 'She's far too feisty for her own good. We wouldn't mind if she won a battle or two but she always ends up the sore loser, and this unfortunately is the result of her latest spat with the neighbours' cat.' Craig and Isla watched in silence as Maggie cradled Donner in her arms like a baby. 'It's okay, she won't bite. That one, however, is another matter entirely. She's had her eye on you since you arrived.' Maggie nodded at Craig. 'Blitz has met Isla, so she's already been given the once-over. But you, she's still trying to work you out.' Blitzen miaowed before walking tentatively towards Craig. 'Oh, here we go,' said Maggie. Craig bent down to stroke Blitzen, and everyone laughed as she rolled about on the floor, clearly enjoying the attention. 'Looks like you've already won her over. Your father's favourite. Remind me to tell him how the cats are doing when we see him later.'

Maggie forgot to tell Hanson about the cats, and Craig and Isla didn't remind her either. She had quickly left them to it after dropping them off at the nursing home, wondering how long it would take to make up for all those years of absence. The truth was, no one knew what to expect or how they would feel. Hanson's first instinct was to take his children in his arms and hold them. Then he gazed at them for a very long time as if he couldn't quite believe that his son and daughter were there in the room with him.

'How are you feeling, Dad?' said Craig. 'Are you thirsty? Hungry? Can we get you anything?'

Hanson waved a hand dismissively as he attempted to sit up in his bed.

'No, Dad, let me,' said Isla, rushing forward. 'Here, I'll prop you up with the pillow. You'll feel more comfortable.'

Hanson smiled appreciatively as he watched Isla pace about – her cream shorts complementing tanned limbs – and he wanted to ask where she had caught her colour. Hanson had wanted to ask a hundred questions that afternoon so that he could start to weave together all the missing pieces in his children's lives until they made sense; the gaps he now so acutely felt.

'Maggie says you have one of the nicest rooms.' Isla walked towards the patio, its corners filled with golden leaves. Hanson nodded again and Isla tried to imagine her father sitting outside on one of the chairs, every day the same, with no end in sight. And she felt an overwhelming sense of sadness for him.

'Congratulations are in order for Yorkshire.' Craig moved a chair next to Hanson's bed. 'Only wish I could say the same for Worcestershire.' Hanson laughed and Craig imagined what humorous quip his father might have batted back. 'I found this cricketing spoof on the internet. It's really funny. Thought you might like to watch it.' Craig took his mobile phone out of his pocket and positioned the screen so they could all watch it together. 'It's already been viewed nearly two million times.'

Looking at the three of them, no one would have realised they had ever been apart. No one would have realised either how it pained Hanson when he saw Craig and Isla get ready to leave. He desperately wanted to ask them if he would see them soon. He desperately wanted to ask Isla how everything was working out for her in Berlin and whether Craig, now that he owned a pub, was less likely to drink elsewhere. He also wanted to tell them how sorry he was for the way things turned out, for all those lost years that could never be brought back. Most of all, he was sorry for leaving that day without telling them why and where he was going. As Hanson waved goodbye, he knew in that moment he would never have the chance. He also knew there was so much beauty in the unspoken, hoping that Craig and Isla understood what he had tried to tell them in these few short hours. And for the first time in a long time, he felt his heart beating again.

Jack   53

Jack spent the best part of his day sleeping now. The old adage about the armchair and the electric chair that was his sage warning to others had turned itself on its head. Still, Jack could be forgiven for being tired. He knew he was at the end of his journey. Indeed, he often joked that having reached a century, he had long surpassed his three score years and ten. If ever there was a time to look back on his life, it was now. All in all, it had been a good life. It was *still* a good life despite the aches and pains, despite the assortment of pills that dictated the daily rhythm of his day and despite the fact he could no longer do the things he used to do. Still, he was alive! Alive for a century! He had lived through two world wars. He'd travelled the globe with his carpet designs. He'd witnessed huge leaps in technology (although he still resisted an email address). He'd had two very happy marriages and he had spent his retirement painting hundreds of pictures. Yet what would a life be without regret?

Jack thought about the futility that came with all those wasted years; of letting the silence with his son fester, both submerged in their own stubbornness. He remembered how he felt after Maggie told him about Hanson, how he had sat down in his chair and stared into the garden, repeatedly saying to Anna: *This is not the natural order of things. That a son should fall ill like this before his father is not the natural order of things.* When Jack called Hanson the following week, it was the first time he had been in touch with his son for fifteen years. Jack tried to imagine him: powerless, vulnerable, weak; his heart ravaged by disease. But it was useless, because within the blurry contours of his mind, the image that had stayed with him all these years was the one of Hanson – charismatic, proud, determined – outside the Connaught. It didn't matter how they had parted. What mattered was that they had found each other again. Even in these most tragic of circumstances. Even if Hanson could no longer communicate.

Jack thought of Tilly, who had kept the family together and now, in retirement, had found herself again – a second renaissance – in Devon. She had been more than a daughter-in-law; she was a *daughter* to him. Craig too, now a married man, navigating the highs and lows of building a business. Yes, there would be difficult days, Jack could see that, but he also knew that Craig would be fine. His grandson had a good head on his shoulders and he knew what he wanted. And Isla? She wasn't quite there yet. Perhaps she would never be. The trouble with Isla was that she never appeared to know what she wanted. Flitting here and there; dipping in and out of things without ever really committing to something. Jack worried for her in Berlin, all alone in that apartment with its views that stretched for miles while she was stuck somewhere in the middle wondering which direction to take. Perhaps, Jack thought, she just needed more time.

And his brother? He wished they had been closer. Of course he did. Perhaps he had been too quick to show resentment, too focused on seeking out their differences. But they were *both* their father's sons. Henry Jagger, their talented, ambitious father, who had taught Jack so many things in his barbershop. And the secret formula, which now lived on in all of the things his family were creating; all living, breathing legacies: Tilly's Devon guesthouse, Craig's business and Isla in Berlin. This was the *Jagger* legacy. The Illingworths would never be able to take that away from them. And yet, were it not for his stepfather, Jack was sure his life would have taken on a different trajectory. Would he have become a designer? Perhaps, but he doubted it. 'Thank you, Albert,' Jack said. 'Thank you for helping me make something of my life.' For that, he would always be grateful.

'Did you think I would forget you?' Jack whispered, his thoughts turning to his mother. 'Did you think I would forget how much you sacrificed too? You, whose unwavering faith in me kept me going those long, dark days.'

Those who betrayed him, Jack had long forgiven. Besides, there was too much beauty in life to waste on the futility of anger. Better to spend it recalling all those wonderful moments, including the day he met his darling Maybelle – all shyness in her blue chiffon dress – for the first time. Darling Belle, her life taken away before she knew her grandchildren. How she had looked forward to them. How she would have delighted in them. How cruel life can be. How fleeting. How precious.

Yes, fleeting and precious. Jack could feel all the years spent living swirl around him. Even though things hadn't always gone to plan, even though he didn't always get things right, he had tried his best.

Jack knew he need not worry about Anna. She had been a good wife, a good choice for his second act: kind and uncomplicated. Then there was Elizabeth – her daughter, his stepdaughter – whom Anna was still on good terms with. And this, Jack knew, was no mean feat. He had learnt that having children was no guarantee of anything. Still, Anna's friends were the real bedrock of her life. They were the ones who provided her with joy. And he knew they would continue to do so long after he had gone.

The Robin

54

One morning, before little shafts of light appeared in between the gaps in the curtains, Anna glanced across at her husband. He was lying on his side, as he often did when he slept, with the blanket partially covering his face. Jack had always been an early riser; liked to be up with the lark, he said. Except lately, it was Anna who was getting up first after realising her husband had fallen over again on his way to the bathroom. Anna was ninety-four years old and Jack was a hundred and one. Jack no longer drove – he had given up driving at ninety-two – nor painted or played bowls, but he still lived in his own home with his wife, and that's how he planned for it to continue. But these nightly falls were beginning to worry Anna. She had never known Jack to be ill, not once during their marriage. Now he seemed to have run out of steam.

Anna lay very still and looked at her husband: the shape of his shoulder, the blue of his night shirt. She could no longer hear the soft, laboured breathing, a sound that was as familiar as it was comforting; a sound that was woven deeply into the fabric of their marriage. There was no movement, no stirring, no twitching muscles. Apprehensively, Anna whispered Jack's name and with slightly trembling hands reached across to where he was lying. She gently pulled the blanket towards her, revealing in the first throes of dawn the light in a life extinguished. The stillness he exuded, a tranquility that resonated from the slight curve of his mouth and the softness around his eyes, was an image she would never forget. He seemed at peace. Anna tenderly touched her husband's face, pressing her clammy hand against his cool alabaster cheek as warm, sticky tears escaped down her own, and gently closed his eyes. 'Sleep well, my love. Sleep well. And thank you. Thank you for sharing your life with me.'

The church where Jack's funeral was held was so full that people had to be turned away. Whether they were people whom Jack had known briefly or for decades, Anna made a point of talking to each and every one of them. There was comfort too in having Elizabeth (who had come back from Singapore for her stepfather's funeral) by her side, along with the family Jack had given Anna through their marriage; all united by grief. Hanson, due to his condition, had been unable to attend the funeral. Harry was recovering from a hip operation, and Maggie, even though she would have wanted to pay her respects to the man she had always been fond of, thought it best for everyone that she remain absent. Alice, Jack's niece, whom he hadn't seen half as much as he would have liked over the years, flew from Dublin where she was now living with her husband and three daughters to say goodbye to her Uncle Jack. Her mother, Molly, had already passed away after suffering from a short illness.

'Mrs Jagger?' Anna turned around and saw a man standing awkwardly under the arch of the church hall door, which had been left slightly ajar. 'I hope I'm not disturbing you...'

'Not at all,' said Anna, brushing away remnants of foliage that had attached themselves to her cardigan. 'Were you looking for someone in particular?'

'Just you,' came the reply. 'I'm very glad I caught you.'

'Oh,' said Anna, taken aback. 'Were you at the service earlier? I did try and get round to everyone...'

'I was at the very back. I am so very sorry for your loss.'

'Did you know Jack?'

'I did, yes.' The man extended his arm towards Anna, before quickly adding, 'Sorry, I should have introduced myself earlier. My name is Giles. Giles Illingworth.'

'Giles Illingworth?' Anna repeated, as she grasped the hand in front of her. 'My goodness, it *is* you.'

'I was hoping you'd remember me. It's been a very long time. We met at Hillmans. But your husband came to visit me some years ago in Leeds.'

'I remember.' Anna could see that Giles was nervous.

'My life, well, it's less rigid now, less complicated—'

'She was here earlier,' Anna interjected. 'She was here with her brother and mother.'

'I know.' Giles paused. 'You must all miss him terribly.'

'Oh, we do,' said Anna 'We miss him every day.'

Giles sensed that Anna wanted to tell him something.

'Do you know, yesterday, while I was doing the dishes, I saw a little robin in the garden...' Giles remained silent, waiting for Anna to continue her story. 'And this little robin flew over to the windowsill and just peered in at me. It was very odd. The same thing happened again this morning. In some way, I believe it was my husband coming to tell me that everything is going to be alright.'

'I believe that too,' said Giles. 'I mean, in the sense that when you've shared a life with someone for so many years, where does the love actually go? I think the answer is that it doesn't go anywhere. I think it stays with us. Only now its spirit can be found in a flower or a sweet garden bird.'

'Yes,' said Anna, pleased that Giles had understood. 'I think you're right.' She walked over to a table, which was filled with various bouquets. 'You wouldn't care to take these, would you? It would be a shame for them to go to waste. You are very welcome to have them.'

'Thank you,' said Giles. 'That's very kind.'

'Are you staying locally this evening?'

'Worcester. I've parked about half a mile away. I'm staying at my uncle's for a few days.'

'Well, that's nice,' said Anna. 'Saves you having to drive all the way back to Yorkshire tonight.'

Giles walked over to the table and helped Anna gather the flowers together. 'I'll give these to my aunt. She loves lilies.' Giles placed a bunch under his arm while Anna fetched her coat and handbag.

'Flowers are always appreciated. Could you bring these out for me too? My taxi should be here.' Anna pointed at a posy of delicate pink roses that had been placed on a chair. 'They're from Lizzie, my daughter.'

'Of course,' said Giles, following Anna outside. 'I'm so sorry again for your loss.'

Anna touched Giles' arm and nodded at the sky. 'He wants you to find her, you know. We all do.'

The church bells had begun to ring and the sweet scent of lilies filled the early-evening air. Giles watched the taxi drive away and waved until he could no longer see Anna's arm waving back at him from the open passenger window. Then he looked up at the hazy sky and thought of Mr Jagger, of redemption and forgiveness and the sheer fragility of life.

*

Several days later, while Anna was in the kitchen washing up the breakfast dishes, she realised that the abrasive clang of crockery was the only sound she had heard all morning. She had never been one to listen to the radio, but now she had taken to having it on all day. The background chatter soothed her and she liked the sound of the broadcaster's voice. Of course, Anna knew the real reason for this. It had been less than a month since Jack passed away and she was trying to adjust to life alone in the house; find a way to fill the gaps in the silence, navigate a new way of being. It would take a while, the vicar told her, and should she ever need a guiding hand to help her through her grief, the church doors would always be open. Still, Anna wasn't sure if the vicar would have understood the story of the little robin, whom she was waiting for today and who had come by to visit her yesterday.

After the dishes had been washed and put away, Anna sat down to drink her tea. The radio was playing an extended programme about the volcanic eruptions in Iceland that she had been half following when she sensed she was being observed. Anna glanced up and the first thing she noticed was the way the robin's head was tilted as it watched her with curiosity from its usual place. *There you are*, she thought. *I knew you would come.* Anna remained very still in her chair and the robin, perched on the windowsill, remained still too save for its delicate wings, which were fluttering in the spring breeze.

'Hello, my love,' Anna said softly. 'What do you think? Isn't it a beautiful day?'

Isla   EPILOGUE

Prenzlauer Berg, Berlin (2010)

Isla sat on the bench, her hands nursing the coffee she had bought from the café around the corner. She wasn't sure why she always drank it at the *kinderspielplatz*. It wasn't as if she could claim she was coming for the quiet and solitude. Yet it had become, to Isla's surprise, her thinking place, a place where she could lose herself in the energy of the children whooshing around her.

It was a dull afternoon and the setting sun had given rise to a cold chill. The wind whipped fallen leaves around in the air, which in the fading light looked like dancing fireflies. In the far corner of the playground a group of older children were watching something on a phone and dancing simultaneously; their youth a wide-open vista still to come. It was the adults Isla found the most fascinating, though, most of whom stood on the periphery of the adventures taking place around them while they played with their gadgets or lost themselves in conversations that drifted towards her: the intricate fabric of female friendship, the mundanity of marriage, the complex ties of family or another failed relationship. Where does the love actually go, Isla thought, as she listened to the individual stories around her, all these endings that break us in half? Where does the love actually go? Isla didn't have the answer but she knew she had seen enough of life to realise that it didn't need to be perfect. It didn't need a perfect beginning or a perfect ending. It was the everything in between we live for. It was too late for her father, alone in the nursing home with his memories. Maybe it was too late for Maggie, left behind in that big house, her future in flames. She still wondered why Maggie had chosen to confide in Max about her father's heart flutters. Why didn't Max tell *her* straightaway? Perhaps she would never know. Maybe one day she'd find out. It didn't matter anymore. What mattered was that she and her brother had reconnected with their father. What mattered was how happy their mother was in Appledean; and good for her, she deserved it. And Christmas! Yes, this year they would all come for Christmas – Mum, Craig, Lia – celebrating with a sky-high tree glittering with baubles in red, gold and purple. *Zauberhaft!*

The cafés and boutiques were already lit when Isla walked home, and she felt comforted by their familiarity: the smells emanating from the local pizzeria which was always full; the clink of glasses toasting *feierabend* in the *weinstube* with its colourful mismatch of tables and chairs outside that withstood all kinds of weather; and the dresses, always so many pretty dresses in the shop windows to look at, fairy lights twinkling around the panes enticing her to come in.

The building where she lived was painted coral – not quite orange, not quite red – but an in-between shade that looked resplendent in the light whenever the sun hit it. It was strange because, by her own admission, Isla had never been one for modern architecture and this was starkly modern. Yet when she was shown around her apartment that first time, she just knew that this was going to be her home. 'Lucky you,' the *Makler* had told her. 'You have snapped up the very last apartment. An investor from Hong Kong has just pulled out and the rest, all seventy-four, have been bought off-plan.' Isla began to feel that the whole thing was, in fact, serendipitous. Her apartment number happened to be the date of her birthday, and the renovated building was formerly a textile design factory. It was also the very last space to be sold, as if it had been waiting for her.

Oh, Grandpa, Isla thought, as she turned the key in the communal door, *if only you'd made it here to see me, because this is all down to you.* One of the last conversations she'd had with him that bright morning in March was about her future. She knew that he worried for her – commit to something, he said, believe in something – and she understood now more than ever what he had meant.

By the time Isla reached her apartment, the bells had begun to ring from the Evangelical church nearby. She opened her balcony doors and stepped into the cool October air; the smell of barbecued meat and the sound of laughter drifting towards her. Isla glanced upwards and saw wisps of smoke coming from the communal roof terrace. For such a social building, she thought, with its endless calendar of barbecues and parties, she could count on one hand the number of conversations she'd had with her neighbours. Perhaps it was the transience of the place – people moving in and out, bars and restaurants opening and closing – which gave the city its undercurrent of impermanence; a city always changing.

But now it was Isla who was changing.

The shift was subtle at first, the feeling that Berlin no longer belonged to her. The laughter that drifted from the rooftop only emphasised Isla's sense of being on the periphery again; her feet in two worlds. And she wondered, watching a solitary starling flit from tree to tree, what it would feel like to come home. That feeling of belonging, whether to a place, person or group, which continued to elude her. She remembered what someone had once told her about starlings, how they were always to be found in large flocks of busy, squabbling groups, never alone. So it was strange to watch this solitary thing, green and purplish from a distance, flying back and forth between the trees as if it too was trying to find its place.

The following morning was a Saturday, and although Isla usually headed to the farmers' market on Kollwitzplatz to buy fresh bread and flowers, today, she was headed to Friedrichshain to the opening of an exhibition. She didn't know much about the artist, apart from the fact that he went by the name of Ile Worth and that the gallery was one of those pop-up places, which were long synonymous with and now ubiquitous in the east of the city. The gallery invitation also intrigued Isla. It was minimalist in design, with a white border and the words *Wanderlust(er)* written on the front in gold lettering above a black and white photograph of what she assumed was a nomad sitting at the top of a mountain. Where the image was taken, Isla couldn't be sure, but she liked its sentiment and simplicity. Still, who on earth holds an exhibition preview on a Saturday? she thought, as she cycled down the Prenzlauer Allee, its long, wide boulevard throbbing with activity as people weaved in and out of cafés, some clutching paper cups and pastries; everyone enjoying the autumn sunshine.

The gallery, once Isla had found it, was nestled in between two derelict buildings in the middle of a courtyard. Two boys were playing football in the far corner and at the opposite end stood a Turkish café, which had a handful of customers queuing up outside. A man in a crisp white tee-shirt and black jeans was waiting at the gallery entrance, balancing a large drinks tray in his hand. Next to him stood a young girl, perhaps no more than fourteen, holding a red clipboard to her chest and wearing a pale blue tea dress and Doc Martens. '*Hi. Wollen Sie einen Sekt haben?*' The man in the white tee-shirt spoke effusively.

'*Gerne,*' replied Isla, reaching for a glass. '*Danke.*'

'*Kann Ich Ihren namen haben?*' The young girl spoke this time, holding the clipboard in an exaggerated manner as if trying to exert an air of authority. Isla noticed that the girl spoke with an accent – English, but not quite – and as she waited for Isla to speak, she smiled in a familiar way.

'Isla Jagger.'

'*Perfekt.*' The girl smiled as she crossed out Isla's name and glanced at her colleague, as if for reassurance.

'*Es gibt noch zum trinken.*' The man nodded behind him. '*Auch zum essen. Brunch style. Soll bestimmt lecker sein.*'

'*Danke.*' Isla nodded politely and took a sip of her apéritif, quickly stepping aside as two large white doors leading to the gallery space suddenly swung open. A couple appeared, holding brochures and catalogues against their chests, and as they held the doors open for Isla, she was immediately struck by the hundreds of black and white images adorning the walls. And the room – it was filled with light, so much light that she almost had to take a step back as she glanced up at the yellow neon words *Fernweh* and *Sehnsucht* dangling above her, drawing her in.

She recognised him immediately. He was standing with his back to her, talking to a small group of people who were looking intently at a large image in front of them; every so often turning their attention back to the man as he told them a story. He was broader than she remembered, and his dark hair was speckled with grey now, but still boyish in the way it softly framed the contours of his face. There was a quiet confidence about him too; a maturity underpinned by contentment and acceptance. When he turned around, for a moment Isla wasn't sure whether he realised it was her; that momentary flicker of acknowledgement between two people whose paths have long since diverged but were back at the starting point again. But he knew. There was so much gladness in his face; the star of the show, who was now walking towards her with intent, every step coming closer to the beginning. 'Hello Isla.' He looked at her as if she were the only person in the room. 'I'm so glad you came.'

'Hi, Giles.' Isla was smiling back at him. 'Thank you for inviting me.'

ACKNOWLEDGEMENTS

Thank you to Lara Reid at the Media Archive for Central England who helped with my initial research on the Kidderminster carpet industry and to everyone at Troubador Publishing who helped to bring this book to life. I am especially grateful to Susan D'Arcy, Vivienne Modebe and Paromita Saha Killelea, who generously gave me their time to read through my early drafts and for their insight and encouragement along the way, and to my mum, my very first reader, for everything. I would also like to thank Christine Douglas, Julia Dunning, Mark Jeffries and Christian "history buff" McCarthy for their support; to Catherine McCarthy and Angela Liebig for buoying me along with their positivity; and to Karla Watkins for her magnificent marketing skills and for serendipitously coming into my life at just the right time. To the brilliant baristas at the Out of Office coffee shop in the Hive Building - thank you for all those refills and for providing the perfect space to write, think and daydream. And finally, thank you to Will, for pushing me to keep going.